HASTUR LORD

HASTUR LORD

BY MARION ZIMMER BRADLEY

AND

DEBORAH J. ROSS

DAW BOOKS, INC.

DONALD A. WOLLHEIM, FOUNDER

375 Hudson Street, New York, NY 10014

ELIZABETH R. WOLLHEIM
SHEILA E. GILBERT
PUBLISHERS

http://www.dawbooks.com

First printing, January 2010
1   2   3   4   5   6   7   8   9

DAW TRADEMARK REGISTERED
U.S. PAT. AND TM. OFF. AND FOREIGN COUNTRIES
—MARCA REGISTRADA
HECHO EN U.S.A.

PRINTED IN THE U.S.A.

DEDICATIONS

Marion Zimmer Bradley: To Cynthia McQuillin, who allows me to indulge my favorite vice, talking about Darkover.

—July 26, 1998

Deborah J. Ross: To Betsy Wollheim, who preserved what Marion had written, until it was to time to finish it.

—December 19, 2008

NOTES

NOTES

Marion Zimmer Bradley: For those with an obsessive need to know which book comes after which on Darkover, these events occur after *The World Wreckers* and before *Exile's Song*—about ten years.

Deborah J. Ross: Marion created Darkover over the span of three decades, from the 1962 publication of *Planet Savers* and *Sword of Aldones* until her death in 1999. Over the years, she developed, matured, and reworked many aspects of this rich, marvelous world. In such a process, given that Marion never let previously published details interfere with a good story, minor inconsistencies of geography and time are inevitable. What is important is that each story be whole in itself and emotionally satisfying.

BOOK I: Regis

1

Above the ancient city of Thendara, the great crimson sun of Dark-over crept toward midday. Winter was drawing to a close, yet even at this hour, shadows stretched across the narrow, twisting streets of the Old Town. Snowfall had been light for the last tenday, and the market-places surged with renewed life, anticipating the approach of spring.

Regis Hastur, the Heir of his Domain, stood on a balcony of Comyn Castle and wrapped his fur-lined cloak more tightly around his shoul-ders. He was a tall man in his mid thirties, with startling white hair and the intense masculine beauty of his clan. His gaze slowly swept from the spires and towers of Thendara to the Terran Trade City, the rising steel edifice of the Empire Headquarters complex and, still farther, the spaceport.

Throughout this past winter, he had divided his time between at-tending sessions of the Cortes, negotiating disputes and trade agree-ments between city magistrates and various guilds, and meeting with representatives of the Terran Empire and diplomatic envoys from the Seven Domains that once had formed Darkover's ruling Council.

Oddly, Regis found himself nostalgic for the days when the Comyn gathered together, debating and discussing, scheming and plotting, planning marriages and trading gossip, even those times when a traditional evening of dancing and music was punctuated by the occasional formal duel.

Those days, he reflected, would never come again. Between a low birth rate, natural decline, and the targeted assassinations of the World Wreckers, the Comyn had been decimated, their remnants scattered. These last ten years had been an unbroken struggle to restore the ecology of the planet while trying to develop a new system of government. In his more pessimistic moments, Regis admitted that his idea for a new ruling Council, one open to telepaths of any caste, had been a singularly lame-brained scheme. What had he been thinking, to exchange men who had been educated for leadership since birth for a patched-together assembly that was inexperienced, sometimes illiterate, often pathologically independent? Even the Keepers, with years of rigorous discipline in the use of their psychic powers, had little training in matters beyond their own Towers.

The only saving grace, he thought ruefully, was that the Telepath Council was so disparate and disorganized, it was unlikely to do anything effective on a large scale. What would happen if a crisis demanded unified action? He supposed the remains of the Comyn would rally; certainly, the people would, if he asked.

If I asked . . .

Regis no longer needed to be on constant guard against an assassin's dagger or Compact-forbidden Terran blaster, but no power under the Bloody Sun could erase the look of awe as he passed through the streets or silence the murmured whispers, *"The Hastur Lord."* The people bowed to him in respect and gratitude, having no idea how their adulation ate like acid into his soul.

Even without the hushed footsteps, Regis knew by the softening of his mood and the lightening of his heart that Danilo Syrtis-Ardais had come into the room behind him. He closed his eyes, opening the space in his mind where their thoughts met.

With a click of the latch, Danilo closed the door and came to stand beside Regis. *"Bredhyu,"* he inflected the *casta* term in a far more intimate mode than the usual meaning of *sworn brother.*

"What troubles you, Regis?"

Regis turned his back on the city to face his paxman. Danilo wore the Hastur colors, blue and silver, with a winter-weight cloak of dark gray wool folded back over one shoulder so that his sword was within easy reach. Concern darkened his eyes.

"Nothing more than this foul mood of mine," Regis replied, trying to keep his voice light. "It will pass soon enough, now that you are here."

Danilo's eyes flickered to the weathered stone wall. The Castle was a city unto itself, a massive accretion of centuries, with towers, courtyards and ballrooms, a mazelike labyrinth of halls and corridors, stairs and archways, fireplaces and parapets, the living quarters once reserved for the use of each Domain during Council season, and the glittering domed ceiling of the Crystal Chamber. The main Guard hall was on the lower level, with its own barracks, armory, and training yards.

Danilo's expressive mouth tightened. "This place is like a tomb."

"Yes, but one that requires constant tending. Even with whole sections shut up, the rest must be maintained. The Castle won't run itself, and Grandfather isn't up to it."

Regis fell silent, deliberately avoiding the logical next point in the discussion. What the Castle needed, as Danvan Hastur reminded Regis on a regular basis, was a chatelaine, a Lady Hastur to see to its orderly function.

With a slight inclination of his head, Danilo opened the balcony door and stepped back so that Regis could precede him.

"The dregs of winter are always depressing," Danilo said. "Things will be better in the spring," alluding not only to the brighter days but also to the old Comyn custom of gathering in Thendara for Council season. Old habits died hard.

"Things," Regis replied, "will be better in about an hour."

They clattered through the chamber behind the balcony, once a pleasant sitting room that formed part of the Hastur quarters, then down the corridor and past the office Regis still maintained, although he did not live in the Castle, and down a flight of stairs.

"Oh?" Danilo arched one eyebrow. "We're bound for the Terran Zone, then?"

Regis grinned like a boy sneaking away from his lessons. He still felt the lure of the spaceport, with its promise of worlds that were strange and deliciously terrifying. Years ago, he had accepted that his duty lay here, on the planet of his birth, with all that implied.

Walking briskly, Regis and Danilo made their way to Terran Headquarters. They were not the only ones taking advantage of the temporary lessening of winter's bitter grip. They passed men in fur cloaks, women muffled to their eyes in layers of wool, an occasional Terran looking miserably chill in his synthetic thermal parka, and wagons pulled by blanket-draped horses or hardy antlered *chervines*. A girl in a red jacket swept a layer of snow, no more than a single night's worth, from the stone steps in front of a shop. On the corner, a woman sold apple fritters, scooped steaming and fragrant from a vat of hot oil and then dusted with Terran sugar.

Danilo stayed close, a flowing shadow yet deadly as the steel he carried. Regis had no doubt that any man approaching them with menace would not live to regret it. From the time they had served together in the City Guards, both men had rarely gone unarmed. Their weapons were honorable, not those of a coward, used to kill from a safe distance. Dagger, knife, and sword all placed the man who used them at equal risk. The Compact that eliminated weapons with far reaching targets and those that could cause vast destruction but permitted personal duels had lasted a thousand years, woven into the fabric of Darkovan ethics.

The border between Darkovan Thendara and the Terran Trade sector had blurred over the years, leaving a zone that was a blend of the two cultures, sometimes exotic, sometimes awkward, sometimes the worst of both worlds. Danilo came alert at the sight of a pair of Spaceforce officers in black leather uniforms, but one whispered to the other and they stepped aside.

As they approached the glass and steel tower of Terran Headquarters, one of the guards stationed there smiled and nodded, "Good morning, Lord Hastur."

Regis refrained from pointing out that as long as his grandfather lived, Danvan remained *Lord Hastur,* but the man was well-meaning. It would be a waste of breath to chide him for simple ignorance.

After exchanging a few pleasantries, Regis and Danilo passed within, where a receptionist informed them that the Legate was expecting them. If Lord Hastur would wait but a moment, she would summon an escort.

"I know the way," Regis said mildly. "As you see, I have brought my own escort." Before she could protest, he and Danilo strode past her into the bowels of the building.

Regis had never been comfortable within Terran walls, but at least here the likelihood of an armed attack was less; the Terrans did not permit their own people to carry weapons inside Headquarters.

Dan Lawton, the Terran Legate, bowed to Regis. Over the years, a sympathy had grown up between the two men, for Lawton was Darkovan-born but had chosen to live as a Terran. Lawton could not have been much more than forty, and that was not old by the standards of Terran medicine, yet his lean, angular face was careworn, etched by the habit of worry.

"It has been too long, Lord Regis," Lawton began, then smiled as Regis invited him with a gesture to move to a less formal basis.

Regis slipped off his heavy outdoor cloak and took the proffered seat. Danilo sat down as well, clearly at ease.

"You look well, Regis. And you, too, as usual, Danilo. How is Mikhail?" Lawton asked.

"My sister writes he is strong and healthy," Regis answered. After finishing his term in the City Guards cadets, Mikhail had spent the winter in Armida, learning the duties of a Domains lord. In choosing Javanne's youngest son for his legal heir, Regis had done better than he expected. Mikhail, although still young enough for occasional foolish high spirits, showed an underlying steadiness of temperament.

In response to a polite inquiry, Lawton replied that he himself was well, that his son and wife had gone for an outing in the Old Town.

Lawton had married a few years prior to the time of the World Wreckers. The couple had met off-world during Lawton's diplomatic certification training and had wed after a brief, intense courtship. Regis had met the woman once or twice. She was strikingly beautiful, with pearl-bright skin and lushly curling black hair, exotic on a world that fostered pale-skinned redheads. Yet Regis found something unsettling in her manner, beyond the expected awkwardness of a wife who has found herself on a world far from home, confronted with strange customs. He had tried without success to draw her out in conversation. She was the wife of a Terran dignitary and, more than that, of his friend.

"I don't believe I have ever met your son," Regis said.

"His name is Felix," Lawton said, and they both smiled, for the name was popular and much-honored on Darkover. Many Comyn, Regis among them, bore it somewhere in their long string of names. "He's eleven, and a handful."

"May the happiness of his name follow him through his lifetime," Danilo said.

"Thank you," Lawton replied. "He's still at the most trying age, no longer a child and not yet a man. If it were up to me, I'd send him to be fostered for a few years at Armida or Carcosa, so that he could use up some of that exuberance learning to ride horses or cutting brush on fire-lines, but his mother won't hear of it. Today they're out looking for 'native treasures' as offerings for her grandfather's saint day."

"I'm not familiar with that custom," Regis said. "Is it proper to offer best wishes?"

Lawton frowned. "Not on Temperance. Tiphani's grandfather has been dead for twenty years now, but his entire family still feels obliged to offer sacrifices for the atonement of his sins. Whatever she sends home will be purified and then burned. It seems a waste to me, but it's their way."

"Was he as terrible as that?" Regis was familiar with the concept of a punitive afterworld. As a youth, he had studied for some years at the monastery school at St.-Valentine's-of-the-Snows. Altogether too aware of the universality of human frailty, Regis had little sympathy with the monks' obsession with purity and perdition.

Or, he added silently, with a quick glance in Danilo's direction, *their condemnation of certain expressions of love.*

"I never met the man," Lawton continued. "For myself, I prefer to be remembered for the good I achieved and the happiness I brought to those I loved."

"So should we all."

Lawton turned back to the console on his desk. He engaged the visiphone with a few efficient strokes. "I've set it to play the priority message that arrived on coded frequency for you. I'm afraid it's formatted as play-and-destruct, so you'll only be able to watch it once. Touch this panel to begin and this one here to record a reply, if any." He got to his feet, bowed again, this time in an abbreviated, less formal manner, and left Regis and Danilo in privacy.

"What's this about?" Danilo asked, coming around to view the screen as Regis took Lawton's seat.

"I assume it's from Lew Alton. I can't imagine who else would want to contact me in such a manner."

Regis pressed the panel Lawton had indicated. The screen's background pattern dissolved into bits of iridescent gray. An instant later, the familiar scarred features of Lewis-Kennard Alton, one of Regis's oldest friends and now the Darkovan Senator to the Terran Empire, came into focus.

Since his ordeal fighting the immensely powerful, illegal matrix known as Sharra nearly twenty years ago, Lew had never looked well. The battle had left him battered, a widower aged beyond his years, and in despair. Time and a happy second marriage had softened his expression, but his gray eyes still looked bleak.

"*Vai dom* Regis," Lew began formally in *casta*. Regis imagined him leaning forward, choosing his words with care, masking the urgency behind them.

"I can't risk sending this through normal channels, although soon enough the news will be broadcast everywhere. You may think me overly cautious. Paranoia is, after all, an asset in this profession. If I'm right, however, you'll need all the advance warning I can give you."

Lew paused and glanced down, consulting his notes. "The debate over changing the constitutional structure of the Empire has been going on for three years now, most of it behind closed doors. The people promoting it, particularly Sandra Nagy and Augustus Verogist—sorry, those names won't mean anything to you, but they are two of the most powerful politicians in the Empire— have managed to keep all reports to the level of rumor so they can move ahead while no one takes the issue seriously. I've just learned through my own sources that the proposal will come up for a vote in the full Senate this session. Nagy and her allies are planning a preemptive strike against their opponents."

Regis and Danilo exchanged glances. Neither had given much attention to the internal politics of the Terran Empire. But Regis had heard, through Lawton and Dr. Jason Allison as well as Lew himself, about the move to change the Empire to a Federation. He had considered it an alteration in name only. Most people didn't really care if the *Terranan* called themselves an Empire or a Federation or an Alliance or a spring dance. But Regis could not mistake the urgency in Lew's voice or the grave expression in his eyes.

"The measure will pass," Lew went on. "Make no mistake about it. This is no mere relabeling of the same system. You will undoubtedly hear propaganda about how the new Federation will extend autonomy to all member worlds, increase interstellar cooperation, and promote free trade—all the persuasive phrases that people want to hear. Even people on Darkover. *Don't fall for it, Regis.* This whole process is a power grab by the Expansionist party. They want free access to developing worlds, and they've as much as admitted that their goal is to bring an end to what they call *special privileges* and *protected status.*"

Regis drew in his breath. Beside him, Danilo tensed. The light in the office was too bright, too yellow, the air tainted with alien chemical vapors.

Regis paused the recording. "Danilo, if what Lew says is true, then Darkover could lose its status as a Class D Closed World."

The immensely powerful corporations that had hired the World Wreckers would like nothing better than to have free access to Darkover. Only the Empire's restrictive laws governing Closed Worlds prevented others from turning Darkover into a colony planet. Without legal protections, nothing would stand in the way of those who wanted to exploit Darkover's resources or its pivotal position in the galactic arm.

Not even the Comyn, Danilo sent the telepathic thought.

"Although I hate to admit it, the Telepath Council is completely inadequate to this challenge." With a sigh, Regis resumed the recorded message.

"The new Federation must tread lightly at first," Lew said. "The Expansionist alliance will be fragile, and they will need every vote. They dare not alienate their supporters by forcing full membership on any planet that does not desire it. Therein lies our hope. If Darkover refuses to change its Closed World status, then we have a chance of surviving this period of instability. Eventually the political pendulum will swing back to a more sane and compassionate balance between the benefits of cooperation and the need for self-determination.

"Regis . . . if anyone can preserve Darkover's independence during this dangerous time, it is you. For the sake of all we hold dear, may the gods walk with you. *Adelandeyo,* my friend."

The screen went blank, then words appeared: MESSAGE DESTROYED. Regis read Terran Standard well enough to make out the words.

They sat for a moment in silence, letting the weight of Lew's words sink in. Disgust rose up in Regis, abhorrence of the glass and metal cage around him, the machines, the regulations, the artificiality, the smug implied superiority. He reminded himself that he had survived crises before. Having been raised and shaped by Darkover's greatest living statesman, he knew the uses of power.

"Let's get out of here," Danilo said. "This place is not good for either of us."

He opened the door and followed Regis into the reception room. Dan Lawton bent over his secretary's desk, going over some documents with her. He looked up, and his expression shifted.

"Is it something you can tell me?" he asked Regis. "Can I be of any service?"

"I'm afraid not." Regis tried not to sound curt, to lash out as he badly wanted to. This man, despite his Terran uniform, was not his enemy. The offer of help had been sincere. "Perhaps later."

"Of course."

"We'll see ourselves out." Danilo strode to the outer door and opened it. He had shifted back into his role as bodyguard, eyes alert, posture fluid and balanced, fingertips brushing the hilt of his sword.

Corridors sped by in a blur of glass and metal, of chemically treated air and people in strange, immodest uniforms. Regis wondered if this was the future of the world he had sworn to defend. Only when they were out on the street, with the swollen red sun casting the sky into a glory of color and the Venza Hills rising like waves of living stone beyond the city, did Regis draw a free breath.

2

Regis waited until they were well away from the Terran sector and once more surrounded by familiar sights and sounds—street vendors calling out their wares, wagon wheels creaking and hoofbeats muffled in the snow. "The problem," he said to Danilo, "is that some people will see this move as a good thing. They will *want* what the Expansionists offer them. The Ridenow in particular have agitated for us to join the Empire—excuse me, the Federation."

Danilo nodded. "It surprised no one when Lerrys and Geremy went off-world for good. They had always been . . ." he hesitated, as if searching for the phrase that conveyed both disdain and proper respect for Comyn lords, ". . . *enamored* of off-world ways and technologies."

"Especially the pleasures of places like Vainwal, where anything can be had, or done, or forgotten," Regis looked away, his mouth curling in distaste, "for a price."

Pedestrians streamed past the two men, hurrying about their business in the brief warmth of midday. The Bloody Sun had passed its zenith. Inky shadows lengthened. Despite his fur-lined cloak, Regis shivered. If Lerrys Ridenow and his allies had their way, Darkover would become nothing more than a Terran colony ruled by Terran laws, the ancient ways eroding under Terran customs.

Our heritage will be bartered for luxuries enjoyed only by those few wealthy enough to afford them!

It did no good to dwell on such things, just as it did no good to stand here on a public street. He must take action, although he did not yet know what.

They reached the townhouse on the edge of the Terran Zone. Regis had maintained it as his residence for some years now. At first, he had hated the place, for it was boxy and cramped, lacking the spaciousness of Castle Hastur. The only good thing about it, besides that it was not Comyn Castle, was its ease of defense. The pair of City Guards on duty at the gates could hold off a small army if need be. At least, Regis thought as he and Danilo handed their cloaks to a servant and stepped through the foyer, it was warm.

In the parlor, a fire had been lit on the unadorned stone hearth. Regis halted before it, stretching his chilled fingers. A moment later, the same servant, a man named Marton, who had grown up on the Carcosa estate, brought in a pitcher of *jaco,* placed it on the little table that stood between two armchairs near the fireplace, and silently withdrew.

"The Ridenow will press for full membership, of course." Danilo poured a mug and settled into his usual chair, cradling it between his hands. "Aldaran will join in, not that they count. Hastur and Elhalyn— well, that's you, for all practical purposes. With Lew off-planet and Gabriel Lanart as conservative as he is, Alton's not a worry, either. Who else is there? Aillard? None of them are left. Ardais?"

"Danilo, you're going through the roll call of the Domains as if there were still a Comyn Council," Regis said, a little pettishly. "I very much doubt this decision will be made in the old way, by the heads of the Domains conferring together. For the last ten years, the Council has not existed."

"*You* exist. *You* are still Heir to Hastur."

Regis shook his head, refusing to be drawn in. He threw himself into the empty chair. "It's not so simple. The Terrans have things of value to offer us. Many of the common people—businessmen, crafters, those who've profited from Terran technology, even some in the Telepath

Council—they'll look favorably on increased access to those benefits. They want things that make a hard life easier: fire-fighting chemicals to protect our forests and the means to deliver them quickly and effectively, fertilizers and nutrients to restore our soil, medicines to prolong life and reduce infant mortality . . ."

"All these things come at a cost," Danilo reminded him.

"One we have been able to pay, so far. You more than anyone know that I'm no isolationist, not like my grandfather or the Di Asturiens. I know that Darkover must change. I had hoped the Telepath Council would have accomplished more by now. Sometimes, getting them to agree on any action is like—how do the Terrans put it? *herding cats?*"

At that, Danilo laughed. They both relaxed. Regis went on, more seriously, "I wish Mikhail were not off at Armida. His generation will have to live with whatever we decide, so we should ask his opinion. If only for his sake, I will not surrender the dream of an independent, *Darkovan* Darkover, safe from the Empire and its soulless technology. I would have us follow our own path into that future."

"So you always said," Danilo smiled, warmth lighting his eyes. He set his half-empty mug on the table. "Many will listen to you. You are Hastur, after all, and you speak with an authority that goes back to the beginning of time."

Regis looked away, uncomfortable with so much power and half-afraid that he might lack the wisdom to use it. Should one man, no matter how noble his motives, ever wield such overwhelming influence over another?

And yet, if he had not stepped into the position he now held, if he had let others make decisions because he mistrusted his own judgment, Darkover itself and all its people would have paid the price. Once he had asked himself if he sought the love of power or the power of love. He wished the answer were as clear now as it had been then.

Meeting Danilo's steady gaze, his heart softening in the pulse of acceptance that flowed through their light rapport, Regis almost believed himself worthy of such trust.

"Let's hope so," he said, "for I have quarrels enough for the moment. Thanks to Lew, we will have time to plan before the matter of

Federation membership becomes public. I should consult my grandfather without delay."

Danilo's expression darkened minutely. They both knew that the irascible old man had never relented in pressing Regis to marry and ensure a proper succession. Nor was he the only one. Ruyven Di Asturien would like nothing better than to see his daughter, Crystal, married to Regis; the son she had borne Regis had not lived past his fourth year, but the fact remained that she was fertile, willing, and acceptable to even the most hidebound conservatives.

Together, Regis and Danilo drew up a plan to meet with those members of the Telepath Council who had remained in Thendara for the winter and to contact others through the Tower relays. Danilo suggested that Regis consult Gabriel Lanart-Hastur. Since assuming lordship of the great house at Armida, Gabriel divided his time between running the estate and his duties as Commander of the Guards.

Regis was happy to be doing something, for he never liked waiting for trouble to come to him. However, he was not looking forward to the debate once spring opened the roads and brought people like Valdir and Haldred Ridenow to Thendara.

Leave tomorrow's sorrows to tomorrow, the old proverb went. He would do his best to follow it.

After a brief midday meal, Regis set off on foot for Comyn Castle, accompanied as always by Danilo. His grandfather maintained a suite of rooms in the Hastur section. One of the tasks Regis had set for himself in overseeing the running of the Castle was to make sure the old man was well cared for.

He should have retired to Castle Hastur years ago, among his own people. But Old Hastur, as he was still called, was not yet ready to surrender the reins of power. He insisted he would remain where he was needed.

A servant greeted them at the entrance to the Hastur apartments. Regis found his grandfather in his study, seated before his writing desk and warmed by a merry fire. Danvan Hastur had once been a tall, strongly built man, but age and care had withered him. His hair was pure white now, thinning but neatly combed. The tunic of supple leather, dyed blue and trimmed with silver fir-tree design embroidery, hung on his bony frame. He looked up from the document he had been reading, tracing the lines of script with one finger. The knuckle was swollen, misaligned.

As he studied his grandfather's face, Regis had the curious feeling that all normal life had been burned out of the old man, leaving Lord Hastur as pure refined will. How old was he, anyway? Over a century, certainly. *Chieri* blood ran in the Hasturs, often granting them exceptionally long lives. To Regis, his grandfather had always seemed immortal, like a force of nature. Now he saw an old man, sustained only by the remains of the fire that had tempered him.

Will I look like this someday? Regis wondered. *Will that be my face . . . my fate?*

"Regis, it is good to see you. No, no formal bowing or anything like that. I'm too tired to get up."

Unexpectedly moved by the warmth of the greeting, Regis moved to the desk and pressed his cheek against the dry, shriveled side of his grandfather's face.

After inquiries about one another's health, mention of the weather and the condition of the streets, Regis and Danilo settled into their respective chairs. The servant came back, bearing a tray with the ubiquitous *jaco* and a plate of custard tarts, the old man's favorite. Regis took one out of politeness.

Regis outlined the situation as he understood it from Lew Alton's message. Danvan listened intently. From time to time, the muscles around Danvan's eyes tightened and he clenched his jaw. Danvan had spent the better part of his very long life engaged in political maneuvering, ever since he had assumed the Regency for the incompetent King Stefan Elhalyn. He had presided over periods of transition and tumult, one crisis after another.

"This is what comes from trying to negotiate with the *Terranan*," he muttered. "To think that we might become a third-rate colony . . ."

"Sir," Regis said, "that is exactly what we must find a way to prevent. We are not without resources. Let us not forget that we have friends within the Empire, men of good will who still believe that each world has the right to determine its own fate. Lew Alton still represents us

in the Senate, and that will not change when the Terran Empire is replaced by a Federation."

"If there still *is* a Senate!" Danvan snapped. "We should have held
firm right from the beginning. We had no choice in allowing them to
land their ships and build their spaceport here. But we should have insisted that the contact end there. We should have forced them to leave
us our own way of life and go about their own business without involv-
ing us."

Regis smothered a sigh. They had been over the old argument too
many times already, and he saw no point in continuing. The Terran
Empire was a fact, impossible to wish away. Banshee chicks could not
be put back into their eggs. Given a generation or more of contact with
a star-spanning civilization, Darkover could never have continued on
its own isolated way.

"Whether we chose rightly or not, we are part of the Empire now,"
Regis said. "If we had refused permission for them to build their spaceport here in Thendara, they would have gone elsewhere. Caer Donn
was bad enough, but what if they had chosen Shainsa? Would the Dry
Town lords, who have never observed the Compact, have hesitated to
trade for blasters and worse?"

Danilo drew in a quick, horrified breath. Danvan masked his own
reaction better. In a flash, Regis understood that his grandfather had
indeed considered the possibility. As long as the Terrans could be re-
stricted to Thendara, could be monitored and regulated, then the possibility of imported, illegal weaponry was minimized. After the Sharra
disaster and the destruction of the Terrans' secondary spaceport at
Caer Donn, the Empire officials had reluctantly agreed to abide by the
Compact. How long would that memory last?

Regis went on, "The Terrans granted us Closed World status so that
we would not suffer debilitating social upheavals from exposure to their
culture."

"Are you defending them?"

Regis shook his head. "No, I am trying to be realistic. Darkover isn't
suitable for industrialization like the city worlds. Between lack of minerals and a fragile ecology, we simply can't sustain certain kinds of technologies. The Terrans know this as well as we do."

Danvan's blue eyes glinted, although his voice sounded as weary as ever. "Do you think that would stop them? It didn't stop the World Wreckers from doing their best to bring us to the brink of ruin."

"Then what would you propose we do . . . sir?" Regis struggled to contain his temper.

"We have only one hope of standing against the power of the Terrans as they play on the ignorance and greed of the people." With each phrase, Danvan gathered momentum like an avalanche in the Hellers. "We need a single, strong man to unite us."

Regis closed his eyes. In that moment, he was a boy again, trying to stand up to the most influential, charismatic, and legendary figure on Darkover. He felt Danilo sitting not far from him and opened his mind to his *bredhyu's* calm resolve.

Just listen, Danilo thought. *He can't force you into anything.*

They both knew what was coming next.

"Why do you think I've held on this long?" Danvan's burst of passion-fueled vigor was fading, and Regis felt, like a shiver in his bones, the brittleness of his grandfather's failing strength. "I should have retired as Regent long ago. I would have if there had been someone to take my place."

Stung, Regis shot back, "What more do you want of me? I stayed on Darkover. I pledged myself to Hastur and to our world." *I'm only one man! There's only so much I can give, or I will end an empty husk!*

"Yes, you have behaved with honor," Danvan admitted. His voice lost some of its urgency. "No one questions that. You have stepped forward, at great cost to yourself, when a crisis demanded it."

Regis sat back, surprised by his grandfather's concession.

"But . . ." Danvan picked up his argument, "you have not fulfilled the one duty that only you, as Heir to Hastur, can perform—to give our caste, our world, our people the leadership to take them safely into the future. Look around you! As you yourself pointed out numerous times, the Comyn are all but gone, a few noble families here and there clinging to the shards of the past. We no longer meet in Council to decide crucial issues and provide guidance. The Towers have never interested themselves in anything beyond their own walls, and now they have to contend with training any ruffian with a trace of *laran*."

Thanks to your Telepath Council, Danvan meant.

Regis gritted his teeth. If the old tyrant insisted on pushing his point to its conclusion, let him be the one to do it.

The charred end of a log broke off and tumbled into the bed of ashes, sending up a tiny spark. The mote of brilliance flared and died.

"Regis, my lad, we both know what you must do," Danvan said, his voice now hoarse with emotion.

No. Did he speak aloud, or only in his heart?

I will not become king. I have never wanted that kind of power.

"You are the only one with the true right." Danvan shifted to smooth persuasion born from deeply-held belief. "Not even if Aldones himself wished it could we place an Elhalyn on the throne. Your claim is legitimate, since your mother was King Stefan's only sister. Not even the most hidebound conservatives will oppose you. Rather, they will gladly unite behind you. How can you not see how they need—they *yearn*—for one voice to bring them together, to speak for Darkover?"

"If they are so eager for a leader," Regis said hotly, "let them choose one themselves!"

Danvan snorted and made a rude, dismissive gesture. "Bah! *Terranan* notions of democracy have no place here. Darkover needs continuation, stability, and, above all, a solution in accord with our own ancient traditions."

He paused, visibly regaining his poise. "It must be you, Regis. There is no other. And it must be soon, so that you are prepared to counter this new attempt to destroy everything we hold precious and honorable."

Regis wished his pulse were not rampaging so insistently. He did not want to wound his grandfather's pride. He searched for a way to tell the truth and yet not be needlessly cruel.

"I will—" *never agree to be king* "—consider what you have said. There may be other options, ones better suited for Darkover as it is now, rather than as it has been in the past."

"Do not take too long," Danvan paused, as if formulating another argument. Then his thin shoulders lifted, his vision cleared, and he went on, "While you are *considering,* give some thought to the necessity of a consort." He raised his voice as Regis began to protest. "Yes, we have been over the reasons why you refuse to take a proper wife."

Near the end of his tolerance, Regis broke in. "And you have not listened to a word I have said on the subject! I have told you more than once that when I actually meet the woman I can accept as a wife, I want to be free to marry her!" He paused, then plunged on. "Not even you, sir, can accuse me of not doing my duty in providing the Domain with an heir. Between naming Mikhail as my son and—" with a glance at Danilo, who had once resented the times Regis had brought himself to have an affair with some woman eager to bear a Hastur child, "and fathering *nedestro* children, I have more than fulfilled my obligations!"

Danvan glared at him, then subsided. "I cannot fault you on that. Mikhail is a fine lad, and you are training him well. But as king, you require a lady at your side. You need not marry her *di catenas*. A consort will suffice."

Regis was about to retort that there was no functional difference. He would be saddled with the woman, no matter what her title. Still, it was a remarkable concession for his grandfather to make.

In all truth, he admitted to himself, he had once thought that in Linnea Storn he had met a woman with whom he could spend the rest of his life. Danilo, surprisingly, had liked her. In the end, the intense flurry of emotional intimacy, fostered by the events surrounding the gathering of telepaths for the new council, had died down. They had parted amicably.

Regis rose, unwilling to pursue the conversation any farther. He bowed to his grandfather, assuring him that he would give the subject of a wife or consort equal consideration with that of the throne, and departed.

With Danilo following close behind, Regis strode down the corridor and through the arched entrance to the stairs. He slowed his pace only when they were well beyond the Castle gates.

Regis recalled Danilo's words on one of the many past occasions when his grandfather had been pressuring him.

"Regis, you are Heir to Hastur and all the burden that comes with it. I would lighten it for you if I could, but no man alive can do that. You yourself would not have it otherwise."

"You lighten it with your understanding," Regis had replied, *"so that I need not face the future alone."*

The old sympathy began to weave itself between them, closer than words, the telepathic bond of *laran*, of sworn brotherhood, and more.

Regis felt the coming of night, the swift veil of crimson-edged darkness that swept across the unseen sky like a vast hush of wings. The earth itself shifted, drawing into itself for the long, lightless cold. Throughout the city, candles and rush torches cast pools of fragile light while above the galactic arm stretched in milky glory across the heavens. Mormallor rose, shimmering in pearly light, followed by mauve Idriel.

This, he thought, *this will endure.* He knew in the fearful recesses of his mind that it might not. Among those points of brilliance, men plotted and schemed, men with knives and blasters and weapons far more dreadful, men with poisons to leave soil and ocean barren, to warp the very nature of living cells, to steal the will and crush the hope of his people.

The bedroom fire had died down, its embers glowing like molten gems, then drifting into ashes with a sound that was softer than a maiden's sigh.

Danilo, who had fallen silent and watchful, reached out to touch Regis on the back of one wrist, a telepath's butterfly-light touch.

Come to bed, beloved. Tomorrow's sorrows will still be there in the morning.

Regis met the other man's gaze. In the psychic rapport catalyzed by touch, he felt as if there were no barriers between them. His heart was joined to Danilo's, as it had been for so many years. They both understood, without the need for speech, that one reason Regis had chosen to remain in this house was that here they might find a modicum of privacy. The love between men was not shameful by Darkovan standards, but their constancy in the face of Regis' refusal to marry made both of them targets for scandal and censure.

They also knew that if the issue of Federation membership was as urgent as they feared, Regis would have to take up his formal position as Regent, as Hastur of Hastur. In order to rule effectively, with all the influence of his position, he must move to his quarters in Comyn Castle, and there they must comport themselves as lord and paxman.

Regis had filled the bedroom with family treasures from Castle Hastur. The bedframe of wood glossy and black with age, the Ardcarran carpet underfoot, the lamps of Shainsa filigree work, the panels of translucent blue stone, all created a haven. The room smelled of leather and spice and love.

They turned to one another with a desperate passion, as if they could lose themselves and all their cares in it.

Long into the night, Regis lay awake in a tumble of bedclothes. Danilo curled on his side, facing away, one shoulder bare. Regis grasped the comforter to cover him. As he moved, Danilo made a small, strangled sound. Regis drew back, for it had been many years since Danilo had cried out in his sleep from the old nightmares. He had learned not to ask, just as Danilo respected his own moments of tortured reflection. Some wounds were best left alone. But what, he wondered, had come back to haunt them now?

3

Heart pounding, Regis jerked awake. Footsteps sounded outside his bedchamber door, not the clatter of heels, but muffled, as if the wearer had no desire to announce his arrival. Darkness shrouded the chamber, and the air was still and heavy. The mattress still bore the faint imprint of Danilo's body, but it it was cold. Such a time, Regis thought, invited despair.

He shook himself free of the dregs of sleep and reached out with his *laran*. Immediately, he sensed Danilo's presence. The door swung open with only the mildest of creaking. The flickering light of a taper shone on Danilo's face. Shadows etched hollows around his eyes, but the slightly haunted look was not all illusion. He wore his ordinary working clothes, a dagger at his belt. Regis ached for him, for whatever old wound had been touched during the night.

Danilo glided to the bedstand and touched the taper to the candle there. "I'm sorry to disturb you, *vai dom,* but there is an urgent matter requiring your attention."

"Meaning something you cannot fend off by yourself?" Regis winced at his own dark mood. His anger was not toward Danilo but toward whatever had so disturbed Danilo's sleep that he should be up and dressed—and armed—at this hour.

The second source of irritation was Danilo's use of the honorific, the shift from lover and equal to loyal paxman.

"What is it?" Regis asked, more gently.

"A messenger from the Legate."

"It's not yet dawn. Couldn't it wait until a decent hour?"

"Apparently not."

"Forgive me, I'm in a beastly mood. You have done nothing to displease me." Regis reached out for the bond between them, heart and mind and body's sated need.

And if I should *displease you?*

"Zandrua's frozen hells, Danilo! What does *that* mean? Look, I don't want to quarrel with you. If I can't rely on you, you of all people—to whom can I turn?"

Danilo drew a breath, almost disguising how his voice trembled. "I will be here at your side as long . . . as long as you want me." When Regis reached out a hand to him, he shifted to avoid the touch.

Regis cursed silently, not caring if Danilo sensed his thoughts. *It's that dream, or the Federation, or old memories. Whatever it is, I won't let it come between us!*

"All right, I'll see the messenger in the downstairs parlor." Regis pulled on a dressing robe and shoved his feet into fleece-lined house boots. "I'll be down in a minute. Make sure the man has something hot to drink."

A few minutes later, Regis joined Danilo and the Terran messenger around a newly lit fire. Shivering in his synthetic parka, the Terran looked vaguely familiar in the way many off-worlders did, but Regis could not recall meeting him before. From the tray with its steaming pitcher and untouched mugs, Regis surmised the messenger had refused refreshment. Danilo, despite the outward nonchalance of his posture, looked ready to draw his dagger any instant.

"I am Regis Hastur. My paxman says you have a message for me."

The poor messenger was not only half frozen, but was terrified at facing an armed and obviously suspicious bodyguard. He could not have been more than twenty, probably on his first tour of duty.

"From the Legate," Regis prompted.

"Your Highness—er, Your Honor—Lord Hastur," the man stammered and attempted a bow.

"We can dispense with titles," Regis told him. "I'm sorry you had to come out here on such a night. What is so pressing it cannot wait until morning?"

Some of the stiffness left the messenger's body. "I don't rightly know, sir. The Legate—Mr. Lawton—he asked if you could please come up to Medical. As soon as possible."

"Medical? He's not ill?" Regis felt a little frisson of fear. Why would Dan Lawton send for him, of all people? He had no medical training and only the most rudimentary knowledge of *laran* healing, so he could be of little use there. If Dan were badly injured, dying, he might send for Regis—to disclose what?

The messenger shook his head. "I wasn't g-given that information, j-just to ask you to come."

Regis nodded, decisive. "I'll be ready shortly. Wait here, and for Evanda's sake, man, get some hot drink into you!"

Outside, clouds had blotted out the stars. Needle-edged rain slashed down, a harbinger of the coming spring. Although the temperature was above freezing, the damp wind penetrated even the warmest woolen clothing.

A motorized ground transport stood waiting for them outside the gated grounds of the town house. Regis sensed Danilo's abhorrence of the machine, an echo to his own. The messenger held the door open. Regis sighed as and he and Danilo slid into their seats. The conveyance was practical, given the hour and the weather. Truthfully, he was glad not to have to walk, to arrive at Terran HQ shivering and soaked.

Danilo, tautly vigilant, eyed the Spaceforce patrolmen as they passed through the checkpoints. Beyond the gates, fences and barricades cut off all view of the spaceport. Stark white lights illuminated the entrance to Central Headquarters. The building was dark, the floors slick. The heels of their boots clattered on the hard synthetic surface. Although an underground power plant heated the complex, the entrance hall was frigid. To Regis, the chill was as much of the spirit as of the flesh.

As they made their way up the strange rising shafts and along the corridors of the Medical section, the lighting shifted, became less harsh. Perhaps the sick required illumination that soothed and sustained instead of assaulting the senses. Unlike the outer areas of the building, the Medical section was as busy at this hour as during the day. Staff in white uniforms, and some in pale green or blue, hurried by, speaking in pairs, clutching recording tablets. A few stared at Regis and Danilo.

The messenger brought them to a halt below a sign that read, INTENSIVE CARE. A young man glanced up from behind a long, curving barrier that served as counter and desk. Regis decided he must be a nurse, because his white uniform bore the staff-and-serpent emblem of the Terran Medics. A musical recording issued from the console behind the counter, a woman singing in a lilting, alien tongue, accompanied by drums and guitar. The snatch of melody reminded Regis of the sea.

Regis tried not to stare, for the nurse's skin was a glossy blue-black and his hair a cap of fuzz. His ears were like ebony shells set on either side of his skull. Dark eyes, bright with intelligence, took in the two Darkovans, their native clothing and pale skins. But there was no judgment in that brief glance, only curiosity and good will.

How insular we are, Regis thought, *and how little we know about the infinite variety of humankind.*

"We have been expecting you," the nurse said in a musical voice. "Please wait here while I page Dr. Allison." He returned to his work at the computer console. Regis caught his flicker of amusement at being the object of curiosity.

He knows what it is to be set apart from his kind, to feel different, and yet he has made his peace with it. Regis would have liked to speak further with the man, but just then Jason Allison emerged around the corner. Jason wore a white coat, unbuttoned and flowing, over ordinary Darkovan clothing.

"*Dom* Regis, Danilo, I can't tell you how glad I am to see you," he said in flawless *casta*, inclining his head but making no effort to shake hands. "Come this way."

Regis had known Jason since they had worked together on finding a vaccine for trailmen's fever. He liked and trusted Jason, who had been born on Darkover and lived several years among the nonhuman aboriginals.

They hurried down the corridor that ran behind the nurse's station and past three or four open doors. Regis glanced in, seeing darkened rooms and empty beds, two to a room. The next door was closed, but Jason entered without preamble.

The first impression Regis had upon entering was that he had stepped onto another planet. The chamber was saturated with light and the clutter of carts and machines. The stink of chemicals masked a miasma of emotions. Before he could raise his *laran* barriers, he caught a whiff of curdled fear from the woman on the other side of the bed. She looked up at him with frightened eyes. Regis recognized Dan Lawton's wife.

From the patient on the single bed, surrounded by machines and a spiderweb of wires and tubing, came the flare of *laran*, wild and unshaped. Frantic, barely contained anguish radiated from the man in the corner chair.

The intensity of the emotions and the utter strangeness of the surroundings battered at Regis. Sensations, raw and intense, flooded through him.

Memories surged up through the tumult. In the recesses of his mind, Regis was once more fifteen and wracked by threshold sickness. He remembered how visions had swept his mind like blasts of a Hellers storm. His head had throbbed, and his eyes had flickered with jags of eerie light, incomprehensible visual traceries . . .

Solid warmth steadied him. Blinking, Regis came back to himself. Danilo stood at his back, leaning into him, supporting him.

Ever there, my faithful friend. You saved me then, and you save me now.

The bizarre sensations had not been solely memories of his own struggles as his *laran* awakened. Regis had been picking them up from the boy who lay on the bed. With his own psychic senses, he tasted the drugs surging through the boy's bloodstream, off-world medicines designed to sedate and numb. All they had accomplished, however, was to blur the boy's mind, to deprive him of any understanding of what was happening to him.

Moved to pity, Regis reached out to touch the boy. His mother shrieked, "Stay away from him!"

At the same time, Dan Lawton, who had been sitting in the corner, leaped to his feet.

Jason ignored the woman's outburst. "Regis, do you know what's wrong with him? Is it threshold sickness?"

"This farce has gone on long enough!" the black-haired woman cried. Her anguish sizzled in the air, panic edged with bitterness and love for her child. "I will not have abominable, superstitious natives treating my son! Felix is critically ill. You said so yourself, Dr. Allison! I insist on proper medical care for him, do you hear?"

Jason guided her toward her husband. "Ms. Lawton, sit down now or leave the room."

"I mean your son no harm," Regis began. "I'm here to help, if I can."

"There's nothing you can do!" Violet eyes blazed at him, molten. "Nothing! Because he cannot possibly have contracted this degenerate alien threshold syndrome!" She jerked away from Jason's hold. "Daniel, *tell them!*"

"Tiphani, we've been over this—" Dan protested.

"No!" Ebony tresses whirling around her pale face, Tiphani faced her husband. "This is all wrong! I will not have my own son exposed to those native—those—*perverts!*" She lunged at Regis as if she would attack him with her bare hands.

Regis recoiled, not only from her words themselves but from the burst of hatred behind them. Danilo placed himself between Regis and the near-hysterical woman. Danilo had not drawn his dagger, but Regis had no doubt that he was now fully protected.

Danilo said, in a voice all the more menacing for its calm, "No one speaks in that manner to the Heir of Hastur. *No one.*"

"That's enough!" Jason said, with all the command of his medical rank. Two nurses, one a woman, appeared in the doorway. "Remove this lady from the room. If she resists, sedate her!"

"What, and leave my son to whatever devil-sorcery—" Tiphani shrieked.

"Go with them," Dan begged. "I'll stay here and make sure nothing happens. You've got to calm down and let the doctor do his work. *Please.*"

"It's all your fault," she raged at her husband. "If you hadn't let him run wild in the gutters, he'd be fine!"

Regis reminded himself that this mother was almost beside herself with worry for her critically ill child. At such times, people often looked for someone to blame.

By this time, the nurses had taken her arms. She tensed, ready to resist. She glanced from her husband's pleading face to Jason Allison's stern authority, to Danilo's poised suspicion. Regis held his silence, believing that anything he said would only provoke the woman further.

As Tiphani disappeared through the doorway, flanked by the nurses, Regis wondered at her reaction. What in Zandru's Seven Frozen Hells was wrong with her? Surely Dan, who was devoted to Darkover, would have chosen a wife who felt the same.

Instead, Tiphani had made a poor adaptation to the world her husband loved and served. Had she been so blinded by love that she did not consider what she was committing herself to, a life on a remote, low-technology planet? Or had she thought she could persuade Dan Lawton to relocate elsewhere, perhaps her own world—what was it called, Temperance? That was obviously not a quality it bestowed upon its inhabitants.

Was happiness in marriage a matter of chance if left to the rages of infatuation? Regis could not help comparing Dan's relationship with his own. He and Danilo were so many things to one another; *bredhin* and companions, lovers and lord and paxman. In Linnea Storn, Regis had found a woman of his own caste who was a trained and powerful telepath as well as a loving person. It was too bad things had not worked out, since he did not know if he would ever find such a good match again.

After a moment of embarrassed silence, Regis bent over the bed. The boy appeared to be eleven or twelve, with the wiry slenderness of adolescence. Reddish tints shone in his brown hair. Sweat covered his skin, which was pale from growing up beneath the crimson sun. He opened his eyes, and Regis thought he looked simultaneously terrified and unaware of his surroundings.

"Is it threshold sickness?" Dan asked.

Carefully, Regis lowered his *laran* shields and touched the boy's mind. Regis had never studied in a Tower, but over the years he had learned not only to master his own psychic powers but to use them in ways no other living Comyn could. To the best of his knowledge, he was the only bearer of the rare and powerful Hastur Gift, that of being a living matrix in himself.

His vision shifted, and he saw not only the white-shrouded form of a pubescent boy but also a tangle of mental energies, streams of color, *laran* surging through its channels, sometimes flowing freely, sometimes pooling, stagnant and festering. The channels in the boy's lower body, which normally carried both *laran* and awakening sexual energy, were dangerously overloaded.

"How long has he been like this?" Regis heard his own words as if whispered from far away.

"He was fine this morning," Dan responded. "Bright, a bit rebellious, a typical adolescent. I thought the trip to the market would do him good. Could he have been made ill by something he ate there?"

Regis shook his head. "I'm not a trained monitor, but I think it's rare for the sickness to come on so fast and strong. Danilo, what do you think?"

With a sense of inexpressible relief, Regis felt his *bredhyu's* mind open to his, a flowing unity that he had never experienced with any other human being. Like Regis, Danilo had not trained in a Tower, and like Regis, he was the sole possessor of a rare gift, that of catalyzing telepathy, of awakening latent talent. Unlike Regis, however, his own passage through the tumult of adolescent threshold sickness had been relatively benign.

Danilo shifted, his mental touch like silk over water, and he said, in a voice that shimmered in Regis's mind, "Where is his starstone?"

"His—you mean a matrix crystal?" Dan said. "As far as I know, he's never had one. Where would he get it?"

Danilo looked directly at Regis. "I'd stake my life this boy has keyed into a starstone. That's why—"

Before he could go further, Felix gave a sudden cry. His body arched upward, straining at the bandages, almost ripping out the needle taped to his arm. Jason sprang into action at the same time Regis did, Danilo a split instant later. Together, the two Darkovans managed to hold the convulsing boy. Regis felt a shock as he touched the boy's skin with his bare hands. Energy, raw and directionless, surged just beneath the surface.

Deftly, Jason adjusted the intravenous apparatus. Regis could not see exactly what the doctor was doing, nor would he have understood if he could. Instead, he sensed a lessening of the frantic surge of *laran* power and a softening of the boy's muscles. A shudder ran the length of Felix's body, and he sank back on the bed.

Regis drew his hands back, frowning. This was not a natural end to the spasm. The convulsions had not run their course, nor had the cause been remedied. He glanced at Jason.

"That will hold him for the moment," Jason said. "I've increased the dosage of antiseizure medication to the maximum for his body mass. I dare not give him any more."

Regis shook his head. "It's not over."

"I know, I know." Sweating visibly, Jason raked his hair back from his forehead. "I don't know what else to do for him. God help him if he has another attack. He could suffer permanent brain damage. That's why I sent for you."

From outside the door came the sound of a woman's voice, taut with strain, and Tiphani's frantic sobs.

"You'd best see to your wife." Regis nodded to Dan, who hurried from the room.

After a few murmured words, footsteps receded down the corridor. The room fell into a hush, the three men and the boy lying so still he seemed to be not breathing.

"Danilo—" Regis began. "You're sure he has a starstone?"

Danilo nodded. "Can't you feel the vibrational pattern?"

"Under all that chaotic flow, who can tell anything?" Regis frowned. "Maybe . . . I'm not nearly as sensitive as you. If you say so, I'll take your word on it."

"I know what a starstone looks like," Jason said, puzzled. "When Felix was admitted, he did not have one on his person or among his possessions. I thought that once a person had keyed into a stone, handling it or taking it away from him could kill him."

For a long beat, neither Regis nor Danilo breathed an answer. Slowly, Jason nodded. "Oh."

If they failed to find and restore the psychoactive gem, the boy's convulsions would get worse. Threshold sickness could be fatal. Regis had lost one of his few remaining *nedestro* children to it.

Regis went to the door. The ebony-skinned nurse, still at his station, pointed toward a room at the end of the corridor. "They went to the chapel."

The door opened soundlessly at a touch. Unlike the chill, antiseptic furnishings of the rest of the building, this room struck Regis as Darkovan. Panels of chestnut-brown wood alternated with hangings in soft greens and blues. At the far end, light glowed softly behind panels of tinted glass patterned like trees and mountains. Even the air smelled fresher. To one side of the glass panels, a red votive light glimmered on a table set with various articles. *Instruments of prayer,* the Father Master at St. Valentine's monastery would have called them. Regis recognized a *cristoforo* rosary, a stack of worn prayer books, a glass vessel filled with flower petals, a bell, and a bronze bowl and stick. Dan sat beside his wife on one of the simple wooden benches, his arm around her. Her back was bowed over so that her hair fell like a cascade of glossy curls over her face.

Something in the tenderness of Dan's posture, the way he stroked Tiphani's hair, and the sweet rumble of his voice touched Regis unexpectedly. Beneath the fear lay a woman who was deeply loved, a mother grievously worried for her child.

Regis took a seat beside her, beyond casual touch, yet close enough to feel the shimmer of almost-*laran* emanating from her shuddering form. She was not Comyn, she was not even Darkovan. He had encountered a range of telepathic talents in off-worlders in the last decade, since he had sent out an invitation throughout the Empire as part of Project Telepath. People with true psychic abilities, not parlor-trick charlatans, were rare, often near psychotic. Tiphani seemed sane enough, just distraught as any mother in this situation might be.

The next moment, the awareness vanished. Tiphani's mind clamped down around her fragmentary gift so completely that she might not have had any telepathic ability at all. In her position as wife to the legate, she must have encountered psychically-Gifted Comyn. Untrained and culturally isolated, she would have had no preparation for contact with other telepaths. The resulting confusion must have fueled discomfort, turning awkwardness into distrust, suspicion into outright hostility.

"I apologize for the intrusion," Regis said, "but for the sake of your son, I must ask you a few questions, *Mestra* Lawton."

She gave a shuddering sigh and lifted her head. Huge violet eyes turned toward him. Even with her cheeks reddened with weeping, she was beautiful.

"You aren't a doctor. What can you do?"

"No," he admitted, "but nonetheless, I am here to help."

"Dearest," Dan said, "it won't hurt to let him try."

Tiphani's hands tightened around the object she held; Regis could not see exactly what it was, most likely some religious token. The hectic color drained from her cheeks, leaving her skin as clear as porcelain.

"I'm sorry," she said in a voice that threatened to break. "I was ungracious when your intentions were kind. I don't know what I can add to Dr. Allison's diagnosis."

"Sometimes, an insignificant detail is the key," Regis said. "While your memory is fresh, tell me as much as you can about your son's activities today. Did he seem in usual health in the morning? What did he buy in the market?"

"You're not suggesting I deliberately poisoned my own child!" Quivering in indignation, Tiphani gathered herself to spring to her feet. "Or exposed him to—I am a decent, God-fearing woman!"

Regis wondered what fear of any of the gods had to do with a sick child. "Let me understand you clearly, *mestra*. Neither of you made any purchases? Could the boy have acquired a small item without your knowledge?"

The woman glanced at her husband, her eyes streaked with red, and then at the altar. She slumped back on the bench. "I did my best. Daniel, believe me! I took the filthy thing away from him as soon as I *realized*. Oh God, it's all my fault! If only I had not been weak in letting Felix have his way! If only I had watched him more closely—"

She broke off, too distraught to continue. Dan did his best to comfort her. She turned her face against his shoulder.

"You took something away from Felix?" Dan murmured into her hair. "What was it?"

Tiphani fumbled in her breast pocket and drew out a wad of fabric tied with a drawstring, on a long loop made to be worn around the neck. The cloth was a handkerchief, the kind that could be purchased for a few *reis* in any market. A crude design had been painted on it. With disgust, Regis realized that it was a tourist's version of the pouches in which many Comyn carried their personal starstones. His own matrix was shielded by triple layers of insulating silk. A piece of blue glass might well have substituted for a genuine matrix stone, which might be offensive but not criminal. Exposed to an unkeyed stone, without guidance or supervision, a latent telepath risked madness or death. Who in their right mind would sell such a thing?

Only a head-blind fool, who could not tell the difference . . . or someone who intended this to happen. Regis suppressed a twinge of paranoia, for the Comyn had been particular targets of the World Wreckers assassins.

Deliberately not looking at Regis, Tiphani thrust the little bag into her husband's hand.

"I'd better take it," Regis said. Handling the bag as if it were a snake that might bite him, Dan passed it over. Regis studied the little bundle for a moment, sensing a pulse of jagged power. The thin cloth provided a barrier to physical touch but none at all to psychic energy.

I'm not a Keeper. I shouldn't even be holding it. But who else was there? Thendara no longer possessed a working Tower, and Linnea Storn was hundreds of miles away. A tendril of longing brushed his heart. When she had left, after only a few years together, he had not realized how much he would miss her.

He closed his fingers around the bag and said to Tiphani, "When you have recovered, join me in the boy's room." He did not dare to say more, to offer even the illusion of hope.

When Regis returned to Felix's room, the boy's condition was unchanged. Danilo let out a low whistle as Regis held out the wad of cloth.

"Is that it?" Jason asked.

Regis nodded. "Open one of the boy's hands. I'll drop it on his palm.

We might need to close his fingers around it, but be careful not to touch the stone."

The boy's fingers were thin, yet long and graceful. There were only five of them, Regis noted, but many of the Comyn had only five. Taking a deep breath, he lowered the bundle to the opened hand and drew out his eating knife.

"Careful," Danilo murmured.

"Pray to your holy saints, Danilo, that he doesn't have another seizure while I'm doing this."

The sharp point of the knife slid easily beneath the knotted cord. The fibers parted with only a little resistance. Regis let out his breath. With his fingertips, he drew apart the folds of cloth. The boy moaned and whipped his head from side to side. Danilo grabbed Felix's forearm to hold it steady.

A flash of blue-white light appeared in the folded cloth. Regis tipped the pouch, sliding the starstone onto Felix's exposed palm.

Immediately, Regis had to look away. Ribbons of liquid light twisted within the heart of the stone. Nausea rose up in him, mixed with something akin to euphoria. Motes of brightness jigged and danced behind his eyes, as they had when he almost died from threshold sickness.

With a practiced mental gesture, Regis raised his barriers. The sensations ended abruptly. He knew that what he had experienced was only a fraction of what raged through the boy's mind. He remembered how his older sister, Javanne, had guided him through attuning his starstone to his mind.

As he curled his fingers over Felix's, closing them around the chip of faceted brilliance, Danilo reached out with one hand and placed it on top.

A shudder ran down the boy's body, very different from his previous convulsive spasms. This was, Regis sensed, a wave of tissue-deep relief, of being made whole again.

Felix opened his eyes and looked directly at Regis. "Where am I?" he asked in an exhausted, thready voice. "What happened?"

Regis almost laughed aloud. "We'll explain later. For now, just keep holding on to that stone. Don't let anyone except your Keeper handle it."

Especially not your mother, he added silently. It was a miracle the boy had survived. Tiphani must not have known what the pouch contained and saw it only as a barbaric talisman.

With a physician's deft touch, Jason taped the stone to Felix's hand. It only took a few moments, but when it was done, the boy drifted into a sound, natural sleep.

Regis felt as if he had just raced from the Wall Around the World to the Dry Towns. Wearily, he said to Jason, "He should be nursed by someone with *laran* training. I don't know of anyone who's studied in a Tower who is in Thendara at the moment. I believe that some of the Bridge Society Renunciates have skill in these matters."

Jason nodded. "Yes, we're fortunate enough to have one or two with that training."

"They will do for the moment," Regis said. "It would be better if we had a Keeper to see to him . . ." Out of the corner of his vision, he caught the fleeting spark behind Danilo's eyes, and knew that his *bredhyu* was also thinking of Linnea.

"I very much suspect that because the Renunciate healer is unconnected with me, *Mestra* Lawton will regard her with favor," Regis said in an attempt to divert the awkward moment. "Can she attend him here?"

"I see no reason why not," Jason said. The three men had reached the doorway. "I won't release Felix until he's recovered from the convulsions. You look exhausted, Regis. I'm sorry to have dragged you out of bed at this hour. Danilo, take him home. I'll speak with the Lawtons."

Jason bowed to Regis, the slight inclination of his body that betokened personal respect rather than the responsibilities of caste. Regis promised to check the boy's progress when he could.

4

During the following tenday, Thendara enjoyed an unseasonably rapid transition to spring, as if winter had suddenly opened its fist. Throughout the Lowlands, the bitter edge of winter softened.

Regis felt the turning toward longer days as a rising hope in his own spirit. Sometimes he paused in the middle of the street while hurrying from one conference or another, or he simply stood looking over the ancient city. All things came in their own season, he reminded himself.

Regis had used Lew's warning as best he could to prepare for the choice that would soon be presented to Darkover. Although the vote in the Empire Senate was not yet official, rumors spread throughout the Terran Zone, spilling over into the city. No formal declaration had yet been made, but that was only a matter of time.

Division on the subject of Federation membership developed much as Regis had expected. His grandfather was not the only one who wanted Darkover to cut off ties with the *Terranan*. Conservatives like Ruyven Di Asturien and Kyril Eldrin immediately made alliances. They saw the reorganization of the Federation as an opportunity to sever all off-world relations.

On the other side of the question were Valdir Ridenow, Regent of Serrais, the Aldarans, the Pan Darkovan League, and many citizens of Thendara. The Terrans stationed on Darkover maintained a carefully neutral public face, but Regis needed no *laran* to tell they were worried.

On one of the visits Regis made to check on Felix Lawton's progress, Dan made him an unexpected offer of assistance.

"This is completely unofficial, you understand," Dan said privately, behind closed doors. "As Legate, I cannot be seen to take sides in the debate. Only the citizens of Darkover may determine their course."

They were alone in Dan Lawton's private office, with Danilo on guard beside the door. Regis remembered again that Dan had a legitimate stake in the debate, for his parentage was part Comyn. The Domains accepted the notion of *citizenship* reluctantly, for the term usually referred to legal rights, rather than the complex web of responsibilities that characterized Darkovan culture. Whatever *laran* Dan possessed was deeply buried and likely to remain so in his Terran role. Yet Regis sensed in the other man a passionate desire to protect the world of his birth.

It was, Regis reflected, not strictly true that Darkover would be allowed to choose without any Terran influence or hint of coercion. If the Terrans decided their own interests were threatened—if, for instance, a disturbance should take place at the spaceport or a Terran patroller should be threatened or injured—then those sympathetic to the Expansionists would seize the excuse to impose martial law. Such a thing had happened on other worlds, according to Lew Alton.

If we do not give them an excuse, they may invent one for themselves.

"I thank you," Regis said carefully, "but there is nothing I need from you now."

Dan nodded. "We still have time before a final decision. However, the prospect of full membership in the Federation may cause . . . unrest."

Dan was saying, in the way he had juxtaposed the offer of help and the warning, *Keep your own people in order, and I will keep mine out of your affairs.*

Revolted by the intricacies of political schemes, Regis changed the subject. "I'm glad your son is better. That, at least, is one area in which our two peoples can work cooperatively for our mutual benefit."

Dan's face relaxed into a smile. "Yes, between Dr. Allison's medical expertise and the care of the Renunciate healer—Ferrika n'ha Margali—he is recovering. It will take time for his *laran* to stabilize, but his life is no longer in danger. Ferrika says that eventually he ought to go to a Tower for proper training."

Regis had sensed the power of the boy's *laran* but had not realized it was so strong. "Indeed? He has the makings of a matrix mechanic or technician?"

"She says . . ." Dan paused, wet his lips, "he could make a Keeper."

Danilo and Regis exchanged startled glances, for both had been taught that only women could hold the demanding centripolar position in a matrix circle. Male Keepers were very rare. Regis had met only one, Jeff Kerwin, now Keeper at Arilinn Tower.

"Do you think it is possible," Dan went on, "that he may have the Ardais Gift?" His Comyn heritage came through that Domain, through his Darkovan mother.

Regis turned thoughtful. "I don't think so, but he could well have another talent. If he does, it must be trained and preserved. There are so few of us, and the old Gifts no longer breed true. I am, to my knowledge, the only living bearer of the Hastur Gift." Again, his eyes sought Danilo's.

And you are the only living catalyst telepath and have no child who might inherit the talent.

Don't rub it in. Danilo looked away, once more the faithful paxman, his features a mask of disciplined vigilance.

Comprehension swept through Regis. He had been a fool not to realize that every time his grandfather pressured him to marry, to father heirs and provide for the succession of the Domain, Danvan also meant the necessity to continue the unique talent of the clan. From there, it was only a small step of logic to the requirement for Danilo to do the same. Catalyst telepathy was the rarest of all the known Gifts. Danilo had the ability to awaken even the most deeply buried latent *laran* in another individual.

Unlike Regis, Danilo had never been able to couple with women for the sole purpose of procreation. He was one of those telepaths for whom a deep mental and emotional closeness was essential to physical intimacy. His heart was focused on Regis, and they were bound not only by love but by the vows of *bredhin* and those of lord and paxman.

"If that is true," Regis turned back to Dan, "then a Tower is the only place Felix can receive the training to properly use his Gift. An untrained telepath is a danger to himself and everyone around him. But someone with the potential to be a Keeper . . . I cannot imagine what that person might suffer if his talent is ignored or suppressed."

"We have already seen the dangers of uncontrolled *laran*," Dan agreed with a touch of grimness. His worried expression returned, tightening the muscles around his eyes. "His mother is opposed to the idea, of course. She has finally come around to see that help from Darkovan telepaths is necessary, but she doesn't like it. She's not . . . she's not a bad person."

"You need not make excuses for your wife's behavior," Regis interrupted, affected by his friend's obvious chagrin. "She acted out of love for her son, as any mother might. I am sorry that our ways are strange and frightening to her."

"Yes," Dan said, "I had hoped that after this long she would have adapted to Darkovan culture. It's my fault for not helping her. I've been so busy with my work, I haven't had the time to help her make Darkovan friends. She's a very strong-willed woman, passionate in her opinions."

"You would not have her any other way, my friend."

Dan's description of his wife reminded Regis of Linnea. For all the years they had been apart, she had never been very far from his thoughts. In a rush, he realized that there was a way to placate his grandfather, temporarily escape the Federation membership debate, and obtain skilled help for Felix.

"There is one thing you could do for me, if your offer extends this far," he said. "Lend me a Terran aircraft."

Dan Lawton had said the Terran pilot was the best, and the man deserved his reputation. He held the small craft on a steady course past the point where most would have turned back. The powerful, unpredictable wind currents of the Hellers made air travel chancy at best.

The land rose as the bones of the earth thrust skyward into uneven, snow-draped peaks. Winds buffeted the little craft, but the cabin was warm. Regis and Danilo had dressed in clothing suitable for mountain travel: knee-length jackets of thick wool, fur-lined hooded cloaks, and stout boots.

Around Regis, the metal device bucked like a badly broken horse. He dug his fingers into the cushioned armrests and felt the safety harness tighten around his chest. His stomach lurched, and he broke out into a cold sweat. Out of the corner of his vision, he glimpsed Danilo's white, set face. Then the aircar leveled out.

Finally, the pilot set down on a frost-whitened field no bigger than the practice yard at the City Guards. Beyond the field stood a village.

Regis clambered out of the aircraft, glad beyond words to be standing once more on firm soil. Wind had scoured away the worst of the snow, leaving the ground almost bare. He turned toward the village, the earth crunching beneath his feet. In the distance, the castle of High Windward perched on a massive outcropping of rock. Regis estimated that it would take a good day's ride to reach it.

A deputation of mountain folk, including one stout graybeard who must be the village headman, hurried out to greet them. From their exclamations, they found the Terran flying machine strange and perplexing. Few of them had seen such a thing, this deep into the Hellers. Their excitement turned to awe when they learned who Regis was. *"The Hastur Lord . . ."*

The pilot, who had thought of Regis only as a native friend of the Legate's, regarded him with new respect.

The headman took them inside his own house, a snug cottage with three separate rooms, its stone walls daubed with mortar to keep out the wind. Like many mountain dwellings, it was situated to make use of the light and to present a solid face to the prevailing wind. After accepting offerings of food, hot drink, and the best place by the fire, Regis asked that riding animals and a guide for the journey to High Windward be provided, and also accommodations in the village for the pilot.

They passed an uneventful night. The headman insisted that the Hastur Lord must sleep in his best bed and would not be persuaded otherwise. As a youth, Regis had slept on the ground while working the fire-lines, and the bunks in the cadet barracks had not been much softer. He would have been just as happy curled up in a blanket before the hearth.

The next morning, as daybreak seeped across the cragged eastern horizon and shadows lay thick across the frozen fields, Regis and Danilo took their leave. The headman's grown son brought out two mountain ponies, clearly the best that could be had, one antlered *chervine* laden with supplies and blankets, and another saddled for riding. The villagers clustered around them, women bundled in layers of woolen shawls, children like round-bellied puppies in their thick jackets, and men with windburned faces and bright eyes.

Regis swung up on his pony. At his height, his feet dangled, and he was already anticipating sore muscles. The beast was unprepossessing in appearance, its rust-black coat so thick and ragged that it looked like a badly shorn sheep. Its long tail brushed the ground, and little could be seen of its eyes through the tangle of its forelock. Danilo's mount could have been its twin, except for a crescent of white on its off-side rump.

They set off, the headman's son in the lead. The bridle rings and the bells on the harnesses of the *chervines* chimed brightly. Regis reined his pony beside Danilo's. To his surprise, the animal had easy gaits and a pleasant, willing manner. Truly, it was the best the village had to offer.

Late in the day, they reached the steep trail leading to the gates of High Windward. Set among chasms and crags, the castle had been originally constructed as a fortress. It was said to date back to the Ages of Chaos, and legend had it that the walls had been raised by *laran* in a single day. Centuries had weathered the stone, leaving the castle like an old toothless dragon, melting back into the rock from which it had sprung. Only the great Sunrise Tower, a soaring structure of translucent stone, seemed untouched by time.

Since Regis could remember, the Storns had been peaceful country lords without any pretense of great power, living amicably with their neighbors and content to trade their fine hawks as well as precious metals from the mountain forges.

They were spotted long before they reached the gates, and a welcoming party emerged. The gates stood open, but they looked in excellent repair. The men who came out to greet them wore swords and looked competent in their use. Regis recognized one of them as having served in the City Guards. A murmur spread through the welcome party.

Regis clamped down his *laran* barriers, but not before he caught the edge of the guards' thoughts. *Hastur . . . The Heir himself . . .*

Would he never be free of it, free to be simply Regis?

After making sure their guide and animals would be properly cared for, fed and given warm shelter, Regis allowed himself to be conducted inside. Danilo followed him like a shadow.

The ancient custom of hospitality still ran strong in the mountains, where life itself depended on the goodwill of strangers against the common enemies of cold and avalanche, wolf and banshee and worse.

The *coridom* welcomed them in true mountain style, refraining from inquiring about their business until their physical needs had been attended to. He escorted them through the vaulted hall, very old by its design, and into a suite of rooms in a more modern section. Panels of wood as golden as sunlight on honey covered the stone walls. Newly lit fires warmed the sitting room and also the two adjacent bedrooms. A servant brought a basin of water scented with herbs, soap, and towels. A moment later, while Regis was still exchanging courtesies with the steward, a second servant arrived with *jaco* and hot spiced wine. After they had warmed themselves and washed, the *coridom* himself returned to conduct them to the solarium, where Lady Linnea waited to receive them.

The *coridom* led them through a series of back hallways, avoiding the major halls where Regis would be easily recognized and a subject of great curiosity, not to mention extravagant hospitality. Linnea knew how much he hated that kind of ostentatious attention.

The solarium, like those common in mountain castles, was a pleasantly intimate room. Carpets cushioned the center of the worn stone floor, and comfortable chairs and divans had been placed for conversation or family activities. Although it was almost dark outside the thick, mullioned windows, the air inside the room still held the sun's warmth. A fire, newly lit, danced in the hearth. Linnea sat on one of the stools before it, picking out a melody on a *ryll,* while a little girl of ten or so accompanied her on a reed flute.

Linnea's head was bent over her instrument, the light of the fire heightening the red-auburn of her curls. The folds of her woolen gown, a shade of green that made her look like a wood sprite, fell gracefully to the floor. An old dog slept at her feet, and a plump middle-aged woman sat knitting in a corner.

For a long moment, Regis could not speak, could not move. The domesticity of the scene, the love evident between mother and daughter, woke a hunger in him. He had never known his parents, for his father had been killed before he was born, ambushed by outlaws wielding Compact-illegal weapons. His mother had died soon afterward, of a broken heart, it was said. In their place, his grandfather had been a stern and undemonstrative guardian only too glad to send his young grandson to be educated at Nevarsin. The only warmth Regis had known as a child had come from his older sister, Javanne, herself thrust too soon into adult responsibilities and a politically advantageous marriage.

Regis had thought that the love he shared with Danilo and the satisfaction of knowing he had done his duty were the best he could expect in life. He had not known, until this moment, that he could want more.

While Regis stood, transfixed by the unfamiliar emotions boiling up within him, Linnea finished the musical phrase and set aside the lap harp. She met his gaze with unaffected directness. Even across the expanse of the room, Regis was struck by the purity of her features, her heart-shaped face, her wide gray eyes, and her air of utter composure. The girl glanced at her mother and got to her feet.

"Lord Regis." Linnea rose, but did not curtsy. As a Keeper, even one who no longer worked as such, she bowed to no man. "You lend us grace. Stelli, this is your father."

She did not ask why he had come.

Before Regis could say anything, the child approached him. She had Linnea's eyes, he saw, but the jawline of his own people. Her hair, the same shade of copper as his had been at her age, fell in two gleaming braids down her back. As she met his gaze, Regis realized that she was younger than he had supposed; she would be eight or nine now. It was her height, her slenderness, and her movement, graceful as a *chieri,* that made her appear older. Her smile brought radiance to her entire face.

Kierestelli. This must be the daughter conceived during the brief, intense time when the World Wreckers almost destroyed their world. That a creature of such grace and beauty could have come from such a black and desperate time amazed Regis.

"Papa, is it really you?" Flute in hand, she ran to him.

For an instant, Regis had no idea how to respond. Surely, she could not remember him, for he and Linnea had separated when she was very young. Could she? He had no time to answer the question before the child flung herself into his arms. He lifted her up, hugging her in return before he realized what he was doing. Her body was agile as a dancer's and her hair smelled like a mountain stream. Awkwardly, he set her down.

"I am sorry if I have offended you, Father," she said. The formal words sounded odd, coming from the mouth of a child. "Mother says I forget myself in gladness."

"And so you do," Linnea said gently. "I think your father is not used to the excitement of children. Make your farewells, and go off to the nursery."

Kierestelli flashed Regis another brilliant smile and skipped cheerfully from the room, accompanied by the middle-aged woman. The room fell silent except for the crackling of the fire.

Linnea gestured to the half-circle of chairs before the hearth. "Regis, will you sit down? And Danilo as well? Shall I send for *jaco* or ale? The ale's quite good; High Windward has a skillful brewmaster."

Her homely reference helped to break the tension. Regis and Danilo settled themselves, and she took a seat opposite them.

"Had you a pleasant journey?" she asked, when they declined refreshment.

"It was well enough, thank you," Regis said. "We came by aircar as far as Black Rock village."

Linnea nodded. "It's a long day's ride at this season, but I remember attending the harvest festivals there as a child." She paused, waiting for him to say more.

"You look well, and so does Kierestelli," he said.

She gave a little laugh. "As you see, we are both very well. Regis, I cannot believe that you came all this way, and risked taking a *Terranan* flying-machine into these mountains, simply to inquire after my health. Please tell me why you have come. Has something happened? Is it your grandfather?"

"No, there is nothing wrong with him beyond his years," Regis hastened to assure her. "I came to ask a favor and also to see you. It has been too long."

"It *has* been a long time." Linnea glanced away, for the first time a trifle unsure; then she gathered herself to face him directly. "What favor?"

He'd forgotten how straightforward she was, how plain and unaffected in her speech. She'd never been rude, having been brought up with all the social niceties of their class, but years as a Keeper, coupled with a natural frankness, had stripped away conventional insincerities.

As simply as he could, Regis told her about Felix Lawton. At the end, he said, "Will you come to Thendara to work with him?"

"Thendara is far away," she said, her tone guarded. "It's hard to believe that there is no qualified *leronis* nearer."

"There is no one else with your training who is not committed to work in the Towers. The Bridge Society healer can help him through the worst of his threshold sickness, but she cannot teach him how to use his *laran*. She thinks he may have the potential to become a Keeper."

You more than anyone knows how important it is to nurture such a talent.

Her gray eyes widened, but only for an instant. "It would not be a simple matter to move to Thendara. I have made a life here. High Windward is my home. And there is Kierestelli to consider. You have seen your daughter, Regis. How do you think she would fare in a city?"

Regis had not considered that Linnea would keep Kierestelli with her. Having seen the two of them together, however, he understood why Linnea would not consider leaving without her.

"I could arrange for accommodations in either the Hastur section of Comyn Castle or my own town house," he said. "Thendara is a large city, with all that implies. At the same time, it offers many resources, art and culture and society, a chance to learn about other worlds and to meet a wide variety of people."

"To be assaulted and exploited by them, you mean." Linnea's gray eyes flashed silver fire. She did not need to remind Regis of his own dead children, slain by World Wrecker assassins before Kierestelli was born.

He leaned forward, resting his elbows on his knees. "That was a long time ago. Yes, any place where large numbers of people live together has problems, but I promise you that our daughter will not be exposed to them. I myself will keep her safe."

There it was, his word on it. The word of a Hastur was still considered more binding than any oath.

Linnea sat very still, with the unearthly calm she had developed in her years at a Tower. "Yes," she said quietly, "I believe you would."

She got to her feet in a swirl of woolen skirts. "I must think about this. Such a decision ought not to be made carelessly or too quickly. Meanwhile, enjoy the hospitality of High Windward. The cooks have been rushing around like headless barnfowl since your arrival, concocting a dinner they believe worthy of you." She smiled with a trace of mischievous spirit. "My kinsmen are also anxious to welcome you properly. Don't worry, they keep to the old ways and will not press you about your business here."

"I believe I can endure an evening of toasts and storytelling," Regis said.

"Then," she said, going to him and laying her fingertips on his arm, "let us go down to join them."

5

The next day brought fine weather, high clear skies of the crystalline brilliance of the mountains. Regis and Danilo went riding with Linnea and Kierestelli, the three adults on shaggy ponies, the girl on a beautiful silver-gray *chervine*. Regis noticed that although the little doe wore a halter, Kierestelli never touched the reins. Girl and animal moved as one, bound by a sympathy of mind.

Linnea took them down the path to the old, deserted village of the forge folk and showed them the caves where she had played as a child. Regis very much suspected that Kierestelli did the same. Once or twice, they came upon a herd of wild *chervines* who stared at them, unafraid, before bounding away. Kierestelli laughed and clapped her hands.

That evening, they took their dinner along with Kierestelli and her nurse in the suite of rooms that Linnea had grown up in. These were in the same wing as the chambers Regis and Danilo had been given. Regis realized that Linnea had a hand in that choice.

"I knew you wouldn't be comfortable in the Royal Suite," she said on the second night, as they sat near the fire over cups of warmed *firi* and bowls of *pitchoo* nuts. Kierestelli had just gone up to bed. "It's huge and echoing and pretentious. They say it was built just in case a Hastur Lord should visit. I think it's been used only once, and that by bandits."

"You're right, I'm much better where I am," Regis answered. Replete with hearty country food, exercise in the cold air, and undemanding companionship, he was far more relaxed than in Thendara.

"I do admit," he went on in a jovial mood, "there is a certain appropriateness in reserving the Royal Suite to the princes of the road, as outlaws are sometimes called."

"The folk who dwelled here would have been far less amused at the prospect," Danilo said.

Linnea glanced at him. "Yes, from all accounts that was a terrible time. The fellow's name was Brynat Scarface, or something like that. You can still see the damage to the inner parapet where his men breached the walls."

"Let us hope those lawless times never come again," Danilo said.

Regis took a sip of his *firi*, finding it too sweet for his taste. The Terrans had brought more effective policing methods, and the Domains had been at peace with one another for decades. The closest they had come to war was during the Sharra business, when Beltran of Aldaran marched on Thendara with an army. Still, Regis reflected grimly, the decline of the Comyn created openings for ruthless men to take advantage of the weak. Petty thieves were one thing, even bandit kings like Brynat Scarface, but should a leader emerge, one bent on conquest and willing to use any means necessary to seize power . . .

He came back to himself as Linnea picked up her *ryll* and tested the tuning of the strings. She picked out the melody of an old lullaby, a tune so haunting that Regis wondered if he had heard it in his dreams. She sang in a light but pleasant voice. Then she shifted into a walking song with a strong rhythm, and Regis sang along, while Danilo accompanied them on a small drum.

Eventually, the silences between songs lengthened. Regis noted that Danilo was yawning. "Go to bed before you fall over."

"I'm all right."

"I'm in no danger here, and you're done in. I don't want to have to carry you."

Danilo's gaze flickered to Linnea, sitting with her *ryll* on her lap.

Are we going to argue because I want a little time with the mother of my daughter? Regis thought.

Danilo pushed himself to his feet. "I'll be off, then. *Vai leronis,*" he bowed to Linnea. "Regis."

After Danilo had departed, Linnea set her harp in its case. "He has no reason to be jealous of me."

"Protective, I think."

She sighed. "Do you remember how we teased him about sleeping across the threshold of our door?"

"Come here." Regis held out his hand to her and indicated the place on the divan beside him. "I remember what happened behind those closed doors."

She came to him, still holding herself apart, but smiling now. "It was glorious, that brief time. I regret none of it. How could I, every time I see Stelli?"

Regis remembered when, in a gesture of compassion and openness of heart, Linnea had offered to give him children to replace those murdered by the World Wreckers. Then, as now, he had thought that a child by her would be precious beyond words.

"I do not regret it, either," he said in a voice made hoarse by emotion. "It is said that when we love someone, they become part of us forever."

What was this fey, romantic mood that had taken hold of him? He felt the yearning harmonics of the ballad thrumming beneath the beating of his heart. On impulse, he said, "Could we ever get it back, do you think?"

She turned to him, gray eyes wide with surprise. His question had caught her off guard. No, he told himself silently, it had caught both of them unprepared and open.

"I—I don't know. Such things do happen. Regis, please don't toy with me. You know I loved you, and I love you still. And *I* know that your first, your primary love will always be Danilo."

"Is that why you left Thendara? Because you could not share me? Was the love I was able to give you not enough?"

Linnea shook her head, refusing to be drawn into a quarrel. "No, it is not that. I simply—" She got up, restless yet still too much in command of herself to give way to pacing. "I wanted more. I thought we loved each other in those first days enough to find our way through any difficulty. How little I knew! It was my first serious love affair and, I suspect, yours with a woman. I didn't anticipate how intense the feelings would be, how sweet, how overwhelming. I think we both went a little mad. I didn't think . . ." Now she turned back to him. Shadows of remembered pain cloaked her eyes.

"I didn't measure what I would lose against what I would gain. In the end, it wasn't enough."

"I don't understand," he said. "You have our daughter and as much of my heart as I am capable of offering to any woman. Is that not sufficient?"

Too late, after the words were said, Regis realized what she had given up. She had been a Keeper, one of the few elite Tower workers capable of occupying the centripolar position in a matrix circle. Through her supple, disciplined mind had run the interwoven psychic powers of every member of the circle. Their lives as well as their sanity had been in her keeping. Once, Keepers had been revered as gods, living apart and virgin, immune to normal human warmth. For a man to lift a hand to a Keeper or even assault her with a lustful glance had been punishable by death. Those times were long past; Keepers no longer trained in the old ways of inhuman restrictions. Linnea had not been a virgin, although she had set aside her work as a *leronis* when she came to him.

"Surely—surely you can still function as a Keeper?" Regis said. "You know how to do so safely?"

She sat down beside him again. The fragrance of her hair, some kind of spicy herb, filled him. "Of course, I know how to keep my channels clear," she said. "I have known that since my first training as a monitor. I did not lose my skills along with my virginity. But, Regis—I cannot be both Keeper and mother."

She paused to let her words sink in. "In a circle," she explained, "I must put all other thought aside, leave all loyalties and considerations outside the door. The slightest lapse or indecision might have disastrous consequences. I cannot abandon Kierestelli, not even for a single night. She is always in my heart, in my thoughts. Can you understand that?"

Slowly, he nodded. He wondered what it was like to be so loved by a woman. His bond with Danilo was of quite another sort, one unique to their histories. Danilo's catalyst telepathy had wakened his deeply suppressed *laran* when they were still teenagers. Danilo was the other half of his mind, of his heart. Yet in his encounters with women, in the happiness he had glimpsed in married couples, he sensed a different balance, a complementarity that both excited and puzzled him.

He felt a stirring of desire and admiration, of respect and then rising pleasure, in her nearness. They sat close enough so he could see the tendrils of hair that had escaped from the clasp at the base of her neck. He remembered touching the soft skin there, tasting her, feeling his own passion in her eager response.

"Could you teach Felix," he asked, "give him the training he might have received in days gone by from a household *leronis*?"

"Yes, I could . . . if I were sure that Kierestelli would come to no harm in Thendara. And," she added in a whisper, "if you wanted me there. I would not subject her—" *and myself*—"to your resentment."

"My—? Linnea, if you do not believe my words, then believe this . . ."

Regis leaned forward and slid one hand beneath the coils of her hair, cupping the back of her head. She sighed and moved toward him. Deliberately, he lowered his *laran* barriers so that his mind was open to hers. He offered her the tenderness now welling up in him, the response of his body to hers.

He had forgotten how soft her mouth was, how smooth her skin. It felt as if she were kissing him with her heart, not just her lips. Her touch was not like a man's, not like Danilo's, and yet it was perfect.

The thought struck Regis that it was impossible to compare one person's loving with another's. How could Linnea take Danilo's place or he hers? Then all rational thought disappeared as he gave himself over to the kiss.

The rapport between them deepened, obliterating all outside awareness. Regis had forgotten how strong her *laran* was, how supple her mind. Echoes rippled through him, wordless emotion and memory of the deep sharing they had once offered one another. In that world of thought, no time had passed. The first moment of their love was still going on, stretching into the future. In the opening of one heart to another, they were still bound.

The wave of passion crested. Linnea drew back, her eyes shining. The light from the fire burnished her hair to dark copper. Lips parted, cheeks flushed, she had never looked lovelier to him.

She rose and took his hand, smiling slightly. "My rooms, I think."

Linnea had taken a suite in the older part of the castle, apart from the rest of the inhabitants. As they made their way down the chilly hallway, Regis sensed the muting of the background psychic chatter. Of course, someone with Linnea's sensitivity and Tower training would prefer a degree of insulation.

As they entered the sitting room, the young maid who had been tending the fire stood up.

"Thank you, Neyrissa," Linnea said. "I won't need you for anything else tonight."

The girl curtsied and hurried away. Linnea stretched her fingers toward the fire. Regis came to stand beside her, although he had no need of bodily warmth.

"Are you sure you want to do this?" he said.

"You mean, will gossip about us fill the castle tomorrow morning?" She looked up at him with a mischievous gleam in her eyes. "I am a *leronis*. I have not granted any of my kinsmen the right to be the keeper of my conscience—or of my virtue, or my reputation—nor am I likely to. I tend to those matters as I myself see fit. My family accepted this when I went to Arilinn."

She paused, somber now. "We are not so different in this, you and I. We do our duty as honor demands but according to our own understanding. It would have been far easier for you to set Danilo aside and marry. I'm sure *Dom* Danvan Hastur and the entire Comyn Council would have been delighted."

"I choose whom I take to my bed and with whom I share my life."

"As do I." Linnea closed the space between them and slipped her hands around his neck. Her fingers parted his hair, caressing the sensitive skin on his nape. Tilting her head back, she stood on tiptoe and whispered, "I choose . . ."

In the echo of her words, Regis realized that he, too, had chosen. This night would not be like so many others, the pleasantry of a few hours, the discharge of his responsibility to produce heirs for his clan and caste. In the past, women had been drawn to him because of his position and power, his beauty, his sensual personality. By the time Linnea entered his life, he had grown cynical about women. Because he could have almost any woman he wanted, he had wanted none of them. She had changed all that with the simple opening of her heart, a woman of his own caste, a trained Keeper willing to set aside her own dreams to ease his grief.

This was no dalliance, this night. Every kiss, every caress, created anew the love that had once flowed between them. Her joy magnified his own through their shared rapport. He danced through the movements, feeling how their differences complemented and enhanced one another.

At the peak of their pleasure, when all the world swirled around him in a rapture of iridescent light, Regis became aware of a change in that radiance, a gathering of energy into a tiny point. Golden light-that-was-more-than-light bathed the mote. Regis felt a sense of imminence, of condensing presence, and knew that Linnea sensed it also.

Regis had once promised himself that he would not marry, would not share his Domain with any woman with whom he was not also content to share his life. This woman now bore his son.

He had been a fool to let her go. This time, he would make sure it turned out differently.

Regis rose early the next morning and found himself whistling under his breath as he broke his fast. The meal was a round, crusty nut-bread, pots of jams and preserves, a platter of browned, steaming sausages, and bowls of pickled redroot.

Danilo had already gone down to the stables, preparing for their departure. He had been asleep when Regis returned in the early hours, so Regis had not had the chance to tell him that he had a private matter to discuss with Linnea. After last night, Regis had no doubt that she would understand his intentions in only a few words. He must return to Thendara, but she and Kierestelli would follow as soon as arrangements could be made.

In times gone by, they would have had to obtain permission to marry from the Comyn Council. Now, with the Council disbanded, that was not possible, but Danvan Hastur must be consulted. The old man would doubtless be delighted. The ceremony itself should take place in the Crystal Chamber of Comyn Castle with as many dignitaries and Comyn as could be assembled.

Regis paused in adjusting folds of his short indoor cloak. In all likelihood, the wedding itself could not be arranged sooner than Midsummer, but that was all for the best, for many of the remaining Comyn still came to Thendara during that time.

Still whistling, he sent a servant ahead to ask Linnea to receive him. After waiting what seemed an appropriate time for the lady to prepare herself, he made his way to her suite of rooms. The same maidservant from last night ushered him inside. Linnea wore a gown of gray that shimmered a little like moonlight. She looked up from the little table on which sat a tray bearing a pitcher of the usual *jaco* and a basket of plain brown bread. She came toward him, her expression puzzled.

Regis took her hand in his and drew her to sit beside the fire.

"Linnea," he began, "we have known one another for a number of years."

She stiffened then, perhaps at his formality or the prospect of unpleasant news. He winced, fearing that he had inadvertently offended her.

"As you know, my grandfather has pressured me to marry for a long time. Until now, I could not bring myself to do so. It has also been suggested that I choose an official consort for ceremonial occasions—"

Linnea did not move. Her skin turned very pale. Her breathing became slow and shallow.

"I want to be frank with you, Linnea. I have not—in the past, I have not had the deepest feelings for women." He swallowed hard. "You know that since boyhood, I have been committed to Danilo."

"I doubt there is a single Comyn in the Seven Domains who is not aware of your preference." Under the calmness of her voice, she gave no hint of her feelings.

"Be that as it may," Regis cleared his throat, "for the sake of my Domain and the necessities of my position, I must have a legitimate heir of my own body."

. . . the son we conceived last night . . .

"You already have an heir," she pointed out.

"My sister's son, Mikhail, yes. But that was an extraordinary circumstance. I thought I might not return from Caer Donn. If anything happened to Mikhail, I could not ask Javanne again—it would be better if . . ."

Linnea turned away. She kept silent for a long moment, leaving Regis hanging in a hellish backwash of uncertainty. Then she said, very quietly, "I am aware of the great honor you do me, Regis. I am grateful for your honesty."

She paused, visibly gathering herself. "As you say, we have known each other for some years now. I think we have been as good friends as a man—particularly a lover of men—can ever be with a woman. But I do not believe . . ." Her voice faltered and grew rough. ". . . that I would care to . . . to be a ceremonial consort . . ."

"I asked you to be my wife!"

"Wife, consort, *barragana*! It is all the same!" she shot back at him. "It would mean binding myself to someone who does not want *me*, only a woman—any well-born one will do!—to fill a position!"

Regis stared at her in dismay. Never had he thought to see the usually calm and self-possessed Comynara in such a state.

"That's not what I meant," he stammered.

"I understand you all too well! You come all the way from Thendara, flouting your position and your wealth. No ordinary Darkovan, even a Comyn lord, could command a Terran aircar. You offer me the one thing I cannot refuse, the one thing you knew I could not turn away from, and that is the means to work, to use the skills for which I trained so hard, and still be a mother to Kierestelli."

Training Felix to use his laran! In the frenzy of the moment, Regis had all but forgotten that request. Obviously, Linnea had not.

"And then you come to me, all romantic. You ply me with memories of the dreams I—we once had. You play with our daughter, you give me hope that we could be together as a family. You kiss me and hold me as if I were the most precious—"

She broke off. Every fiber in her slender body quivered in outrage. He realized the depth of her sense of betrayal. Had she thought he had given himself entirely to her? Had he created that impression?

Had he not been in love with her last night? What kind of inconstant villain was he?

Between one heartbeat and the next, Regis realized that, as a Keeper, Linnea must have been well aware of her own fertility. She had deliberately allowed herself to conceive—she had *chosen*—because she believed so fully in his love for her. His mind had been open to hers, as hers to his. How could they have come to such a misunderstanding?

"I'm s-sorry," he stammered. "I h-had no idea you would find my proposal so distressing."

His stilted words only made matters worse. What little experience he had with women failed him now. He blundered on.

"You see, I thought that since we were friends, it would be all right." Trying to keep the rising panic from his voice, he reached out to lay his fingertips lightly on her wrist. She jerked away. "If I must have a wife, surely it should be someone I care for, rather than a stranger."

"A *stranger*!" Her eyes brimmed with hot, angry tears. "So now I am little better than a stranger?"

"I do care for you, Linnea. I give you my word, the word of a Hastur, that no other woman has ever meant as much to me. Or ever will."

"Is this supposed to make me feel better?" she raged. "Can't you see that only makes things worse?"

"Linnea, what is wrong? I don't understand why you are so upset. You've always been so calm, so—"

"So in control of myself? I am—I *was* a Keeper and celibate. Why do you think I must choose between that work and sexual intimacy?" Wringing her hands, she surged to her feet and began to pace while Regis watched, helpless and aghast. "Regis, I know I'm overly emotional. I *know* I'm being unfair to you. But that doesn't mean I am not also telling the truth. It's not just that we made love last night, it's that we *made love*. I didn't *just* have sex with you."

She was right. Their union had been more, not just the pleasure of the body, but a joining of their hearts and psychic energy. And more . . . If he closed his eyes, he could still see the tiny glowing point of new life. No wonder she was reactive, brittle, with nothing left for dealing with the troubles of ordinary life, let alone a proposal of marriage.

"Please," he pleaded, "sit down. I spoke clumsily, but I meant well. The situation cannot be that bad."

Linnea turned, her gray eyes pools of shadow, and lowered herself to the divan beside him. She was still trembling, but she was no longer weeping.

"I know you care for me," she said, her voice rough, "but I don't think it is enough."

"What would you have me do?"

Linnea took a handkerchief from her sleeve and wiped her eyes. "I do understand. But *you* must also understand that I have needs and feelings, too. Even if—even if I could make a life for myself in the shadow of your love for Danilo—always second, never allowed to forget that you two are sworn to one another, *bredhin,* that no woman could ever come between you—even then, there are others to consider."

He raised his head.

"There is Kierestelli . . ." she said gently, "and our unborn son. I must provide for both of them—"

"As my wife, you will want for nothing—"

Impatiently, she brushed aside his offer. "I meant that I must provide for their emotional needs, not their physical comfort. What do you think it would do to them, growing up in a family where their parents merely tolerate one another? It would be a cold house indeed, and I alone cannot change that."

In a moment of insight, the words *cold house* echoed through his mind, and his own childhood came rushing up. He had grown up in such a *cold house,* starved for affection, constantly measured and censured, first by his grandfather and then by the monks at Nevarsin. Surely, she must be wrong—he would never allow that to happen to his own children! How could she believe such a thing?

"I can't court you with fancy words," he said, wrestling his anger under control. "Linnea, look into my heart and see if I am such a monster. I love you . . . and I would love our children."

And give them a better home than I ever knew.

"You say that now, when I have something you want, when I still have it within my power to say no!" Her fury had returned, edged with desperation. "Once I give in, you will make me an appendage, an ornament. You said so yourself—*an official consort for ceremonial occasions!* A toy to be paraded before the court and then set aside. I will sleep like a prisoner every night, while you—you—I will not have even half of your heart, I will have none!"

What did the woman want? How could he make her understand? Was there any woman in the world worth this kind of humiliation?

Again, he tried. "You spoke of my heart. Is a heart divisible? Can it not be big enough for more than one person? Do we not each love many people in our lives—parents, cherished friends, children, lovers?" The words came rushing out from deep within him. "Can one beloved ever truly take the place of another? I have already said that I love you as much as I can love any woman. Is that not enough to build a life together?"

Eyes glittering like ice, wild mood spent, she turned back to him. "But you did not ask me to marry you out of *love,* Regis. You asked out of duty, out of convenience, out of *political necessity.*"

"I made a mistake. I spoke badly, I admit it! Does that matter if the love is there?"

"I hope that you and Danilo find the happiness you deserve, or at least a measure of peace," Linnea said, striding to the door and laying her hand on the latch. "But you must find it without me. I shall always be your friend, as you will always be the father of my children."

"I suppose I had no right to a better answer," Regis muttered. "If that is your final word on the subject, then I wish you a long and prosperous life and that you may find more joy in it than I have found in mine!"

He bowed to her, his cheeks burning with anger and shame. Then he withdrew from the chamber without another word, vowing that he would never put himself through such an ordeal again.

6

Wrapped in his fur-lined travel cloak, Regis stormed across High Windward's courtyard. Danilo stood talking with one of the grooms and the headman's son from the village. The ponies and pack animal were saddled and ready to go. The Red Sun was well up, radiating a tentative warmth.

Danilo smiled pleasantly as Regis approached. "Good morning, my lord. Did—"

"Let's get out of here!" Regis snapped. He did not wait for any assistance but grabbed the reins of his pony from the groom, thrust the toe of his left boot in the near stirrup, and swung into the saddle.

Danilo's eyes widened for an instant. He gestured to the headman's son and handed a small purse to the groom. Regis had already booted his pony into a trot, headed for the outer gates, when Danilo caught up with him. The ponies, fresh and eager, jogged down the ice-hard trail.

Despite the easy gait of his mount, each step jarred his clenched teeth. He knew he should not press the ponies so early in the day, that they would require their strength to reach the village or risk having to camp overnight in the open. The need to get away as fast as possible consumed him.

"Regis! *Vai dom,* what is wrong?" Danilo's voice held a note of true concern. "Has something happened?"

"She said no!"

"*No*? I don't understand. Will you slow down and talk to me? You're upset . . ."

A harmonic of distress in Danilo's voice brought Regis back to himself. When he touched the reins, the pony dropped back into a walk and heaved a sigh at this return to sanity.

"She said *no,*" Danilo prompted. "She will not come to Thendara and work with Lawton's son? Why not?"

Glancing back, Regis made certain that the headman's son was far enough behind so that they would not be easily overheard. "I asked her to marry me, and she refused, quite emphatically."

With his nerves still raw from the interview with Linnea, Regis felt Danilo's emotional reaction, astonishment and anger.

"I am surprised to hear it," Danilo said, his eyes focused between the ears of his mount. "Indeed, I cannot imagine what she must be thinking. I was under the impression that there was not a woman in all the Seven Domains, except a few among the Renunciates, who would not leap at the chance to become Lady Hastur."

Regis could think of no reply. He did not know if he were more angry at Linnea or at himself, for having mishandled the proposal so badly. For good or ill, the words were spoken, the offer rejected.

You can't put a banshee chick back into its egg, ran the old proverb. At the moment, he would much rather have tackled one of the giant carnivorous birds than his own feelings.

Several minutes passed in silence, broken only by the muted clop of the ponies' hooves and the creak of the leather harnesses. The breath of men and beasts made plumes of mist in the cold dry air. The trail steepened, and the animals slowed.

Their way wound along the side of the mountain, from which sprang an enormous knuckle of bare rock, the outcropping on which High Windward perched. From time to time, they caught glimpses of the peaks beyond, the sloping meadows draped in layers of hardened snow.

Morning sun turned the ice-encased trees into confections of crystalline beauty.

Regis sensed Danilo's storm cloud mood. "Let's have it. Are you *glad* she rejected me?"

"When were you going to tell me?" Danilo said tightly. "On your wedding night? Or when you ordered me to find housing elsewhere?"

"I *am* telling you, now. I swear to you I did not come here with the intention of proposing marriage to her, or even asking her to become my ceremonial consort—"

"Or your seamstress, for all that matters! You owe me no explanations, *vai dom*."

"Danilo, don't go all formal, my-lord-this, my-lord-that, on me. I only decided on it last night."

I know what you were doing last night.

"Stop it!" Regis cried. "If I've given you cause to be jealous, tell me. I won't have it festering between us. If all the malicious gossip of the court, not to mention Grandfather's machinations, could not drive a wedge between us, how can one failed marriage proposal?"

"You think I'm *jealous*?" Danilo turned to him, and Regis saw the hurt in his paxman's eyes. "That's not it at all! I know very well that you are expected to furnish the Comyn with as many sons as you can. I accepted your liaisons with women over the years, even the *malicious gossip* you spoke of. Did I complain when you and Linnea became lovers? Did I do anything to make life more difficult for you? Did I ever—once—ask you to set her or any other woman aside?"

"No, you have ever been faithful to the vows we swore to one another." *If there has been a failing, it has been mine.*

"Then why this sudden change?" Danilo demanded. "Why, when you were so opposed to marriage, when you consistently defied your grandfather and the entire Council on the matter, did you suddenly take it into your head to propose? Why did you keep it secret? Do you have so little trust in me? What else are you hiding?"

Regis rocked back in the saddle, causing the pony to flick its tail in protest. Danilo's anguish brought back the wretched fight surrounding Crystal Di Asturien's pregnancy. Regis ought to have told Danilo himself, but the news had come, in the most spiteful manner, from Dyan

Ardais. Danilo had been hurt and outraged, then as now. His sense of betrayal had not arisen from Regis sleeping with a woman but from the secrecy about an event that had the power to drastically alter both their lives.

"I've never kept my relationship with Linnea secret," Regis protested. "You knew that if I ever gave in to Grandfather's demands, she would be the one. You and she get along tolerably well, and I thought of her as a friend. More than that, she is of my own choosing, not some brood mare selected for me by the Council."

"What a nice, convenient solution!" Danilo barked. "You get your grandfather and the Council off your back, and Comyn Castle gets a chatelaine, all at very little trouble to yourself!"

Regis bit back a hot reply. His temper had been in shreds when they began this conversation, and it was increasingly difficult not to take out his frustration on Danilo.

"I suppose what decided me," Regis said, trying his best to speak calmly, "was seeing little Kierestelli. I had no idea a child could bring me such delight. I don't want her to grow up not knowing me."

"And this is why you proposed to her mother, without so much as mentioning the possibility? Excuse me, *vai dom,* but that is nonsense. You could have ordered the child to be fostered in Thendara, where you might see her at your convenience."

In his memory, Regis saw the snug little room, heard the lilt of Linnea's harp and the sweetness of Kierestelli's flute. In a low voice, he said, "It would not be the same."

Had he finally encountered something in life in which Danilo had no part? Sadness shivered through him.

How can I choose between them . . . the man I love, to whom I am sworn, and the family I never knew I longed for?

It came to him, in a rush that left him breathless and his hands limp on the reins, that Danilo had made exactly this choice. Made it with without hesitation, without a backward glance, without ever a hint of recrimination at the cost.

"Danilo, do you ever regret what you have given up? I know you were raised *cristoforo,* and they do not look kindly upon lovers of men. You must have been taught to want a wife and family . . ."

"I am hardly an observant *cristoforo*. It was my father's faith, one I accepted without question when I was a child," Danilo said with such bleak finality that Regis could think of nothing that would reach him. "As for the other matter, do not trouble yourself. I have never thought to marry, my lord. I am entirely at your service. Perhaps next time you will see fit to advise me before you decide to marry."

Regis raised one hand to his heart to ease the ache there. He could not remember such a gulf between them. And he did not know what to do to bridge this one.

"Danilo . . ."

"Regis, let it go. Please. We're both hurt and angry, but it will pass."

Danilo was right. The proposal had touched a sore point, one that might never be resolved. It was best to let the matter rest and to go on as best they could, knowing they would always have each other.

The interview with Danvan Hastur did not go well. Regis had delayed as long as he could, stopping first at the Terran Headquarters to meet with Dan Lawton. Dan had masked his disappointment well. Felix was making slow progress and would have greatly benefited from having a Keeper as a guide and mentor. Perhaps, as the remnants of the Comyn returned to Thendara during the old Council season, another teacher could be found.

Regis could not help thinking that if only he had handled the situation better, Linnea would at this moment be preparing to come to Thendara. *My clumsiness has cost more than my own pride.*

Once the visit with Lawton was concluded, the baggage sent on its way, and the pilot given an additional gift for his excellent services, Regis had returned to the townhouse on the pretext of making himself presentable to his grandfather. Danilo performed his duties as paxman and bodyguard with faultless precision and not a hint of personal feeling.

Danvan's personal servant, a quiet, meticulous man named Rondo, who had come from Castle Hastur about three years ago, ushered Regis into the master suite of the Hastur apartments in Comyn Castle. After the intimacy of Linnea's chambers at High Windward, the rooms felt emotionally barren. They were certainly comfortable, warm and well-appointed, the stone walls covered in tapestries. Regis remembered staring at the hanging beside the door leading to his grandfather's study, trying to decipher which of the two women portrayed was the Blessed Cassilda and which was Camilla, but the threads were so faded, he could not be sure. He imagined the accumulation of years, the unrelenting demands of Comyn honor, blending into an oppressive weight. These walls were no better than the bars of a cage, one that pressed closer with each passing year.

Some day, will I be like Grandfather, an irascible old tyrant with only dreams of past Comyn glories for comfort? Danvan Hastur was revered throughout the Seven Domains. Regis knew that his own unhappiness put such thoughts into his mind.

The servant gestured for Regis to enter his grandfather's study. Wincing at the formality, Regis turned to Danilo. "You'd better wait here. He'll be upset enough, and I don't want him to take it out on you."

"As you wish." An unreadable emotion flickered behind Danilo's eyes. Then he added, in a voice low enough so the servant could not overhear, "Don't let him bully you, *bredhyu*."

Regis felt a smile rise from his heart, stopping just short of his lips. He nodded to Danilo and followed the servant inside. The room, like the rest of the suite, was very much as Regis remembered it, untouched by time. A faint aroma of beeswax polish, paper, and leather book bindings hung in the air. A fire brightened the hearth, and ranks of candles produced enough light for even aged eyes to read easily.

Danvan Hastur stood beside his writing table, bracing himself on one hand, a man who once had been strongly built, of commanding presence, but who had now shriveled into a husk. Looking at his grandfather, Regis felt a wave of pity. Time and too many seasons had quenched the fire that once burned in those blue eyes. How many years did the old man have left, and how many of those would he insist on wasting in service to a world that, very possibly, no longer wanted it?

Regis paused, bowed formally, and then approached. Danvan held out his free hand. Regis took it, feeling the bony joints, the slight trembling in the withered muscles.

"Good morning, sir."

"So you're back from seeing the Storn woman," Danvan lowered himself into his chair and gestured for Regis to be seated as well.

"News travels fast," Regis said neutrally.

Danvan's scowl deepened. "What a dreadful mess you've made of it! You've managed to lose a perfectly eligible young woman, one who's already borne you a child so we know she's fertile, and, of course, there's not the slightest question of her parentage or *laran*. Did you deliberately offend her so that she wouldn't have you? And do you intend to do that with every other suitable young woman—" Danvan broke off, wheezing and coughing.

"Grandfather, please calm yourself," Regis said, alarmed at the old man's breathing. "You mustn't make yourself ill."

"It isn't *me* that's making myself ill," Danvan snarled.

"I regret that you think I arranged for my proposal to be refused in order to annoy you," Regis said hotly. "My offer to *Domna* Linnea was quite genuine. I am as—as distressed by her answer as you are."

"I doubt it."

"Nonetheless, it is done. Are you sure you are well? Can I get you *jaco?* A tisane? Hot wine?"

Danvan leaned heavily on one armrest, still breathing with difficulty. At the mention of hot wine, he nodded, and Regis called Rondo to bring some. A few minutes later, the servant returned with the drinks. He hovered, face furrowed with worry, as Regis poured out a goblet. A little of the wine spilled as Danvan grasped the cup in both hands and brought it to his lips. He took a large gulp, closed his eyes, and sagged in his chair.

"Rondo, don't linger," Danvan grumbled. "My grandson can tend to me." The servant glided away.

"You aren't well, sir," Regis said. "Have you seen a healer?" There was no point in asking if Danvan had consulted a Terran physician.

"I'm fit enough for the work before us," Danvan muttered. "The only thing wrong with me, other than the passage of time, is I was foolish enough to think that when you went to High Windward, you'd finally acquired sense: marriage, then accepting the throne, standing up to the Federation . . . But I was mistaken. You haven't come around to my way of thinking, have you?"

Regis shook his head. "We've had this discussion a dozen times before. Nothing you can say will change my mind. I don't believe returning to a monarchy will solve anything. In fact, I believe the opposite, that we must move toward broader participation, increased literacy and communication, not a concentration of authority."

"Spare me your degenerate notions! Clearly, you've been contaminated by your *Terranan* friends. Next you'll be saying we should look to the common people for leadership, against all our history and traditions."

"If you'll forgive me saying so," Regis said stubbornly, "the days when we Comyn were regarded as descended from the gods are long over. Darkover is in transition, and such times are never easy. The old ways are gone, and we must create new ones, a culture that embodies the finest of who we are. I have a great deal more trust in the people than you do. If we allowed them more education, if they understood what was at stake, then they could fully take part—"

"Where would that get us? The rabble see only the advantages of Terran citizenship, the luxuries. They have no concept of the price. It's up to *us* to maintain our integrity in the face of these temptations—we, the Comyn, what is left of us." The old man subsided. He had half-risen from his seat in the heat of the argument, but now he sank back. Under his breath, he muttered something that sounded to Regis like, "—if you won't do your duty, there is another who will—"

What was the old man talking about? Had he not emphasized, time and again, that Regis had the only legitimate claim to the throne? The only other possibilities were the minor Elhalyn children, hidden away by their reclusive mother.

"Grandfather, I think it prudent that we discontinue this conversation. Clearly, it is distressing to you, and neither of us can possibly say anything that will change the other's mind. I wish you good day, then, and take my leave of you." Without waiting for an answer, Regis bowed and strode out of the room.

Regis passed Rondo outside the door. "Look after him." Rondo nodded and went inside.

7

When Regis returned to his townhouse, a message was waiting for him. Dan Lawton had sent word of the vote in the Terran Senate. The Empire was now a Federation. Pending the reformulation of planetary classification protocols, all Class D Closed Worlds, including Darkover, were now Protectorates of the new Terran Federation.

Regis barely had a moment to sleep in the next tenday. Half the people he talked to reacted with outrage to Protectorate status as a *de facto* military takeover, and the other half rejoiced in it as a step toward full Federation membership. Several small riots had taken place in the markets, for the warming weather had brought a stream of traders and farmers who feared its impact on their livelihoods.

Working closely with Gabriel Lanart, Commander of the City Guards, Regis was able to disperse the worst of the gatherings with a minimum of violence. It had been a decade since he had led Darkover through the World Wreckers crisis, and many people still remembered him. He began walking the streets when he wasn't meeting with Telepath Council members, Guild masters, or Cortes judges. His height, features, and distinctive white hair made him stand out in any crowd. Danilo was not happy about this public vulnerability, but he assumed his role as bodyguard with good grace. In a way, it was like old times, the two of them together.

Felix Lawton improved enough to be discharged from Medical, although he remained housebound. Regis visited from time to time, which allowed him to hold informal discussions with Lawton. The Terran Legate hinted that the newly reconstituted Federation Senate was unlikely to take immediate action on Darkover's planetary status. They had time to plan their strategy, but plan they must, for the reprieve could not last.

With the lengthening days, the roads through the mountains became passable once more. Word had gone out about the Senate vote, by telepathic relay or by simple messenger. By this time, almost all the remaining Comyn knew about the new Federation, and some journeyed to Thendara to make their voices heard. Just as Regis was making preparations for an informal gathering of Comyn that summer, Rondo arrived at the town house with a private message that Danvan Hastur had been taken suddenly, seriously ill.

Regis raced through the hallways of Comyn Castle, Danilo at his heels.

If he dies, it's my fault! If I hadn't provoked him when he was ill, and then ignored him . . .

Regis could not imagine Darkover without the old man.

Rondo waited at the entrance to the Hastur apartments. The servant had no perceptible *laran,* but grief surrounded him like a dark halo. He opened the door to the bedroom and stood back for Regis and Danilo to enter. This time, Regis would not ask Danilo to wait outside. *I go to make my farewells as I am, not as he would have me.*

Regis could not remember the last time he had stepped into the ornately furnished bedchamber. By far, the majority of his visits had been conducted in the presence-chamber or the study. Light filtered through the windows with their thick, irregular panes of glass. A film of dust lingered on the polished surfaces of the chairs and desk, the huge blackwood armoire, the immense old-fashioned bed with its headboard carved in a scene of a stag leaping through a stylized forest. Over the headboard, a coat of arms bore the Hastur device, the silver fir-tree, and motto in the archaic plural form: *Permanedó*.

We shall remain.

Rondo closed the door behind them. The room, although spacious, seemed filled with people, Danvan's secretary, looking very agitated, a couple of servant women, and three or four young pages. One of the women was wringing out a cloth over a basin on the washing stand, and the other was measuring a tincture into a goblet.

For a terrible instant, Regis feared he had come too late. His grandfather lay so still, it was impossible to tell whether he was still breathing. Then the old man groaned and shifted. Regis crossed the room in a few long strides and bent over the bed.

Pale blue eyes opened, blank and unfocused, without a hint of recognition. One withered hand pawed the bedcovers. The gesture moved Regis unexpectedly.

"Grandfather," he murmured, "it's Regis. Don't you know me?"

He almost expected the old man to sit up and berate him for one thing or another, mocking his concern as weakness. As the seconds blended into minutes, Regis knew this would not happen. In fact, his grandfather very possibly would never recognize him again.

Regis turned to Rondo, who had come to stand, like a mute sentinel, at the foot of the bed. "What's wrong with him? Has a healer been consulted? Why isn't someone attending him properly?"

"It was a stroke, a seizure of the brain." One of the women that Regis had taken for a servant stepped forward, goblet in hand. She looked vaguely familiar, and he realized that he had seen her in the Terran Medical Building. She was one of the Bridge Society Renunciates, although garbed in ordinary women's clothing.

"I am sorry," she said, "there's very little we can do for him."

"Surely, the Terrans have treatments—I must apologize, *mestra,* I have not greeted you properly. I don't know your name."

"Ferrika n'ha Margali."

"The same who helped Felix Lawton?"

She smiled, a lightening of the corners of her mouth. As she stepped closer to the bed, the light shone on her ruddy hair.

"Then I am doubly in your debt. Has Dr. Allison been sent for?"

"*Dom* Danvan would never permit it," Rondo interrupted.

"My grandfather is in no condition to protest."

Rondo glared at Regis for an instant before bowing his head.

Ferrika gestured for Regis to come apart from the others. "Lord Regis, not even the most sophisticated Terran medical technology can reverse old age. If your grandfather had not suffered a stroke, then it would be something else. I am sorry to sound harsh, but neither do I wish to offer you false hope. After a century of living, the body falls apart; it is only a matter of which organ system will fail first."

Regis could not tell whether his grandfather was aware of their conversation, and if so, what he thought. The old man would doubtless make a caustic comment about the weakness of will that could not overcome such a trivial inconvenience as death.

"How long does he have?" Regis asked.

Ferrika glanced away. "Only Avarra knows the length of a man's years. If he improves in the next two days, then he may live on for a time. But not, I think, for very long."

"Live on . . .?" Regis echoed her words. "Like this?"

How Grandfather would hate to be trapped in a shell of unresponsive flesh, dependent on others for the simplest care.

Ferrika's gaze met his with a disconcerting directness that reminded Regis of Linnea. "Sometimes, a swift ending is a blessing."

He nodded, unable to speak. Ferrika began ushering the others from the room. Danvan's secretary protested, but not too vigorously. Rondo set his jaw and looked as if he would refuse, until she reassured him that he would be summoned if there was any change. In the end, only Danilo remained, on guard just inside the door. Ferrika left the two of them alone with Danvan.

Regis found a chair and drew it up near his grandfather's head. His mind had gone blank, as it had when he was a boy called to account by this stern, disapproving old man.

Moments slipped by, marked by the halting rise and fall of the old man's chest. With his psychic barriers down, Regis felt Danilo's steady presence. Danilo believed in him, believed that he could rise above the past. Therefore, Regis must find a way to see the best in this old man, as he had in so many others.

One of Danvan's hands lay on top of the covers. The fingers, with their arthritic joints, quivered like the wings of a misshapen bird. On impulse, Regis grasped the hand. Its lightness surprised him, the softness of the paper-thin skin, the frailness of the bones.

"Grandfather . . ." He could not force the words through his lips, even if he knew what to say.

Grandfather, there's so much I never told you . . .

Tears stung his eyes, but Regis refused to look away. He focused on the pale blue irises that glimmered between crepey lids.

See me, hear me. Forgive me.

"I know I often disappointed you," Regis said aloud. "I couldn't live up to my father's reputation—" *which grew in glory with each retelling and which you never let me forget.* "I couldn't be the king you so fiercely wanted me to be. I'm sorry if I let you down."

Regis paused, unable to overcome the resentments that surged within him. Certainly, he admired his grandfather, for who of the Comyn did not, even when they disagreed with him? Part of him still craved the old man's approval, although he knew he would never have it. Nothing he did would ever be good enough, nor would any sacrifice of his dreams ever be great enough.

He had run out of time. Unless he spoke now, he might never have another chance to set aside the old rancor, to summon all his compassion, to send his grandfather to whatever came beyond life with a clear conscience.

"Grandfather . . ."

Suddenly, the blue eyes cleared, and the withered mouth moved silently. Regis tensed, and bony fingers closed around his own with desperate, brittle strength. *Regis . . .*

Regis gasped, taken by surprise. Danvan Hastur, for all his force of will and personality and his extraordinary statesmanship, had very little of the *laran* that characterized the Comyn. He had been able to lead the Domains for three generations by diplomacy, wily cunning, and reasoned argumentation. For him to now speak mind-to-mind required almost superhuman effort.

Regis . . .

Grandfather, I am here.

I . . . am dying . . . have . . . very little time . . .

One mind, linked directly to another, could not lie about a matter of such importance.

. . . secret I have carried . . . these many years . . . your brother . . . you have a brother . . .

Regis startled, almost dropping out of telepathic rapport. A brother? How was that possible? He had always believed that he, like Danilo, was the only son of his parents. To the best of his knowledge, his parents had been so devoted to each other that when Rafael Hastur had been killed, his wife Alanna had lived only long enough to deliver Regis and then had died of a broken heart.

. . . your father's son . . . nedestro *. . .*

Lord of Light! Had his mother known?

Danvan's gaze wavered in intensity.

No, it was . . . before they married . . . Regis! . . . find Rinaldo . . . bring him to Thendara, ensure his rights . . . as Hastur . . .

The old man's mental presence, which had strengthened for a moment, now thinned like mist.

An older brother! Regis reeled under the thought. For so much of his life, he had struggled under the weight of believing himself the sole Hastur son. *Nedestro* children were often legitimatized; Regis had done this for his own offspring, those that survived infancy.

Promise me . . . came Danvan's fading thought, more plea than command.

"Of course, I will. A brother, I never thought to have a brother!" *And a brother with a claim to Hastur, a place among the Comyn.*

Then . . . what would his life be like, as a second son? Might he at last be free to choose for himself?

Swear . . .

Regis wrenched his thoughts away from the tumult of possibilities. He felt as if his entire world had just turned inside out. What sort of man would his brother be, after all these years? No, Regis thought, he must set aside these questions for the moment. All would be revealed in the proper time.

Although he did not know if his grandfather could feel it, he tightened his grasp around the limp hand.

"I swear."

There was no response, neither of the flesh nor of the spirit.

Regis sat there, holding his grandfather's hand as it began to cool. His eyes were parched, his heart empty and aching, until Danilo touched his shoulder.

8

Over the next tenday, Comyn and minor nobility streamed into Thendara to attend the funeral of Danvan Hastur. One of the first to arrive was Javanne Lanart-Hastur, older sister to Regis. Her husband, Gabriel, who commanded the City Guards, had sent word to her immediately. By a feat of organizational skill, she singlehandedly managed the journey from Armida for herself and her household. Her two older sons were already in Thendara, serving as officers in the Guards under their father's stern eye, and her daughter Liriel was a novice at Tramontana Tower.

As soon as Javanne had settled in, Regis and Danilo paid her a visit. With Lew Alton and his only child off-world and no other Heir to Alton, Gabriel held the position of Warden of that Domain, and his family now occupied a spacious suite in that section of the Castle. The rooms, although newly cleaned, still retained a musty, disused smell. They had not been in regular use since the days of Lord Kennard.

Javanne, a bevy of serving women, and her daughter, Ariel, were unpacking a chest of household linens when Regis entered the sitting room. Her features were taut with strain. Awkwardly, he took her in his arms. She drew in her breath as if to speak, but the words choked in her throat. Ariel, a thin girl of fourteen or so, was too nervous and shy to look directly at Regis.

"I didn't think to see you so soon, nor under such circumstances," Regis began.

"Mother, I can't find—" Mikhail, sturdy and golden-haired, burst from one of the inner rooms. His face came alight. "Uncle Regis!"

"Come here, lad." Regis gave the boy a kinsman's embrace. No, Regis realized, not a boy. Mikhail had grown into a young man. The season at Armida, a working horse ranch, had added muscle to his body and a steady judgment to his gaze. He had open, generous features and an air of calm beyond his years, sensitivity combined with a naturally even temper.

I have not done my duty in training him as he deserves, Regis thought, for although he had seen to it that Mikhail had a proper Darkovan education and service in the cadets, he had acted out of his own convenience and not Mikhail's need for a thorough apprenticeship in statecraft. Now, with Danvan's death, all that changed. Once the funeral and attendant period of official mourning had passed, he must make arrangements for Mikhail to move into the townhouse.

No, not the townhouse, Regis corrected himself. It was one thing for the Heir to Hastur to indulge himself in the isolation of a private residence. He was now the Head of his Domain and must live here, in Comyn Castle, in his grandfather's old quarters. He shuddered at the thought of those cheerless rooms.

Regis clapped Mikhail on the arm and stepped back. "We must discuss your future, but this is not the time."

Mikhail nodded. "I expected as much. With Great-grandfather's death, your situation and mine have changed. I expect that you will want me here in Thendara year-round now, and I intend to be of as much assistance to you as I can."

Gods, the boy was sharp!

"Mikhail!" Javanne burst out. "How can you say such things at a time like this! Where are your proper feelings?"

"What else should he say but the truth?" Regis turned to his older sister. "Mikhail is thinking of the future, as a Hastur must. It's exactly what Grandfather would have expected of him."

"You are right, of course. We must all look ahead, even in the midst of . . ." Javanne went back to the table and picked up a length of fine embroidered *linex,* as if she would wring it between her hands. "It's all so sudden and difficult. My entire life, Grandfather has been there, as dependable and enduring as the Wall Around the World."

And as unforgiving.

Her head jerked up, eyes white for an instant. Regis remembered that she had trained for a season or so at Neskaya Tower. He'd have to be more guarded in his thoughts around her. Certainly, she was distressed by their grandfather's death, but Regis pulled back from a subtle change in her. He could not identify it precisely, only that she was no longer the same sister he once trusted.

"Ariel, come away with me . . ." Mikhail motioned to his younger sister, and a moment later, they retreated to an inner room and closed the door.

Regis took Javanne's hand and led her to a divan. He had to move an armful of shawls and a cloak to make room for both of them.

"I, too, once believed that Grandfather would last forever," he said gently. "I put off assuming my full responsibilities because he was always here. The best way we can honor his memory is to strive for the highest standards of honor and duty. Even as he did."

Javanne sniffed and wiped her eyes with the corner of one shawl. "You were never unworthy, Regis. He should have told you he was proud of you. I know he was, he was just too—" a sob came out as a hiccough, "—too stubborn to admit it. To either of us."

Regis felt his heart give a little jump. He had always thought that Javanne had had an easier life, simply because she was a woman and less was expected of her. She had already fulfilled her primary duty, that of producing sons. She'd given birth to three fine boys and two daughters, one of them with enough *laran* to be accepted at a Tower. In that moment, Regis realized that she had had no more encouragement or approval from the old man than he himself had. No one, least of all Danvan Hastur, had ever consulted her on her own wishes. Had she wanted to remain at Neskaya? Or choose her own husband? Or not bear one child after another until all her youth and beauty were spent?

"Javanne . . . did Grandfather ever talk to you . . . about our family?"

She startled. "Why do you ask?"

"Before he died, Grandfather revealed to me . . . Javanne, prepare yourself for startling news."

Her eyes widened, and Regis caught the flicker of her fears. *What terrible secret did the old man lay upon us now? Scandal, rebellion, poison from the skies?*

"No, nothing like that. *Breda,* we are not alone. We have a brother."

"A—no, surely that's not possible! Mother—"

"No, not hers. Father's son."

"Father would never have . . ." She collected herself. "Such things happen. In the old days, when a woman was heavy with child, or ill, it was no shame if her husband took another to bed to spare her the burden."

The burden? Regis brushed the thought aside. Had Linnea thought their lovemaking a *burden?*

"An older brother," he continued, "conceived most likely before our parents were wed. He is, of course, *nedestro.* I don't even know if he's aware of his parentage. All I have is a name. Rinaldo."

"Rinaldo." Javanne frowned, her brows drawing together, as if she did not quite like the taste of the name. "It's an old family name, to be sure. I'm certain I've never heard of him. Where has he been all these years?"

"That's the problem, Grandfather died before he could tell me." Regis sighed. "But not before he made me promise to find Rinaldo and secure his rights."

Javanne's eyebrows lifted, and her mouth formed a moue of surprise. "Bless Evanda I was born a woman and exempt from such duties. I don't envy you. Where will you start?"

"With Grandfather's private papers, most likely. It's too much to hope that he kept a record, but the search must be made. I would like Mikhail's help, and it would give him exposure to the not-so-public history of Grandfather's Regency."

"That's a good idea," she said. "You'll want to keep Mikhail with you, and not just in Council season and Midwinter. While I have appreciated the extra time with him at home, I can't look at him without thinking he is no longer mine."

"Sister, in his heart, he will always be yours."

"That is as it may be." Pain flickered behind her eyes, quickly masked.

Regis, struck by the vehemence behind her words, looked away. "There is another matter on which I would ask your help." He did not mean the words to sound so stilted.

Her expression turned polite. "You are now the Head of our Domain. You have only to ask."

"In a few days, the Castle will have more Comyn residing here than it has in years," he began. "The *coridom*'s overwhelmed as it is, and the housekeeping staff isn't adequate to that many. In addition, I must move my own household into Grandfather's old quarters." He searched for the right way to phrase his request.

She nodded. "You can't possibly oversee all that and attend to the funeral, not to mention your new duties. As sister to the new Head of Hastur, it would not be improper for me to take on the duties of Castle chatelaine."

Regis closed his eyes, trying not to sigh audibly in relief. Javanne had capably managed the great estate of Armida.

"This is only temporary," she cautioned him, "until you have a wife or an official consort to take over the position."

"That event will be a long time coming," Regis said with an edge of bitterness. "After the season, most of the Comyn will return to their own homes, and we will manage with the staff we have. Perhaps you can recommend additional housekeepers to the *coridom*."

Shrugging, she got to her feet. "Now, if you have no further startling revelations, I really must get back to unpacking."

The funeral procession for Danvan-Valentine, Lord Hastur, Warden of Elhalyn and Regent of the Seven Domains, left Thendara along the Old North Road. Except for the Aldarans, all the Domains were represented, for the weather had been mild enough to permit travel. In addition, Dan Lawton attended for the new Terran Federation.

For the moment, the debate over Federation membership had been set aside. Whatever their differences, the various parties had agreed on the traditional period of mourning. A man of Danvan Hastur's stature deserved no less. He had not only ruled the Hastur Domain through three generations, but had guided the Domains through the most turbulent and uncertain times in memory.

Slowly, the cavalcade proceded past the cloud-lake at Hali. Across the seething mists stood the ruins of Hali Tower, a silent testimony to the horrors of unbridled *laran*. Regis wondered if it would ever be rebuilt, or the Tower in Comyn Castle occupied once more. Beneath him, his fine Armida-bred mare tossed her head, sensing his unease. Something terrible had happened in this place, or something was about to happen, he could not tell which. Only when they moved off, nearing the *rhu fead*, did he draw an easy breath.

Regis found himself astonished at the quality of his grief. For so many years, he had resented the old man's meddling. Why should he now feel such a poignant loss? It was beyond comprehension. Danvan Hastur had never had a kind word for his grandson and had never ceased trying to part Regis from Danilo. Now that Regis was finally free of his grandfather's interference, he missed the old man more than he could put into words.

Following the ancient custom, Danvan's body was lowered into an unmarked grave. The hole gaped like a wound in the world. The mourners gathered around. As the highest-ranking person present, Regis was expected to speak first.

"When I was a child, my grandfather seemed indestructible," he began, remembering Javanne's words, "like an elemental force of nature. He was the only father I ever knew, and he wanted me to be an honorable man and a good Son of Hastur. I can only hope to do as well by my own children." He couldn't think of anything else to say, and he wanted to finish before tears choked his voice. "Let this memory lighten grief."

Javanne came forward, leaning on her husband's arm. "I was eleven when my parents died, and Grandfather was there when I needed him. He chose a wonderful husband for me," her hand tightened briefly on Gabriel's, "and once . . . *once*, he told me that he was proud of me, that

I was a good wife and mother, and that my sons did me credit. Let this memory lighten grief."

"When both my sisters died, and I unexpectedly became the head of my Domain," said Marilla Lindir-Aillard, "Lord Hastur called on me, putting aside his own grief, to help me adjust to my new position. Let this memory lighten grief."

Valdir Ridenow, Warden of Serrais, stood a little apart from the others, surrounded by a couple of his kinsmen and his favorite nephew, Francisco. "Some have called Lord Hastur antiquated and hopelessly out-of-date, but that was neither kind nor true. He lived a long time and guided Darkover through many difficult challenges. He always tried to make sure that any change—or lack thereof—was what was best for all of us. Let this memory lighten grief."

Ruyven Di Asturien observed, "Lord Hastur oversaw a great deal of change over his lifetime, but he still held to the values of the Comyn. When we last spoke, he told me how proud he was of his grandson, that he trusted Regis to defend and maintain the Comyn. Let this memory lighten grief."

Regis heard the unspoken warning. The Di Asturiens had played a pivotal role in Comyn politics for as long as Regis could remember. Theirs was an ancient and dignified family, but as conservative and scheming as any. It was said they never did anything without at least two hidden motives. What had Grandfather and Di Asturien been plotting?

When Dan Lawton came forward, a few muttered that a *Terranan* had no business speaking. Their neighbors quickly hushed them, reminding them that since his mother had been Ardais, he had as much right to be there as any of them. He waited until the flurry died down.

"Danvan Hastur once told me that it was his ill fortune to rule over a period of upheaval," he said, "but I cannot think of any man more capable. He did not choose to be chief Councillor to King Stephan, nor to assume the Regency on that King's death, nor to negotiate with the Terran Empire for over three generations. He never shirked his duty, and his determination and loyalty preserved the Darkover we all love to this day. Let this memory lighten grief."

As the other mourners spoke, Danilo had hung back. As the former Warden of Ardais, he had the right to be among the first to speak.

Through the turmoil of emotions, Regis could not sense his friend's thoughts. Danvan Hastur had never found personal fault with Danilo except for his relationship to Regis. Danvan had long since advanced the opinion that the Heir of Hastur ought not to have the reputation of a lover of men, and the sooner Regis married, the better.

With his face tightly set, Danilo stepped forward. He gathered himself in a moment of silence, and when he spoke, his voice was rough. "I knew Lord Hastur as a man of honor. When I was wronged, he saw to it that justice was done. Let this memory lighten grief."

On the journey back to Thendara, rain began to fall, at first a mist, then a sprinkle of ice-edged tears. Finally, sheets of rain slashed down from the darkening skies. Water pooled in the ruts of the road, turning solid ground to mud. The horses snorted and clamped their tails to their rumps. Woolen cloaks were soon soaked, but they retained their warmth.

About half the party, including Javanne and the other women, stopped at an inn in one of the villages. Regis and Danilo, along with the Ridenow party, pushed on.

As Danilo dropped back to rearguard position, Valdir Ridenow reined his horse beside Regis. The overcast sky and icy rain made his skin even paler than usual. His hooded cloak and the saddle blanket of his horse were of fine orange and green wool. In the shadow of his hood, his hair gleamed like pale gold, as fair as that of a Dry Towns lord. The reins hung loose in his hands, and from the way he sat his horse, a rangy blood-bay without a speck of white, he clearly possessed the Ridenow empathy with beasts. Regis thought him maybe ten years older than himself, a well-favored man who had been strong and active all his life, but he could not recall ever seeing Valdir in any meeting of the defunct Comyn Council.

Politely, Regis nodded. As the new Lord of Hastur, he held higher rank, and it was his prerogative to initiate a conversation. Feeling emotionally exhausted, wrung out like a rag, he would have preferred to ride back in solitude. Yet curiosity stirred as Valdir returned the greeting.

"I did not have a proper chance to greet you on your arrival in Thendara," Regis said. "You must have had a hard ride from Serrais."

"This early in the season, yes. I thank you for your concern, *vai dom,*"

Valdir replied, somewhat formally. "Faced with the two gravest situations in the last decade, I could do no less."

He meant the coincidence of the death of Danvan Hastur and the Terran Federation question. "I have no wish to be rude," Regis said wearily, "but my grandfather is not yet cold in his grave, and we are both chilled and drenched. I have not the slightest intention of discussing the future of Darkover under these circumstances."

Valdir's horse threw up his head, as if reflecting his rider's reaction. But the Ridenow lord said, "My deepest apologies if I gave that impression. Surely, such matters as *the future of Darkover* merit serious attention and thoughtful debate."

A debate you intend to be part of? Regis smothered a sigh. "We will speak at the proper time, in the proper setting."

With an enigmatic smile, Valdir returned to his own kinsmen.

Mikhail, who had been riding close enough to overhear the conversation, guided his horse forward. "Was that something I should know about? I can't tell if *Dom* Valdir meant he was your ally or your enemy."

"If he is anything like his cousins, we will find ourselves on opposite sides of the Federation membership debate," Regis said, frowning. "However, men have been known to change their minds. We must wait until we hear what he has to say before placing him in either camp."

Mikhail glanced back, peering through the rain at the green and gold cloaks of the Ridenow party. "Francisco Ridenow seems to be a pleasant enough sort. I think I might have a word or two with him, if you don't mind."

"By all means, get to know him. Unless *Dom* Valdir produces a son, young Francisco stands in the line of succession, so if you are already on friendly terms, you may be of support to one another."

Regis arrived back at his townhouse to find a hot bath waiting. He waved away the help of his servant and stripped off his sodden clothing himself. Danilo helped with his boots.

Fresh-smelling herbs had been added to the steaming water. He eased himself in, wishing it were large enough for two.

"I'll get mine later, once the horses are properly seen to," Danilo said with a hint of a grin. "Don't fall asleep."

Regis closed his eyes, feeling the heat seep into his aching muscles. The day's ride had been long, but not beyond his strength. Emotional intensity, not physical exertion, had drained him. Around him, he sensed the house with all its familiar and alien aspects. Like so many other things in modern Darkover, it represented an uneasy compromise between the past and the interstellar present. Reluctantly, Regis admitted he would miss the place, but he could not maintain a residence separate from Comyn Castle. Shuddering, he slid deeper into the water. Even the most cheerful Castle rooms had the power to oppress him. As a child, he had fancied the ancient stone walls rising like mountains on all sides, crushing life and breath and hope.

At least, Regis thought wearily, he had resisted Grandfather's schemes to make him king.

He was almost asleep when Danilo glided into the bathroom with a mug of honey-sweetened chamomile tisane.

Spring lurched to a standstill as cold, damp weather settled over Thendara. It seemed to Regis that Darkover itself mourned the passing of his grandfather. The few social gatherings were subdued. Regis attended only a few, those he could not in all civility decline. With Javanne's help, he moved his household into the Hastur quarters of Comyn Castle.

Regis stood in the middle of his grandfather's study, alone yet hemmed in on every side by memories. The chamber was pleasant enough, designed and furnished for intimate meetings and research. Between the heavy glass windows and the perfectly situated fireplace, the room was warm even in the depths of winter. He would not change the massive desk or the bookcases that looked at least as old as his grandfather had been. The huge bed, on the other hand, he had already ordered moved to another part of the Hastur suite and his own brought from the townhouse.

Papers and bound ledgers, along with writing supplies and reference books, covered most of the desk. Regis had avoided going through them, as if he would be invading his grandfather's privacy, snooping where he had no right. A part of him could not comprehend that this room, this library, this archival midden spanning three generations of Comyn history, was now his. He had dreaded this day and dreamed of escaping it. Yet now that it was here, he found himself resigned. He would not have chosen it for himself—indeed, he would have chosen almost anything else—but over the last years, he had become reconciled. He was Hastur, and there was no one else.

A tap on the door brought him alert. Mikhail stepped in, backlit so that he appeared to be enveloped in his own golden aura. Regis smiled and gestured for him to come in.

Mikhail surveyed the room with an expression bordering on awe. "So this is where Darkover's destiny was plotted. And it's yours now."

"No," Regis said, shaking his head, "it's *ours.* I have no intention of sitting here alone, spinning out schemes like a spider in the center of a planet-spanning web. The reason I formed the Telepath Council in the first place was to ensure that many voices be heard. Together, we will plan our future." With a light touch, he guided Mikhail into the chair behind the desk.

"Uncle Regis, I can't sit here! This is your place now!"

"Someday, my lad, it will be yours. I want you to have the best training I can give you."

"I'm not ready!"

"Not now, but you will be," Regis said, reflecting that no honest man ever felt truly prepared for such a position. He himself certainly did not. Changing the subject, he pointed to a sheaf of papers covered with Danvan Hastur's circular scrawl.

Mikhail could read and write the two primary Darkovan languages, *casta* and informal *cahuenga,* as well as Terran Standard. "I think I could make out this handwriting with a little practice. It's Lord Hastur's, isn't it?"

"Unfortunately, yes. He also employed a secretary, sometimes two or three, most of them trained at the Nevarsin monastery, so their script is quite clear." Regis himself wrote a barely legible scrawl, but Danilo, who had also studied at St. Valentine's, still had the clearest writing of any of them.

"Much of this is of historical value," Regis said, "but some will help us now. I'll spend some time going through the documents, but I cannot do it alone."

And I dare not trust anyone besides you and Danilo.

Mikhail looked up, eyes wide. "Where do you want me to begin? How should I sort all this?"

"Let's start by making an inventory. Use general categories—personal, Hastur Domain, Comyn Council, like that. Set aside anything that strikes you as pertinent to the Federation membership. And . . ."

"Yes?"

"There may be a reference to a man named Rinaldo. He'd be in his early forties now. Please show me anything you find, even the slightest mention . . . and I trust your discretion. Mention this to no one."

The light in Mikhail's eyes gave Regis confidence in the younger man's probity. Again, he blessed the impulse that led him to choose Mikhail over his brothers. They had turned into sturdy, reliable, unimaginative men, a credit to their family and caste. Mikhail . . . Mikhail was something more. Regis determined that, no matter what happened, Mikhail must not be pushed aside.

9

A few days later, as Mikhail continued to sort and catalog Danvan's papers, Regis received another coded message from Lew Alton. As before, this was delivered through Dan Lawton's office. Unlike the previous message, however, this one began with Lew's request that the Legate listen to its content.

Regis had thought it was not possible for Lew to look any more haggard. With his scarred face and eyes etched with sorrow, Lew had always appeared older than his years. Tightly bottled anger now flushed his features.

"Regis . . . and Dan, I am assuming you are listening to this together." Lew's normal voice was hoarse because of his damaged vocal cords. "First of all, Regis, I'm sorry about your grandfather. I wish I could have spoken at the *rhu fead*, but that is for another life. In all sincerity, I wish him peace."

Regis, knowing the struggles Lew had endured with his own father's death, bowed his head.

Lew went on, his voice more gravelly than before, "I have made no secret about my opposition to Darkover's membership in the new Federation. As you can imagine, this has not been well received in some quarters. Darkover's location on the galactic arm makes it a rich prize. I've heard speculation about turning the entire planet into a military base."

As Lew drew in his breath, a vision came to Regis of forests razed, villages cemented over and rivers dammed, fields of permacrete covered by an armada of ships, blasting off again and again until the earth cried out like a wounded beast . . . the native peoples, from the shy arboreal trailmen to the ethereal *chieri* extinct . . . the Comyn preserved like zoo specimens . . .

That must never come to pass. Not so long as I have breath and strength to prevent it.

"I swear to you, Regis," Lew was speaking again now, and it seemed to Regis that the other man echoed his own thoughts, "that I will be damned in Zandru's coldest Hell before I let that happen. But three days ago . . . they came for me in the night, here in the Diplomatic Sector. Only two of them," and here, Lew's lips twisted in a feral grimace, and Regis remembered that even one-handed, Lew was a formidable opponent with Darkovan weapons. "My wife and daughter are shaken but unharmed," Lew ended. "I don't think they'll try again, but I've sent Dio and Marja off-world for safety."

Lawton, standing beside Regis, drew in his breath. His hands had curled into fists, and he was almost shaking with outrage.

"As Senator and *as Alton,* I will do *whatever* I can," Lew said, putting a faint, suggestive emphasis on the words. "Darkover must stand firm. Any sign of weakness or division and the Expansionists will seize the opening. I won't be able to stop them. Regis, we're counting on you."

So it had come at last, the fate Regis had struggled so long to avoid.

The screen flickered into blankness as the play-and-destroy program ran to completion. For a long moment, none of the three men said anything. Regis sensed Danilo's unvoiced thought, *I am with you, no matter where this takes us.*

To be king, you mean. Desperation boiled up in Regis. *There must be another way to keep Darkover free! We must not exchange one kind of tyranny for another.*

"Dan, leave us for a moment," Regis said. "I want to send a private reply."

"Play-and-destruct?"

Grimly, Regis nodded. Dan set the console to encrypt the return message and then left. Danilo glanced at the closed door, but Regis had no doubt of the Legate's integrity.

Regis leaned back in the console chair. The plasteen and metal gave slightly under his weight. He wished, not for the first time, that the interstellar void was not such a barrier to mental communication. Only the most extraordinary telepaths could contact one another over more than the shortest distances. He and Lew must used nuanced words to convey what would be so simple face-to-face.

Lew's message, although forthright enough on the surface, carried a deeper meaning, that slight emphasis on the word *whatever* coupled with the deliberate mention of Lew's Domain. Lew was the only adult known to possess the Alton Gift, the ability to force mental rapport, even with nontelepaths.

Regis paused, his fingertip hovering above the panel that would begin the recording. Lew, like every other Darkovan who had trained at a Tower, had taken an oath never to enter the mind of another except to help or heal and then only with consent.

Was Lew serious about using *laran* to sway the Federation politicians? To convince them that Darkover was not worth bothering with, that it would be better to let Darkover go its own way and remain a Closed World?

He knows I would never ask such a thing, Regis thought, *but clearly, he feels the situation might require it.*

Regis had sometimes wondered why the Alton Gift had been bred into the Comyn during the Ages of Chaos. The *leroni* of the Towers recognized it as dangerous but had not seen fit to eliminate it. Instead, it had been preserved through the centuries.

As a final weapon? Or as a last defense when all else failed?
A defense when the future of Darkover hung in the balance?

It went against his training and personal ethics to order Lew to use the Alton Gift in this way.

At the back of his mind, Regis felt Danilo's steady support, his abiding trust. Regis drew in his breath and touched the panel.

"*Dom* Lewis-Kennard Alton," he said, using the formal title to convey his understanding of Lew's reference. "The situation is indeed distressing. I am glad that you have taken those precautions you deem necessary. During these difficult times, Darkover could have no better spokesman and protector. I have always known you to be a man of honor. You have my authority to act as you see fit."

Before he could say anything more, Regis cut off the recording. He would neither command nor forbid Lew in such a matter of conscience. He was not Lew's Keeper, nor would he ever wish to wield that kind of power over another.

With a silent prayer to whatever god might be listening, or whatever power could span the light-years, he tapped the panel to send the message. It was done, for good or ill.

And, for good or ill, if Darkover was to remain free, he must take up the full power and influence of the Lord of Hastur.

Outside the Headquarters Building, the Terran Sector seemed bleaker than ever. Structures of steel and glass rose like the walls of canyons where the sun never shone. The wind tasted like dust and metal; as it swept through the streets, it sounded like keening.

Regis said little as he and Danilo made their way back to Comyn Castle. They were, as usual, in light rapport, so Danilo sensed his mood. "Has Mikhail found any clue as to your brother's whereabouts?"

Regis shook his head. "I am beginning to think Grandfather invented Rinaldo in order to get me to do what he wanted. I can hear him saying, from his grave, 'If you don't take your responsibilities as the Heir of Hastur seriously, then I'll find someone else who will!'"

"Not even Lord Hastur would fabricate a lost brother for such a purpose," Danilo said.

They passed the borders of the Terran Zone under the watchful eyes of a Spaceforce patrol.

"I have been considering the problem," Danilo said, "and I think it likely that if Lord Hastur recorded this knowledge, it would have been not on paper, which could be stolen and used against him, but to someone he trusted without reservation."

Who might that have been? Danvan Hastur had outlived any cousins or comrades who came to manhood with him, and his only son was dead.

When Regis voiced his question, Danilo shook his head and said he would look into it before venturing more. Regis knew his *bredhyu's* stubborn nature well enough to not press him.

Regis paced his sitting room, waiting for the signal that the meeting of the Telepath Council was ready to begin. It would not take place in the Crystal Chamber, for the remaining Comyn would object strenuously if an assembly such as the Telepath Council met there, and Regis needed their support. Instead, he had chosen one of the newer, less formal halls.

As usual, when faced with addressing a large group, his thoughts tangled like one of Javanne's childhood embroidery samplers. He had given enough public speeches to know that the feeling would pass. The trick was to make eye contact with a few people and speak directly to them. Moreover, he must speak from his heart.

How, in all the world, could he speak from his heart when he wore the mantle of Hastur? He threw himself into a chair beside the door, then heaved himself up again. One thought returned to him again and again.

There is no one else. I alone must do this!

Only the day before, official word had come through the Legate's office. All worlds previously classified as Class D Closed were now subject to automatic Open citizenship unless they requested an exemption.

Request? We must demand *it!*

Regis was so distracted that he heard the knock at the door before he felt Danilo's presence.

Danilo cracked the door open. "*Vai dom,* it's time."

Regis straightened his shoulders and glanced down at his attire, a formal suit of suede, with high boots to match, all dyed in Hastur blue, the jacket embroidered in silver thread with the fir-tree emblem of his Domain. A bejeweled ceremonial sword hung from an equally flamboyant belt. Javanne had urged him to add a court-length cloak trimmed with *marl* fur, but he had refused.

"How do I look?"

One corner of Danilo's mouth quirked upward. He stepped back and gestured for Regis to lead the way.

The four Guards stationed outside the door were seasoned veterans, for theirs was a post of honor. They bowed to Regis and stood back.

Gabriel Lanart-Hastur announced, "Regis-Rafael Felix Alar Hastur y Elhalyn, Hastur of Hastur!" In the old times, the title would have included, "Regent of the Crown of the Seven Domains," but Regis would not permit it.

Regis forced himself to a stately pace. The crowd drew back to let him pass. He waded through a sea of faces crowned with hair in a hundred shades of red, from flaming fire to pale-rose-tinted flax to burnt copper.

Here and there, Regis recognized friend or kin. Javanne stood in the center of a knot of glittering nobles, including Marilla Lindir and Valdir Ridenow. The earnest young man at Valdir's side must be Francisco. Mikhail, standing a little apart from the others, smiled as Regis passed, as did a Renunciate with an open, generous face. Regis did not see any Tower folk. He wished Linnea were here.

Unlike the Crystal Chamber, this room had not been equipped with telepathic dampers. Even through his *laran* barriers, Regis felt the vast, unfocused presence of so many minds. He clenched his jaw, forced himself to breathe, and stepped onto the platform at the far end of the chamber.

Most of the audience knew that the time had come for Darkover to choose or reject full Federation membership. Even so, Regis began with a brief discussion of the particulars involved, the drawbacks and costs as well as the benefits of such a move.

The Telepath Council included traders and merchants as well as aristocrats. The pro-Terran Pan Darkovan League, while not officially present, spoke through its sympathizers. Those whose livelihood depended upon interstellar trade made no secret of welcoming greater access to foreign markets and suppliers. As Regis expected, they presented their concerns in carefully calculated, rehearsed phrases.

"Darkover must take its rightful place among the great worlds of the new Federation," said an aging man with more gray than rust-red in his hair. Regis knew him from the lower Cortes and by reputation as a sound judge of character, respected by the community. Even without *laran,* the man's sincerity rang out; he truly believed what he said.

"We should not have to beg for the privileges and rights that are due to us," the man went on. "Many of the Federation welcome us like the long-parted kinsmen we are. We should rectify the mistake of confining ourselves to Closed World status."

Murmurs of agreement spread through the chamber. The League spokesman had appealed to their pride, offering a vision of Darkover as one among equals, no longer a second-rate backwater world but a great among greats.

"I do not speak solely for those whose businesses depend upon off-world trade and travel. Every one of us, throughout the Domains, will benefit from the superior technology of the Terrans, as well as their medicine and science. More than that, the Federation offers education for all our sons, not just those fortunate enough to have been born Comyn!"

As the man spoke, Regis felt the old longing to take passage in one of those starfaring vessels, to walk upon strange worlds and meet people to whom the name *Hastur* meant nothing. Since that was not possible—he had long since given his oath to his Domain and the Comyn—he had made sure that Mikhail benefited from Terran education. How many boys—and girls, too—still hungered for that knowledge?

Modern techniques of weather control could transform Darkovan agriculture, make travel throughout the Hellers possible, and bring the lands beyond the Wall Around the World into contact with the Domains. Some day, the deserts of the Dry Towns might be reclaimed, as well.

Regis paused and the crowd grew still. He drew in his breath, willing his heart to be still. An unnamed force rose up in him, flowed *through* him, a force that came from beyond his own limited physical and intellectual powers. He felt himself reaching out to his audience with mental touch as well as words. Phrases rolled through his mind.

"Everything that this good man has said is true. If it were not, there would be no difficulty in making this decision." Regis sensed the ripple of surprise and outrage from the conservatives among the Comyn. None of them had expected him to agree with the pro-Federationists.

"At the same time, these benefits come with a price. The Federation will demand that in return, we acknowledge them as our lawful government. Do we truly wish to be ruled not by our own people but by men who have never walked beneath our Bloody Sun, never seen snow on the Hellers peaks, never dreamed of *chieri* singing beneath the Four Moons? Men who know nothing of our customs and history, our honor, our gods? To them, the Compact is no more than a backward superstition. I need not remind you that the *Terranan* think it honorable to settle their differences with blasters and nerve guns and far more terrible weapons that kill indiscriminately and at a distance, while those who give the orders hide in safety."

The murmurs shifted now, like the soft growl of a cloud leopard scenting danger. Regis held out his hands, and it felt as if his heart opened as well. Eyes shining, Danilo looked up at him. Emotion flushed Javanne's cheeks. Gabriel was nodding, and even stolid Ruyven Di Asturien looked moved.

He had them . . . almost.

"My friend has offered a vision of greatness and equality, of riches and opportunity. Who would not want that? But in a Federation spanning a thousand worlds, Darkover will become one more poor, backward world. We will be reduced to accepting handouts from those who care nothing for our dreams.

"I am not saying that we can never have progress and prosperity, a better future for our children. We can do all this, but in our own way and in our own time.

"Once I asked you to join together, Comyn and commoner, peasant and lord, Renunciate and mountain folk. I promised you that we would not become another lockstep world of the Empire. I swore that I would never allow the *Terranan* to remake us in their image. Together, we agreed to restore our world."

Around the room, heads nodded in memory of that intoxicating time. Anything had seemed possible, and they had accomplished more than anyone believed possible. For a brief golden age, the telepaths of

Darkover had acted as one, rejoiced as one, and defended their world as one.

Regis had no idea if he could summon that same commitment again. In asking them to stand beside him, he risked fracturing what remained of that unity. He sensed the currents of discord, of dissension. For too many of them, the Empire—and now the Federation—represented an end to the rule of the aristocratic Comyn and the old feudal system.

For what seemed like an eternity, Regis spoke. He felt the shift in the audience, yielding to the ingrained reverence for the Hastur Lord. Under ordinary conditions, the patchwork assent would have been enough. Now he could not afford even the appearance of disunity. If what Lew said was true, the Expansionist party of the Federation would seize upon the flimsiest excuse to impose their will.

Darkover must speak with one voice, even if that one voice was his.

He could command it. As Regent. As Hastur. As King. Was this why his grandfather had urged him to claim the throne, so that no one could contest his decisions?

Echoes of that first gathering resonated through his voice. They lifted him, carried him. Throughout the chamber, he felt a storm gathering. But would it bear them all to a safe haven or shatter them upon the rocks?

"I ask you to join together again, to answer any outside power that we shall always belong to ourselves first. Darkover must and shall forge its own destiny."

For a long moment, no one spoke. A word, a gesture, could tip the balance and fracture the tenuous momentum.

Gabriel moved to stand before the platform. He looked imposing in his Guards Commander uniform, and his features were set in an expression of determination. "The Lord of Hastur has asked for our support. I say we owe him our loyalty, as has been the custom from the time of our fathers. Who stands with me?"

"I do." Ruyven Di Asturien came forward. The crowd melted back and swirled to close up behind him. He carried himself with quiet authority.

"And I!"

"I!"

"I!" cried Javanne, then one of the Castamirs joined in, then Kyril Eldrin and a chorus of men and women in ordinary commoner clothing.

Valdir Ridenow was one of the last Comyn to speak up. "If it is the will of this Council, I will not stand in the way." He paused. "For the time being."

"So be it, then," Regis said. "With your support, I hereby direct the Terran Federation Legate to inform the Senate of our decision to retain our status as a Class D Closed World."

Cheering broke out throughout the chamber. Dan Lawton applauded, grinning. Regis stepped off the platform to accept congratulations and thanks. He sensed as well as saw the flickers of dissatisfaction, of grudging acceptance. Some of those opinions might change with time as Darkover continued to evolve into a new society and the planetary ecology attained a new balance.

But nothing gave Regis a deeper sense of unease than the smoothly bland expression on the Ridenow lord's features.

It took a long time for the chamber to empty. Regis felt obliged to remain as long as anyone wanted to speak with him. The experience was exhausting, for he had never enjoyed the attention of crowds. He knew that his ability to persuade rather than to coerce depended on personal contact. It was part of the cost of victory.

Javanne hugged Regis, a brief, distracted embrace before she departed with Gabriel. Mikhail stayed to watch and listen. Valdir Ridenow gave a brief salute through the thinning crowd and then strode off. The Cortes judge bowed deeply to Regis and said that, although he was not entirely convinced, he had the greatest respect for the arguments Regis had put forth. Time would tell, the man concluded.

Time is what I have asked for, Regis replied, *time to find our own way.*

Through it all, Danilo never left his side. From time to time, someone would try to draw Danilo into conversation, but Danilo gracefully deflected their overtures.

Finally, when only a few pockets of conversation lingered and the servants were clearly impatient to begin cleaning the chamber, Danilo guided Regis to the back entrance. Regis was so tired that only habit and momentum kept him on his feet. He ached, not only in body but in spirit.

The corridor was narrow and poorly lit but blessedly quiet. A threadbare carpet, too poor for public use, cushioned their footfalls.

"Gods, Danilo, I need a drink!" Regis said. "My head's about to explode!"

"As long as it doesn't turn you into a *blockhead,*" Danilo quipped, referring to an old joke between them, from their earliest days as cadets.

Laughter bubbled up from a half-forgotten place within Regis. How long had it been since he had heard anything silly?

"I'm glad you haven't lost your sense of perspective," Danilo said, more seriously. "There's one more item to be dealt with."

Regis groaned. "Haven't I done enough already? Surely, whatever it is can wait until tomorrow."

Now that they were moving, Regis felt a renewal of physical vigor. Side by side, they swept up the back stairs, wending their way through the labyrinth of the Castle to the Hastur quarters.

Danilo paused at the door leading to the suite of rooms that had been Danvan's and now belonged to Regis. "You'll want to hear this."

"If you say so."

Danilo led the way into the most intimate of the sitting rooms, more a parlor than the formal presence-chamber Danvan had favored. A fire and a bank of beeswax candles filled the room with comforting light. A meal had been laid out on a table before the hearth. Candlelight gleamed on silver utensils, the curve of a glazed pottery bowl, the glass vase holding a cluster of dawn lilies.

A man perched on the end of the armchair as if he expected to be hauled off and punished for sitting there. A stout cane lay on the carpet beside him. Backlit by the fire, Regis saw him in silhouette, the thin, hunched shoulders, the wisps of downy hair.

"*Vai dom!*" The man struggled to push himself to his feet.

"Good uncle, do not rise," Regis said, going to him. "Please, be at your ease. I am sorry, but although your face is familiar to me, I cannot recall when we have met."

"My lord Regis," Danilo said, "allow me to present Caradoc from Castle Hastur. You would have known him when you were a lad."

"You served my grandfather, then," Regis said, taking the nearest chair.

"That I did, young master, for many a long year."

Regis glanced quizzically at Danilo.

Danilo bent over the old man. "Tell Lord Hastur what you told me . . . about the secret the old lord entrusted to you."

"Ah, that." The rheumy eyes brightened. "I swore I'd never tell, as my lord bade me. But you're the new Lord Hastur, so that's all right. You see, a long time ago, it must be forty year now, I were much younger. In the dead of night, he summons me, the Old Hastur Lord, he does. He gives into my charge a boy child, no more than three winters old."

Astonishment swept away the last dregs of fatigue. "Rinaldo?"

"Don't recall that were his name. Valenton? Valentine? Summat like that. Anyways, he bids me, the old lord does, to take the child to Nevarsin and give him to the monks. Now, what was I to think? What kind of life is that for a Comyn, to be reared by *cristoforos* in the City of Snows? But I dares not say anything. I takes the child, and a fine healthy boy he is, too, and I gives him to the brothers there. And nary a word have I spoke of it these many years," Caradoc concluded with a look of satisfaction.

"You have kept your word, like a true and loyal man," Regis murmured. "Did my grandfather give any reason for the secrecy?"

The old servant shook his head. "Oh, I've had thoughts aplenty, but who am I to ask questions? I serve—served—my good lord. And he never saw fit to confide in the likes of me."

Danilo went to the side cupboard and took out a purse that clinked softly. "The *coridom* will see you're given supper and a soft bed, and here's for your trouble."

"No trouble at all, *vai domyn*," the old man replied, bobbing bows as he tucked away the purse. Deftly maneuvering his cane, he made his way to the door. "No trouble at all."

The latch clicked shut behind him. For a long moment, Regis stared at the fire, hardly seeing it, hardly daring to believe what he had just heard. When he looked up, Danilo returned his glance, unsmiling.

"Nevarsin?"

BOOK II: Rinaldo

10

As the customary period of mourning for a man of Danvan Hastur's rank came to an end, spring settled over Thendara. Rain fell most evenings and occasionally snow, but the air softened a little more each day. Flowers brightened gardens throughout the city. Girls went about with blossoms tucked in their hair, and singers and street performers appeared in every market place. The courtyards of Comyn Castle sprouted arbors of fragrant twining rosalys and sweet-mint.

With the end of winter, the passes through the mountains opened, permitting messengers to travel to and from Nevarsin. Regis received an answer to his inquiry from the Father Master of the monastery. He had to read it several times to fully comprehend its content.

The letter confirmed that one of the brothers of St.-Valentine's-of-the-Snows was indeed named Rinaldo, the unacknowledged son of Rafael Hastur and Rebekah Lanart, placed there as a young child about forty years ago at the command of Danvan Hastur himself.

As soon as a suitable escort could be arranged, Regis and Danilo set out for Nevarsin. Regis dispensed with the banner bearers, taking only a few Guards, men trained and selected by Gabriel for their discretion.

Danilo frowned as the Castle grooms led out Melisande, the Armida-bred mare that Kennard Alton, Lew's father, had given to Regis many years ago. White frosted the mare's muzzle, and her coat, once solid black, was now the color of pewter. She pricked up her ears as she recognized Regis.

"Are you sure it's wise to take so old a horse into the Hellers?" Danilo said. His own mount, a big-boned gelding, its white hide flecked with irregular brown spots, was old enough to have good trail sense and yet young enough to endure the mountain journey.

"Probably not." Regis grinned as he checked the girth and blanket, making sure there were no wrinkles to cause saddle sores. Affectionately, he rubbed the mare's forehead. She lipped his hand, searching for morsels of apple. "It will be the old girl's last journey, that's certain. But there's no need to push our pace. We'll go slow enough for her."

The towers and ramparts of Thendara fell behind as they climbed into the Venza Hills. As happy as Regis was to be away from court and Castle, he could not entirely enjoy the journey. What would he find at Nevarsin, what sort of man might his brother be after so many years among the monks? His own time there had been both lonely and rewarding. A few of his teachers had been kind to the shy, awkward boy he had been, but most had been demanding, often harsh.

Danilo had endured the same discipline but to a greater degree. As heir to a great Domain, Regis had been allowed certain privileges, including better food and exemption from religious observances. But Danilo, born into the *cristoforo* faith, had been subject to every requirement. The monks had hammered a rigid set of moral rules into their charges.

Including the absolute condemnation of homosexuality. Regis had never asked Danilo how he reconciled the doctrines of his faith and their enduring bond. He had never understood why a faith that espoused compassion for all one's fellows should single out and forbid one particular expression of love.

Regis sensed Danilo's concern as their first meeting with Rinaldo drew nearer. For most of his life, Regis had lived with the knowledge that he was the last living son of Hastur. Now that situation had changed, although in what way remained to be seen.

How would Rinaldo react to his relationship with Danilo after a lifetime of being taught that sexual or romantic love between men was sinful? In public, Regis and Danilo behaved discreetly, with only that degree of intimacy proper for lord and paxman, but most of Thendaran society knew they were lovers. Sooner or later, Rinaldo would hear rumors, if such had not already reached the monastery.

Regis did not want to antagonize his brother with a premature confrontation. They should get to know one another before facing such a sensitive issue. The topic must be introduced carefully. With time and patience, Rinaldo would surely accept that not everyone followed the same stern code and that all men—even his own brother—had the right to follow their own hearts.

They left the Lowlands, climbing higher into the mountains. Snow-laced peaks rose on either side. Inns became scarcer and fellow travelers few. There seemed to be no end to the mountains, for as soon as they scaled one pass, another line of cragged heights came into view. The air grew thinner, and the black mare stumbled with fatigue toward the end of each day.

Around midmorning, they reached the village of Nevarsin. Markets offered ice-melons, furs, and small items of carved *chervine* antler. Vendors did a brisk business in statues of St. Christopher bearing the World Child on his shoulders. Danilo pointed out an old woman selling leaf-cones of roasted nuts, a treat they had relished as students.

The monastery itself lay some distance beyond the village, up a narrow trail. Glacial snow covered the rocks above. Indeed, with its gray stone walls, weathered by centuries, the monastery seemed to spring from the mountain itself.

A cold, hard place for a cold, hard land, Regis thought gloomily. *And not much warmer than Zandru's hells.* Yet men had found peace here, as well as useful work in service to their fellows. Who was he to judge them, based on a few tormented years as a student and an aversion to their narrow discipline?

The monk who greeted them at the gates looked overawed at the sight of so many armed men. He could not have been twenty, with a pale, homely face with a wine-colored mark over one side of his forehead.

"Come this way, *vai dom* Hastur, *Dom* Syrtis," he stammered in accented *casta*. "Father Master, he awaits you. In fact, he warned me this very morning that you soon would be arriving. He instructed me to make you comfortable and to bring word to him. If you will please for to follow me—"

"Gladly, but first I must see to my men and our horses," Regis pointed out.

The monk ran off to one of the stark gray stone buildings, leaving them standing in the paved courtyard. Regis glanced up at the buildings, remembering that the founders of the monastery prided themselves on placing every single stone by human hands without the use of *laran*. Such could not be said for any Comyn dwelling.

A few moments later, the young monk returned with several older brothers, who took away the horses and directed the Guardsmen to the kitchen.

Blinking and stammering, the young monk led Regis and Danilo to the Stranger's Room, luxurious by monastery standards but modest compared to Comyn Castle. Unlike the other rooms in the monastery, it boasted a fireplace and cushioned chairs. Wood had been laid on the andirons, with flint and tinder nearby. The monk set about lighting the fire, then asked if he could be of further service.

Regis sent him off to let the Father Master know of their arrival. Shortly thereafter, Regis and Danilo found themselves in the study of the venerable old monk. Regis was struck by the sensation that time had been suspended since he had last passed the monastery gates. Sun flooded the room, touching the battered surface of the desk and the alcove where a statue of the Bearer of Burdens stood eternal vigil. The figure looked as if it had never been dusted, or perhaps it was so ancient and fragile that it might fall to pieces at the slightest touch.

"Lord Regis—Lord Hastur you are now, I bid you welcome back to St. Valentine's." The Father Master remained in his seat and gestured for Regis to take the single cushioned visitor's chair. Danilo remained by the door.

"It has been a long time," Regis replied with a practiced smile. "You must also remember Danilo Syrtis, my sworn paxman."

The Father Master inclined his head in Danilo's direction. "No doubt, you are eager to meet with Brother Valentine. You will find him in the scriptorium."

Thanking the old monk for his kindness, the two young Comyn took their leave. They knew the way as intimately as the path to their own chambers. As they threaded their way along the narrow corridors, the stone walls rough and unadorned, they passed a number of monks. Almost all the brothers covered their faces with their cowls; they might have been the very same ones as years ago.

If anything, the scriptorium was brighter than the Father Master's study, for the windows were situated to take advantage of every moment of daylight. A handful of students bent over their desks. A fat, elderly monk strolled up one aisle and down the next, pausing now and again to inspect a line of text, to reposition a pen in clenched fingers, or to draw a wandering gaze back to its purpose.

Regis remembered the hours that he, too, had labored to produce a legible document. Perhaps the Terrans, with their instruments for perfect duplicates or vocal recordings, had the right idea. Why, in this age of starfaring ships and technological marvels, must young boys strain their eyes at such a task?

The thought came to him that the benefit lay not only in the creation of beautiful letters but in the mastery of discipline and concentration.

At the far end of the chamber, beside the unlit fireplace, a monk sat alone at a copying table. Light streamed from a high window, bathing his tonsured head. For an instant, he looked like a carven figure, silver and palest gilt. Unlike the students, who fidgeted at their desks and cast surreptitious glances at the two lords who had just entered, this monk gave no sign he was aware of the intrusion.

The monk supervising the boys came forward, a smile lighting his wide, generous features. "Good friends," he said, using the inflection of *beloved comrades* with a naturalness that touched Regis deeply, "you are most welcome."

When Regis introduced himself and Danilo, the brother nodded in obvious delight. With a conspiratorial wink, he turned and clapped his hands three times. The boys scrambled to put aside their work, cap their inkwells, and file out of the room. Regis gathered, from their excited whispers, that their practice session had been cut short and that now they were at leisure for a few brief hours. He remembered how precious such times were.

The fat monk crossed the room to wait silently beside his brother at the fireplace. After a long moment, the other monk lifted his head. Bathed in the overhead light, his skin was as pale as milk, as if he had never walked beneath the sun, only in twilit forest. In those thin, almost delicate features, Regis saw echoes of the ethereal, nonhuman *chieri,* the ancient Beautiful People who had inhabited Darkover since before the lost colony ship crashed in these hills. They were now all but extinct, yet their blood and their telepathic abilities flowed in Comyn veins.

Rinaldo? Or rather, Brother Valentine?

No, the tall, thin man was no *chieri,* but that graceful hermaphroditic race had left their mark in other ways . . . in the six fingered hands of many of their descendants . . . and in the occasional *emmasca.* Was Rinaldo such a one?

Regis could not be sure. General appearance was not proof. Many Comyn were thin and pale, and decades indoors might bleach the color from any man's face.

The *emmasca* condition was much rarer now than in former times, but the old attitudes lingered. Such individuals were said to be long-lived but sterile, and therefore in the past they had been barred from holding Domain-right. Regis thought it barbaric to measure the worth of a man by his reproductive performance. As to the requirement of fathering sons, or even being capable of lying with a woman, Regis had already provided Hastur with an heir, Mikhail, without doing either.

Yet the prejudice would explain why Danvan had hidden Rinaldo away, rather than raising him as a member of the family. The old man must have believed him to be *emmasca,* although male enough in appearance to be acceptable to the monks.

Regis ached for his brother. He determined not to add in any way to Rinaldo's lifetime of shame and rejection.

Smiling with evident pleasure, the fat monk left them. Regis came forward. The other monk rose, tall and slender in his shapeless robe. His eyes, steely gray, had a slightly distracted expression. As he reached out to touch hands with Regis, he smiled.

"Good brother—" Regis began, then laughed, a little unnerved. "My brother in truth, as I understand."

"True, indeed," the monk replied with an air of composure. "Forgive my lack of manners. I know you already, you see, from the time you were a student here."

Regis blinked in surprise. "Were—could it be—were you one of my teachers?"

"Indeed, I was privileged to instruct the younger boys how to read and write. If memory serves, you never achieved a very good hand, little brother. To compare it to the scratchings of a barnyard fowl would be unkind to the hen."

Regis flushed, feeling once more the diffident, lonely boy he had once been. But Brother Valentine went on, without taking any notice of his discomfort.

"Your companion—Danilo Syrtis, is it not?—wrote a more acceptable hand."

"And does so still," Regis replied, grateful to change the subject from his own shortcomings. "Danilo serves as my paxman and attends to my official correspondence. In fact, it might be said that although the will of a Hastur might be law, without Danilo's pen to set it down, no one would be able to read it."

A flicker of emotion passed over the monk's features. Regis sensed no trace of *laran,* no mental presence, so he could not tell what his brother might be thinking.

"You have the better of us, Brother Valentine," Danilo interjected. "You remember the two of us well enough, but I have no memory of you at all."

The monk turned to Danilo with a good-humored smile. "It would surprise me if you did. When I first came to St. Valentine's, it was many months before I could tell the brothers one from another. No doubt, we looked as much alike as so many fleas."

"Hardly fleas," Danilo muttered.

"When I was here all those years ago," Regis said, "why did you not make yourself known to me? I would have welcomed a brother's company."

"It was for you to speak, if you wished to claim me as kin."

The first thing Regis thought was that this answer was very much what he himself might have said in like circumstances. Then the world slipped sideways for a heartbeat—

—but I didn't know, and he did, I was a child and he was grown—

—and then resumed its normal course.

In that brief pause, Brother Valentine lifted his head in an attitude of listening. "It is time for prayer."

Regis caught the deep, throbbing sound of a bell from afar.

"Our reunion must yield to a greater obligation." Brother Valentine set aside his work materials. "You used to worship with us, little brother. Will you join us now?"

"I think not." Regis did not add that as a son of Hastur and a member of the Comyn, he had been raised to follow the four traditional gods of Darkover. Aldones, Lord of Light, was reputed to be the ancestor of the first Hastur. But Regis could not say so aloud and risk the implication that his brother might have to choose between his heritage and the demands of his caste on the one hand and his religious vows on the other. How deep that commitment ran, Regis could not tell.

A man ought to be able to follow his own conscience!

Brother Valentine turned to Danilo. "Come, we must hurry."

"I beg your leave," Danilo replied with a stiff bow. "My duty is to my lord."

The monk's gaze swept from one to the other. Whatever he thought of Danilo's refusal, he kept it to himself. "Then, with Father Master's permission, I will come to you in the Stranger's Room afterward."

The monk's sandals made no sound as he strode down the stone-floored corridor. Without discussion, Regis and Danilo headed back to the visitors' quarters. Regis felt pulled by conflicting feelings. Certainly, he was disappointed and beset by memories of an unhappy childhood. He told himself that his brother was an exemplary monk, dutiful and observant, that these same qualities bespoke an honorable nature.

When they were alone, Regis lowered himself onto one of the cushioned chairs. In their absence, someone had left a tray with *jaco* and slices of coarse nut-bread.

"Well, Danilo, what do you think of my brother? Or have you formed an opinion from so brief an encounter? Did you truly not remember him from before?"

"*Vai dom,* he is not my brother, but yours. Therefore, your opinion is the only one that counts."

Regis frowned. "Don't go all *vai dom* on me! It's clear you don't like him, but I don't understand why. He was perfectly polite."

"He was perfectly glib."

"What the devil do you mean by that?"

"Regis, you can't have it both ways. If you ask for my opinion and I offer it against my better judgment, you have only yourself to blame if you dislike what you hear. Or would you have me bow and scrape and agree with every blockheaded thing you say, like a courtier?"

"I expect—" Regis realized he was on the edge of losing his temper. What was wrong with Danilo? Why was he acting this way? Regis drew in a breath and began again. "I *expect* you to give my brother a fair chance, taking into consideration his lack of worldly experience. If you won't do it as a matter of fairness, then do it as a personal favor to me. He's going to have enough difficulties adjusting to his new life without you censuring him before you even know him!"

With a snort of exasperation, Danilo got up and went to the door leading to the bedroom. From where he sat, Regis could see four narrow beds, straw-tick mattresses on simple wooden frames, a washstand and a couple of chairs. Their baggage had been stacked neatly beside the nearest bed. Without another word, Danilo began unpacking and making up two of the beds with a precision that would have made a Cadet Master proud.

Regis poured himself a mug of *jaco* and sipped it, staring into the fire. Why could there not be peace between the people he loved? Why did it always come down to a choice?

Regis was still turning over these depressing questions when Brother Valentine arrived. Danilo, having finished preparing for the coming night, joined them in the sitting room.

At the insistence of Regis, Valentine took one of the chairs. He smiled as he settled against the cushions, clearly enjoying the unaccustomed comfort.

"You may not remember me," the monk said, once they had resumed their conversation, "but I have kept myself informed about you, little brother. Although they call me Valentine, after the holy saint who founded this order, I was named Rinaldo. You may call me that if you would claim me as kin."

"I am in need of kinsmen, for we are so few," Regis said with a sigh. "Tell me, have you thought—would you be willing to come with me to Thendara, to take up your place as a Hastur?"

Rinaldo regarded him with those strange gray eyes. "Until your message arrived, I never expected to enter the world. I understood there is little acceptance for one such as I."

"I intend to have you formally legitimatized," Regis said quickly. "Then no one will question your right—"

"No, no, that is not what I meant." Rinaldo protested. "Our grandfather could have done the same, but he chose not to, for reasons that seemed good to him."

"Your . . . difference, you mean."

"You are too courteous to ask," Rinaldo said, "so I will tell you straight out. I would not have you think I withheld the truth in order to curry your favor. We do not speak of such things here at St. Valentine's, but I believe I am *emmasca*. That is, I am shaped as other men, or I could not live among the brothers. Although I admit to being curious, I have never had the opportunity to lie with a woman, but I am not indifferent to the prospect. As to fathering a child, who can say, but from everything I know about my condition, I cannot believe it possible."

Regis looked away. So his first impression was correct. Yet to be born *emmasca* and without *laran* would be very strange indeed, since the telepathic genes ran so strongly in their *chieri* ancestors.

Rinaldo paused. "Do you wish to withdraw your offer, now that you know what I am?"

"We are not living in the Ages of Chaos, when a man's value was measured by his pedigree, his *laran,* his ability to father children, or anything else except the quality of his character," Regis said with feeling.

Rinaldo gave him a long, measuring look. "Bare is a brotherless back, as they say?"

"As they say. Hastur does not need another stud horse to breed heirs, but *I* have need of a brother."

"It seems that I am indeed called to be of service in the outer world. To my family . . . to my brother," Rinaldo inflected the word with a warmth that brought a rush of pleasure to Regis. "In that case, I will petition Father Master for a release from my vows. He has already indicated he would do so if I wished."

"I welcome you to the family with a joyful heart," Regis said.

Rinaldo bowed his head in a gracious gesture. "As you know, we monks are not permitted to own property. Even my robe and sandals and the wooden bowl and spoon I eat with do not belong to me. You must provide me with clothing suitable to my rank and a means of transportation."

Was there a hint of reproach beneath the words delivered with all civility? Although of equal blood, Regis had enjoyed all the privileges and luxuries that the Heir to a Domain might expect, while his brother had languished in obscure poverty.

"It will be my pleasure to furnish you with all that you require," Regis gently assured his brother. "Danilo, I leave the matter in your capable hands. There must be a stable or horse market where you can obtain a mount for my brother."

"You can ride, I suppose?" Danilo asked Rinaldo, a little stiffly.

"I have made sure I could, although I learned on a stag-pony, not a proper horse. I will do my best not to disgrace you."

As they sat at their ease, Regis went on, "I am afraid that any clothing to be found in Nevarsin will fall short of the elegance proper to a son of Hastur. Once we reach Thendara, I will order an appropriate wardrobe for you."

"That is most generous of you, little brother."

"It is no more than you deserve," Regis returned with a smile.

"You have convinced me," Rinaldo replied. "I believe you are right. I deserve the best, even if I must wait to receive it."

In the presence of the monastery community, gathered together in the chapel, the Father Master performed the ceremony that formally released Rinaldo from his vows. He would no longer bear the name of Brother Valentine or be bound by the rules of the order. If only, Regis thought, there were such a Comyn ritual for himself.

The monks embraced their former brother for the last time, exchanging blessings and wishes for peace. The ceremony concluded with a speech by the Father Master exhorting Rinaldo and every other man present to faithfully and scrupulously adhere to the principles set forth by the holy saints, to emulate the Holy Bearer of Burdens, to keep themselves pure through the Creed of Chastity, and to redeem their sins by acts of charity and penance.

"Never stray from the path of righteousness!" The Father Master's thunderous voice filled the chapel. "Accept your burdens . . . no, rejoice in them! Remember always—*Righteousness flourishes under the lash of discipline!*"

A lifetime of sitting through formal events had given Regis the ability to look interested no matter how bored or irritated he felt. He allowed the lecture to wash over him, paying little heed to its content. He was a guest here, an observer only.

But Danilo, who was an adherent to this faith, what must this tirade be like for him? Regis stole a glance at his companion, sitting a short distance away. Danilo's cheeks had gone pale.

As they made ready to depart, Danilo was taut and silent. He answered Regis in monosyllables. Regis did not press the issue. Danilo would speak to him in his own time or deal with his feelings in his own way.

Rinaldo was in high spirits, excited by every aspect of the journey. When he was presented with his mount, however, he seemed less than pleased. The horse Danilo had found for him was almost as small and shaggy as the local ponies. The rust-brown gelding had a scrawny neck and a loose, hanging lower lip, but the slope of his shoulders and the sturdy bone beneath the knee promised an easy gait. Regis knew enough of the mountain breeds to have confidence in the animal's ability to carry a large man over rough terrain and to thrive on poor forage. This horse was a practical choice, if less than beautiful.

Danilo had also obtained warm, serviceable clothing, trousers, jacket, and riding cloak of mixed sheep and *chervine* wool for extra water repellence. Neither the garments nor the boots were new; the pants were stained, and the leather was worn to softness that would minimize blisters.

Regis caught a flash of quickly masked disappointment in his brother's face. It was gone in an instant, as if it had never been, a faint tightening of eyes and mouth, a glace at Danilo. Regis opened his mouth to explain that such clothing and such a horse were the best that could be had and would be far more comfortable than anything new or flashy. He stopped himself. What was he doing, making excuses for Danilo? Surely, Rinaldo could see the true quality of these things, and when they were settled in Thendara, more elaborate garb, suitable for a Hastur Lord, could readily be ordered.

11

Several days later, the party set off from Nevarsin, traveling at an easy pace. As a peace offering to Danilo, Regis suggested that they break their return journey at Syrtis, Danilo's ancestral home.

"There's no need to hurry back." Regis did not need to add that it might be a long time before he had another opportunity to escape the city and the weight of his new duties.

"I would appreciate that," Danilo replied. "Since my father's death, I have had few opportunities to oversee the estate. My *coridom* manages well enough, but it is still my responsibility to examine the accounts and ascertain for myself that all is in order. It—" and here a shade of emotion crept into his voice, "—it will be good to be home again."

Rinaldo responded with easy-going cheerfulness to the change in plans. Regis supposed that his brother had traveled so little in the world that any new place must be a pleasure. Despite his disappointment at being given worn clothing and an ugly mount, Rinaldo was a pleasant traveling companion. Regis never heard him utter a syllable of complaint.

Syrtis lay half a mile off the road to Edelweiss, where Javanne and her family had once lived. The manor was situated at the end of a valley, leading downward to the lake country around Mariposa. Grass grew lush along the road. Mice and rabbithorns scurried away at their approach. Cattle grazed in the fields, lazily swishing away flies. One of the Guardsmen, a fine baritone, began an old ballad from the Kilghard Hills.

As they traveled through a little village, Danilo was instantly recognized and welcomed. Drawing near the main house, the party passed orchards of apple, pear, and ambernuts. The trees looked well-pruned and healthy, laden with fruit.

"It will be a good harvest," Regis commented.

Danilo, who had been riding silently at his side, turned to Regis with an expression of bittersweet contentment. "Yes." *But I will not be here to see it.*

"Perhaps . . ." Regis hesitated, his boyhood diffidence rising once more, "perhaps you could return this fall."

Dark eyes hardened. *And leave you to the wolves?*

Dani, I will not be alone. I have Rinaldo now.

Danilo looked away, his *laran* barriers tight. Regis kept silent with an effort.

Seeing the house, it was impossible for Regis not to remember his first visit to Syrtis, so many years and so many sorrows ago . . . At the time, he had not realized how poor Danilo's family was. One wing of the house had fallen into such disrepair that it was not safe for human habitation. Now the house sat like a jewel amid its gardens. The old moat had been drained, ditched, and turned into plots of vegetables and pot-herbs. Rosalys and star-lilies glowed like bits of sun-touched colored glass. Bees hung in the air. Regis took a deep breath, drinking in the fragrances of flowers and rich earth. A layer of tension slipped from his shoulders.

A stone barn, with its snug roof and new siding, led to a paddock in which several horses stood dozing in the sun. Beyond it lay a mews, and Regis remembered the splendid hawks bred and trained by Danilo's father. Old *Dom* Felix had been hawkmaster to Danvan Hastur.

The thought came to Regis, *Dani's brother and my own father died together. 'The two Rafaels,' they were called.*

Past and present overlapped in his vision. There, down the path that led to an apple orchard, now so old the trees in all likelihood no longer bore fruit, he and Danilo had exchanged vows as liege and paxman, had bound themselves with honor.

Our lives were woven together even before our hearts knew one another.

Was that about to change?

The *coridom,* a wiry middle-aged man, welcomed them. He seemed neither surprised nor distressed not to have had advance warning of the visit, nor was his manner obsequious. He held himself like a man who took pride in his work. From the ease of his manner and his clear respect for Danilo, they understood one another. There would be no last-minute repairs or beautification; what they saw was how the estate was run every day.

Danilo took his father's suite, Regis and Rinaldo were given the two best guest rooms, and the Guardsmen were housed in a snug outbuilding. The rooms were in the oldest part of the house, walled in dark gray stone but refurbished with wooden paneling and carpets. Regis suspected the tapestry in his room had been a gift from Dyan Ardais. The furniture was most likely original, so darkened with age and polish that the wood appeared black. With the shutters thrown wide in the warm twilight, the air quickly became fresh.

At Danilo's insistence, the *coridom* joined them for dinner. The meal was simple but nourishing: a stew of shell beans and vegetables from the garden, made savory with herbs and dusted with finely grated cheese, several freshly-baked round country loaves called *barrabrack,* and bowls of deep purple brambleberries and clotted cream. Regis ate slowly, savoring every bite.

Through the meal, Danilo chatted with his steward. Regis found himself drawn into the litany of stories, the daily events and routines of country living. No wonder Danilo spoke of home with longing. Such a place was an oasis, a refuge, a restorer.

With the swift fall of night, the temperature dropped enough to make a small fire delightful. The *coridom* excused himself, saying he had more business to attend to, and left the three guests to enjoy glasses of *firi* before the dancing flames.

Rinaldo had been quiet through the meal, often glancing between Danilo and the *coridom*. He swirled the pale amber liqueur in his glass and looked thoughtfully at Regis.

"Now that we have comfort as well as leisure and need not attend to the menial labors of the trail," Rinaldo said to Regis, "perhaps you will tell me more about yourself."

"What can I say? You told me you were well informed about my life."

"I am, indeed, but only about such things as any man may know. I would become acquainted with you as a man—a brother—and not merely a figure of political importance and common gossip."

A brother in more than name . . . Regis thought with an astonishing sense of joy. At the same time, the part of his mind that had become accustomed to rumor and insinuation wondered exactly what sort of gossip Rinaldo had heard, cloistered away in a monastery all these years.

Common gossip . . . Danilo had flinched visibly at the last comment. From his expression, Regis knew that Danilo was certain it had been aimed at him, at them both.

"Is there any particular gossip you wish to ask me about?" Regis asked carefully.

Rinaldo looked uncomfortable. "I hardly know what to believe. Envy may have caused others to spread malicious lies about you."

"Power attracts some and stirs resentment in others. We live in a world of many sorts of people. But in my experience, true friends accept that we need not think—or feel—or conduct our private affairs— alike. We each do our best with what we have been given by birth and inclination. Do you not agree?" Regis was acutely aware of Danilo, sitting so still, measuring Rinaldo's reactions.

"A man can hardly be held responsible for the shape of his features or whether he is naturally talented in music or gardening," Rinaldo said. "Or giving sermons, for that matter. But this is why we have the guidance of those older and wiser, that we may endeavor to improve ourselves by discipline, study, and prayer."

"By your leave, my lords," Danilo said, setting down his glass and rising. "I must make an early start tomorrow if I am to inspect the boundaries."

"By all means." Regis smiled in encouragement, but Danilo would not meet his eyes. "It has been a long day, and tomorrow will be tiring for you while we laze about. You must get what rest you can. I will sit with my brother a while longer."

Wishing them both a good night and assuring them that they had only to ask for whatever they might desire, Danilo withdrew. Rinaldo acknowledged his departure with a tight-lipped smile. When the door closed and the sitting room once more fell silent, he turned to Regis.

"Your paxman does not like me, I fear. But then, it is only reasonable that he should not."

"Why might that be?"

"What man in his position would care for anyone with the power to displace him in your affections? I cannot help but think that it displeased him greatly to be sent on errands for my sake like a common servant."

Regis gave a little, dismissive laugh. "Danilo is not like that at all."

"You are amazingly unworldly for a man raised and educated in the midst of a political hotbed, my brother. I see you are the kind of person who wishes to think the best of everyone." Rinaldo grew grave as he continued, "Beware that you do not come to regret your trusting disposition."

Regis sat back, for a moment speechless. He was as dismayed by his brother's comment as by his misgivings about Danilo.

"I am no courtier, to couch unpleasant truths in flowery language," Rinaldo said. "I speak simply, as I think. You have been too sheltered from the realities of life. That is, if you truly believe what you say, and I have no reason to believe otherwise. You are too open, too innocent."

Regis wanted to laugh. He had been called many things since coming into his majority and accepting the responsibilities of Heir to his Domain. *Open* and *innocent* were not among them.

"I have had much time in which to study the ways of men," Rinaldo went on, his tone shifting now to conciliation. "I tell you plainly that all men are indeed *like that*. Your Danilo is no exception. Did you see the clothing he got for me?" His voice took on a sullen edge. "It was poor stuff, hardly suitable for a servant. Bah! His actions have betrayed him."

"There was no intent to slight you," Regis hurried to explain. Perhaps Rinaldo felt like an interloper, unsure of his welcome, needing tangible proof. Regis did not want to accuse Rinaldo of ingratitude, but at the same time, he could not ignore the insult to Danilo. "After all, Nevarsin is a small town. This was the best available at such short notice. When we arrive in Thendara, we will have fine clothing made to your own measure."

Rinaldo looked as if he would protest further, then smiled. "Of course, you must be right."

For an uncomfortably long moment, the two brothers sat in silence. Finally, Regis said, "So you want to know more about me. Ask what you wish and I will do my best to satisfy you."

"No, no, I do not mean to interrogate you! I have no right to question what I do not yet understand. But I have wondered . . . there are so few of us Comyn left . . ."

"Yes, we are far too few to form a Council or to divide our resources between ruling our own Domains and Darkover. Even before the World Wreckers sent their assassins, the great houses of the Seven Domains had dwindled. Grandfather needed me as Heir to Hastur. I set aside my own dreams of a private life. I thought . . ." Regis stumbled, surprised by the sudden burst of emotion, "I thought I was the only male Hastur heir."

Now I have a brother to share that burden. But it would be premature to say so, before he knew Rinaldo's temperament and desires. What could a man who had spent more than three decades behind monastery walls know about the greater world, about power and diplomacy, the skills required of a Hastur of Hastur? More to the point, would Rinaldo want that kind of life?

I will not inflict the same expectations that Grandfather—the Council— Darkover—placed upon me. I will not make him forswear his dreams even before he has had time to discover what they are!

"Dreams?" As if catching the thought, Rinaldo lifted one eyebrow expressively.

Regis paused for a moment, wondering if Rinaldo might have a trace of *laran* after all. Or perhaps it was only a facility of observation and following the natural course of the conversation.

He considered the question. It had been so many years since he had lifted his eyes to the stars, hungry to journey among them. He remembered that argument with his grandfather, the old man raging.

"Choice? If you wanted a choice, Regis, you should have arranged to be born somewhere else! I never chose *to be chief councillor and Regent to the Elhalyns. None of us has* ever *been free to choose!"*

Although it was like peeling a long-hardened scab from an unhealed wound, Regis met his brother's gaze. "Yes, dreams. When I was young, I wanted more than anything to travel the stars, to see other planets and other peoples. But, as Grandfather told me in no uncertain terms and upon many occasions, I should have chosen other parents." He sketched a sigh to lighten the mood. "There you have it. Regis Hastur, the great Comyn lord, is at heart a frustrated spaceman."

"I would not belittle any man's dreams, let alone those of my brother," Rinaldo said. "One of the benefits of having lived as I have, cloistered in unvarying routine, is faith in the unpredictability of life. A year ago, I had nothing to look forward to beyond teaching recalcitrant novices and praying on my knees through one winter after another until death took me. Now—" with a gesture, he encompassed the comfortable room, the fire, the glass of *firi* held lightly between his long fingers, "now an entirely new life unfolds before me. I see not just its sensual pleasures, but new opportunities to be of service. To you, to our family . . . to the Comyn as well. In a world where such miracles can come to pass, who can say?"

Regis did not comment again that the Comyn no longer existed as a power on Darkover. He was too moved by Rinaldo's offer. It was indeed a miracle to have found a brother, to be able to share the burden of his rank . . . an older brother who had every right to the power and prestige of Hastur . . .

"Perhaps, in good time, you will discover your proper place in this world," Regis said, acutely aware of how clumsy he sounded. "The important thing is to heed what is in your heart—your dreams—and not be pressured or tricked or flattered into what is burdensome to you."

"Regis, I have spent my life being told *not* to consider my own desires. What has given me greatest satisfaction, and I presume will continue to do so, is to make myself useful to others. At St. Valentine's that meant performing any task set before me, no matter how menial. Now you have given me the chance to do something of importance in the larger world."

Rinaldo leaned forward. "I know I am unsophisticated and inexperienced, but I am not ignorant. Do you think the monastery is a place devoid of ambition, free from the failures of human nature? You studied there long enough to know better. It is the world distilled, with all its vanities and cruelty. I know it very well, its strengths and truths as well as its follies."

Slowly, Regis nodded. "I beg your forgiveness if I sounded patronizing. I meant only to protect you against the harsh demands that have beset me in my own life."

"I wanted to know you better, and so I do. You have a kind and generous heart. Perhaps too generous. I will not abuse your love. Instead, together we will accomplish—" Rinaldo broke off in a little self-deprecating laugh. "Just listen to me! I do not even know what needs doing! And you have not asked me anything about myself."

"There is something . . . I could not ask you when the matter first arose because we were still at Nevarsin and you had not yet been released from your vows." Regis paused, watching his brother's reaction and noting nothing beyond bland interest. "You freely told me you are *emmasca,* so I assume the subject is not too difficult to discuss."

"You mean *painful,* don't you? It is not, only a bit awkward. I have never—we did not speak of such matters, you understand. I'd rehearsed that little speech ever since I heard you were coming. I knew it would come up and thought it best to get it over with at the earliest opportunity. I suppose I must be prepared to face more questions at Thendara."

"Let them keep their questions to themselves! Other than an explanation of why Grandfather hid you away, and that only for my own understanding, it is none of anyone's business. I won't have you harassed because of it!" Regis saw Rinaldo's eyes widen at the vehemence behind his words. He gentled his tone. "I know how it feels to be judged for what I cannot change."

He was thinking now not only of his sexual preference but also of the late awakening of his *laran*. For too many years he had believed he had none, and if Danilo had not reached his mind, that might still be the case.

"I wondered how the monks treated your being *emmasca* and therefore different," Regis finished.

"You mean if I was made to feel unworthy because of how I was born?" Rinaldo shook his head. "Then how little you understand of the deep, encompassing love of He Who Bears the Burdens of the World. He gathers us all into his righteousness. Of course, boys tease one another, but they also do a great many things that they repent when they are wiser. It is not our bodies or our temperaments that are unacceptable, only the uses to which we put them. Therein lies our sin or our salvation."

Regis sensed an opening. "Just as men have bodies of varying shapes and strength and talents for one thing or another, do you not agree that our hearts can lead us in different directions without one being right and the other wrong? Surely, men of honor can hold different opinions. Honesty and integrity are more important than conformity."

With a faint, humorless smile, Rinaldo shook his head. "I had no idea you were such a philosopher, my brother."

"As a Hastur, I must deal with many sorts of men and women," Regis said. "Not all differences are harmful. Some enrich us all, and others are simply none of anyone's business. The *Terranan,* for example—what we see as immodest or bizarre, they consider normal. Yet they have brought us riches and knowledge. What they choose to think or how they behave in the privacy of their own chambers causes us no grief. Sometimes I think their greatest gift is a tolerant, welcoming attitude toward the unknown."

"Strange, indeed," Rinaldo murmured and then fell silent.

"We've had a long day," Regis said, "and you have had to deal with many changes. If the journey thus far has been filled with new experiences, Thendara will be far worse. Remember that you do not face them alone. I will be at your side."

"Indeed." Rinaldo's thin lips spread in a smile. "And now, we had best renew our strength for that new adventure." He yawned. "I'm afraid the habit of early rising is still upon me."

"I have kept you talking past your usual hour of sleep," Regis apologized. He himself had no duties to wake him early, as Danilo did, and had not considered the schedule his brother had kept at the monastery.

"It is no matter," Rinaldo said lightly. "I must expect to become accustomed to different hours, among other things."

As they came up over the pass leading down from the Venza Hills into the valley of Thendara, Regis signaled for the party to halt. He wanted to see his brother's expression at the first sight of the city, huge and sprawling and ancient. Beyond the old Darkovan town lay the Terran Trade City and the spaceport.

What did Rinaldo see? Were the towers of steel and glass ugly in their alienness, or did they present a strange, austere beauty? Regis himself was never sure.

"I did not realize it was so big," Rinaldo murmured. "So many people, such riches! You must think me even more rustic than ever, for saying so."

"Not at all," Regis said. "I value that you speak as you think. Such honesty is rare in the city."

"So I have been warned all my life." Rinaldo grinned. "Father Master described Thendara as a cesspool of fleshly indulgence and deceit, rife with every form of sinfulness. I wonder what he would have said about Shainsa or Ardcarran, should he have been induced to pollute his tongue with their names. But I have no fear for my soul, with a brother to guide me." He straightened his shoulders. "In fact, if Father Master's assessment was at all correct, I will consider this a challenge."

"A challenge?" Regis was not sure if he had understood or if the breath of chill that touched the nape of his neck were a premonition. Rinaldo's easy smile set his fears to rest.

"To test what a man of determination and virtue can do in such a place," Rinaldo answered.

"Let us hope for compassion and an open mind, as well." Regis nudged his horse forward, and they began the long descent. The City Guards stationed at the gate recognized him long before he drew to a halt.

"Lord Hastur, welcome back to Thendara." The senior officer bowed respectfully. "*Dom* Danilo." His eyes flickered to Rinaldo, taking in the poor quality of his horse, the worn clothing, and the fact that this disreputable-appearing person rode at the side of the most honored man in Thendara.

Regis noticed the officer's reaction, the confusion that flickered momentarily across his face. He knew, too, that Rinaldo had seen it.

Indignation stirred. *I will not make excuses for my brother's appearance or anything else. Rinaldo is here under my protection.*

Soon enough, everyone of any consequence in Thendara—in all the Domains, most likely—would know who Rinaldo was. It was better to let the poor man enjoy a little peace before they descended upon him, the courtiers and power seekers, the sycophants and schemers.

Regis wondered if he had done his brother a favor by taking him away from the peace of Nevarsin.

Still, the ordinary world was not all bad. If Thendara teemed with unscrupulous men, it also held those who valued honor and justice, the bonds of blood and integrity. If Regis had suffered from the demands of his rank, he had also known great kindness here. At least, he could count on Javanne to extend a gracious welcome to Rinaldo.

Javanne did not fail Regis. In his absence, she had completed the transfer of his possessions from the townhouse to his grandfather's rooms in Comyn Castle. A second suite, the best available, had been scrubbed spotless and refurnished for Rinaldo, and a body-servant engaged as well. Regis was astonished at her energy and efficiency, but he was also concerned at the new lines around her eyes. She was using work as a way of holding her grief at bay. She had always thrived when she felt needed.

After making sure the horses were properly tended and Rinaldo escorted to his new quarters and given everything he needed, and after thanking Javanne for her efforts, Regis was at last free to seek his own rest. He was so tired that even the strangeness of Danvan's bedchamber could not keep him awake for long. He undressed without the help of a servant, sponged away the worst of the travel dirt, and tumbled into the enormous bed. As he drifted into unconsciousness, he wished it were possible for Danilo to slip between the soft *linex* sheets beside him. This wasn't the townhouse, where they might enjoy a certain latitude of behavior, not to mention privacy. This was Comyn Castle, where the servants knew and gossiped about everything, and Regis was not longer Heir but Hastur of Hastur.

The next morning, Regis awoke to the sound of a servant lighting the fire in the bedroom. He jerked upright. The poor man startled, bowed, and retreated.

Regis raked his hair back from his face, pulled on the dressing robe that lay across the foot of the bed, and stumbled about in a semblance of his usual morning ablutions. Shortly his body-servant brought in a breakfast tray and an armload of clothing. Suppressing his irritation, for it was hardly the poor man's fault that proprieties must be observed for the Hastur of Hastur, Regis allowed himself to be dressed, his hair combed into place, and his meal placed before him in the parlor. He forced himself to sip the steaming *jaco* without burning his mouth. When he had finished, he asked the servant to send for Danilo as his paxman to discuss the day's schedule. Then he went into his grandfather's study, now his own.

Where to begin? The brief respite was over. The question of Terran Federation membership, while settled for the moment, must be carefully monitored; he should send a message to Lew Alton and find out if there was more news. As the Head of his Domain, he now bore the responsibility for running Carcosa and Castle Hastur. His departure for Nevarsin had postponed a number of ceremonial duties that could no longer be put off—reviewing the cadets, meeting with Gabriel in his capacity as Commander of the City Guards, holding audiences with those Comyn still in the city, and speaking with the Pan-Darkovan League and the trade delegation from the Dry Towns. Regis began pacing to keep his head from spinning at the sheer number of tasks. He should arrange for more help in the management of Comyn Castle, but subtly, so that Javanne would not take it as a criticism.

Linnea rose in his memory, and his heart ached. If things had gone otherwise, if he had not made such a botch of the marriage proposal, she would be here, relieving Javanne as Castle chatelaine. It could not be helped; no amount of self-recrimination would change the past.

All the smiths in Zandru's Forge cannot put a hatched chick back into its egg.

What was taking Danilo so long?

And Rinaldo . . . Regis could not leave his brother alone and unguided in the treacherous maze of Castle and city. He must carve out time to continue getting to know his brother, helping him to find his place. The first thing was to have Rinaldo recognized as a legitimate son of their father. In the old times, this would have been a matter for the Comyn Council, but that body no longer existed. The Cortes? The Telepath Council? A simple written declaration?

Danilo halted at the library door and bowed. *"Vai dom."*

Regis strode over to his grandfather's desk, now *his* as well, and sat down. "Close the door."

Danilo held out his hands. Regis, in a spasm of inexpressible relief, took them. Danilo's fingers felt warm, so his own must be half-frozen.

"It will be hard at first," Danilo said softly, "adjusting to new arrangements, but that cannot change how I feel, what I want . . . You are the lord of my heart as well as of my sword. Nothing can take that away from us."

Although he had heard these words before and had spoken them in his own turn, Regis could not respond aloud. He did not need to. A pulse of wordless understanding gathered them both. Regis felt his heart grow calmer.

"Meanwhile, I have need of my paxman, my friend and advisor."

Danilo gestured theatrically. "He stands before you."

"Then we had best get to work." Regis outlined his thoughts on the duties ahead of him. Danilo nodded, making suggestions about what must be attended to first and what could be easily put off.

"No one will expect you to pick up where old Lord Hastur left off," Danilo observed. "People will understand. They'll give you time to find your feet."

"Bless Aldones and anyone else who will take credit, I don't have to deal with the Regency as well," Regis said fervently.

"The Elhalyns aren't going to storm Thendara, demanding the throne. Some may expect you to take on the title for ceremonial purposes, but that shouldn't be onerous."

Regis shook his head. "I won't do it, not even as a token. I told Grandfather I would never be king, and I meant it! *Regent* is entirely too close to *king* for my taste."

"Can you justifiably refuse a title that means nothing?"

"I can and will," Regis repeated with a touch of savage heat.

Danilo would not be derailed. "At the same time, you cannot escape the fact that you are now Hastur of Hastur. You shake your head, Regis, but it is true. The Comyn may be less than we once were, but we are still here."

"Not for long."

Danilo shrugged, refusing to argue further.

"Be that as it may, the absence of a formal Comyn Council does present a problem." Regis briefly described his intention to create a place for Rinaldo in the Domains.

At the mention of Rinaldo, Danilo stiffened. The warmth that had sprung up between the two men chilled. Danilo agreed that it would not be appropriate to bring the matter of Rinaldo's legitimacy before the Telepath Council. Traditionally, the Comyn had governed themselves, especially in matters of inheritance, Domain-right, and marriage. Less than a generation ago, the Heir to a Domain could not have chosen a wife without the consent of the Council. Now, there was no authority to petition.

"There is a precedent," Danilo pointed out after a little thought. "Historically, when urgent matters arose in between Council sessions, those Comyn still in Thendara would convene an informal decision-making body. They would in due course submit their actions to ratification by the full Council."

Regis did not have a full tally of who had remained in Thendara after his grandfather's funeral, enjoying the fair weather and summer festivities. Even one or two would be enough. Rinaldo's status was as much social as it was legal. Documents could be drawn up and filed with the Cortes to ensure the latter.

"I will see to it," Danilo said. "You have only to fix a date."

"As soon as it can be arranged, after I have discussed the matter with my brother."

The next moment, a tap sounded at the door. At a command from Regis, one of the Castle Guards stepped in. Regis did not know him but thought him to be one of Gabriel's rising young officers.

"Vai domyn." The Guardsman bowed in turn to Regis and then to Danilo. "There is a person wishing an audience with Lord Hastur. He is not known to me, but he claims to be Rinaldo Hastur."

"He is my brother," Regis said, "and I expect him to be treated with proper courtesy."

The Guardsman bowed again, more deeply. A moment later, he escorted Rinaldo into the library, this time with almost obsequious attention. Rinaldo wore the same suit of clothing in which he had traveled, although it had been cleaned and pressed.

Before either Regis or Rinaldo could say anything, Danilo begged leave to be about his duties and hurried out of the room.

"Please make yourself comfortable." Regis gestured to the chairs drawn up by the fireplace. "This was Grandfather's library."

"It's very impressive," Rinaldo said. His gaze lingered on the rows of books.

"You will of course have full access to the collection," Regis said.

"Thank you, brother. That is most kind. But I wonder if I might prevail upon your generosity—" With a sheepish expression, he indicated his clothing.

"I will have my own tailor get to work immediately. Other than that, are you well? Your quarters are adequate?"

"More than adequate," Rinaldo assured him. "I am ready to take on whatever work you assign me."

"Rinaldo, you are my brother, not my secretary. It is for others to serve, not you."

"But I cannot remain idle. I must make myself useful, as I have been accustomed."

"I welcome your assistance once you have familiarized yourself with the way things are done here in Thendara," Regis said. "One man alone cannot hope to perform all the duties expected of a Hastur. I don't know how Grandfather managed it all and the Regency as well.

Our first step must be to secure your position and inheritance." Regis outlined what he and Danilo had discussed. Excitement and pleasure flared in Rinaldo's face.

"I will have the legal documents drawn up and filed with the Cortes. You will not need to make an appearance. My declaration should be sufficient. Javanne is eager to arrange a ball in your honor. Have you had much opportunity to dance?"

Rinaldo shrugged. "Only as much as is seemly for a monk. Which is to say, none at all. I do not object to dancing if it is modest and innocent in nature. But the third thing you mentioned, presenting me to a body of Comyn as in olden times—I think that is the most important of all. Even though the Comyn Council no longer rules Darkover, their consent is essential, is it not?"

"It is of less importance than in the past," Regis agreed guardedly. "Certainly, it would smooth things to have their approval. Do not underestimate the power of our family. Grandfather managed to ram all kinds of unpalatable truths down their collective throats. I am no Danvan Hastur, but I have had some experience in the arts of persuasion."

"As Hastur or as Regent?"

Regis suppressed a grimace of exasperation, reminding himself that his brother could have no way of knowing how sensitive that issue was. "The Regency," he explained patiently, "no longer exists. The Elhalyn, what is left of them, are scattered. No one even knows what the proper lineage is, except maybe a few moldy old scholars. There hasn't been a single one capable of ruling since Grandfather's time."

"If there are no Elhalyn contenders for the throne," Rinaldo said thoughtfully, "then the honor would pass to Hastur, would it not? One of us could be king . . ."

"There is nothing to be king *of*," Regis said wearily. "The Comyn have collapsed as a power, the Council is gone, and we ought to direct our energies toward Darkover's future, not reenacting her past."

"Yes, yes, I see your point. Still, it is a pity the Council has been replaced by a less prestigious body. I would have liked to see the Crystal Chamber in all its glory, the color and pageantry, everything I have missed in my life. Now it is gone, and I have lost my chance."

Regis shook his head, unable to come up with a way of explaining that no rational man would *want* to attend a meeting in that ancient hall. Even with the *laran* dampers to block out psychic energy, the memories of so many painful conflicts, schemes and coercions, even deaths, lingered. He said, "I hope that a ball will provide a happy substitute."

"It is overwhelming; I have never been an observer, let alone the object, of such an honor."

12

Later that day, Regis sent for his personal tailor and instructed the man to furnish Rinaldo with a wardrobe suitable for his rank. Whatever Rinaldo wished, even silver lace or Ardcarran rubies, he was to have. No expense was to be spared, and all materials must be of the finest. Additional sewing women and tailors were engaged so that Rinaldo might be properly resplendent for the ball.

Danilo reported on the progress of the various arrangements. "I've set the date to allow sufficient time for the guests to respond and make their preparations. If it meets with your approval, I'll send out the invitations today."

Regis glanced through the notes, written in Danilo's graceful script, and nodded his approval. "As usual, your efficiency and thoughtfulness are everything I could wish for. What about the formal presentation?"

"I've tallied up those Comyn known to be in the city. This is only an approximation, with additional information from your sister and *Dom* Gabriel. Undoubtedly, there are more, and I shall endeavor to locate them."

"Mmmm. There are more than I expected. The Ridenow are still here?" Regis wished they had stayed in Serrais.

"We can't very well exclude them."

"No, I suppose not." Regis handed the written plans to Danilo. "When you have a moment in the next few days, send a letter to Armida. I'd like Rinaldo to have one of the blacks as a gift. I know they are bespoken for years in advance, often before they are foaled, so it's best to put in my order as soon as possible. In the meanwhile, Rinaldo is to have the free use of any of my horses in the Castle stables."

"My lord, surely this is excessive—" Danilo began.

Regis cut him off. "What would you have me do, Danilo, leave him with the nag you got for him in Nevarsin? He is my brother, a Hastur! I cannot allow him to ride through the streets of Thendara as ill-mounted as a farmer!"

"Are you saying that I slighted him? That I deliberately chose a horse *unworthy* of a Comyn lord?"

"By no means. For mountain travel, a horse like the one you found, strong and trail-seasoned, is far preferable to a prancing, ninny-brained beauty. But this is Thendara, and appearances must be maintained. Rinaldo may have been hidden away and forgotten, but I will not allow him to be treated that way any longer. By *anyone*."

Danilo recoiled. "I did not mean to imply . . . I am altogether conscious of the honor of Hastur, but—"

"I suppose now you will tell me," Regis said, his voice laced with sarcasm, "that if I make him such gifts he will succumb at once to greed and ambition. His only thought, of course, is to take my place as Head of Hastur—a place I never wanted in any case!" He began pacing with such energy that the wind of his passing sent a pile of papers slithering to the floor.

Danilo made no attempt to pick up the fallen documents, although normally he would have done so without thought. "Such things have been known to happen."

"Gods, Danilo!" Regis forced a laugh. "Until a tenday ago, the man was a cloistered monk! What kind of monstrous ambitions do you think they foster within the hallowed halls of Nevarsin?"

"You should know as well as I," was Danilo's sullen answer.

Regis quieted, pensive. He thought of his own life, one of luxury and privilege but also beset by unrelenting responsibility. If Rinaldo's childhood had been one of prayer and discipline, his own had been even more bleak.

"Actually," Regis said, "I wish Rinaldo were capable—could be induced—that he might be permitted to take Grandfather's place instead of me. I have lost all heart for scheming. Even if he were willing, how could I wish such a life on him?"

What must life have been like for the unacknowledged bastard son of a Comyn lord? Rinaldo had been too young to understand why he was hidden away like a shameful secret. Had he waited for a token of recognition from his father, a message that never came? How had he felt all those years, watching from obscurity while Regis occupied the place of the eldest son and Heir—forced to keep silent, even when set to teaching young Regis his letters?

Holy Bearer of Burdens, Danilo's thought shimmered through the light rapport, *what resentments, what secret desires must have festered in such a wounded heart? And how dangerous might such a man become?*

When Regis turned to meet Danilo's gaze, the dark eyes were shuttered, the moment of compassion fled. Danilo's mind was as tightly barriered as a fortress.

"Danilo—" Tentatively, Regis lifted one hand in his direction but dropped it when there was no response. Regis hardened his voice. "Of what, exactly, do you suspect my brother?

"Greed, ambition, envy, I don't know! I don't trust him. Can't you see how he says one thing and does another? He utters the pious words of a monk and then complains about the quality of his garments. I know he's had a difficult life, but he seems to have learned more about self-interest than brotherly love."

Danilo swept up the fallen papers. "When are you going to tell him about us? Don't fool yourself into believing he won't figure it out. How do you think he'll respond? Will he rejoice that his brother is a lover of men?"

"He needs time to accept the larger world. I've been cautiously introducing the topic—"

"And every time, he turns the conversation into a sermon on righteousness and salvation!" Danilo stormed. "Underneath those oily words, he's no different from Father Master!"

"Are you quite finished?" Regis asked in a clipped, taut voice. Danilo nodded. "Then I must make one thing clear. This is the last discussion of this kind that you and I will ever have. Whatever your opinions about my brother, I *require,*" placing an unmistakable emphasis on the word, "that you keep them to yourself. You are not to criticize him in word or action. I never want to hear of this again."

For a long moment, Danilo stood immobile. If he wrestled with his own thoughts, he gave no outward sign. "As you wish, *vai dom.*"

Some demon prodded Regis to say, "I am not asking you, Danilo. I am telling you." He tore his eyes from Danilo's face and threw himself into the desk chair. "Now, go about your work. I expect that the next time you present yourself to me, everything I have assigned to you will be accomplished."

Without a word, Danilo bowed and strode to the door. Hand on the latch, shoulders rigid, he paused.

In a spasm of guilt for having provoked yet another quarrel, Regis cried out telepathically. *Bredhyu . . .*

To his relief, Danilo did not shut him out. Danilo had been waiting—hoping—for Regis to make the overture that he himself could not.

Danilo's posture softened. He turned back, tenderness warming his eyes. His *laran* shields dissolved in an outpouring of solace. The air shimmered with their psychic bond. Then Danilo bowed again and withdrew.

Regis stared at the age-darkened wood of the desk, the piles of documents, the papers Danilo had neatly replaced. Despite the season, an insidious chill seeped into his bones. He wondered if he would ever be warm in this place.

That evening, dusk fell quickly. The sudden deepening of the shadows, for which Darkover had been named, shrouded the castle halls. Regis tried to shrug off the sense of foreboding that had dogged him since his fight with Danilo. Stubbornly, it grew stronger with every passing hour. With relief, he set aside the day's work and returned to his own quarters.

Javanne—*May Evanda and Avarra bless her!*—had prepared a family dinner, so he need not change into formal courtly wear. He would have a chance to relax, to set aside the myriad administrative details of the day.

His mood lightened as he strode down the corridor toward the apartments taken by his sister's family. The carpet runner was new, green with an ivy pattern down the center. The corridor led into another, twisting as one architectural style gave way to the next. What a warren the old castle was! Regis hoped Rinaldo would be able to find his way. To his surprise, Gabriel met him at the corner just before the entrance.

Gabriel had changed little since Regis had last seen him, a sturdy, russet-haired man with a hint of squareness in his jaw and the strongly muscled shoulders of a man who had spent his life in military office. He was reputed to at one time have been the best wrestler in the City Guards.

"Lord Hastur, may I have a private word with you before we go in?"

"There is no need for formality between kinsmen," Regis answered. The knot of foreboding in his gut tightened.

"I would speak to you on affairs of the Comyn, and I would rather not do so in front of Javanne and . . . others."

"Gabriel," Regis said, deliberately using his personal name, "you may discuss any matter you wish."

"Very well, then." Gabriel moved aside, into the shadowed corner. "Javanne tells me that you plan to not only welcome a *nedestro* relative into the family but to have him declared the legitimate son of your father . . . which would make him the *eldest* son. Is this true?"

"No doubt, the existence of Rinaldo will come as a surprise to many. Grandfather confided it to me on his deathbed." Regis paused, trying not to sound defensive. "I fear a great injustice has been done. My father undoubtedly meant to recognize Rinaldo, but he died too soon. Grandfather, in his turn, could have done so but chose not to. I do not wish to speak ill of my own relations, but together they have done my brother great harm in denying him his rightful place in society and his inheritance as a Hastur. I intend to make things right."

"Speaking as both your kinsman and your friend, I beg you to consider whether this is wise," Gabriel said, his voice lowering with urgency. "Since you left, even this tenday . . . the political balance in Thendara is volatile. The *Terranan* have shifted their tactics. They are now trying to purchase the good will of the people with promises of technological miracles and Federation citizenship. Half the old Comyn Council, those who are not outright senile, want to take us back to the Ages of Chaos. The Ridenow are out for all they can get. I fear they see themselves as the next great power in the Domains. You know as well as I that they want to turn Darkover into a Federation puppet state."

"Surely, things cannot have deteriorated so badly."

Gabriel pressed his lips together. "Not only that, Valdir Ridenow and his allies are doing all they can to consolidate the Comyn against you. He's been arguing that the Telepath Council is incapable of making a decision and should be done away with. If the remaining Comyn unite with the Pan Darkovan League and malcontents in recognizing Rinaldo's claim over yours, thinking him more easily bent to their will, then—"

"Gabriel, I must do what I feel is right. Besides, who is to say that Rinaldo might not be the better man, trained as he is in modesty and service? I never wanted such responsibility. It was thrust upon me. You, who have known me for so many years, must understand."

"What I understand," Gabriel said in a heavy, sardonic tone, "is that you are quite mad. Such a change would throw the Domains into chaos."

Wearily, Regis shook his head. "If we are so dependent upon any one man, then we Comyn have outlived our usefulness. It would be better for Darkover if we all disappeared."

Before Gabriel could respond, the door swung open. Javanne peered out. Despite the gown of cream wool trimmed with delicate silver and blue embroidery at neckline and cuffs and the garland of tiny white flowers tucked into the coiled braids covering the nape of her neck, she looked tense and weary.

"Are you two going to stand there while dinner gets cold? We are all assembled, waiting for you. Men's talk is very well," she said, slipping one hand through her husband's elbow, "but folk must be fed, and roasted meat is not improved by congealing."

Gabriel nodded and, patting her hand affectionately, allowed himself to be led inside.

"You, too, Regis." Javanne affected a stern expression. "Our brother has superceded you and is anxious for us all to be together. And—" when he opened his mouth to reply, "no mention of politics, do you hear me? This is a *family* dinner, and I'll not have everyone's appetite destroyed by talk of Councils and trade delegations and *Terranan!*"

With a trickle of relief, Regis bowed his head and yielded to the inevitable.

Some demon from Zandru's Seventh Hell had prompted Regis to don his court finery for the presentation of Rinaldo to the Comyn. The suit of velvet in Hastur blue embellished with silver-trimmed lace was the most ornate garment he had ever worn. He refused to wear the matching sword, however, with its hilt and scabbard filigreed in the same lacy design as the jacket trim. As a small blessing, the boots were comfortable, if impractical for outdoor wear. Danilo wore more modest clothing, a bit on the somber side but still tasteful enough for the occasion.

At least the meeting would not take place in the Crystal Chamber or the chamber in which he had addressed the Telepath Council. Instead, Danilo had prepared a smaller room, one designed for informal gatherings and furnished with comfortable chairs around a central table. Instead of the echoing spaciousness of the stately chamber, this room afforded a degree of intimacy. Regis would be able to make easy eye contact. There would be no telepathic dampers, nor would any be needed. This was not a debate, but a simple introduction. It was as much an honor for the other Comyn as it was for Rinaldo, so there was no reason why it should not be a pleasant and enjoyable affair.

Bless Danilo, there was but a single Guardsman standing at attention at the door. Regis waited until he could be reasonably sure the others were already assembled. Then Rinaldo arrived.

The tailor had done his best. Rinaldo's raiment, although minimally ornamented, was of exquisite quality, the gray wool so fine it shimmered like snowfox fur. The jacket had been shaped to enhance Rinaldo's spare frame. Had he been dressed as Regis was, the sumptuousness would have turned his complexion gaunt and rendered him pretentious. As it was, he looked grave and dignified, a man who had lived simply but meaningfully.

Rinaldo bowed, the salute of one of noble birth to another of higher rank. He took no notice of Danilo. Regis inclined his head and together they went in.

Regis did not expect a formal announcement of their entrance, complete with the recitation of all his titles, and he received none. Instead, the reaction was exactly what he had hoped for: conversations paused, heads swiveled, and eyes brightened as he took his place at the head of the table with Rinaldo beside him. Danilo slipped into the chair beside Marilla Lindir-Aillard, whose son, Kennard-Dyan, was to inherit Ardais. Whether this gesture on Danilo's part was a subtle reminder that, as former Warden of Ardais, he claimed the right to sit among the Comyn lords or simply that it was the most convenient unoccupied chair, Regis could not tell.

Not everyone who had attended the funeral for Danvan Hastur had remained in Thendara, but most of the great houses were represented: Regis himself, Javanne and Gabriel, who was acting as Warden of Alton, Marilla Lindir-Aillard, Ruyven Di Asturien, one of the Eldrins, and a few from lesser families—Castamir, Lindir, and a very elderly man from the Montereys, distant cousins of the Altons. At the far end of the table, Valdir Ridenow watched calmly, his nephew Francisco at his right elbow.

Where Danilo had found all of them, Regis had no idea. Most wore courtly dress in the beautiful colors of their houses, like a flock of exotic birds filling the otherwise somber chamber. Jewels and precious metals glinted in the headdresses of the women. Chains draped the chests of the men. Their expressions ranged from distantly polite to courteous. In the absence of telepathic dampers, their emotions curled like smoke through the room. Regis did his best to block them out. Danilo's face was a shade paler than usual; he had always been the more sensitive of the two. It must be costing him an enormous amount of psychic energy to remain free of the outside mental influences.

"*Vai domyn,* kinsmen, lords and ladies," Regis said. "Thank you for coming and on such short notice."

"The honor is ours." Ordinarily, it would fall to the member of the next highest-ranking Domain to speak, but in this informal setting, Ruyven Di Asturien answered. His dignified gaze took in the assembly. "You have brought us together, as we Comyn have always gathered at this season since before our sun turned red. We never thought to do so again. But now, we welcome you, Lord Hastur . . ."

"And the man who sits beside you," Valdir Ridenow broke in.

Regis rose with all the dignity at his command. "It is my pleasure to present to you my father's *nedestro* son, Rinaldo Lanart-Hastur. I declare Rinaldo legitimate and desire that he should enjoy all the privileges and responsibilities of our caste. It is my intention that my brother take his place among us, and I call upon you to acknowledge him now."

The announcement could not have come as news. Regis knew all too well the pervasive and insidious currents of gossip that saturated Thendara in general and the Comyn in particular. Yet there was no mistaking the unease that rippled around the room.

"*Dom* Regis," Lady Marilla began tentatively, then corrected herself, "Lord Hastur. We are of course delighted to receive any kinsman to our midst. There are so few of us that every new addition must be precious. Your brother looks to be a fine, sober man, a credit to your Domain and to us all. But . . ." Her eyes shifted between Regis and Rinaldo, although her composure did not waver. "You are proposing more than a simple welcome. Such a step requires careful consideration of all the . . . implications."

Regis found the woman's indirection maddening. What she meant was she thought it inappropriate to discuss Rinaldo's position in front of him. He sensed, from *Dom* Ruyven's air of disapproval and the downturned curve of the old man's lips, that he was not at all in favor of what Regis proposed. Despite the barriers Regis had summoned in his mind, he could not escape the surge of emotion from where Valdir Ridenow sat.

"Some might say," one of the Lindir lords put in, "that the Hasturs had too much power even before the demise of the Council."

"Speak plainly, my lord," Gabriel said. "What are you insinuating?"

"Why, nothing more than what everyone already knows. The Telepath Council was created by Lord Hastur, and they answer to him with an almost slavish devotion. It is bad enough that the Hasturs have traditionally been the most powerful of all the Domains, more so than their royal Elhalyn cousins. But when personal charisma is combined with exemplary leadership—I say nothing against Lord Hastur, you understand—we are all cognizant of the debt owed to him—when all this is added to political influence and the legends that have grown up over the last few years . . . can it be wise for one man to possess so much power?"

"My reputation is not at issue here," Regis said tightly. "Do you accuse me of deliberately creating a cult of personality? I assure you, I never sought or wanted—"

He reined in his tongue before spilling out that he would far rather have lived an ordinary life. No one would have believed him. A nasty impulse led him to add, "Or are you saying that it's bad enough to have one Hastur lording it over you without adding another?"

A moment of silence answered him, of indrawn breaths, of sudden stillness of hands. That was exactly what they *had* thought. In that hush, Danilo leaned forward.

"If any of you wish to accuse Regis Hastur of an abuse of rank and power, do so properly, openly, but not at this time. We are here at Lord Hastur's behest and in the presence of one newly come among us. Decency and dignity require that we give Rinaldo Hastur a fair hearing."

All eyes now turned toward Rinaldo. He had listened, quiet and serious, to the debate. Now he rose to his feet, a movement both supple and dignified. He lifted his head so that they could all see his milk-pale skin, his eyes colorless as an overcast sky, and his delicate, almost ethereal features.

Emmasca . . . ? whispered through their minds.

Just as I suspected when I first saw him!

But if he cannot father an heir—

Regis cannot possible expect us to—

Regis can, Regis formed the thought and dropped his barriers so that his mental communication resounded through the ambient psychic space. *And Regis does!*

"Vai domyn." If Rinaldo had sensed any of the roiling thoughts, he gave no sign. "I am not here to challenge the established order. Indeed,

I have spent my life in obedience to authority. Judge me if you will, as you will, but I beg of you, cast no aspersions upon my brother. He has been the soul of kindness to me. I would hear no evil spoken of him."

Rinaldo waited for his words to sink in. "As for myself, you see me as I am. I have no ambition for myself nor any desire to found a dynasty."

With a gentle smile, he invited their agreement and was rewarded by a nod here and there.

Regis did not like the way Valdir watched, careful and intent, as if assessing how hard it would be to mold Rinaldo to his own ends. Now, where had *that* thought come from? Regis wondered. He had caught no *laran* thoughts from the Ridenow lord.

"My work at Nevarsin was primarily copying ancient manuscripts and teaching those younger than I to do the same," Rinaldo explained. "So you see, I know a fair amount of history and very little of current worldly affairs."

At this, someone chuckled. Regis felt the iron tension across his shoulders relax a fraction.

"If you have lived your life cloistered at Nevarsin, you are *cristoforo,* are you not?" *Dom* Ruyven kept his voice neutral, but he could not disguise the challenge in the carriage of his shoulders, the suggestive angle of his chin.

By ancient law, the sole surviving heir to an estate was forbidden to become a monk, owing to the required vow of celibacy. But Rinaldo was no longer a monk, he was not the only son of Hastur, and those days were long past.

Rinaldo met Ruyven's stare. "Although I have been released from my vows and am free to marry and lead a secular life, I am now and always will be the servant of the Holy Bearer of Burdens."

"My brother's faith or lack thereof is not an issue for public debate," Regis said, before anyone else could jump into the discussion. "We are not living in the Ages of Chaos. Darkover is part of a confederation of planets, and it is time we behaved like civilized people, not superstitious savages."

"A *confederation?*" Valdir's voice was soft, but it filled the room. At his side, Francisco straightened in his chair.

"A fellowship, if you will," Regis replied, instantly regretting his choice of words. "An alliance. But on equal footing, on our own terms, not as a poor relation."

"Change comes upon us, whether we invite it or not," Valdir said. "Reason dictates that we would be better off to control as much of it as we can. Perhaps our best hope is to return to the days when each Domain was free to direct its own destiny."

On the surface, Valdir was discussing the right of the Hastur Domain to run its own affairs, to satisfy itself as to the legitimacy of any *nedestro* heirs and to grant them whatever rights it saw fit. Regis had learned through years of painful experience, of betrayals and schemes and hidden meanings, never to take anything a Comyn lord said at face value. His Grandfather had begun the lessons, and the unfolding politics of Domain and Council had reinforced them.

The implication of Valdir's argument was clear. If Regis agreed for the sake of Rinaldo's inheritance, then Valdir could—and most likely was even now readying himself to—apply the same principle of Domain autonomy to negotiations with the Terrans.

Ridenow will join the Federation as an independent nation, whether the rest of the Domains follow or not. The prospect was beyond terrifying. Division would follow, then civil war and the disintegration of social order. The Federation would eagerly intervene. They would send troops armed with Compact-banned weapons. The Expansionist agents would seize whatever resources they could. They would be worse than the World Wreckers, for they would have no need for secrecy and no reward for restraint.

Was *that* what Valdir wanted? Or did he simply not see the logical progression of consequences?

Wishing he could be anywhere but in that suddenly hostile chamber, Regis conceded that Rinaldo had been right. He had been a very unworldly, optimistic person after all.

Regis could see only one way of avoiding the destruction of the world he loved. "*Vai comyn,* these are indeed unpredictable times, and as *Dom* Valdir has so eloquently pointed out, change breeds uncertainty. We must look to our strengths for guidance and stability: our connections with one another and with the past, our unique Gifts, our love for this world and its people. Now more than ever, Darkover needs all our leaders."

"No one questions your qualifications, Lord Hastur," said the Castamir lord. Others nodded agreement, Ruyven among them.

"I have called you here out of respect for our ancient traditions. Set your minds at rest, I have no intention of relinquishing my responsibilities as Head of my Domain. Honor demands no less. As has been pointed out, we are not so many that we can afford to exclude one who has so much to contribute. For this reason, I ask for your approval of full Comyn rights for my brother as a member of Hastur."

"There is ample precedent for a younger son to hold a Domain," Danilo said, looking pointedly at Valdir.

"Yes, that is true," the Monterey lord agreed in a quavering voice. "Lord Regis Hastur has already been recognized as Head of his Domain. The legitimacy of his brother, whose attributes, however worthy of a devotional life, hardly qualify him to administer a Domain, does not alter that fact. Of course, if *Dom* Regis himself were to abdicate, that would be an entirely different matter. Or if Rinaldo were to marry and produce a male heir, which is . . . ah, unlikely . . . the legal precedents . . . ah, yes. But neither of these situations pertains."

"Put that way, I see no reason to object," Ruyven said. "It seems to me as good a compromise as any. *Dom* Regis will retain the position he already holds, and Hastur will gain another member, but one out of the line of succession."

"Aye . . ." Murmurs of agreement filled the room. Some, including Lady Marilla, looked frankly relieved. Valdir held back, his expression unreadable. To Regis, he did not have the air of a man entirely pleased with the outcome. He'd wanted Regis out of the way, that much was clear, and now he had not one but two Hasturs to contend with.

Valdir was too crafty to let any trace of disappointment show. As everyone rose to leave, he congratulated Regis on a matter well handled and then spoke to Rinaldo, but for somewhat longer than courtesy required.

When, at last, the socializing came to an end, Regis felt thoroughly wrung out, like an old rag that had been used too many times and left soggy all winter. The last time he had used such an object was in his time as a cadet. Danilo, he recalled, had been far more adept at scrubbing stone floors.

Danilo . . .

There he was, standing just outside the door. Regis yearned for a private moment, to feel the strength of his *bredhyu,* that sense of acceptance deeper than words. Of all the men in Thendara, none would understand better than Danilo what Regis had done, the price he had paid. The corridor was far too public for any semblance of intimacy, however, and Rinaldo was waiting, overflowing with excitement, wanting to discuss every detail of the meeting. Regis had only a moment to meet Danilo's dark, compassionate gaze.

13

Summer descended on Thendara, and lengthening days brightened the city. The social season enjoyed a brief, frenzied renewal with the ball held in Rinaldo's honor. Almost every dignitary in Thendara attended, those few from major Comyn houses and any minor nobility who could be found, wealthy commoners, and a good portion of the Telepath Council. Only the Terrans were lacking; Dan Lawton had been invited, but he had declined. Regis was not entirely sure why, but he sensed some continuing family difficulty.

As the evening approached, Regis found himself uneasy, although he rejoiced in the evident pleasure of his brother. He had never felt comfortable in large assemblies. Since his first entry into society, people had stared at him, openly or covertly, out of curiosity or envy. He felt himself measured against his grandfather and the lineage of great Hastur leaders, against the prowess of the other cadets, against the stories that sprang up wherever he went. He hated the whispers and insinuations, but worst of all was the adulation. How could one man live up to everything they said he had done?

As Regis moved through the glittering crowd in the main ballroom of Comyn Castle, he was not sure whether the shift of public interest from himself to Rinaldo was a good thing. Mostly, he felt a sense of relief at not being the sole object of gossip.

Danilo shadowed him, discreet as usual, the exemplary paxman.

Despite the lively music and air of festivity, Regis danced little and only with his sister. Javanne loved to dance and had few opportunities. She had grown up in a generation when it was improper for a woman to dance with any man not a kinsman or husband. This night, Gabriel had been called away at the last minute to sort out a disturbance in the Trade City. Regis did not want Javanne to be too disappointed. If Linnea had been there, he would have asked her as well, but she was not.

Although he did not dance, Rinaldo took great apparent delight in watching. His eyes followed the ladies gliding through the patterned steps. *Not indifferent, indeed,* Regis thought. It was a shame that as a novice and then a monk, his brother had never learned to dance. The old Darkovan proverb went, *"Only men laugh, only men weep, only men dance."* During his three years of study at Nevarsin, Regis had returned home for Midsummer and Midwinter Festivals, so he had never thought about how the monks might celebrate. He stood at Rinaldo's side, watching two of the cadet officers begin the Hellers Sword Dance. Rinaldo, who had been smiling and tapping one foot in time to the music, stiffened.

"Is something amiss, brother?" Regis asked. "All this elegance must be a bit bewildering to you."

Rinaldo looked abashed, but did not lower his gaze. "The evening was enjoyable enough, until . . ." His gaze flickered to the two cadets, now dancing very close to one another, leaping and twirling with such precision that they seemed to be one being.

"The Sword Dance is a bit barbaric, I admit," Regis said, "but it is very old, from the deep Hellers, and traditional at Comyn gatherings. When I was young, Dyan Ardais was famous for his performance. Rest assured, the swords are not used as weapons; if anyone gets hurt, it is from overexertion and muscle strain."

"The swords do not offend me."

"What then?" Regis wondered at the use of the word *offend*.

Rinaldo inclined his head toward Regis, so that they could not be easily overheard. "It is indecent for two men to—to comport themselves in such an unseemly fashion."

What, dancing together? Even as Regis thought this, the two dancers came together for one of the complicated duet figures, arms flung over one another's shoulders, each in turn using the other for balance and support during the increasingly wild acrobatics. Both men were breathing hard, their faces flushed and gleaming with sweat, their eyes alight with savage joy as they threw themselves into the stylized martial movements. From their excitement, the intensity of their awareness of one another, and the closeness of their bodies, they might almost be lovers . . .

"They are not—" Regis began. "And even if they were, that is hardly *indecent.* This is Thendara, not St. Valentine's."

Regis faced his brother directly. He could no longer put off addressing the *cristoforo* attitude toward homosexuality, although he was not ready to confront Rinaldo with his own nature in the middle of such a public gathering.

"Among the Comyn, it is not considered disgraceful but proper for young unmarried men to turn to one another rather than to such women who are common to all. Most set aside the physical joining when they marry, but the ties of devotion and loyalty remain. A few continue to find their deepest connection to other men, but they are no less honorable for it."

Rinaldo was trembling, visibly fighting for control. Regis could not read the emotion beneath the outward physical signs, only its intensity. Could it be that Rinaldo, like himself, struggled between his sexual preferences and the deeply implanted guilt from years of indoctrination?

No, whatever passions drove Rinaldo, Regis did not think that suppressed love of men was one of them. He must give his brother more time to accustom himself to life outside the monastery.

"I know you have been taught otherwise, and so was I," Regis said as kindly as he could, "but the world is far larger and more varied than one isolated snowbound corner. In time, I hope you will see that such private, individual choices pose no threat to anyone else and that you can respect and even admire those who are made differently. It is a difficult adjustment, but for tonight, you need not remain if the dance offends you." Deliberately, Regis repeated the same word. *Offend.*

If thy right arm offend thee, cut it from thy body. The words of the ancient *cristoforo* scripture echoed in memory. As an adolescent, Regis had been appalled at the injunction, and perhaps that was why he could never forget it.

"No one will think ill of you if you retire early." Regis kept his voice encouraging. "You are not accustomed to such energetic activity late at night. Shall I ask Danilo to attend you, or do you remember your way back to your rooms?"

"I am indeed overtired. A period of cleansing prayer will restore me. Do not trouble your paxman on my account. If it is improper for me to walk alone from one part of the Castle to another, then one of the Guardsmen can do as well."

With that, Rinaldo bowed to Regis and went to take his leave of Javanne, as the evening's hostess. Regis watched with relief as Javanne smiled and patted Rinaldo's arm in a sisterly way. A moment later, Rinaldo disappeared through the archway at the back of the ballroom, one of the older Guardsman marching smartly in his wake.

The following morning, Regis breakfasted late with Javanne and her family. She had transformed the blandly impersonal parlor into an intimate family room. Cushions with brightly colored needlepoint, some of it obviously the work of her daughters, were piled on the divan. A table nearby held a vase of flowers and several open books; a flute had been left on the divan itself.

Gabriel had already left for morning roster, but Mikhail and Ariel greeted Regis warmly. Ariel had not been allowed to attend the dance and was bursting with questions that, she insisted, her older brother was incapable of answering properly. Who had worn what and danced with whom? Regis did his best, despite her growing impatience with his answers.

At last Javanne called a halt to the interrogation. Regis yawned and sipped his second cup of bitter *jaco*. He had not slept well since returning to Thendara. Although they worked together every day, Danilo kept to his own chambers at night. Eventually, they would have to find some private time, before irritations and misunderstandings began to fester.

The maid swung open the outer door and Rinaldo entered. As before, he was simply but richly dressed. If the colors of his garments were somber, the quality was unmistakable.

"Please join us," Regis said, adding, "or perhaps I overstep the prerogative of my sister, since this is her apartment and her breakfast."

"Oh, Regis! We are family and must not be so formal!" Javanne began handing Rinaldo plates of sausages and cold sliced meat pie and bowls of stewed mountain peaches and fresh cheese, followed by baskets of spiced pastries.

"I looked for you this morning." Rinaldo's tone was even, but the words came out as an accusation. "They told me you were here."

Regis shrugged. "It's far more pleasant to spend the morning after a ball relaxing with one's family than returning immediately to work." He started to say, *Even if one is not exhausted from dancing,* but thought better of it. "You look as if you have rested well."

"I have indeed."

"What did you think of the ball, Uncle Rinaldo?" Mikhail asked.

"Yes!" Ariel joined in, clapping her hands. "Were the ladies dressed very grandly? *No one* has been able to tell me!"

Rinaldo paused in cutting a sausage into tiny slivers. "I have been a monk for most of my life," he said, avoiding looking directly at his young niece, "and know little of how to judge such things. But if *grandness* can be measured by the brightness of the silks and the number of bows and frills, then yes, very grand indeed."

"That is enough," Javanne interrupted before Ariel could pose another question on the latest fashions. "Your uncle is our guest, not our entertainer."

In the awkward silence that followed, Regis said, "Rinaldo, was there something you wanted?"

Rinaldo finished the last bite of sausage and mopped up the juices with a bit of bread. "Only a trifle. Nothing worthy of taking you from your work. But since you are at leisure and you have asked . . . I have seen many things in this city, some admirable, some otherwise. I suppose such behavior is to be expected without firm moral guidance."

Ariel lifted her head with a puzzled expression. Mikhail pretended to whisper to her, "He means houses where——"

Javanne cut him off. "Mikhail! We do not speak of such things in front of children! I am so sorry, Rinaldo. Mikhail really knows better. But boys will be curious, and he is of an age . . ."

"Let us hope his curiosity extends only to vocabulary and not *experience*," Rinaldo said severely. "Once he is married, he will have no cause to pollute his thoughts in this way."

Mikhail's flush was all the more obvious because of his fair complexion. He looked as if he wanted to sink through the carpeted floor and into the Castle's forgotten dungeons. Regis felt a surge of sympathy for the boy. When he was Mikhail's age, he would never have spoken the word *brothel* before any person of his parents' generation.

And so, we were left to our own companions and the ravages of adolescent hormones. Not that it would have made much difference in his case.

"Mikhail is a fine young man," Regis said temperately, "and would never do anything to bring shame to his family. As you say, sister, he is still learning the habits of discretion." Mikhail shot him a look of gratitude.

"See that he is taught well," Rinaldo said, not to Javanne but to Regis. "I did not come here to instruct you in the proper discipline of your family. I'm afraid my purpose is far less serious. Self-indulgent, I must confess."

Regis smiled at his brother's habitual self-deprecation. A lifetime of self-effacement could not be erased in a few tendays "What is your pleasure?"

"Last night, and from time to time, I have heard much discussion of the Terran Federation. Until I came here I had never set eyes upon an out-worlder. What exotic beings I imaged them to be, these creatures from the stars! Now I find they are men much like ourselves."

"In some ways," Regis agreed cautiously. He did not want to give the impression there were no differences between Federation races and Darkovans. Certainly, there were many political differences. Out of the corner of his vision, Regis saw that Mikhail was following the conversation closely.

"But not all ways, is that your meaning, brother?" Rinaldo smiled as Regis nodded. "Yes, yes, that makes sense. If I am to take my place in Comyn society, I must not remain ignorant of the issues that divide us."

"I cannot tell you how happy I am to hear you say that," Regis replied. "On the surface, the Federation offer of membership is tempting. When you understand the cost to our culture, our independence, even the ecology of our planet, things look very different."

"That is a simplistic way of putting it," Rinaldo said.

"I am sorry to interrupt what must be a long, involved conversation," Javanne said, "but I really must get to work. There is a great deal to do, cleaning up after the ball in addition to the normal daily housekeeping."

Regis rose. "Please, do not let us keep you. Your work is deeply appreciated."

Javanne gathered up her daughter and swept from the room. Mikhail remained behind, very much on his best behavior, perhaps hoping to escape any suggestion that he might assist his mother.

Regis turned back to Rinaldo. "So you would learn more of the Terran Federation situation?"

"I must begin by becoming acquainted with these Terrans themselves. The Holy St. Christopher bears the burdens of all who pray to him, regardless of their worldly allegiances. Do you not try to see these star travelers as fellow creatures, with their gifts and sorrows, rather than as a single nameless adversary?"

Regis nodded. All too many tragedies might have been prevented, had the parties thought as his brother did. He proposed a visit to the Federation Legate and a tour of the Terran Zone. Rinaldo was openly delighted with the prospect, as was Mikhail with being asked to accompany them.

14

Regis strolled beside his brother through the Trade City, which lay between the older part of Thendara and the Terran Zone. Mikhail followed half a pace behind, serious with the weight of his new responsibility. Since Regis had decided against summoning Danilo or a pair of the Castle Guards to accompany them, Mikhail had taken it upon himself to protect his two uncles from any possible harm. Regis suspected that if there were any danger he and Mikhail could not handle together, the addition of two or even twenty swordsmen would make no difference. The Terran authorities did all they could to prevent the illegal sale of blasters and other Compact-banned weapons, but it was still possible to obtain them on permit.

Regis did not want his brother's experience of Thendara, both the Darkovan and Terran portions, to be one of constant vigilance against real and imagined threats. He himself had spent too much of his life either a prisoner in a gilded cage or looking over his shoulder to see who might be hunting him. His fears were not all paranoid imagination. The World Wreckers assassins had threatened him on at least seven occasions and had succeeded in killing half a dozen Comyn . . . and, Aldones help him, two of his *nedestro* children.

Now, as Regis remembered the loss of those two babes, slaughtered in their cradles, he felt renewed grief. He had not thought of them in years, had never really known them. Their mothers had been young women of good birth, eager for the honor of bearing a child to a Hastur lord. Nonetheless, he had mourned their passing and still did.

And Kierestelli, would he ever know her, watch her grow to womanhood, share her dreams? The sense of loss shifted, now something far more chilling, something akin to prescience.

Danger . . . a child in danger . . . Stelli? Some other child? The impression slipped away like snowmelt.

"Regis? Is something the matter?" Rinaldo peered at him anxiously.

Regis felt himself once again standing in a street lined with houses and shops in Terran-style architecture. They were only a short distance from the Terran checkpoint.

"A stray worry, nothing more." Regis followed Rinaldo and Mikhail to a planter filled with summer blooms, surrounded with benches for the ease of travelers enjoying the miniature garden. It was a Terran innovation he found particularly pleasing.

Regis sat down and inhaled the sweet, moist scents. Mikhail bent over him, clearly anxious. A crease formed between his fair brows.

"Let me summon Uncle Danilo," Mikhail said. "Or get you some *jaco* or Terran coffee. I saw a shop a couple of blocks back."

"I'm all right, just a little troubled in spirit. It's hereditary with us Hasturs. I don't like coffee, but *jaco* would be welcome. And some for you, as well, Rinaldo?"

Rinaldo shook his head as Mikhail hurried off. "He's a good lad."

"That he is."

"But he should not refer to your paxman in such an intimate way. It is not respectful."

Regis made a dismissive gesture. "Mikhail has known Danilo since he was a small child. We do not stand upon ceremony among such close friends."

"But *Dom* Syrtis is not, after all, a member of your family." Rinaldo inflected the words to invite agreement that Danilo was no more to Regis than a bodyguard.

Regis felt his spine stiffen instinctively. He could not allow that comment to go unanswered. "Danilo and I have been pledged to one another, as *bredhin* and as lord and paxman, since we were cadets." His voice sounded rusty to his own ears. "Our father and his older brother also swore such a vow. Rafael Syrtis died trying to save our father's life, and they are buried together in the Field of Kilghairlie. Danilo and I are bound by blood, by honor, and more than that—"

Just then, Mikhail appeared at the end of the street, carrying two cheap mugs, the sort one could buy for a few *reis* at a cook shop.

Uncle Regis? came the boy's tentative mental touch. *What happened?*

Leave it, chiyu. *It has nothing to do with you.*

They finished their *jaco* and proceeded to the Terran Headquarters. Mikhail did his best to keep up a lively chatter, pointing out various shops. The Spaceforce guards at the checkpoint recognized Regis and admitted his party without question.

By the time they reached the Headquarters building, a rectangular tower of steel and glass instead of Darkovan stone, Regis had wrestled himself into a better mood. Security had been increased since his last visit, doubtless as a result of the volatile debate regarding Federation membership. The Terran guards looked humorless to the point of belligerence. They were armed with nerve guns as well as blasters. Even Regis, as Lord Hastur, was not allowed entry without an escort.

The Legate was not in his office, but after a wait and a number of radio communications back and forth, a Spaceforce officer accompanied Regis and his party to the Lawton family living quarters. Regis had never seen where his friend lived. It must be strange to sleep, eat, and work all within the same walls, bathed in the unrelenting yellow light and breathing the tasteless reconditioned air. The floor, a slick synthetic material, felt as unyielding as granite, unlike the carpet Javanne had installed in the Castle, a touch of living green.

The Headquarters tower was almost as confusing as the Castle, although less labyrinthine. There were no stone cul-de-sacs, no blind corners or hidden doors. They proceeded upward in a series of interconnecting elevators. Such devices, Regis supposed, were necessary for a structure twenty or thirty floors high, but that did not make him enjoy riding in one. Mikhail did his best to disguise his delight, and Rinaldo was openly filled with wonder.

"Such marvels!" he murmured as they emerged into a hallway bounded by an immense glass window that gave a view of half the city. "Such grandeur!"

"I'll tell Dan Lawton you're impressed," Regis said with a humorous lilt. "He'll be pleased to hear it."

They reached a doorway, and the officer stood to one side. The door looked like any of the many they'd passed, distinguished only by a small plaque bearing the occupant's name. A small copper charm had been affixed to the wall. Regis noticed it, since that metal was rare and expensive on Darkover, but thought nothing more of it. Rinaldo, however, bent to examine it with an exclamation of unaffected delight.

The door slid open. "Regis—Lord Hastur! This is an unexpected pleasure! Please come in. I had no idea you intended to make us a visit." Dan Lawton stepped back to gesture them inside.

Instead of his formal uniform, Dan wore a Darkovan shirt falling in loose folds from a shoulder yoke and trimmed with simple geometric embroidery at collar and cuffs, Terran-style pants, and low house boots. He ushered them through a mirror-lined passage that Regis had no doubt was laden with security devices and into a large chamber, a parlor of sorts. Windows faced west. The carpet was dense and springy but drab in color, mottled tones of mud and ash, a combination of luxury and unimaginative ugliness. There was no fireplace, but the air was uncomfortably warm by Darkovan standards.

The room was not without beauty. Against one interior corner stood a display case of carved red-hued wood. Shaped like a tree, its branches interlaced to create niches for polished crystals, too large and clear to be anything but quartz, little porcelain statues of unfamiliar animals or hooded, cloaked dancers, and on the topmost, a stylized *cristoforo* symbol of yellowed bone. Rinaldo glanced at it, a peculiar expression lighting his features.

As they entered, Tiphani Lawton rose from the divanlike structure on which she'd been sitting beside Felix. Felix looked pale, but the gaze that greeted Regis was steady.

The divan, it turned out, was mechanized, so that with a touch of a few panels, it rearranged itself into seating for everyone. Mikhail, although still on his best adult behavior, looked as if he would like to see how many different configurations were possible.

"I'd heard about your discovery, Lord Hastur," Dan said, "and was looking forward to meeting—" turning to Rinaldo, "Please forgive me, is the proper form of address for you, *Dom* Rinaldo?"

"Just Rinaldo, please." With a faint smile: "It is difficult enough answering to that name after so many years as Brother Valentine. I doubt I would recognize myself as *Dom* anything."

"Since we are here informally, let's leave *Lord Hastur* outside, too," Regis said. Everyone laughed. "Dan, you and I have known each other for too many years to insist upon protocol in your own home. And you know my nephew, Mikhail Lanart-Hastur."

Tiphani peered at Rinaldo, pointedly ignoring Mikhail as someone of little consequence. "Brother Valentine, you said. I don't understand."

"Forgive me," Regis said, "I felt sure the gossip must have reached you by now. Rinaldo is indeed a brother, but he is mine. He was once called Brother Valentine after the *cristoforo* saint, because he was a monk. Grandfather kept his existence a secret until shortly before died."

Since the original introductions, Felix had been sitting quietly, but now he began to fidget. Regis doubted the boy had any interest in Rinaldo's religious calling. At that age, Regis would have been desperately bored. He interrupted the conversation long enough to ask if he might have a word with the boy about his progress. Mikhail glanced at Regis as if to protest being left with sole responsibility for Rinaldo, and then he solved the problem by inquiring where the sanitary facility was.

The three went into the hallway leading deeper into the apartment toward the bathroom and, presumably, the sleeping areas. Mikhail disappeared through an open doorway, leaving Regis and Felix to themselves.

Regis smiled encouragingly at Felix. "How have you been getting on? Any more trouble with threshold sickness?"

"I'm feeling much better now, thank you, sir. As long as—" Felix's hand went to the front closure of his shirt, where his starstone made a small bulge in the clinging off-world fabric.

At least the boy was keeping it close to him. "May I see your matrix?" Regis asked.

Felix opened the top of his shirt. Regis noted with approval that neither the cord nor its clasp was made of energy-conducting metal. Layers of gray silk cushioned the stone, acting as a psychic insulator. When Felix removed the stone and held it up, a pattern of blue light flickered in its heart. The facets were clear, not clouded. As far as Regis could tell, the stone was properly keyed, betraying no illness of the mind to which it was linked, nor could he detect any distortions of *laran* energy in its depths.

From the parlor came the sound of a chime and Dan's voice, "I'm sorry, I must take this call," and another door whispering closed.

"I am no Keeper," Regis told Felix, "but to my eyes, this looks as it should."

Felix closed his fingers around the matrix stone. "I can't do much with it. Ferrika is nice, and I appreciate everything she's done, but she doesn't know very much about—about what *laran* is good for. Except healing."

Behind the boy's awkward words, Regis heard a hunger. It was not the same one he had known at that age, but it was yearning nonetheless. If only Linnea were here to teach him, if only—

No. He would *not* think about her.

From the parlor, he caught Tiphani's voice raised in excitement. "Those are almost the same words from the sacred texts of Megaera!"

Regis and Felix exchanged conspiratorial glances. The brief respite was over. Regis led the way back to the others. Rinaldo, seeing him, called, "Brother, the wonders of the world are many! Here is *Domna* Tiphani from a distant world, speaking the same eternal truths as taught by our own saints."

Regis had never seen Tiphani Lawton so animated. Her eyes glowed, and a high color suffused her cheeks. Were she other than she was and were Rinaldo any other man, Regis could have sworn the two had just fallen in love.

"Is it possible," she said breathlessly, "that your St. Christopher is St. Christopher of Centaurus? From what you just told me, his teachings are not precisely the same, but the moral bedrock upon which they are founded—the law of righteousness, the promise of salvation and the certainty of damnation—all these are mirrors of one another!"

As she spoke, Rinaldo nodded. Mikhail came back and stood quietly listening. From the wetness on his neck and shirt front, he had been experimenting with the washing fixtures.

"It is very possible," Regis said temperately. "The first humans to settle Darkover came from a lost colony ship millennia ago. I believe the Nevarsin monastery dates from that time and has been relatively isolated from the larger world. Many of the traditions and beliefs of the first *cristoforos* may have come down to us with very little change."

"Look," Rinaldo exclaimed, "here is a holy reliquary, in form and symbolic ornament very like our own. If I saw it in the chapel at St. Valentine's, I would not think it out of place. I cannot believe the resemblance is accidental . . . Now I know why I have been brought here to Thendara! I might have lived my entire life at Nevarsin without learning the universal truth of our teachings."

He turned to Tiphani. "We must pray for guidance and knowledge of the work we are called to accomplish."

Although Regis was glad his brother had discovered a way to integrate his religious and worldly lives, he was also disturbed that the connection should be a woman who had shown herself to be so volatile of temper.

Rinaldo, as if sensing his brother's mood, hastened to say, "Our work will become a powerful instrument of understanding between our two planets or rather between Darkover and the Federation. I can think of no better way to serve my people."

Having no ready answer, Regis said nothing. Mikhail looked politely uninterested. Felix shuffled from one foot to the other.

"Brother Valentine—Rinaldo, that is," Tiphani rushed on, oblivious, "will you help me to build a chapel where people of faith from both our communities may worship together?"

"Most gladly, lady. That is, if my brother consents."

Finding no graceful way to refuse, Regis said he thought it a fine project. "But," he warned, "both Darkovan and Terran authorities must agree on the final plans."

"Oh, there will be no problem from this side," Tiphani said. "My husband will ensure the approval of the Federation."

Just then, Dan returned through a side door. "I won't trouble you with details, my dear, but I'm afraid my presence is required."

"We must take our leave as well," Regis said, with the short bow of a Comyn lord to one of equal rank.

Rinaldo came away cheerfully after making arrangements for a properly chaperoned visit with Tiphani a few days later.

Regis did not draw an easy breath until they were once more under the great red sun instead of glaring yellow lights. For what he had inadvertently overheard, as much with his mind as his ears, was his brother saying to Tiphani Lawton,

"*. . . forbidden black arts . . . none so lost . . . cannot be saved . . . if the will is strong enough . . .*"

15

On one of these rare afternoons when he was able to finish work early, Regis found himself low in spirit. He had determined to dine alone, savoring a few hours of quiet. Javanne had organized so many family dinners that Regis had begun making excuses not to attend. Rinaldo had stepped into the vacuum, regaling Regis with his day's exploration of the city, work on the Chapel of All Worlds, and meetings with Tiphani Lawton, with whom he was developing an increasing closeness. Regis had heard enough theological discussions in the last tenday to last a lifetime. He no longer cared about the liturgical differences between the *cristoforos* and the priests of Tiphani's faith.

The parlor felt empty and too quiet; Regis chuckled at himself for having become unaccustomed to his own company and poured himself a goblet of unwatered wine. He sipped it meditatively, remembering the tavern near the gates of the Guards Hall, where he and Danilo used to sneak away for a tankard of pear cider. It was one of the few places where they could enjoy an evening without people constantly staring. The cadets would throng the outer room, but the back was reserved for officers. It was dark and closed-in, but the Guardsmen understood that even a Hastur needed a little privacy.

Sighing, Regis set down his wine. He no longer wanted it, although the vintage was as fine as any on Darkover. What was the Terran proverb, something about, "Better a crust of bread in a hovel where there is peace than a banquet where there is none"?

A familiar tap sounded on the door. At his greeting, Danilo entered. "Your brother is not here?"

Regis gestured, *As you see, I am alone.* Danilo had good reason to expect Rinaldo's presence, for Regis had been spending his little available leisure time with his brother.

Taking a goblet from the sideboard, Regis poured it half full and held it out. Danilo settled on the opposite chair and raised the cup to his lips. "It's good."

"Better than we used to drink when we were cadets," Regis said. Danilo shuddered theatrically. "But the point wasn't the taste, was it? Not in those days."

The two men sipped their wine. Regis felt the coiled tension within him ease slightly.

"Regis, I am glad to find you alone. I want to talk privately. No, not about Rinaldo, at least, not directly. About this Chapel of All Worlds that he and Dan Lawton's wife are building."

"What of it?" The completed structure would take time, even with Terran construction methods. Once a circle of *laran* workers under a skilled Keeper could have raised such a structure in a day. Meanwhile, services were held in an old mansion in the Trade City, accessible to all.

"It's an excellent way to foster understanding between our peoples." Regis said.

"I thought so too, at first. I was curious to learn more of the off-worlders' faith, which seems so close to that of the *cristoforos*, and what wisdom they might have to teach us. I even allowed myself to believe in an all-embracing god who lifts every man's burdens, no matter what sun we live under."

Beneath Danilo's calm words, Regis sensed ambivalence and . . . fear. *Fear?*

"Danilo, what is wrong?"

Danilo began pacing, wine goblet in hand. The garnet liquid sloshed perilously close to spilling as he gestured. "You know—from our years at Nevarsin, from all we have been through—how I have been at odds with certain aspects of my faith."

"The injunction against homosexuality, you mean." Outright phobia was more the case, but Regis did not need to say so.

Danilo paused in his stride, his back to Regis. His shoulders rose and then fell. He nodded, then turned back, dark eyes filled with light.

And love, Regis realized as his own heart responded. *How could I ever doubt that?*

"I hoped," Danilo continued, "that since the *Terranan* are said to be more tolerant, that this coming together of faiths might result in greater openness and acceptance."

"Not all *Terranan*," Regis reminded Danilo. "Remember when Grandfather had to intervene after an off-worlder stabbed a Guardsman who had, he claimed, made him an 'indecent proposition.' The Guardsman's brother quite justifiably filed an intent-to-murder."

Danilo shook his head in incredulity. "I'd forgotten that incident, it was so long ago. Wasn't the Terran deported to save his life? He nearly caused an interstellar scandal because he had not the wit to simply decline the invitation."

"Perhaps," Regis said delicately, "he did not see that as an option. Or perhaps he was brought up like a *cristoforo*, unable to consider bedding another man without moral disgust. I've never asked you—how did you reconcile what you were taught with what you feel, what we have together? For a time, I thought you might have set aside your *cristoforo* beliefs, but you did not."

Danilo took a moment to compose his answer. "For a long time, I made excuses to myself. I told myself that when you married—and each season made that more inevitable—that I too would take a wife. Do my duty as a member of the Comyn. Pass on this damnable telepathic Gift to the next generation.

"Redeem my . . . sin and become a good *cristoforo*." He paused, his voice on the edge of trembling. "In the end, I came to understand that the sin was not in the love or the act of love but in the misuse of it. Like *laran,* a thing of good that can also be abused."

Or twisted. Regis closed his eyes. *Or suppressed, with deadly consequences.*

The *laran* bond between them shimmered with memory, of how Regis had brought himself to the point of death, rather than approach Danilo in a way that would offend him. They had each come close to destroying themselves, trying to hide their true feelings.

Danilo's voice dropped to a hush. "Nothing is going to change that, *bredhyu.* Nothing. Ever."

They did not need to touch one another, so strong and clear was the telepathic embrace.

After a time, their minds drew apart. Returning to his chair, Danilo lowered his eyes to the wine swirling in the cup, like a miniature sea storm. "Regis, something is going on in that chapel. People see it as having the full sanction of the Federation. Every day, more worshipers come. They come to hear your brother preach."

"That's a good thing, isn't it? For Rinaldo to use his monastery training? He's an educated man; should he not share his knowledge of an ancient and venerable tradition?"

"Look, it's one thing to submit oneself to the tenets and teachings of one's faith, but it's another matter to insist that this is the *only* way to live. And that anyone who says otherwise has no legitimate authority."

Regis sat back in his chair. The burned end of one log collapsed into embers, sending up a cloud of ash. "If I understand rightly, you accuse Rinaldo of publicly preaching against any faith but his own. I can't believe he would do such a thing, no matter how he may personally feel. It will take him time to emerge from the cloister, but he is a fair-minded man."

"Of course, he makes every effort to appear reasonable to *you.*" Hardness shaded Danilo's voice. "He still needs you."

Regis made an impatient gesture. "Rinaldo may have spent the better part of his life as a monk, but he is not a child. He most certainly does not need me. Even now, he is exploring the city on his own."

Danilo looked away, his features stony.

"Can we just drop the subject?" Regis said. "I don't want to quarrel with you again."

"Nor I with you," Danilo said quietly.

"Why then do we keep tearing at each other this way?"

"I don't know! In truth, I can't blame Rinaldo. We fought even before we knew of his existence."

"Maybe it's the times or being Comyn in a world that no longer has a place for us," Regis said. "If our way is hard for you and me, who were born to it, how much more difficult must it be for my brother? To be wrenched from a life of quiet and contemplation into this madness?"

Danilo nodded, thoughtful. "I admit there is much good in him. He is earnest and intelligent, and he has faithfully performed his duties as a teacher. But, Regis, he is still inexperienced. Is it is wise to let him wander through the city on his own?"

"Rinaldo is a grown man," Regis insisted, "and I will *not* subject him to the kind of tyrannical restrictions that have plagued my own life!"

"No," Danilo said gently, "you would not wish that on your dearest enemy."

Regis felt a trickle of foreboding. Danilo might have a valid point. The streets were not as safe as they once were, even by day. "Rinaldo should have been back by now."

"We would have heard from the watch if he were in trouble," Danilo said. "Doubtless he has forgotten the time or lost his way. In some districts, the streets are like a maze even to those of us who know them well."

"I should send a Guardsman to search for him," Regis said.

"Let me go instead," Danilo offered. "I know he thinks I dislike him, but that is not true. I simply do not trust him. If I look for him myself, that may show him that I have his best interest—as well as yours—at heart. And if he has become lost, I promise I will not tease him. Anyone can lose his way in the old city."

Regis nodded. With a bow, Danilo took his leave. Alone with no distraction but his own thoughts, Regis struggled against the sense of something terrible looming over him.

My brother is a grown man, he silently repeated to himself. *Danilo is a skilled fighter, more than capable of dispatching a trained assassin, let alone a hapless footpad. He saved my own life more times than I can count. I should not worry.*

Regis sat, watching the pattern of reflections cast by the flames. Minutes slipped by. The fire died.

Suddenly, a clamor of intense, desperate emotion burst upon his mind. Deeper and quicker than thought, Regis *felt* Danilo cry out. In warning—in surprise? In alarm?

Regis was not a strong telepath. There were only a few people with whom he could speak mind-to-mind, even at short distances. Linnea, with her powerful and trained Keeper's *laran*, was one of them.

Danilo was the other.

A series of flashing images, like bits of shattered glass and leaves blown in a Hellers gale, flooded Regis.

Shadows cloaking the streets, shop windows grimy in the nightly drizzle . . . searching for a familiar landmark, glancing up at the lighted towers of Comyn Castle through the gloom . . . A flash of recognition: The Starry Plough tavern on Music Street . . .

"Danilo!" called a man's voice.

Not Rinaldo . . .

His own voice—Dani's voice: "I am looking for Rinaldo Hastur . . . went off without an escort . . ."

The answering voice was silky and tantalizingly familiar." . . my duty to assist you in your search . . ."

A man stepped from the shadows into the light cast by the lantern above the tavern door . . . by his movement, a trained swordsman . . . a sword slipping free . . .

Danilo's hand reaching for his own blade . . . the weight of the world crashing down on his head . . . cobblestones hard beneath his cheek . . .

A dim, vanishing thought: *Did they get Rinaldo, too?*

The next moment, the thought-touch disappeared, sending Regis reeling into oblivion.

Regis gasped as he jerked back to consciousness. He had fallen across the little table. One of the wine goblets lay on its side, spilling dark liquid on the carpet. For a sickening moment, his eyes would not focus. Nausea clawed the back of his throat. He had not felt such wrenching disorientation in a long time.

Danilo—*Danilo* was in danger, needed him! He had to do something, but his mind was too muddled to determine what. He should summon help—a Guardsman. Speech seemed impossible.

Although the fire had died into coals, multicolored light filled the room, shifting, surging, and then dissolving into sparkling motes. His breath wheezed through his lungs.

Move, he urged himself. Walking would help stabilize the balance centers in his brain and keep his focus from drifting. With a poignant twist, he remembered that Javanne had been the one to tell him that.

Praying he would not give in to the waves of stomach sickness, Regis clambered to his feet, one foot and then the other, resenting each moment of delay. Minutes later, the worst of the distortions faded, and he felt solid again.

It was time to make plans, to act quickly. The attack on Danilo had occurred in front of The Starry Plough. With a message to Gabriel, a suitably armed escort would be ready in minutes.

A servant answered his summons promptly, but before Regis could issue the message, he heard a muffled shriek coming from another part of the Hastur section.

Mikhail!

Regis raced down the corridors toward Mikhail's room. The door was open. Inside, a servant lay senseless on the floor. Regis rushed inside.

The room was filled with strange men, their faces concealed behind strips of cloth.

Bandits? Here, within Comyn Castle?

Regis could hardly believe what was happening. Then he was no longer thinking, he had whipped out his dagger and was fighting for his life. Twisting, lunging—at nothing.

As suddenly as they had appeared, the men vanished. Regis was alone once more, crouched in a fighting stance, his dagger in his hand. The residue of battle-adrenaline still saturated the air.

Mikhail—attacked here, in his own chamber? Dragged away half-conscious . . . gagged, unable to call for help, reaching out in the only way possible before losing consciousness—

Blessed Cassilda! How had this happened? First Danilo, now Mikhail . . . and Rinaldo as well—lost in the city? Taken captive?

The attacks must be related. Had Rinaldo been lured into a trap?

Whoever set it might have guessed that someone would come after him. Mikhail's abduction must have been planned in advance and therefore was part of a coordinated plan. Anyone might be the traitor. *Anyone!*

The servant, a maid barely in her teens, roused and opened her eyes. When she saw Regis with a weapon in his hand, breathing hard, his face flushed, she gave a yelp of terror.

He slipped the dagger back into its sheath and lifted the girl to her feet. It took him a moment to remember her name, Merilys. She'd come from Armida with Javanne as part of the household, a plain, hard-working country girl.

"It's all right," he murmured. "I won't hurt you."

"Lord Hastur," the girl answered in a whisper. She gulped, righted herself, tidied her apron with a few deft tugs, and bobbed an awkward curtsy. Unfortunately, she remembered nothing about the attack, beyond being knocked unconscious. She nodded in a calm, practical way when he asked her to get someone else to help.

Within minutes, three other servants and a Guardsman arrived. Regis set up the outer sitting room, easily accessible from the hallway, as a base of operations. He issued a stream of orders, to seal off the Hastur section and gather everyone within, to send word to Gabriel as Commander of the Guards and also to Javanne. Merilys took this last upon herself and showed her country good sense, for at the news that Mikhail had been abducted, Javanne came close to hysterics. She recovered enough to count off the servants and identify the one missing, a Thendara native she had hired for the season.

"Find him!" Regis snapped.

Before he could say anything more, young Kennard-Dyan Ardais stumbled through the door, closely escorted by two grim-faced Guardsmen. Regis did not know Kennard-Dyan well, although Danilo did; the lad was Mikhail's friend, as well as Heir to Ardais. Word had it that his mother, Lady Marilla, was educating him in the Terran manner. Annoyance vied with concern on the youth's face, both fading into confusion as he recognized Regis.

"Lord Hastur, we found this one coming up the back staircase," said one of the Guardsmen.

"I'll have you know I am—" and here, Kennard-Dyan rattled off a string of names and titles. He pulled his arms free. "Dom Regis, what is going on? I came to meet Mikhail, not to be mauled by—" He broke off, glaring at the Guards.

"That's all right, I'll handle it," Regis said. At his nod, the Guardsmen retreated. "You and Mikhail had agreed to meet? Here, at this hour?"

The youth flushed slightly. "We were to go . . . um . . . hawking."

"Hawking? At night? Is that what they're calling it now?" Could it be a coincidence that the Ardais youth had come looking for Mikhail at this hour? Regis eyed Kennard-Dyan's shamefaced countenance. Whom would he suspect next?

Wetting his lips, Kennard-Dyan glanced around the room. "Sir, please . . . is something wrong?"

Regis hesitated, for a moment tempted to enlist Kennard-Dyan's help. Just then, Gabriel stormed into the sitting room. From his expression, he had already heard news of the kidnapping. His glance took in the scene.

Regis laid one hand on Kennard-Dyan's shoulder and propelled him toward the door. "There is no time to explain, and in any event, it will all come out soon enough. I require your word of honor that you will say nothing to anyone, not even your mother, until I myself or Commander Lanart-Hastur make an announcement."

Kennard-Dyan straightened his shoulders. "The word of an Ardais may not carry the same legendary weight as that of a Hastur, but to me it is as precious."

Regis bade the youth return to his own apartments, then turned to Gabriel. "I don't know what you've heard, but it's probably true. Mikhail's been kidnapped, by whom or for what purpose, I have no idea. I heard a scream—the servant girl had been knocked unconscious by the time I got here. I picked up the *laran* residue of the assault."

He did not add that his mind was already open, sensitized by Danilo's anguished mental cry.

"You're sure no one has entered or left?" Gabriel's voice was rough with barely masked emotion. "Good."

"There's more." Regis found his legs suddenly unsteady. He lowered himself to the nearest chair. "Danilo has been taken as well . . . and maybe Rinaldo, I'm not sure. There's no trace of him, but he's only been gone a few hours. Danilo went in search of him. To a tavern on Music Street—The Starry Plough."

"I'll dispatch my best men there at once."

Saying the words aloud, hearing them in his own voice, gave them a terrible reality. Dimly, Regis realized he needed to eat, that use of *laran* exhausted physical as well as mental energies. Cold shivered through his gut. He swayed in his chair.

Gabriel bent to steady him. "You've had a shock. Let me get you some wine."

Regis shook his head, trying to remember what was needed. What had Linnea said? Not wine. "Food, I think. Something sweet."

Regis slumped forward, head in his hands. What a weakling he was and what a fool! Silently he cursed his traitor body for collapsing just when the people he loved most needed him.

He heard voices, people moving through the room, the door opening and closing. Someone shoved a plate into his hands. It smelled of honey-eyed pastry. With shaking fingers, he broke off a morsel and chewed it. The sweetness melted over his tongue. Moments later, the trembling eased. He was able to sit up, to focus.

". . . to see Lord Hastur . . . should we . . ." One of the Guardsmen who had captured Kennard-Dyan stood talking to Gabriel just outside the door.

"Yes," Gabriel said. "Send her in at once."

Regis got to his feet. "Send who in?"

A clatter of feet at the top of the stairway drew his attention. The next moment, Linnea came running down the strip of carpet toward him. Her green traveling cloak and the leafy pattern underfoot made her look like a wild creature of the forest. Her hood had fallen back, revealing flushed cheeks.

Regis! Her mind touched his, that light, supple contact he remembered so well.

Linnea, here? Of all the people he could have wished for—

Incredulity melted into relief. Disregarding all propriety, forgetting the audience of Guardsmen and servants, Regis caught her in his arms and buried his face in the auburn tangle of her hair.

16

"How could you come so quickly?" Regis murmured. "How did you know?"

They were sitting together in his private parlor, their chairs drawn up so that her slim fingers could easily rest in his. Within moments of Linnea's arrival, Regis had ordered the tightest security and the best guest quarters for her party. He had wanted Gabriel himself to stand guard over Kierestelli, but Linnea had insisted on keeping the girl with her. Regis had forgotten or not allowed himself to remember the shimmering beauty of the child, the quickness of her mind, the calm, almost inhuman serenity of those silvery-gray eyes. Kierestelli sat on the carpet beside her mother, long legs tucked with unselfconscious grace beneath her, one hand resting on Linnea's knee.

She knows more than she reveals, Regis thought with a pang. He too had been forced to set aside his childhood far too early.

Linnea caught his glance. "Would you have her face this world ignorant and unprepared?"

Did she mean a world in which children—and Mikhail was barely more than a boy, although adult in Comyn eyes—were abducted from their own homes? A world in which others could be set aside, consigned without their consent to lives of privation and servitude? A world in which a boy like Felix Lawton, immensely Gifted, could be brought near death by the superstition of a parent?

"I did not know," Linnea said, returning to his question, "not when I set out from High Windward. I was on my way, almost at the city gates, when your telepathic sending reached me."

"Then you know what happened?"

"I know that your mind was linked to Danilo's when he was assaulted. I did not know about Mikhail until I reached the Castle." She stroked his wrist with a featherlight touch, a Keeper's touch. "I am so sorry about Danilo. This must be dreadful for you. I will help in any way I can. And with Mikhail's disappearance as well."

As she spoke, she lowered her *laran* shields, opening her mind, inviting his presence. The simplicity and trust of the gesture was more than Regis could bear. The contact of skin on skin intensified his feelings. He pulled his hand away, but gently, so as not to affront her.

"What is to be done?" he asked, heaving himself to his feet. "They have taken everyone in Thendara dear to me. If you had been here—"

"Could I have prevented it?" she said. "Sensed it coming, used my Keeper's sensitivity to give warning?"

He saw that she had misunderstood his meaning. *If you had been here, they would have kidnapped you as well. You and Stelli.*

Linnea's gray eyes widened. Regis sensed her horror, her outrage, and then her dawning recognition. *She* was one of those most dear to him. In a distracted, emotional moment, he had been able to communicate what he had never been able to say aloud. Her face softened, her heart opening like a rosalys in the sun. From Kierestelli, at her side, came a mental starburst of joy.

It was too much, too intense, all a tangle in his mind. He had to think clearly, to plan, to act decisively. He forced himself to sit down again.

"From the beginning, then. If you did not come to Thendara because of this night's events—and how could you travel all the way from High Windward in a night?—then what brings you here?"

"It seems foolish to think of personal concerns now," she said, lowering her gaze for an instant. "I came to set things right between us.

We parted so bitterly, I could not let matters rest. Especially when—when I had had a time to consider things other than my own vanity and temper."

"You are not the only one with a temper," Regis said.

For a moment, she regarded him with that cool, direct Keeper's gaze. "No, but I am responsible for what I say and do when I am in the grip of mine. I rejected you so cruelly and sent you on your way without a shred of hope. I acted selfishly as well as rashly."

Regis thought she was the least selfish person he had ever met, but his tongue had gone inert. He could only hope his admiration for her showed in his eyes. Mentally cursing his clumsiness, he said, "I did you no honor in the manner of my address."

"That does not excuse my behavior," she responded. "I thought about—I considered what I was throwing away because, like a spoiled child, I wanted everything. And so I lost much of value, too much. Here in Thendara, I can be both mother and *leronis*. At home, as you know, my choices are limited. And—and you want to know your children and be a good father to them. How could I deprive them of your care? I decided that I would rather have a life with as much love you can give me than a life without you in it."

Her voice wavered. She glanced away, blinked hard, then met his gaze again.

I will never ask you to choose. I will only ask you to love me as much as you can.

Carya . . . His fingertips brushed her lips, soft and firm.

Her next words jarred him back to the present moment. "Now Danilo has been seized, dragged away—as prisoner, as hostage? Has a message come? And Mikhail is gone as well."

"And my brother," Regis added grimly.

"Your *brother*?"

He had never seen her so astonished. "My older brother, my father's son but not my mother's." Quickly he told her of his grandfather's deathbed confession, of the search and discovery, and of the journey to Nevarsin.

"A Hastur *cristoforo*? This is very strange," she murmured. "Are you sure he is missing?"

"I think it certain by now. It may be that these three abductions were carried out by different people and for various reasons, but I do not believe it. Not on the same night."

"Why would anyone want so many hostages?"

Regis glanced down at Kierestelli, who had been following the discussion. How much more could he reveal in front of the child?

"She stays," Linnea said. "For the moment, anyway. She may have need of this knowledge."

"Danilo. Mikhail, my heir. Rinaldo, my brother," Regis ticked off the names on his fingers. "Abductions, not murders. Obviously, whoever is behind this wants them alive. That can mean only that he—or they—aim to force me into some action."

Linnea's expression darkened. "You have never lacked enemies, a hazard of being who and what you are. Is there anyone you suspect? Surely they will contact you with their demands."

"No doubt they will," Regis agreed. "But if I can find out who is behind this and what he wants, I will be far better prepared to act when the time comes. Gabriel and his men are scouring the city, but I do not think he will find them. With your help—"

"You have it without asking. What do you want me to do?"

Regis hesitated. Of the three men, his closest bond was with Danilo. Would Linnea agree to contact her rival?

I meant what I said about never asking you to choose! Her thought shimmered in his mind. *I do not love Danilo as you do, nor do I think I ever could, but I will do whatever is necessary to protect him for your sake.*

Regis closed his eyes, gathering his thoughts. "When Danilo was captured, he was looking for Rinaldo, who had been gone for hours. He searched one of the poorer areas of the city. There he met someone he recognized, a man I think—I hope—who can provide key evidence. I sensed images, bits of speech, emotions, but not enough to identify the other man. It was all too quick. If you could help me to recover those mental impressions—maybe even contact Danilo . . ."

"That would mean submitting yourself to me as your Keeper. Are you willing to do that, Regis? How much do you trust me? With your mind? Your life? With *his* life?"

With her cool, steady gaze, she measured him. Regis remembered one of the many arguments with his grandfather, when the old man had been pressuring him to marry. He remembered shouting, *"When I meet the woman I wish to marry—"* and realized he had indeed met her.

"For this, we must be alone." Linnea bent to the girl at her side. "You understand, *chiya preciosa*? This is *leronis* work."

Gravely the girl got to her feet. Regis did not know how much she had understood, certainly far more than any other child her age. She was too young for her *laran* to have fully developed, according to what he had been taught, and yet . . .

"With your approval, I will place her in my sister's care," Regis said, then to Kierestelli: "You do not yet know your Aunt Javanne, but she is as fierce as a mother cloud leopard."

Kierestelli giggled.

In only a few minutes, Javanne bustled into the room. She was clearly affected by all that had happened, but she held herself together. An impeccably correct copper butterfly clasp held her hair smoothly coiled on the nape of her neck, and she wore a dark green gown, plainly styled. For moment, Regis thought there was something wrong with her eyes, as if something in her had broken at losing Mikhail a second time, something that might never be mended. Then the moment passed, and Javanne was gathering the little girl with brisk motherly competence.

"It's past your bedtime, little one. Are you hungry? I'll have warm honey-milk sent up and then straight to bed with you."

In her wake, Javanne left a turbulence of psychic currents. Regis had *laran* enough to feel his sister's distress even after she had left. The room fell quiet. He took a breath.

Linnea's back was as straight and poised as a dancer's. She had been looking down at her folded hands, her eyelids half lowered. Only the slow, controlled rise and fall of her breathing indicated she was not a beautifully carved statue. Her face, shadowed beneath the braided auburn crown, betrayed nothing.

"Are you sure this is safe?" he asked, lowering his gaze to her softly rounded belly.

"I would not have agreed if I had any doubts of my control. It would be better if we had a monitor, but I can manage for a short time without one. I could not do this work regularly, and I will have to rest and clear my channels afterward, but yes, for this great a cause, I can keep our son from harm."

She lifted her head, and Regis saw the steel in her eyes. When she spoke, her voice rang like a tempered sword, a Keeper's voice resonant with power. She was no longer the sweet, impulsive girl or the passionate woman, or even the friend so generous with herself and her heart.

"Now we will begin."

"You have never worked in a matrix circle, I think," Linnea said.

Regis shook his head. After he had come to terms with the reasons he had suppressed his *laran,* he had never felt the need to study at a Tower. In any event, it would have been impossible for the Heir to Hastur to shut himself away even if he had wished it.

"Normally, each member of the circle focuses her or his *laran* through his starstone. The psychoactive crystals amplify psychic energies." Linnea sounded as if she were lecturing a class of novices, but Regis did not interrupt her. She was not being patronizing; as she spoke, he felt her thoughts spin a subtle web between them.

"The Keeper functions as the centripolar point for the diverse mental patterns. She gathers them, weaves them together, harmonizes them . . . controls them."

It was the ultimate test of trust to turn one's mind over to another without reservation, without holding anything back. To become utterly vulnerable. Could he do it for Danilo's sake? For Mikhail's? For Rinaldo's? Regis was willing, but did not know if he could overcome the barriers forged over a lifetime.

One of the servants had stoked the fire, and now the flickering orange light reflected on Linnea's eyes and burnished her skin with coppery shades.

I have to try, no matter what the price to myself.

"We will begin with your memories of the attack on Danilo," Linnea said. "I will not alter your mind, I will only clarify what is there. You may already have the answers you seek, and we need not go farther."

Regis nodded. "What must I do?"

"Take out your starstone and look into it. Let your gaze rest lightly on it."

Opening the silken pouch from where it hung on a cord around his neck, Regis slipped his starstone into the palm of his hand. The crystal awoke with a shimmer of cool blue light. On contact with his bare skin, it warmed immediately.

"That's right," she said, her voice taking on a hypnotic quality. "Follow the patterns of light. Do not force the memory. Simply wish to remember . . . allow it to fill your mind . . ."

Drawing a breath, Regis imagined himself floating on her words, even as his eyes floated on the light. Deeper and deeper he went, until the stone came alive. Patterns of brilliance pulsed within its faceted core.

"Gently now . . ." Linnea's voice sounded far away, and Regis could not be sure whether he heard it with his ears or his mind.

As the blue light swelled and brightened, he felt the power of the crystal infuse him. The stone filled him with fire.

"Think of Danilo . . . the last contact you had with him . . ." Linnea's *laran* caressed his own psychic energy fields, as deft as a feather brushing the breast of a newly tamed hawk . . .

Regis remembered his first view of *Dom* Felix Syrtis, the stubborn pride of the old man, the dark eyes so like his son's . . . He drifted with the images.

Danilo standing on a ladder in the apple orchards, wearing a much patched farmer's smock—

Abruptly, the scene changed. *Danilo walking in a darkened street, his figure outlined by lamps to either side. Underfoot, cobblestones gleamed wetly.*

Concentrate on the image, Linnea's thought touched him like spidersilk. *Hold it steady . . .*

Then he was inside Danilo's mind, seeing the street through Danilo's eyes . . . *men in fur-lined cloaks, the thin drizzle of rain . . . the smell of wet cobblestones and grime. In his gut, a rising sense of urgency. Thinking,* This district isn't safe for a man alone and unarmed, an innocent with a purse worth the taking. *He could just make out the towers of Comyn Castle, glittering above him in the gloom.*

"*Whatever possessed Rinaldo to wander into this pit?*" *he muttered.*

Peering into shadows, searching . . . Breathing, "Thank the blessed St. Christopher!" *as he hurried toward the tavern with its brightly painted sign of stars.*

"Dom *Danilo Syrtis?*"

At the sound of his name, he paused. Instead of Rinaldo, grateful to be rescued, he saw it was one of the Ridenow cousins by the green and gold trim of his cloak. Haldred, he thought, but could not be sure. For a moment, it seemed there were more men hiding in the shadows.

"What brings you here alone at this hour, my lord?" Yes, it was Haldred by his voice.

"I am looking for Lord Hastur's brother, Rinaldo. He has taken it into his head to go sightseeing and went off without an escort. Or even a guide . . ."

"Between ourselves," Haldred replied, slyness edging his voice, "that loss would not grieve me much."

Danilo felt a touch of anger that anyone would speak so of any Hastur. "Be that as it may, Dom *Haldred, he is one of our own caste. I ask you in all charity and honor to help me. I do not know these streets well."*

"I suppose you are right." Haldred stepped from the shadows into the pooled light beneath the tavern lanterns. Teeth glinted in a humorless, almost feral grin. "It is indeed my duty to assist you—"

Haldred's shoulders twisted, then steel whined as he pulled his blade free.

Instinct and training sent Danilo reaching for his own sword. Even as he drew on Haldred, he sensed a second assailant coming at him from behind, and another—

Darkness.

*. . . lying on a thinly carpeted floor, by its lack of vile smells not a tavern . . . leather thongs tight around his wrists . . . pain throbbing through his head . . . voices, too distorted to recognize . . . struggling to clear his vision—the huddled forms of two other people. Sleeping? Abducted as he had been—or even—*O Blessed Bearer of Burdens, may it not be so!—*dead!*

. . . more voices . . . Some time must have elapsed, for now there was but one other body. *Slender as a youth, flax-pale hair like a golden waterfall—Mikhail?*

I was right! Regis thought. *They are together!* Was the third man Rinaldo? What had the scoundrels done with him?

The link was weakening, the images falling away with every passing second. He had run out of time.

Rinaldo! Regis made one last desperate cry, throwing all his waning power behind it.

Light flashed, blue and white, and then he caught a glimpse of his half-brother's startled face. Behind Rinaldo, he spotted not the dimly lit room, but a place bright with off-world yellow light, the corner of a luxurious tapestry of Shainsa weaving. Another man moved in the shadows.

A cry of alarm—"What is it? *Dom* Rinaldo—"

Valdir Ridenow! It had to be his voice.

The connection vanished.

Then Regis was spinning, tumbling into a maelstrom of sickening darkness that clawed at his mind . . . dim sparks from Zandru's own Forge . . . demonic chattering filling his skull—

"Regis. Enough." Words rang through his mind, haloed in starstone-blue fire. "Open your eyes. *Now.*"

Without his conscious intent, Regis felt his lids jerk open. Orange firelight swept away the last images.

His fingers clenched his starstone so tightly that the hard edges of the crystal dug into his flesh. Linnea took his joined hands in hers. Her skin felt warm and unexpectedly soft. Firelight turned her eyes to amber.

"I'm all right," he mumbled.

She released him. Without needing to ask, Regis knew she had seen and felt everything he had.

"Valdir." The name came rumbling up through his throat like the growl of a wolf. "Valdir Ridenow has taken them. By Aldones and Zandru, by the Dark Lady Avarra, if he has harmed any of them, I will have his blood!"

It took the combined efforts of Linnea, Javanne, and Gabriel, returning with the news that Danilo had been seen near The Starry Plough, to convince Regis not to go storming off to confront Valdir immediately. Linnea pointed out that he could as well send a company of Guards-

men to summon Valdir to *him*, while another group searched and secured the Ridenow quarters.

When Regis left Linnea, she had lain down in her bedchamber with
Kierestelli wrapped in her arms. The delicate skin around her eyes and
mouth had taken on an unhealthy tinge of gray. She had smiled a little
as Regis bade her good night.

*She should not have exposed herself to such stress. Not when she is carrying our
child!* But if she had not, he would be no closer to rescuing Danilo or
the other captives. Moreover, it had been her decision, based on her
judgment as a Keeper.

After a few hours' fitful sleep, Regis forced down a meager breakfast and allowed himself to be dressed as befitted a Lord of Hastur.
Gabriel waited with Regis in Danvan Hastur's old presence-chamber,
while the Guardsmen tramped across the wealthy district to the Ridenow mansion.

Time took on a bizarre, elastic quality, passing both too quickly and
with agonizing slowness. Regis could not recall having been this anxious since—since Danilo had been seized by the Aldarans for their ill-
fated Sharra circle. They had been newly pledged to one another, and
Regis had had little confidence in his own abilities. All he had known at
the time was that he must do whatever it took to find Danilo. Now . . .
now there was more at stake than just Danilo's freedom. He must think
of Mikhail as well, and the future of Darkover, and his brother.

Rinaldo was an innocent, a sheltered monk. What a rude awakening
to the dangers of the world, to be taken prisoner! Regis would not be
surprised if, once this mess was resolved, Rinaldo retreated back to the
security of Nevarsin.

Rinaldo . . . Rinaldo, who had no *laran* and yet had responded with
surprise to that last desperate mental outreach. Linnea had suggested
the possibility that the combined psychic strength of a trained Keeper
and a Hastur might well have broken through to the thoughts of even
a nontelepath.

Rinaldo . . . and the voice in the background. If Rinaldo had suddenly heard a voice in his head—his own brother's voice— would he
have realized Regis was searching for him? More importantly, would

his reaction have revealed that contact to another person, to the other man? To *Valdir?*

Regis could not have wished for a better man to wait with him than Gabriel. Whether from natural reserve or a lifetime of discretion as a Guards officer, Gabriel kept his own worries to himself. From time to time, a messenger would appear at the door, and Gabriel would step outside to receive the news.

Nothing . . . no trace at The Starry Plough . . . no witnesses . . .

Leaving the door open, Gabriel returned to Regis. Gabriel's expression was as unreadable as ever, but Regis sensed something new.

"*Vai dom,* my men have just returned from the Ridenow mansion," Gabriel said. "They searched the entire house twice, as well as the surrounding garden and outbuildings. Neither Danilo nor my—nor Mikhail, nor your brother were to be found. The only person there, aside from a few servants, was *Dom* Haldred Ridenow. They have brought him. He did not seem in the least reluctant. In fact, he has *demanded* an audience with you." Gabriel spat out the word as if it were a serpent.

Haldred Ridenow was the man in Danilo's vision. Haldred had sprung the trap that snared him. What did he want, or did he come on behalf of someone else? Did he speak for his kinsman, Valdir?

What will Valdir demand in exchange for the hostages?

"I had better see him without delay." Years of training slipped into place. Regis squared his shoulders, sitting tall in his grandfather's chair. The muscles of his face hardened; he imagined Danvan whispering in his mind, pouring resolve into his veins.

At Gabriel's command, the Guardsmen escorted their prisoner into the presence-chamber. Haldred's wrists had been bound, but he was unharmed. He seemed to be in no great discomfort as he came to a halt before Regis.

Regis had met Haldred at the ball held in Rinaldo's honor, and on a few other social occasions. Haldred was a minor Ridenow cousin from a collateral branch, not likely ever to be in line for rulership but deriving his importance and most likely his wealth from the patronage of Valdir.

Haldred's fair hair betrayed his Dry Towns ancestry. Regis sensed only a trace of the Ridenow empathic Gift, enough to make Haldred a good horseman or hawkmaster but not enough to sensitize him to the emotions of other men. Or, Regis thought darkly, perhaps his talent allowed him to glimpse the pain and fear of his fellows, and he enjoyed it.

"Z'par servu." Haldred bowed only as low as custom required, when in the presence of a fellow Comyn of higher rank.

"You requested an audience, and I have granted it. What do you have to say to me?"

"On my own behalf, nothing, *vai dom*. I carry a message. A private message."

"From Valdir Ridenow, your master." Regis did not bother turning the statement into a question.

Haldred inclined his head and raised his bound wrists, as if indicating that, as a mere courier, he merited respectful treatment. Dangerously close to losing his temper, Regis satisfied himself with ignoring the hint.

"By all means, fulfill your commission." Regis indicated with a jerk of his chin that the Guardsmen were to withdraw. Gabriel provided more than enough protection against one bound man. The door closed behind the Guardsmen with a click.

The Ridenow lordling cleared his throat. *"Dom* Valdir Ridenow, speaking on behalf of the entire Comyn, desires me to say that for the good of Darkover, your high-handed tyranny must cease. He declares that you are no longer the legitimate Lord of Hastur and have no right, either legal or by prestige, to influence the affairs of the other Domains."

Gabriel remained standing, outwardly imperturbable, but Regis could feel his outrage simmering just beneath the surface. Keeping his voice mild, Regis said, "That is a very improbable viewpoint. Exactly why should *Dom* Valdir's delusions concern me?"

"Isn't it obvious?" Irritation tempered with fear edged Haldred's voice. "You are to renounce your position in favor of the true and lawful Hastur Lord."

"And that is . . ." Even as the words escaped his lips, Regis saw the thrust of Valdir's attack, as surely as if it had been a precisely aimed dagger.

"As the elder and now legitimate son, *Dom* Rinaldo Hastur is the rightful Heir to the Hastur Domain." Haldred made no effort to suppress a smirk. "The Ridenow have vowed to uphold his right by force of arms. However, in the interest of the common welfare, we trust it will not be necessary. The last thing we wish is to plunge Darkover into civil war, one Domain against the other."

"That sounds like a threat to me," Gabriel said in the moment of stunned silence.

"Why would I accede to such a preposterous demand?" Regis said, although he already knew the answer. "What does my brother say to this?"

"My lord reminds you that your paxman and your heir are in his custody. If you resist, they will suffer for it. As for the new Lord Hastur, he has given his full consent."

The matter-of-fact manner in which Haldred spoke chilled Regis worse than any number of boastful threats. These truly were not Haldred's words but those of his master.

"Valdir Ridenow is a fool."

Regis knew in his heart that he had been a bigger one. How many times had he longed to set aside his rank and position, to live a simple life, to follow his private dreams? Had he not secretly hoped Rinaldo might be the one to ease his burden? Was that not his subconscious motive in pressing for his brother's legitimate status? But now . . . he could not allow the lordship of Hastur to be wrested from him and given to Rinaldo. Unpracticed in the ways of the world, Rinaldo would be a puppet in Ridenow hands.

Regis harbored no illusions about the intentions of Valdir Ridenow and his allies. They wanted full Federation membership, with everything that implied.

Angrily Regis said, "There is another way to solve this problem, and that is to have the location of the hostages wrenched from your mind. Unfortunately, the only known possessor of the Alton Gift is off-world at the moment, but I am more than happy to try the powers of the *Hastur* Gift."

Haldred paled. "M-m-my lord—*vai dom*! I beg you to reconsider. I cannot reveal what I do not know. I will swear by Aldones or St. Christopher or Nebran the toad god of Shainsa that *I do not know* where they are!"

Valdir Ridenow might be a fool, but he was too wily to entrust such a secret to anyone who might be put to the question. In truth, Regis would slit his own throat before he forced his mind upon another, but Valdir did not know that.

Regis sat very straight, resisting the impulse to cover his face with his hands. In despair, in shame.

This is my fault, my responsibility. I should be the one to suffer for it, not Rinaldo, not Mikhail. Not—oh gods, not Danilo. But he would be seventimes damned to each of Zandru's frozen Hells before he would give this arrogant pup the satisfaction of seeing him grovel.

Regis allowed the memory of his grandfather's arrogance and unbending resolve to flow through him. "I will meet with *Dom* Valdir to discuss his proposal."

"But—" Haldred had clearly expected a capitulation. "But I have already told you the terms—"

Regis glared at him. Haldred lowered his eyes and stammered that he would arrange an interview at the earliest convenience of the *vai domyn*. Only when Haldred had bowed himself out and the room fell silent did Regis allow himself to breathe again.

The meeting with Valdir Ridenow took place a few hours later. In the interim, Regis and Linnea tried a number of times to establish *laran* contact with the prisoners, without success. Linnea was still exhausted from her previous efforts and dared not do too much. In her opinion, their minds were shielded by a telepathic damper.

Regis had more to worry about than two individuals, regardless of how precious they were to him. If Valdir ended up in power through a naive and malleable Rinaldo, the Ridenow lord would surely move for Federation membership. Regis did not know how he might prevent it, once set in motion. He was having difficulty focusing his thoughts on anything beyond the moment. His mind filled with dire imaginings. No matter how often he told himself that Danilo and Mikhail were of no value to Valdir dead, his heart would not believe the hollow reassurances of his head.

Ordinarily, Danilo would have taken care of the details, arranged the meeting place and ensured its security. Regis wondered how he had managed when Danilo had served as Warden of Ardais. In the end, ironically, the Ardais quarters of the Castle proved to be the best, mutually acceptable location. Lady Marilla, acting most likely at the behest of her son, who was in a frenzy of worry about his friend, offered the largest of their chambers. She pointed out, quite rightly, that it lent itself to privacy and was as difficult to infiltrate as any place in the Castle.

Regis found clothing laid out for him by his body-servant: a suit of discreet elegance, pants and jacket and short indoor cloak of suede in muted blue over a shirt of ivory spidersilk. Regis sighed; he could not remember having worn this ensemble, and yet it so perfectly fit the occasion. Danilo would have approved. Yet, Regis admitted as he began dressing, all was not mere decoration. He could move—and fight, if need be—in these clothes. The boots, a subtly darker shade of blue and cut lower than was fashionable, were comfortable, the sword in its bejeweled sheath of good steel and well balanced. He had wielded far worse in his cadet days. The edge, he noticed, was sharp.

Gabriel came with him as advisor and kinsman, plus four Guardsmen, veterans all. The walk took them through a maze of corridors, over Javanne's leaf-patterned carpets, under arched doorways studded with pale blue stone that made it seem they passed through the heart of an immense starstone before plunging back into torchlight-studded gloom.

Regis bent toward Gabriel to speak privately. "If this meeting goes badly, I will need your help. We may not have another chance to speak."

Gabriel nodded. The Guardsmen gave no sign they had overheard.

Even if Regis achieved his goal of getting both Danilo and Mikhail released, he could not allow Valdir to continue with his schemes. He did not know how closely he would be watched, whether or not he would be able to come and go as he wished. Valdir was no innocent in the ways of Comyn politics. He would not leave a deposed Hastur Lord free to plot his way back into power. The Word of a Hastur might be as unbreakable as the Wall Around the World, but oaths could be phrased to a legal nicety.

"I don't want you tainted by association with me," Regis cautioned Gabriel, "at least, no more than you already are. It won't help either of us if Valdir finds another Commander of the Guards."

"That may be inevitable, but I know which officers can be trusted and which will think only of their own advantage."

Regis understood that Gabriel included his escort among the loyal. "It would be good to establish a meeting place outside the Castle."

"It is already done, and passwords put into place. As the Dry-Towners are fond of saying, *Trust in Nebran, but tie up your* oudrakhi.*"

"Can you get a message to Dan Lawton? I don't know how fast Valdir will move on Federation membership, but Lawton must find an excuse to delay action. I need time to straighten things out."

Gabriel gave Regis a darkly appraising look, one that said, *If anyone can sort out this mess, it's you.* "I'll do what I can."

The party paused at the Ardais entrance. Gabriel and the most senior of the Guardsmen went inside, verifying the safety of the premises. The last time Regis had entered this room, it had belonged to Dyan Ardais. In his time, Dyan had been and done many things, not all of them honorable.

Gabriel reported that all was as it should be and that *Dom* Valdir and Rinaldo were waiting. He stepped back for Regis to enter. At first glance, the two men inside appeared dressed for a funeral. Valdir wore a suit of green velvet so dark it looked black and a gold chain around his neck. Rinaldo was dressed in a simple belted robe reminiscent of his monkish habit.

The room was comfortably furnished, used more as a living and entertaining space than the more formal presence-chamber in Dyan's day. Regis recognized a few pieces of furniture from those times. Dyan's taste had been heavily masculine, leaning to heavy wood glossy with polish. The newer pieces reflected a woman's more delicate hand.

Valdir sat on a brocaded divan, Rinaldo on a more modest straight-backed chair. Two men in Ridenow green and orange leathers stood along the far wall.

Dyan's favorite chair, which must have dated as far back as old Gabriel-Dyan Ardais, was unoccupied. Gesturing for his escort to assume their positions, Regis strode to the center of the room and paused for Valdir and Rinaldo to rise.

After a moment of uncertainty, they did so. Tradition and protocol demanded it. Valdir had grown up in a world that respected the Hastur Domain above all others, and as for Rinaldo, he might well become the next Lord Hastur, but he did not possess that prestige yet.

Regis held the tableau for a moment longer than necessary, enough to see the faint tension in Valdir's jaw muscles. He lowered himself into Dyan's chair and gestured for them to sit.

"Now that we are all here together," Regis said, "I would hear what you have to say to me from your own mouth."

Let's not play games, Valdir's expression said. He had more self-control than Regis had given him credit for.

"*Dom* Regis, I speak not only for the Domain of Ridenow but for the people of Darkover. If I had my way, the Comyn would be as truly equal as we once were. Unfortunately, the common people require a ruler."

Valdir paused, perhaps awaiting a response. Regis did not give him that satisfaction. Valdir gave a little shrug. "Since the people cling to their adulation of the Hasturs, they shall have one—but one who looks to the future." He leaned forward, his face tightening. "Not one who would have Darkover remain frozen in time, while the rest of the in-habited worlds move forward."

Rinaldo had been sitting motionless, hands folded on his knees in the manner of a monk. Regis imagined a flicker of discomfort in his expression. Perhaps his brother did not agree with Valdir's argument.

"It was a mistake to reject the benefits of Federation membership," Valdir declared, "just as it was a mistake to abandon the Comyn Council and give so much power to that flock of squabbling barnfowl you call the Telepath Council."

"*Dom* Valdir," Rinaldo said earnestly, "my brother acted from the best of intentions. He and our grandfather served the Domains through many crises. Once a man has been forced to take extreme measures, one cannot fault him for continuing on as he has before. I will not hear my dear brother censured or his achievements so lightly dismissed."

"So you would put Rinaldo in my place," Regis said to Valdir, "think-ing him easier to bend to your will."

Rinaldo flushed visibly. Valdir said, "I would elevate him to his right-ful place, completing what you yourself began by declaring him your father's legitimate firstborn son. But there would be no point in sup-porting his cause if he were not also a man of vision."

A moment passed. Regis shifted in his seat. "If you speak for the people of Thendara and you truly represent their interests, then why abduct three—two innocent men? Are these not the acts of a man who has placed himself outside law and custom? Why should I reward these crimes with my cooperation?"

"No man such as yourself, accustomed to unquestioned authority and power, surrenders his position simply because it is *right*," Valdir replied. "Do you expect me to believe you are willing to have Rinaldo become Head of Hastur?"

"I think you do not know me at all, if you need to ask."

"*Dom* Valdir, let me speak privately with my brother." Rinaldo's voice betrayed his agitation. "I am sure that once he understands the necessity of such safeguards and that no harm has come to either guest, he will be agreeable."

Valdir scowled. "This is not wise, *vai dom*. Your brother wears a sword and has been trained in its use, whereas you are a man of peace. Should he turn on you—"

Regis wanted to laugh, except for the bitterness welling up in his mouth. Did Valdir think him such a villain as that? A man who would murder his own kin for gain? A tendril of suspicion brushed his thoughts, and he wondered at how easily Valdir had come into power in his own Domain, how conveniently those in the line of succession had fallen, one by one. What lessons must Francisco, still young and impressionable, be learning?

Rinaldo was reassuring Valdir in such animated tones that it would have been impossible to resist without restraining the monk. Valdir agreed, although reluctantly. Within a few minutes, Gabriel, Valdir, and both sets of guards had withdrawn.

Rinaldo picked up his chair and brought it closer. "I am sorry the situation has come to this—"

"*What happened?* Rinaldo, how in the name of—" he could not invoke *Aldones* as he would with any other kinsman, "—the Holy Bearer of Burdens did you come to ally yourself with that man? Have you been deceiving me all along, waiting for your chance? Or has even a brief captivity softened your mind?"

"You cannot believe I *planned* this!" Rinaldo shot back with the first sign of temper during that meeting. "*Planned* to be seized, bound, hauled away like a piece of meat? *Planned* to be used against the brother who has shown me nothing but kindness?"

Regis let out his breath. Rinaldo had been taken by force, like Danilo and Mikhail. That fact eased his sense of betrayal. Eased it, but did not entirely erase it.

"Does it matter?" Rinaldo moderated his tone. "However we have been thrust into this situation, we must work together now. Valdir is not an evil man, although somewhat prone to extreme measures. I will teach him better."

"You intend to collaborate with him, then?" Regis did not know whether to feel relieved or appalled.

"I mean to use whatever St. Christopher has placed in my hands to do good. Why else would the blessed saints have brought me from St. Valentine's and yet preserved the fire of righteousness in my breast? Look at me, brother. I could never be a military commander or a great statesman like Grandfather. I am not fitted to caper about in finery or sing ballads to ladies, although in my new position, I might soon enjoy the blessings of marriage. Valdir has spoken of an eligible young kins-woman . . . Be that as it may, I have been shaped for better things than frivolity—and what more holy purpose than to bring the teachings of St. Christopher to the larger world? Do you not see all around you the evidence of ignorance and sin? Pride, greed, deceit, lust, violence—do they not stalk the streets in human form?"

"I am glad you see the opportunity to wrest some good from the situation," Regis said carefully. "But I fear for you and for our world. You know so little of Comyn politics, and Valdir means to influence you, to shape you to his own ends. Those ends do not bode well for Darkover."

"Valdir is mistaken. It is I who will rule, not he. It will take time to consolidate my position. In order to do that, I must lull his vigilance while I retain his confidence."

"It seems neither of us has any choice in the matter."

Rinaldo's expression turned grim. "Although it pains me to admit it, Valdir does not trust you, and nothing I have said has changed his mind. He means to reform the Comyn Council and become my chief councillor. Mikhail will be released as a token of his good will, but your paxman must remain a prisoner—"

Remain a prisoner—Regis hardly heard the end of Rinaldo's sentence.

It took every scrap of discipline that Regis had forged over the years not to leap up and throttle the man who had uttered those words. Rinaldo was not to blame. He was merely repeating what Valdir had said.

Valdir, that snake-brain! That scorpion-ant!

Regis gripped the carved wooden armrests so hard, his joints cracked. Valdir was wrong, damnably wrong, if he thought Regis would give in as long as Danilo still remained a prisoner.

Rinaldo leaned forward, concern furrowing his brow. His eyes were very bright, and his long scholar's fingers hung gracelessly loose. *Let us try to make the best we can of this terrible dilemma,* he seemed to plead. *Together, as brothers.*

"I believe we have said everything we can on this subject," Regis said. "I understand your viewpoint," *although it is clear you have no comprehension of mine,* "and would speak further with *Dom* Valdir."

Valdir was the one he had to face down, and he refused to make any agreement without getting Danilo back.

At Rinaldo's summons, Valdir and the others returned. Gabriel sought Regis with his gaze, but Regis made no response. He needed all his concentration for Valdir.

With an expression of triumph, the Ridenow lord resumed his place. "Are you now convinced of the necessity of sensible cooperation, *Dom* Regis?"

"I am convinced of the sincerity of my brother's motives," Regis replied, "but not of yours. You have stated your demands and my brother has told me your conditions—that my paxman will remain your hostage, regardless of my agreement."

"Correct." Valdir's half-smile did not waver.

"Now I will state *my* conditions."

Valdir blinked, for a moment looking unsure. Then his face hardened. "*You* are in no position to dictate terms to *me.*"

"On the contrary," Regis riposted, "you need me. You need my public participation in this mad scheme. Not even you, *Dom* Valdir Ridenow, are arrogant enough to fake my abdication. If you simply had me killed, the rest of the Domains would rise up against you."

By the whitening of Valdir's pale skin, Regis saw he'd made his point. He pressed on. "You want me to cede the ruling of Hastur to my brother. Very well, if he is fool enough to want it. I will do so only when my paxman is free and back at my side."

No one moved. No one breathed.

"You do not realize you have no say in this matter." Valdir shifted in his chair, although his gaze remained steady.

"You have nothing to gain by holding the man," Rinaldo pointed out.

Valdir shot Rinaldo a warning look before turning back to Regis. "How do I know you'll keep your part of the bargain?"

"I have already said I would."

"Ah! The fabled Word of a Hastur! I'm afraid that isn't sufficient. There's too much at stake. I can't risk your changing your mind or agreeing now and then blocking me at every turn. I respect your ability to generate all kinds of trouble."

With a wrenching effort, Regis waited to hear what further demands Valdir would make. Instead, Valdir smiled, an unctuous rictus that left his eyes cold.

"Come now, I have no animosity against your paxman. I hold him only to ensure your good behavior. But if you cross me, if you continue this obstinate defiance . . ." the pale cheeks, which had drained of all color, now turned dusky with emotion, "I will hang Danilo Syrtis and display his body from the Castle battlements as a warning to all who stand in the way of progress."

For a heart-stopping instant, terror blurred all thought. Then icy certainty swept away all other emotion. Regis dared not deliberate, dared not feel. Dared only to act. "*Dom* Danilo Syrtis-Ardais is Comyn. He served in the City Guards and as Warden of Ardais. The Comyn will never stand for such an outrage against one of our own."

If a man as well-born and respected as Danilo could be treated like a nameless outlaw, who would be next? And then Regis realized this was exactly the reaction Valdir wanted.

"Who's going to stop me? You?" Valdir growled. "Are you willing to wager this man's life that I am bluffing? That I cannot produce a convincing public justification for whatever I choose to do with him?

Or do you care so little for your paxman after all? Are you thinking that once he is dead, I will have no further hold over you? I do not believe you have *no* other loved ones."

And what I have done to one, I can do to another.

"You would not dare—" Regis pushed himself half out of the chair.

"I would."

Valdir wasn't bluffing. He would do it.

What choice do I have? Oh gods—Danilo!

Slowly, Regis stood up. Gabriel came alert. His Guardsmen looked to him for a signal. The air hummed with adrenaline.

"Commander Lanart, this is not your affair." Valdir's tone dropped menacingly. He lifted one hand and four more men in Ridenow colors filed in, swords drawn.

Gabriel's glance flickered to Regis. *Say the word.*

Regis shook his head. *This is a fight we cannot win.*

Gabriel's expression turned stormy, but he bowed to Regis and withdrew, his men after him.

"How can I be sure Danilo Syrtis is still alive?" Regis said.

A faint lightening passed over Valdir's features, not rising to the level of a smile. "I anticipated that you would require assurance." He offered a folded paper to Regis.

The note was unsealed so that anyone could read it. For a moment, Regis could not focus on the words, only on the exquisite, flowing script. As cadets, they had joked that Danilo wrote with the finest hand of any of them.

The words were undoubtedly dictated by Valdir. But the hand that had written them was as familiar as the rhythm of his own heart.

"I would like to keep this." Regis folded the note again.

Valdir made a gesture of assent. "And of course, your Heir will be returned to his family."

"Then," Regis said, gathering himself, "I agree to your terms. I will formally abdicate my position as Lord Hastur in my brother's favor at whatever venue you see fit, and I will not oppose the reconstitution of the Comyn Council. I think it is a foolish move," *both of them foolish moves,* "but clearly, I have no say in the matter."

Valdir put forth his most charming, amiable manner as he praised Regis for his difficult and honorable decision. With a little discussion on the logistics of the transfer of power, the meeting ended.

The hectic energy that had driven Regis soon dissipated. The corridors had never seemed so long nor the steps so steep. He felt as if he had been living underground for so long, he would never see the sun again. He was too overwrought to attempt a conversation with the two Ridenow guards or to learn their names.

The guards made no objection as he headed not to his own rooms but to those of his sister, so that he could personally inform Javanne that Mikhail was to be freed.

Javanne lay on the divan in the family room, swathed in a thick shawl. A table had been drawn up beside her, bearing a decanter of wine and flasks of various tinctures. Linnea sat on a bench beside the divan, holding Javanne's hand and speaking softly to her. Sunlight sifted through the mullioned windows, touching Linnea's hair with red-gold light.

As Regis entered, Linnea turned toward him. Weariness softened her features, blurring the beauty of bone and flesh to reveal the shining spirit within. He had known her as generous, honest, stubborn, and passionate, but until this moment he had not seen how deeply compassionate she was, how willing to give of herself. She was, he reflected, exactly the woman who could accept his relationship with Danilo.

At the same time, he sensed—he *knew*—her vision pierced his diffidence and guilt, even as it did the layers of lace and silver-trimmed suede. She truly saw him. All this, he had thrown away in a spasm of awkward pride.

The next thought that came to him, in the moment between one heartbeat and the next, was what kind of monster was he, to think such a thing while the man who had shared his life for these many years was a hostage under threat of death?

Their eyes met, and his heart stopped. And he knew that she would never see him as a monster.

All this happened in an instant, and before he could draw breath, Javanne raised her head. Whipcord-taut, she sat up. Questions brimmed in her swollen, tear-reddened eyes.

"Mikhail is alive and will be released," he blurted out.

"Oh!" Then, as if she did not care, *could not* pay the price for caring, she demanded, "Regis, what did that terrible man want?"

"Why, to restore the true and just succession of the Hasturs, not to mention the traditional power of the Comyn and Aldones knows what else." Regis threw himself into the nearest chair. His spine creaked with prolonged strain.

"It is unkind of you to tease me—" Javanne burst out, "to mock the situation!"

Regis swept the sarcasm from his voice. "I do not mock you, sister, nor do I mean to increase your distress. The situation is as I have said. Valdir Ridenow intends to replace me as Head of Hastur and to elevate our brother into my place. To ensure my—how did he put it? my *good behavior?* my *sensible cooperation*—he has taken Mikhail hostage, as well as Danilo."

"Oh!" Javanne cried out again and swayed on her seat. Linnea reached out to steady her but drew back when it was clear that Javanne was not faint but furious.

"How dare he? That power-mad, overinflated Dry-Towns upstart, that—And *you,* Regis—I suppose *you* let him get away with it!"

"What would you have had him do?" Linnea asked. "Challenge *Dom* Valdir to a duel? Put the life of your son at risk, to say nothing of that of his own paxman?"

Silently Regis thanked Linnea for her calm words. At this point, anything he said would only further inflame his sister's temper.

Javanne reasserted control of her emotions, taking one gulping breath after another. Linnea handed her a goblet of water from the little table.

"For the time being, the hostages are safe," Regis said. "Valdir wants my willing abdication, and he knows that he would lose any hope of that if he were to harm them. I dare not risk it. Valdir's demands are not intolerable, and Rinaldo seems optimistic that he can make the best of the situation."

"Rinaldo? A monk, sitting in Grandfather's place?" Javanne made no attempt to mask her incredulity.

"He's an educated man," Regis pointed out. "Naive, but not a fool. He does mean well."

"That will not help him if he becomes *Dom* Valdir's puppet," Linnea remarked.

"Perhaps," Regis agreed. "But the monastery is not so unworldly as that. There, as everywhere, some men scheme and others collaborate to their own advantage or abuse the trust of others. Rinaldo may have led a sheltered life in some respects, but he is not inexperienced in the ways of men. Besides, he trusts me and wants my good will. If Valdir is content to have me gone, and if Rinaldo is then free to seek the guidance and advice of worthy men, the result may not be so terrible after all. And Mikhail will be restored to us."

But Danilo will not . . .

Surely, Valdir will not hold him once he has what he wants, Linnea said to Regis mentally.

I—I do not know.

"I do not know Rinaldo," Linnea mused, "but I cannot imagine any brother of yours being entirely lacking in firm opinions."

Javanne snorted, and Linnea glanced at Regis, a touch of mischief in her eyes, as if to say that proved her point about the Hastur wilfulness.

"It is too soon to tell," Regis said, trying to sound hopeful. "Valdir may find Rinaldo less malleable than he hoped. Power changes men and none so much as the lordship of Hastur. I admit I will not be entirely sorry to be free of it."

In answer to Javanne's question, Regis added, "The abdication announcement will take place in the Crystal Chamber. Valdir's delusional if he thinks he can resurrect the Comyn Council, but I don't expect him to take my word for it."

At this, Linnea smiled wryly, perhaps remembering the struggles that led to the abandonment of that body and the establishment of the Telepath Council.

"I don't know if I would do any better in your place, Regis," Javanne said after a pause. "What is to become of the rest of us?"

"You and Gabriel and your other children, nothing. I hope Valdir does not mean to overturn all order in Thendara. As Rinaldo has no wife, he had asked me to convey his hope that you will continue as chatelaine of the Castle. There is no question of Gabriel's position as Commander of the Guards. Half the city would rise in outrage if he were to be dismissed. Once Mikhail is freed, I will make provision for his safety in case Valdir changes his mind."

"The estate at Armida—" Javanne began.

Regis shook his head. "—cannot be well defended, and I would rather not create a reason for it to be attacked. It would be better to convince Valdir that Mikhail poses no threat."

Linnea looked at him as if she had had the same thought, that few places in the Domain were truly safe, even if Mikhail had the aptitude for Tower work and could shut himself away at Arilinn or Neskaya.

And Linnea herself, Regis thought with a frisson of panic. *What if Valdir decides his hold on me is not sufficient and goes after her? If she were still a Keeper, she might defy him, but as she is . . . carrying our son . . .*

He thrust the idea from his mind, praying she had not sensed his fear.

Meanwhile, Javanne had gotten to her feet, rearranged her hair and skirts, and set about putting the room to rights. Work would steady her, Regis thought.

Regis departed to make his own preparations for his move back to the townhouse. He dared not ask Linnea to come with him. Her best hope lay in the illusion that he no longer cared for her. How long that deception would hold, he did not know.

18

The Crystal Chamber was the last place Regis wanted to be, and he thought it ironically fitting that Valdir Ridenow had chosen it for the abdication speech. The chamber had been the meeting place of the Comyn Council from time out of memory, and it struck Regis as nothing short of pretentious for the small remnants to gather as if they were still the ruling faction in the Domains. True, the Telepath Council had not lived up to his hopes of a broadly inclusive fellowship of those with psychic talent, and true, its internal bickering and inertia, its inability to unite in common cause, had paralyzed any hope of effective leadership. As he waited in the private entrance to the Hastur section, Regis wondered if a smaller, unified Comyn Council might be able to accomplish something. But was that a good thing or an invitation to tyranny?

Beyond the dusty curtain that once shielded Hastur women from public view, Regis heard the sounds of people entering and taking their places in the sections reserved for their Domains. Footfalls echoed, for the chamber held only a fraction of the assembly for which it had been designed. If he closed his eyes and reached out with his *laran,* he could feel the ghosts of the great Comyn lords and ladies, Keepers, and *leroni* whose lives had been given meaning in this place. Were they watching him now, waiting to see how he would conduct himself?

Did the spirit of his grandfather watch him as well? For an instant, Regis almost believed it.

He felt the assembly waiting—Gabriel by the massive double doors, Javanne boldly in the front of the Hastur section, Linnea—*ah! Linnea!*—in the dim recesses under the Alton banner, Valdir like a glowing ember across the room. The others were phantoms with less substance than the echoes of the great men and powerful Keepers of the past.

The telepathic dampers hummed into life, and he sensed nothing beyond the sickness in the pit of his own belly. Although the waiting was a torment in itself, he held himself still until he heard a booming male voice, one of Gabriel's lieutenants, rolling out his many names and titles. At any other time, he would have shrunk from such ostentation.

"Regis-Rafael Felix Alar Hastur y Elhalyn . . . Warden of Hastur . . ."

Regis had never wanted spectacle and mythic adoration, and yet these were what his Grandfather had drilled into him, what the people on the street expected. So many times he had longed to be free of it, and now that his wish was granted, he felt nothing.

He pushed aside the curtain and took his seat in the front row of the Hastur enclosure, the same seat his Grandfather had used. Rinaldo would enter later, on Valdir's summons.

Regis took a moment to survey the Crystal Chamber and the faces washed by the pastel rainbow light from the prismed ceiling. Some looked grave, others confused, a few desolate. He glanced toward the Ridenow area long enough to notice Mikhail there, sitting between two burly men. The boy looked shaken but well enough to stand on his own. Valdir had kept his word.

"Kinsmen, nobles, Comynarii," Regis began, "I welcome you to Council." These were the same words his Grandfather had used. He could think of no more fitting farewell.

After he finished the formal greeting and the roll call of the Domains, such as it was, Regis drew out the paper bearing the speech he was to deliver. He had not written it; Valdir had, and Regis saw no reason to pretend otherwise. He would read it word for word, giving his enemies no cause to charge him with equivocation. If this was what they required as the price of Danilo's life and Mikhail's freedom, then they would have it.

The words came awkwardly to his tongue. Valdir was not much of a writer, although the legalistic language was inescapable. There was nothing that could be misinterpreted, no vague stipulations, no euphemisms. All intention was made clear, even as Valdir had commanded.

In his misery, Regis had given no thought to how deeply the silence, the horrified *listening,* would affect him. Not a hand twitched or a murmur breathed during the entire speech.

At last, it was over. The speech had not been a long one. Sweat dampened his neck. He was glad he had not eaten. Then the same officer shouted out Rinaldo's name, the great double doors parted with a distant booming sound, and Rinaldo entered.

To his credit, Rinaldo carried himself well. Instead of ornate courtly dress, he wore a long belted robe in the Hastur colors, of costly materials but simply cut, subtly evoking the life he was now to leave behind forever. The fabric flowed with his stately strides. He came to a halt under the central prism, facing the Hastur section.

Now came the most difficult part of the ceremony. To Regis, it was enough that he state in public the validity of his older brother's claim. But Valdir insisted on a more powerful symbol of the transfer of power.

Regis opened the railing gate, crossed the polished floor and stood before his brother. Then, with numbed dignity, he knelt.

The only saving grace was that Danilo was not here to see it. Or Grandfather or Lew, or even Dyan Ardais.

He heard a sob, muffled and indistinct, from somewhere in the Chamber.

The formal oath of fealty was brief. Regis had heard it a hundred times, mostly when it was offered to himself. His throat went dry and his voice felt like parchment over stone, but he held steady. He would not disgrace those for whom he did this thing. His own vanity meant nothing and if Valdir thought to humble him, the man did not know him at all. There was no false pride in him to mortify, no humiliation to inflict. The only honor of the moment, the only true honor in his life, was in service to those he loved.

Rinaldo stood like a man of ice. Regis blessed the *laran*-smothering dampers as well as his brother's lack of psychic Gifts. He very much did not want to know what Rinaldo was feeling at this moment. Mercifully brief was the moment when Rinaldo placed his hands in the correct position, one brother's flesh pressing the other's.

Regis finished, "The gods witness it, and the holy things at Hali."

Rinaldo responded, not with the traditional formula, but with, "May the one true God bless you for this selfless act and keep you on the path of virtue, my brother."

Rinaldo lifted Regis to his feet and kissed him on either cheek. "I want everyone to know you are an honorable man. Blessings beyond measure will spring from your sacrifice."

"I pray it may be so," Regis replied.

Regis followed Rinaldo back to the Hastur enclosure, where Rinaldo now took the place of honor. Rinaldo seemed at ease in the enormous chair. No one protested that a *cristoforo* monk could not be Head of his Domain, for Valdir had made it widely known that Rinaldo had been re-leased from his vows. The issue of whether he could produce an heir must eventually be addressed. Doubtless that was Valdir's intent in suggesting a Ridenow bride. For the time being, Hastur still had an heir in Mikhail.

The assembly then proceeded to the formal recognition of Rinaldo as the new Lord of Hastur. One of those permitted to come forth was Mikhail, unfettered and unaccompanied. He bowed to his uncle. Rinaldo responded courteously with an invitation to join him in the enclosure. Javanne gave no response as Mikhail moved past her to one of the lesser places in the back.

By the time Rinaldo dismissed the Council, his first act as the Head of Hastur, Regis was so wrung-out it took an effort to stand. He man-aged to get to his feet and wait, his face frozen in polite attention, as one and then another of the lords approached him with carefully phrased greetings.

Valdir hung back, his expression hooded, as Rinaldo dismissed the last of the well-wishers.

Rinaldo said to Regis, "I return you now to the life you desired for so long, a *private* life. May the Holy Bearer of Burdens look into your heart and lift your sorrows in proportion to your penance."

Before Regis could summon a response, Rinaldo added, "We must speak soon, you and I, in private. There is much to be done, much good to be accomplished. I would seek your counsel in many things. I must also consult with *Mestra* Lawton. And . . ." grasping Regis by the forearms with a sudden, fierce gaze, "I have not forgotten your paxman. He will not languish in captivity one day longer than I have the power to free him. I promise you!"

With that, the stunned calm inside Regis gave way like a broken floodgate. A dozen jumbled emotions sluiced through him. He could not speak.

Valdir and his men swept Rinaldo from the chamber. Regis could not see Linnea, for the Alton enclosure was empty. The next instant, Gabriel rushed across the room and caught Mikhail in a wordless embrace, pounding the boy's back.

"Let's get away from this place," Javanne said to her husband, "before anyone changes his mind."

Regis could not have agreed more.

19

Before Regis left the Crystal Chamber, Valdir took him aside and informed him that he might choose to remain in the Castle under guard or to move to another location. Either way, he would not be permitted free movement in the city or private access with those who might plot against the new order. Regis listened politely and expressed his desire to retire to a secluded life in his own residence. He asked if he might be allowed to visit his family, but he did not mention Danilo. He was afraid that any inquiry might sound too much like begging. Valdir admitted the rationale for coordination with Javanne as Castle chatelaine but waved away the subject of Rinaldo. That meeting would not happen, Regis thought as he took his leave, until Valdir had the new Hastur Lord securely under his influence.

The next tenday went by in a blur. Regis was glad of an excuse to decline invitations to the usual summer festivities. He had no intention of sitting idly by while Valdir consolidated his position, but he must move carefully while lulling the Ridenow into thinking he had given in.

Regis formulated a plan to bring charges against Valdir in the Cortes. The matter should properly have been heard by the Comyn Council, since it involved the kidnapping of two of its members as well as extortion and possibly treason, but the Council was not yet reinstated. Valdir would most likely refuse to cooperate in a civil suit, but the hearings and resulting scandal would cripple his position as Rinaldo's councillor. The Cortes might even order Valdir confined to his city mansion or, if he refused, which was likely, freeze his assets and threaten his guards as co-conspirators with fines or imprisonment. The first step was to find a judge with the courage and integrity to investigate a member of the Comyn.

Regis began removing his household to the townhouse. One of Gabriel's officers, an earnest young man named Brunin Sandoval, contrived to encounter Regis during one of his many trips back and forth. Regis was able to communicate his plan and the officer agreed to make discreet contact with a judge who had a staunch reputation for upholding justice.

Meanwhile, Gabriel was quietly continuing the search for Danilo's location. None of his attempts had been successful, nor had he been able to escape the surveillance of Valdir's men long enough to speak with Dan Lawton.

The *coridom* had kept the town house tidy and in good repair. He had tracked down those servants who had been let go or sent to the estate at Carcosa when Regis moved into the Castle. Soon the house was made comfortable, far more than the drafty, gloomy chambers in the Castle.

Set in its walled garden, now jewel-bright with summer blossoms, the townhouse exuded the aura of safety. The dangers, and there were many, would come from without. Here Regis felt no fear of betrayal. He breathed more easily and slept more deeply between his own sheets, on which lingered the faint, musky scent of love.

Once, in a spasm of masochistic longing, Regis wandered into the room Danilo had used. The air was shrouded in ghosts. A trick of light created the appearance of a fine layer of dust on fabric and wood, although the *coridom* would never have sanctioned such careless housekeeping.

In the corner beyond the narrow, little-used bed, Danilo's cadet chest huddled as if in grief. Regis smoothed his fingers over the worn lid and lifted it. He would never have dared even so slight an invasion if Danilo had been here. In that moment of half-crazed heartache, his hands moved of their own accord. If this was all he had of Danilo, it must suffice. He recognized most of the contents, threadbare handed-down clothing and mementos from Syrtis.

There, wrapped in shimmering spidersilk, was the dagger Regis had given Danilo when they first swore themselves to one another. Why had Danilo left it? It had not been so much buried as thrust into hiding. Holding the slender blade and knowing it would never fall into Valdir's hands brought a surge of irrational joy.

"In your service alone do I bear this," Danilo had said as he accepted the blade. Then he had pressed his lips against the naked steel. Regis echoed the gesture, tasting the imprint of that long-ago kiss. The instant of pleasure fled, leaving only cold metal and the slow, churning fear in his heart.

With the exception of the Terran Zone, from which he was strictly banned, Regis was still able to come and go. He was always escorted, not by the usual City Guardsmen, but by men assigned to him by Valdir, men whose accents and gold-tinted hair bespoke their Ridenow lineage.

The loss of contact with Dan Lawton and Dr. Jay Allison was bad enough, but it also meant Regis could not speak with Lew or send him a message. He had no way of knowing how the transfer of the Hastur Lordship had been portrayed. What possible explanation could Valdir have offered?

More than that, Regis missed the counsel and longstanding rapport with his oldest friend. Never before had he been so painfully aware of how few friends he had; his rank and lineage had kept most of his contemporaries at arm's length. Of those who had found their way through the convoluted politics, too many were dead, off-world . . . or beyond his reach.

Regis tried several times to speak with the Legate, only to find the Terran sector barred to him. The Ridenow guards, who had until then resembled silent shadows, closed briskly with him, leaving little doubt that any attempt would be met with instant failure.

Within the Castle, the guards would not allow Regis to enter the corridors leading to the Ridenow section or, for that matter, the environs of their mansion in the city. From this, Regis deduced that Valdir had moved his quarters to the Castle, but he could not be sure. He received no inkling of where Danilo was kept. As for Rinaldo, Regis was told repeatedly that his brother was occupied at the moment and would send word when he desired an interview.

Regis often had business in the Castle during this time of shifting residences and preparing the quarters that would now belong to Rinaldo. When at last he had removed all traces of his own occupancy, he lingered in the study. It had never felt as though it belonged to anyone except his grandfather. Danvan Hastur had served the Comyn for longer than most men now alive could recall, and his presence whispered through every scroll and ledger. Now the man who would sit at this ancient desk and handle these pens might be kin, but he had never known the person behind the legend.

The thought had come to Regis that he ought to take the more sensitive items with him for safekeeping, for instance his grandfather's personal records.

He was Rinaldo's grandfather, too, he reminded himself. Moreover, Rinaldo was a man of learning, a scholar. He would not damage or misplace any documents, no matter how strenuously he disagreed with their contents.

On this occasion, Haldred Ridenow had accompanied Regis, remaining at a watchful distance. Regis handed him the keys to the desk and the locked cabinets and closed the door behind him. He paused, weighing his next move.

He had seen nothing of Linnea since that awful spectacle at the Crystal Chamber. There was nothing he could do to protect her, he knew that. Although he felt sure his *laran* would have alerted him if anything had happened to her, he wanted to see her with his own eyes.

"Now that I have no further reason to come to the Castle except to visit my sister," Regis began, facing Haldred with an expression of innocence. It rankled to subordinate himself to such an arrogant bootlick. "I would take my leave of an old acquaintance. A lady of the Storns and hence a distant relation of the Altons. Is this permissible?"

Haldred shrugged, bowed, and left Regis to the care of his usual escort.

The central hall of the Alton quarters had always struck Regis as dreary and sepulchral, even when old Kennard had still been alive. The lights in this part of the Castle were very old, chunks of luminous rock hacked from deep caves; charged with daylight, they gave off a cold radiance for hours into the evening. Regis preferred the warmer light of flame or torch or even the yellow incandescence of the Terran buildings.

Linnea had avoided the main chambers for the smaller, more intimate rooms once used by Lew Alton. After the chill of the corridors, the small bright fire filled the parlor with cheer. The furniture was heavy and masculine. Linnea had added little except her own presence. Except for the herbal scent and the honey-tinge of beeswax, she might have been only a passing guest.

After exchanging awkward pleasantries with her, Regis put forth his offer. "I cannot guarantee your safety or Kierestelli's. Here in the Castle, anything can happen. Mikhail was seized in his family's own quarters. At least, in the townhouse, I know every face."

Linnea set down her cup of the spiced pear cider she had served. "Regis, if I move in with you, I will destroy what is left of my reputation—and hence, my position of respect—and have it cried from every street corner that I am Regis Hastur's *barragana*."

Regis searched for a graceful way to point out that there was an alternative, as his wife *di catenas*.

Catching his thought, she shook her head and gestured negation. "Let us not discuss *that* any further. Regardless of recent events, I believe we have each said all we care to on the subject."

Regis looked away. The fire, so merry and comforting only a moment ago, now cast blood-lit shadows across his thoughts. He thought of the people he loved and who were now kept from him—Lew. Mikhail. Even Dan Lawton.

Danilo . . .

"I have tried to reach Danilo," she said softly. "We will not abandon him."

At least, Mikhail is no longer in Valdir's clutches.

"Since you have given thought to such matters, perhaps you would advise me concerning Mikhail." To his own ears, Regis sounded clumsy, Would he ever be able to speak with her without making a fool of himself? "I cannot take the risk that, should I do something to displease him, Valdir will imprison Mikhail again. This time, Valdir might not be as concerned for his welfare."

Linnea looked thoughtful or perhaps grateful they had abandoned a painful subject. "Have you considered sending Mikhail home to Armida?"

Regis replied that he had judged the Alton country estate too poorly defensible. "As long as he's my Heir, he can hardly apply to the Federation for protective asylum."

"I agree." She picked up her cup, no longer steaming, and swirled its contents meditatively. "Mikhail remains at risk as long as Valdir believes he is important to you. What if you were to set him aside? I know the oaths you swore when you took him for your Heir cannot be lightly nullified—"

"The issue is not Mikhail's legal inheritance but the claim he has on my heart," Regis said. "I pledged myself to protect him as I would any child of my own flesh."

"I know that," Linnea made the words into a caress, "and you know that. The question is what might cause Valdir to disbelieve it? What if—what if you were to transfer Mikhail's fealty elsewhere?"

"I'm not sure I understand you."

"You might give him to Kennard-Dyan as paxman and then send them both back to Ardais."

For a long moment, Regis stared at her. For a young, gently reared woman who had spent the better part of her life in a Tower, her grasp of Comyn politics was astonishing. Mikhail would object, of course. Regis might have to command him with all the force of past authority and present love. Javanne would support him, he was sure. The young Ardais lord truly cared for Mikhail, of that Regis was also certain.

The estate house at Ardais was no more defensible than Armida, but it was considerably more remote, being three days' ride beyond Scaravel Pass in the Hellers. Not even Valdir would dare to violate its sovereignty in order to abduct the paxman of the Heir of Ardais. That was, unless he intended outright warfare between Domains, for that would surely be the result.

The air became less oppressive to Regis, his shoulders less burdened. At the same time, he felt a deepening of his sorrow at the thought that after this day, he would no longer be able to speak with Linnea in this way, to seek out her advice. One visit might be ignored, but a second would surely attract notice.

She brushed the back of his wrist with her fingertips. "I hope it will be for only a little while. Until—until Danilo is safe and no one you hold dear is under threat. In the meantime, I will use my position here to best advantage."

Regis raised one eyebrow in inquiry.

Her laughter rippled, a sweet arpeggio. "Why, gossip, of course! I can listen to all the things women and their servants never say to men!"

At last, Regis received word from Brunin Sandoval that he had contacted a respected and fair-minded Cortes judge who had agreed to review the complaints. Regis was under too close watch by Valdir's men to meet at the judge's chambers or residence without arousing suspicion. He arranged for the judge to come to the townhouse, with the caution to wear casual clothing, as if the matter were no more grave than an informal opinion regarding grazing rights.

That same day, a second message arrived from Rinaldo, requesting that Regis attend him in the Hastur presence-chamber the next morning.

Regis readied himself at the appointed time. The sun had barely cleared the spires of the city, and shadows clung to all but the broadest streets. Last night's rain gleamed on the cobblestones. The air smelled fresh, washed clean.

Walking quietly between the Ridenow guards, Regis gave up trying to make polite conversation. They looked at him as if he carried poison in his tongue. When necessary to speak at all, they answered him in monosyllables. The common people on the street moved away at their approach. Valdir might claim to speak for Darkover, but no one had informed the townfolk.

Regis tried to keep an open mind, to not anticipate what he would find or what Rinaldo might say. Had Rinaldo become Valdir's willing pawn?

He is my brother. I must give him a fair hearing. In turn, he may listen to what I have to say, and that will strengthen him against Valdir's influence.

The Ridenow guards conducted Regis to the apartment that had briefly been his. A man Regis recognized as one of the understewards, now wearing a tabard of Hastur blue and silver, escorted Regis inside, leaving the guards in the hallway. The understeward swung the door open and stepped back for Regis to enter. "*Vai dom,* Lord Regis is here."

Regis smiled inwardly, for the title that had been his for most of his life was now proper again. He walked into a room that was at once familiar and altered. No fire burned in the fieldstone hearth, although ample wood had been laid and the night's chill still hung in the air. Some of the furnishings were gone, and the walls were now bare of their former tapestries. A massive wooden chair dominated the center of the room, facing two or three more modest seats, none of them softened by cushions.

A wooden *cristoforo* altar had been erected upon the sideboard, where decanters of *firi* and *shallan* had once stood. Regis found the style repellent, emphasizing in sculptural detail the sufferings of the Bearer of Burdens. From the candle stubs, the layers of melted wax, the lingering smell of incense, and the indented pillow on the floor, the altar had been in recent use.

Rinaldo entered through the door that led to the library. Regis had only a moment to take in the flushed, excited look on his brother's face and the robe very similar if not identical to the one Rinaldo had worn at the abdication ceremony. Then Rinaldo caught him up in a brother's embrace, just a fraction of a second too brief.

"Regis! Sit down, be at your ease." Rinaldo indicated the smaller chairs and settled into the larger. "I had not meant for so much time to pass. Valdir concocted his own schedule for me, and I myself have discovered many more things to do in each day than there are grains of sand in Shainsa. I would not for the world have you believe I had forgotten you! Have you been well? Has the move to a private residence after the comforts of the Castle been very difficult for you?"

Regis refrained from commenting that the townhouse was considerably more comfortable than these quarters. "I do not envy your burden in assuming Grandfather's quarters or his duties. Once Hastur was the most powerful Domain among many. Now that the Comyn are so few, the Head of Hastur speaks for all Darkover. Your opinion on a matter as crucial and far-reaching as Federation membership must be given with great care. Others will try to influence you for their own gain, including Valdir Ridenow. You must not simply do what he says. As Hastur, you are beholden to no one—"

Rinaldo shrugged carelessly. "Oh, as for that, Valdir advises me when he can, and when he cannot—or when he spouts utter nonsense— then I have my own counselors. Lady Lawton's insights have been most enlightening, even though she has a woman's delicate sensibilities and limited understanding."

From his limited experience with Terran women, Regis doubted that either description was applicable, but he said nothing.

"I must ask you to keep what I am about to say in strictest confidence," Rinaldo continued. "I am thinking of bringing three or four of my Nevarsin brothers here to Thendara. This Castle is so big and empty, it will be a small matter to find them quarters and a chamber big enough to hold services. It's only a temporary measure until I can locate the right building—or have one constructed—for a proper chapel. What a relief it will be to have their spiritual fellowship and the daily sustenance of our faith! I know you do not adhere to it yourself, but you must have seen how the influence of the holy St. Christopher transforms the lives of all who live under his rule."

Regis listened to this remarkable speech with a mixture of reactions. While he was happy that Rinaldo did not seem to be entirely in Valdir's power, he felt uneasy with the direction of his brother's thoughts. His grandfather would have turned apoplectic at the notion of a *cristoforo* chapel in Comyn Castle; nor could Regis imagine the traditionalists welcoming such an incursion. For himself, although he acknowledged the benefit of his education at Nevarsin, he harbored no illusions about the harm he had suffered there.

Trying to keep his tone neutral, he said, "You must follow your own conscience in this and all other matters, my brother. That is what it means to be Lord Hastur. It is your responsibility to safeguard the future of Darkover and all its people."

"Yes, yes, exactly." Rinaldo leaned forward, elbows resting on his knees, face alight. "There is so much I must make right in the world, so many ways I feel myself called. You understand the need to do what is right. It would have been easy for you to ignore my existence and leave me at Nevarsin. You could have accorded me only the meager status of an unfortunate, neglected relation. But you followed a higher standard of honor, and so will I. You have inspired me!"

Regis murmured that he deserved no such praise.

Taking no notice, Rinaldo said, "I wonder . . . did it never strike you as unjust that not all men are free to worship as their hearts dictate? That you yourself were prevented from following the one true faith?"

He meant that as a Comyn and the Heir to Hastur, Regis was expected to worship Aldones and the other gods.

"When I was a humble monk," Rinaldo said, his expression pensive, "I thought the highest calling was to bring men into the path of righteousness. As the years passed, I labored at the tasks set to me, but I never surrendered that hope. Now the blessed saints have placed the means within my power.

"I intend—" Rinaldo's voice dropped dramatically, "—to grant full equality to every *cristoforo* in the Domains. I wish to see the true faith raised up in law and in respect. No longer will we gather in dark, cold, remote places but here in the cities, where our message can be heard by multitudes."

"Your sincerity is admirable," Regis said, since Rinaldo expected a response and there seemed no hope of a serious discussion of Federation membership at this time.

"I knew you would be sympathetic! You see, I cannot do this alone. Valdir has no interest in matters of the spirit, and *Domna* Lawton, for all her inspired insight, is a woman and an off-worlder, not one of us. I need *your* help and advice."

Regis could not think of what to say. The room, once spacious and echoing, had shrunk, suddenly too narrow. He felt as if he were a wild beast being herded to the slaughtering pen. The *cristoforo* faith had always existed on the margins of Darkovan society, with its central establishment the remote monastery at Nevarsin. As far as Regis knew, there had never been any overt interference with its practice except that the sole heir to an estate could not be a celibate monk; but there was nothing to prevent any ordinary person from worshiping as he pleased.

"I believe that each man must answer to his own conscience," Regis said carefully. "At the same time, change comes slowly. One cannot reverse millennia of tradition in a single year. From the dawn of history, the Comyn have worshiped the Lord of Light."

According to legend, Aldones had fathered the first Hastur, progenitor of the Comyn. Nowadays, however, few people doubted the evidence that Darkover was a lost Terran colony.

"Pah! Aldones!" Rinaldo's mouth twisted in disgust. "Evanda of the springtime, Avarra the Dark Lady, and Zandru of the Seven Frozen Hells! They're all nonsense, vile superstition!"

"Sharra was not a superstition," Regis said. "Nor was this." He gestured to his hair, long enough to brush his shoulders. Behind his eyes rose the memory of being drenched in living light, of giving himself over to that power. Whether it had been the embodiment of Aldones or something else, he did not know. A single hour in its grip had turned his hair from red to pure, shimmering white.

Rinaldo seemed not to have heard. "This is why we need the one true faith! For too long, ignorance and degrading practices have lured our people into wickedness. Every day, precious souls are lost to sin. *This* is why I was brought from Nevarsin, why such power was given into my hands, not to use for my own pleasure or aggrandizement but for the salvation of our world!"

He paused, visibly gathering himself. "Now we come to a subject I greatly regret, but I would be failing in my duty if I avoided it. Saying this gives me no pleasure, but . . . I have heard rumors. I did not believe them at first. It was impossible that my own brother should be accused of—of—" Wringing his hands, Rinaldo catapulted from his chair and began pacing.

Regis swallowed hard. Keeping his voice calm, he asked, "Exactly what are you talking about?"

"Your . . . relationship with . . . that man. Your paxman. And he a *cristoforo!*"

Regis had hoped that his brother had understood their discussions on the acceptance of differences, whether of Rinaldo's *emmasca* condition or the Comyn tolerance of *donas amizu* between men. True, Regis and Danilo had always maintained a modicum of discretion. They did not share a bed while staying in public accommodations or at Syrtis. Was Rinaldo so oblivious he had not noticed the bond between them? Or did he, lacking *laran,* think it no more than the loyalty of lord and paxman?

Or did Rinaldo's religious training render him blind to what he could not accept?

"Do you wish me to address these rumors?" Regis asked. "Think for a moment. Do you really want to hear the truth?"

Rinaldo glanced away, his jaw clenching so that the muscles leaped into stark relief. "These accusations cannot be true, or if they are . . . You must have been deceived, misled, s-sed—" His mouth worked, as if he could not bring himself to pronounce the word *seduced.* "You did not know what you were doing."

"I beg to differ. I knew *exactly* what I was doing. What I wanted. *Who* I wanted. In all the years since I gave my oath to Danilo and he gave his to me, I have never had a moment's regret."

Regis paused to let the words sink in and was met by tight-faced silence.

"I know that this is difficult for you to accept," Regis went on, "having lived your life according to the *cristoforo* faith. I am not ignorant of the prohibitions against . . ." out of consideration for Rinaldo's obvious distress, he tempered his words, "against certain relationships. We've talked about this a number of times. Among the Comyn, as I have told you, these feelings are not judged sinful. Such a bond between men too young to marry is considered far more suitable than frequenting women who are common to all—"

"Stop!" Rinaldo cried. "Do not speak of such things!"

Regis regrouped his thoughts. "Perhaps later, when we know one another better, I can find words to make this truth less . . . offensive to you."

"You—you would make such a sin an *acceptable topic of conversation?*"

"Rinaldo," Regis said as gently as he could, "St. Valentine was a holy man, but in this matter, he was either ignorant or just plain wrong. Each of us, men and women, love in the way the gods shaped our nature. The only sin, as I see it, is pretending what we do not feel." *Or hiding, even from ourselves, what we do feel.*

"No, no, I will not listen to such blasphemy!" Rinaldo threw himself back into his chair and glared at Regis. Regis wondered if he would be allowed to leave without giving some sort of pledge, one he had no intention or ability to keep.

"How do you propose to save me? Will you lecture me until I say what you want? Or send me back to St. Valentine's? Three years among the monks could not alter what I am, and I was a boy then. Now I am a man and know myself. A hundred years of sermons will make no difference."

"No, no, you misunderstand me!" Rinaldo exclaimed, his tone shifting like quicksilver. "I spoke from brotherly love, out of my desire to free you from sin. Virtue cannot be coerced. For all my zeal, I would not see you mistreated or shamed. What would that accomplish except to harden your resistance? I do not believe you a vicious man at heart. I myself have experienced your generosity."

And this is how you repay me? Regis clenched his fists at his sides.

"You have been led astray, polluted by the loose morals of your upbringing, the victim of a decadent society. I must—I *will* save you from such evil impulses!"

Something inside Regis snapped. He launched himself to his feet. "You and your ally have extorted my cooperation only by the most cowardly and dishonorable threats against those I hold dear. You have my place—you are Lord Hastur now. Do what you like, I will not challenge you, so let this be an end to squabbling. There is no further need to hold anyone prisoner. Release the last hostage, and let us be quit of one another."

"The last one . . . that is the problem, is it not?" Rinaldo's voice turned silky. "How can I permit you, my dearest brother, to plunge back into a life of perversion?"

"This is ridiculous! You have no authority over my private life!"

"Please sit down. I truly do not mean you ill. In fact, I have every intention of freeing Danilo Syrtis." At an incredulous look from Regis, he added mildly, "I assure you, I have the power to do so."

Wrestling his temper under control, Regis lowered himself back into the chair. If what Rinaldo said was true, if he could restore Danilo's liberty, then what would be the price?

"I am sorry for my heated words," Regis said. "I . . . misunderstood you."

"It is a difficult situation, and no man relishes being powerless. Listen to me, Regis. I may not know everything about the niceties of court etiquette, but I do know the nature of men and how hearts may be reformed. You are correct, we do not choose the impulses that arise within us, but we *can* decide whether and how to act upon them. I myself have done penance many times for my wayward thoughts. I prayed I might overcome the weakness of my flesh, but now I see that I was made as other men for a reason, that someday I might enjoy the blessed delights of marriage."

As Regis tried to formulate an appropriate response, Rinaldo waved him to silence.

"I am willing to release your paxman, but only if I can be assured that neither of you will return to your former ways. As a sign of submission to the true moral precepts of the *cristoforo* faith, you must give up your abhorrent and unnatural practices. Even your own people consider them scandalous."

Regis held his tongue. How dared Rinaldo lecture him on what *his own people* thought? It was better to say nothing. The important thing was to agree, as long as that did not require an outright lie.

"Proximity and habit create a powerful temptation," Rinaldo continued. "Therefore, I am not willing to send him back into your service. He will join mine."

"What does Danilo say? Does he consent?"

"He will if you command him. There will be no negotiation or compromise on this point."

Regis forced himself to breathe. "Then I can see him? Speak with him?"

Rinaldo nodded. "You may, but only with witnesses present

and in a decorous manner. Habits take time to reform, but it is not impossible."

"If I must agree in order to see him free and unharmed, then I will give him up. That is the condition, then?"

"One of them."

Regis felt his heart sink.

"In order to effect a true rehabilitation, you must focus your affections on a more appropriate person. I am not so naive to think a man such as yourself can be celibate. Therefore, you must marry decently. You must take a wife."

With great effort, Regis kept himself from laughing. Did Rinaldo mean to accomplish what Danvan Hastur himself had failed to do? Yes, he did. And he wielded the only leverage that would force Regis to it. Danvan Hastur had never threatened Danilo's freedom . . . or his life.

The pause in the conversation had drawn on overlong. Savagely, Regis said, "What does *Dom* Valdir think about this arrangement?"

"I assured him that you will be cooperative, little brother, as I am certain you will. There is no need to be brutish, but the truth is that otherwise, your paxman might not continue to ah . . . prosper." Rinaldo's lips stretched into a smile, one that did not change the hardness in his eyes. "I cannot guarantee what may befall Danilo Syrtis should he remain in present custody. Valdir Ridenow's threat to hang him was not an empty one."

A feeling of helplessness swept through Regis, so intense he thought he would choke on it. Finally he managed to speak.

"Rinaldo, Grandfather tried for years to induce me to marry. I am not indifferent to women. As all the world knows, I have done my duty in producing sons and daughters for Hastur. Unfortunately, almost all died or were killed by the World Wreckers assassins. In the end, it seemed wrong to continue to father babes with such a fate. But I tell you now what I told him then: I will not marry a woman I cannot love."

"Love? Love comes after marriage more often than not. When it comes before, the illusion of happiness ends when lust burns itself out," Rinaldo commented with a faintly lascivious glint in his eyes. "Do you seriously mean that you have *never* met a woman you could marry?"

A quick retort rose up, but Regis knew it for a lie. He could say nothing, and that would also be untrue. "I have, and I have asked her to marry me. She refused."

Rinaldo's expression wavered between surprise and triumph. "You said nothing of this before."

"Should I have offered her to Valdir's ruffians as another hostage? Even if I no longer cared for her, I would not do such a thing."

Regis prayed that he had not made a colossal blunder in revealing Linnea's existence. Now the only way to ensure her continued safety was to change her mind, and that was as poor a way to begin a marriage as any he could imagine.

"You must ask her again," Rinaldo said, clearly pleased. "You must be persuasive. You must woo her."

Regis shook his head. "That would only jeopardize what good will remains between us."

"Come now, I cannot believe that a man of your physical attributes— you are very handsome, if one cares for such things, which I do not— your wealth and lineage, cannot secure the affections of any woman you desire. Who is this obstinate female? She must be of high rank. I know so little of our caste . . . but I did notice one very pretty woman on the day of my ascension. An Alton, I thought, but Valdir said they are all off-world. She was watching you."

The truth would come out, one way or another. Frankness might be the best policy, and Rinaldo valued honesty.

Taking a deep breath, Regis admitted that the lady Rinaldo had noticed was indeed the one. "Linnea Storn-Lanart was trained as a Keeper and served in that capacity at Arilinn. During the World Wreckers crisis, she gave up her work to bear me a child and now carries another. A son, she believes. Rinaldo, I beg your patience in this. I hope that, given time, she and I may find our way back to one another."

"With your—the other one—out of the picture, I should hope so."

Regis felt his face harden. "*Domna* Linnea is not a woman to be se- duced or coerced. I would rather set her aside then see her harmed. I fear that in naming her, I have placed her at risk. I have opened my heart to you, trusting you not to abuse the confidence. For the sake of the love you bear me as a brother, for the sake of my children, I beg your protection for her."

Without a moment's pause, Rinaldo replied, "Set your mind at rest. Your lady will be safe in my care."

"Thank you." The words came out in a whisper.

"*Dom* Valdir is a man of few scruples, and I cannot condone his methods. I know you think I am his servant, but it is the other way around. My allegiance is pledged to a higher master. As for Lady Linnea, I promise you I will not expose another innocent to Valdir's schemes or let her be used against you. Some provision must be made for her, one way or another, for it is not seemly for a mother to be unmarried."

"I intend to have both children legitimized, as is the custom," Regis protested.

"The matter of *your* marriage is too important to leave to a woman's uncertain favor." Rinaldo looked down, his brow furrowed in thought. Clearly, he was weighing whether to demand that Regis find another bride or whether to concede. Did Rinaldo believe a man's affections could be easily shifted to another? He had already expressed his belief that marriage need not include love.

Regis thought spitefully that his brother would be satisfied with a wife who was no more to him than a dutiful bed partner.

At last, Rinaldo made up his mind. "You have one month to either persuade this lady or find another. You may suit yourself. If it is not to be *Domna* Linnea, then I will make other arrangements for her."

"But—"

"I promise you, my brother. On the day you wed, I will secure the release of Danilo Syrtis. You may depend upon it."

I will depend on it when I see it done, Regis thought. Yet what choice did he have?

Rinaldo was not finished. "Once he is no longer under guard, will you give me your sworn oath you will make no attempt at private communication with him? No secret assignations? No stipulations in the transfer of his services to me?"

Levelly Regis met his brother's gaze. He saw no deception there, only a frank and ardent desire to do what he saw as good. "Will you in your turn treat Danilo with honor? Will you defend him as your sworn man, as I do?"

"I will deal fairly with him, acting in accord with his highest welfare."

Regis felt his mouth go dry. From this point, there would be no turning back. Gods, what would Danilo think? That he had been bartered like goods in the market? Like a horse or a fine sword, without feelings or honor?

And Linnea? How could he possibly propose to her again in any way that would not be an even graver insult than before?

"If these are truly your terms," Regis said at last, "then I must accept them. But I swear by all that is sacred that if you play me false, Rinaldo, you will die by my own hand."

"Never fear, little brother," Rinaldo said, giving him a brilliant smile. "I too am a Hastur, and my honor is as precious to me as yours is to you."

"It is done, then," Regis said, wanting it finished before he lost his nerve.

"It is done."

Solemnly, Regis took his leave, knowing that he had bartered away the best part of his soul for the two people he loved most in the world.

20

Regis paced the length of his townhouse parlor before a hearth as cold and desolate as his heart. One of the servants would have rushed to light the fire, but he had stormed in and locked the door behind him. What was a little cold, a little dark, compared to the monstrous action he had just taken?

He was equally furious at Valdir Ridenow and Rinaldo but most of all at himself. He had saved Danilo's life but sold him into servitude. He had kept Linnea as safe as he could at the likely cost of a final refusal and then no option but to chain himself to another. That he had not been given a choice was of no importance. He should have found another way to save them. Now he had made his bargain and must live with it.

It was impossible to think clearly when all he wanted to do was hit something. Sick and trembling, he lowered himself to one of the chairs. Not the one he usually sat in, just the nearest. Its unfamiliarity felt right. He did not belong here, in such comfort, in his own home.

Stop it! Self-pity helps no one! he railed silently. He must bide his time, wait for a chance . . . outlast Valdir's ambition—*as if that were possible!—*

reason with Rinaldo when they were both calmer . . . get Linnea safely out of the city—*No, don't even think about her or Stelli!* . . . and find a wife.

He slumped against the rigid chair back. *A wife.* Wouldn't the gossips of all seven Domains be thrilled with *that* news?

A month. A thrice-damned month. Where was he going to come up with a marriageable woman by then? Javanne would be happy to suggest someone. How she would relish it!

Regis ground his teeth so hard that pain shot through his jaw. Javanne wasn't his enemy. It would not be fair to ask her advice and then take out his frustrations on her.

He had not slept with any woman besides Linnea since that terrible time of the World Wreckers. The sight of his children, murdered in their cradles, had haunted him. He could not take the chance again. But there might be one or two women from before then . . . Crystal Di Asturien, perhaps. She was a pleasant young woman, although now he remembered how she had made her disapproval of Danilo all too evident.

Crystal, assuming she was still unwed, would be thrilled to become his wife. Even though he was no longer Lord Hastur, she would flaunt her status as if she were a queen. She would never allow him a moment with Danilo, even if Rinaldo relaxed his watch.

And Linnea—

Gods, what was he thinking? *Linnea!*

He buried his face in his hands. The knowledge that he had chosen another would wound her deeply. It would be a repudiation not only of herself but of Kierestelli and their unborn son.

What was he to do?

The following days brought Regis no closer to resolution. The longer he delayed, the more insulting his proposal would be, giving the bride little time to do anything but catch her breath and don her slippers before the wedding. He forced himself back into society, accepting invitations to one social event after another, but never anything small or intimate. The Ridenow guards accompanied him. Danilo's absence left an emptiness, an ache like a missing limb. Valdir sometimes attended these events, as well as Rinaldo. Once Regis glimpsed Linnea across the room, but she shook her head, warning him off.

The judge, Estill MacNarron, arrived as agreed, entering through the servants' gate. They sat together in the room Regis used for business. MacNarron was a heavyset man of middle years and grave countenance with a habit of pausing, one finger pressed to the side of his prominent nose, before speaking.

As Regis presented his case against Valdir, MacNarron's expression shifted, no longer unreadable but visibly concerned. "I see why you hesitated to put any of this in writing. These are very serious charges but without substantive evidentiary proof. I have only your own testimony, and you were neither victim nor direct witness to the kidnappings. You assert you are the victim of extortion but can produce no corroboration. The Word of a Hastur may be proverbial, but I must adhere to a more practical standard. We cannot value the sworn word of any one man above another. In justice, all must be equal. You understand my point, Lord Regis?"

Regis nodded. The situation was very much as he'd feared. Without physical evidence or other witnesses, his case was weak at best. Valdir and Haldred would hardly testify against themselves, Rinaldo saw nothing amiss with the transfer of power, and if Regis brought Mikhail back from Ardais, he would place the boy once more at risk. If he moved forward without proof, he would alert Valdir.

"I'm afraid I've brought you here needlessly," Regis admitted. "I have only my own knowledge of these actions, and anything I say will be denied. The case will be reduced to one man's word against another, suit and countersuit."

"We understand each other," the judge nodded. "Yet I do not consider this conversation *needless* or in vain. It is always of benefit to discuss perplexing matters, to reason things out with someone you can trust. No harm has been done this day, and nothing that was said here shall pass the confines of these walls."

MacNarron rose, gathering up his outer garments. "I sincerely hope we will have further opportunities to converse, if not on this subject then on another. You have a very interesting mind, Regis Hastur, and I look forward to seeing what you will make of this challenging situation."

About a tenday after the meeting with Rinaldo, Regis stood beside Javanne and Gabriel, welcoming guests to the main ballroom of Comyn Castle. The party was Javanne's idea, and Regis hoped she would have the chance to enjoy herself. She clearly derived satisfaction from her work, although the stress left her preoccupied and irritable. She had not even wished Mikhail farewell when he and Kennard-Dyan had departed for Ardais. Now she had organized a resplendent evening, the hall as brilliant and lavishly decorated as it would be for a Midsummer festival, the music lively, the food and drink all the best.

Dan Lawton and his wife arrived along with several other Terran dignitaries and joined the queue to greet their hosts. Tiphani, having murmured brief thanks, headed for Rinaldo.

The Legate watched them, his mouth frozen in perfect diplomatic cordiality, then turned back. "Lord Regis, it's good to see you again." He held out his right hand, Terran style.

Regis hesitated. Dan had been on Darkover long enough to know how disturbing casual physical touch was for telepaths. The gesture had been deliberate. Regis slipped his hand into Dan's and felt the rush of thoughts and emotions, catalyzed by the direct skin contact.

Regis, I've heard . . . rumors . . . hostages, this change of power—are you all right?—Danilo—

Regis cut off the mental contact. He could bear many things, but to reveal his personal torment was not one of them. Quickly he composed himself, aware that the Ridenow guards were close enough to overhear the conversation.

"I'm well, as you see," Regis said smoothly. "How is *Mestra* Lawton? And your son?"

From the flicker in Dan's eyes and the residue of psychic contact, Regis sensed his friend's concern. Not for Felix—the mental image had been encouraging, if complex.

Tiphani—

Regis glanced in her direction. She was still talking with Rinaldo, their heads bent together. Her face was flushed, her eyes a little too bright, her gestures a little too wild. He could not read her emotions in the swirl of partygoers.

The next guests in the reception line inched forward. In a moment, Regis would be obliged by politeness to greet them.

"Has there been any news from our mutual friend?" Regis asked.

Does Lew know what happened? Has Valdir attempted to change Darkover's status?

"Nothing but routine business." By his tone, Dan implied the matter was of no importance. "All is quiet for the moment."

You must delay—find any excuse—

"Your Excellency." Valdir Ridenow appeared at Dan's shoulder, dressed in Ridenow orange and green. A chain of heavy copper links set with enamel medallions in the same colors, of the finest Carthon artisanship and worth a small fortune, hung around his neck. His smile did not touch his eyes.

"*Dom* Valdir, it's a pleasure," Dan replied, returning the Ridenow lord's bow with the correct degree of formality.

"I've been hoping for a word with you," Valdir said, holding out one arm to invite the Legate to step aside.

"Oh, surely there can be no occasion for serious talk on an evening like this." Without a backward glance, Dan guided Valdir toward the table where lavish refreshments had been laid out. "I've come prepared to relax and enjoy myself. Is it true that whenever three Darkovans get together, they hold a dance?"

Regis turned to the next guests. Properly cordial greetings flowed from his mouth without him having to think of what to say.

As usual, a dozen or so young ladies of good birth and fortune competed for Regis as a dance partner. They did it with varying degrees of flirtation. In any other circumstances, he might have enjoyed their attentions. Now he could not help wondering, with each sidelong glance, each heave of youthful breasts, whether they knew of his urgent need to find a wife.

Nauseated at the entire business, he forced himself to respond graciously even as he avoided any appearance of preference. He never danced with the same woman twice and only danced those sets that involved changing partners.

In one of these, he found himself unexpectedly paired with Linnea. Her gown of pale green silk, cut full around the waist, could not disguise her pregnancy. The color ought to have turned her skin the color of cream against the glory of her hair, but she looked ashen, her eyes huge and dark, almost bruised. Despite this, or perhaps because of it, his heart opened to her. He thought she had never looked so beautiful or so brave.

They moved through the figures of the dance, passing shoulders, never touching. Her skirts swung gracefully, giving her the aspect of a woodland creature. At the end of a slow spin, she stumbled. He reached out to steady her. His fingers closed around hers, and in that instant, her powerful trained *laran* rushed into his mind.

Regis, I must speak with you.

He sent a pulse of unconditional assent. *When? Where?*

Tonight. An hour past the rise of Kyrrdis. Your townhouse.

Before he could reply, the movement of the dance swirled them away from one another and on to new partners.

Later, Regis noticed Rinaldo crossing the floor with Javanne on his arm. From what he glimpsed between the patterns of the dancers, Javanne was performing introductions between Rinaldo and Linnea. Linnea inclined her head, the abbreviated acknowledgment of a Keeper who bows to no man, and glided from the room.

At the appointed time, when the blue-green moon of Kyrrdis swung above the rooftops of Thendara, Regis waited in his parlor, too wrought up to rest and unwilling to dull his wits with wine. Linnea would not have asked for a meeting for any trivial reason. The urgency of her mental communication had made it clear that something was terribly wrong.

A tap roused him. The *coridom* swung the door open and stood back for Linnea to enter, then closed it behind her.

Linnea wore a traveling cloak over her green gown. Droplets beaded the thick wool. She smelled of rain and fresh air and lilias blossoms.

The hood, which had been drawn forward to hide her features, tumbled back. In the firelight, her hair glowed like spun copper.

"Regis! I'm so sorry to impose on you like this—"

Her words, almost breathless, shook him more than her unexpected plea. With a rush of tenderness, he stepped behind her, unfastened her cloak and laid it aside, took her hands and brought her to the chair nearest the fire. Her fingers were cold. He wanted to warm them between his own, but she pulled away, sitting tall and remote.

He pulled a second chair next to hers. "Can I get you anything? Hot wine? A blanket?"

Linnea shook her head. "Thank you, I would rather skip the preliminaries. If I wanted physical comfort, I would have stayed in my own rooms."

Regis sat back, praying he would not say anything stupid. He was acutely aware of the trust implicit in her presence. "If you are in distress, I will do whatever I can to help. You will always have a claim on me."

"I do not want *a claim* on you!" With a visible effort, she calmed herself. "Regis, matters between us have been awkward, to say the least. Matters regarding our . . . relationship. I believe we have each spoken in haste."

In the fractional pause that followed, a breath only, he said, "And regretted it."

Her eyes met his, light-filled gray. She took in his words, nodded. "Yes. For my part."

Linnea's fingers twisted the fabric of her skirts. She noticed and folded them neatly in her lap. "Regis . . . I need your help."

Her voice was been so low, so resonant with emotion, that he could hardly believe what she had said. He thought how difficult it must be for her to ask aloud. To ask *him*.

"Tell me," he said.

"I feel so foolish after the way I rejected you. I—"

"Just tell me. Whatever it is."

She lifted her chin. Something inside her grew very still. "I have heard rumors from sources I trust of a plan to force a marriage between myself and your brother."

"How is that possible without your consent?"

Linnea's expression turned wry. "Once such things were not uncommon. The Comyn Council approved all such unions and imposed not a few. My wishes mean nothing, and the one protection I might have is no longer available to me." She meant being a Keeper, for as an ordinary matrix worker, she would be subject to Council decree. Not so long ago, another Keeper, Callina Aillard, had been forced into an unwelcome alliance with Beltran of Aldaran.

"I'm not sure I understand," Regis stammered, trying to think. "Oh. Rinaldo was released from his vows."

"He may not have any use for a wife, but in order to solidify his position, he needs an heir. If he marries me, he can claim your unborn son as the next Hastur Lord and thus insure the succession." She paused to let the words sink in.

Regis was so appalled, he could not speak. He felt like a fish thrown up on a wharf, gasping for the air it could not breathe. Could Rinaldo have hatched such a plot? Condoned it? He did not know, but he had no doubts about Valdir's willingness.

He sat motionless while thoughts tumbled through his mind . . . Rinaldo remarking on Linnea's presence at the Crystal Chamber ceremony, *"a very pretty woman."* And then, *"Some provision must be made for her, one way or another, for it is not seemly for a mother to be unmarried."*

Rinaldo had sought her out this very evening . . .

Rinaldo was interested in women, his desires long denied by his vow of chastity. While he might be able to function sexually—and his comments had suggested to Regis that he could—that did not necessarily mean he was fertile. Linnea's pregnancy removed that difficulty.

Linnea's eyes shifted. In her glance, in the fragile dignity of her posture, Regis saw how she clung to her pride for both their sakes. She could not beg, she could not even ask if he still wanted her.

The only sure way to place her beyond Rinaldo's reach was for Regis to marry her himself. But he could not—*would* not—do so without her full understanding.

He had botched his last attempt. Now, when honesty and plain speaking was essential, would the right words fail him?

"Once I asked you to marry me," he began, praying he would not commit another colossal blunder, "and that offer still holds. I can think of no other—I have never met any other woman with whom I want to spend my life, no woman capable of understanding—"

No, too dangerous to bring up Danilo so soon. But it must be done.

"But . . .?" she prompted, fear and hope warring in her voice.

"There is no *but.* No hesitation on my part. Only a desire to make sure you understand *all* the circumstances."

Linnea said nothing. The crackling of the fire seemed very loud, or perhaps it was the hammering of his pulse.

"You know that Valdir Ridenow took Danilo hostage *'to ensure my cooperation'.*"

She nodded. "Along with Mikhail and your brother."

"Who have both since been freed, Mikhail on my abdication. Rinaldo—well, I'm not sure how much of a prisoner he ever was. Valdir thinks to rule him and through him, push Darkover to join the Federation. Rinaldo believes otherwise or at least has his own goals."

He paused, gathered himself. Gods, this was harder than he had thought!

"One of those . . . *goals* seems to be ridding me of what he sees as my sexual perversion. Rinaldo claims he has the power to free Danilo and that he will do so when I promise to give him up and marry decently."

Linnea's lips soundlessly echoed his last words.

"If I do not," Regis went on, knowing that if he stopped now, he could not finish, "he hinted that Danilo will—Valdir threatened—"

Light and swift as silk unrolling, she reached out to touch the back of his wrist. "I know. I know what Valdir said."

With the contact, fingertips soft as a butterfly's kiss, Regis felt her presence in his own mind. His normal *laran* barriers had been shredded by worry and fear. If she would have him, despite everything, she should know what she was getting.

Oh, my dear, she spoke with her mind to his. *My dearest. I have known that from the first time I saw you. How could I let harm come to someone you love as you love Danilo when I have the power to prevent it?*

It was too much, the wave of tenderness and acceptance flooding into him from her mind. He wrenched his hand away, shot up from his chair, and strode to the hearth. He stood, chest heaving, facing away from her.

The intensity of their psychic rapport diminished but did not disappear. She came closer, carefully not touching him. His body tingled with her breath.

"Is it possible?" he muttered, as much to himself as to her. "Can you love me—want me—knowing the better part of my heart will always belong to him?"

Regis felt the slightest pressure, her cheek on his back, not at all intrusive but nonetheless compelling, as if he were a mountain and she a weary traveler, as if he were a straw in the wind and she a sheltering tree. He closed his eyes.

I have known, from the first time we met, she said telepathically, *that your heart was big enough for more than one love. I needed to be sure that it is me you love, for myself, and not a substitute for another.*

At this, he turned to face her. Tears filled her eyes with liquid light. One spilled over, leaving a glistening trail down her cheek. He brushed it away, lifted her chin. Bent to brush her lips with his. She answered him but utterly without demand, without desperation.

He remembered the moment, years ago, when he had stood desolate at the ruin of his world, aching with grief for his dead children.

"Regis, I heard—" She had raised her eyes to his, and suddenly they were in deep rapport. *"Let me give you others."*

For an instant, they had stood outside of time, more deeply joined than in any act of love. She had come to him in neither pride nor pity nor ambition for the status that bearing a Hastur child would bring, but a sharing of his most profound emotions. She had sensed how difficult his life had become and through that moment of mental union had simply wanted to ease his burden.

He remembered thinking that a child of Linnea's would be too precious to risk . . .

The image of that child, that daughter who was as fair as a *chieri* and as filled with grace, rose in both their minds.

Regis' arms slipped around Linnea as if she had always belonged there. As he pressed her to him, he felt the softness of her breasts, fuller than he remembered. She took his hand and placed his palm over the small roundness below her waist.

Our son. Our Dani.

Linnea drew back, regarding Regis with the inhuman composure of a Keeper. "We will get through this. No matter what happens with Lord Rinaldo Hastur or his Ridenow confederates, they cannot touch what we have together."

An emotion akin to gratitude welled up in Regis. He had almost lost her, this woman with all her courage and understanding. She was with him now, and he sensed that never again would there be such a misunderstanding between them. For the first time in longer than he could remember, he began to hope.

BOOK III: Danilo

21

Danilo Syrtis-Ardais roused at the sound of footsteps. He had been in the dark, or at least in the dim, uncertain light of this foul cell, for more days than he could count. His head had stopped throbbing where he had been struck, but the lump on his scalp was still tender. At first, he had been bound like a common criminal. He remembered feeling sick and dizzy, but whether from the blow to his head or from something poured down his throat, he could not tell.

He had a dim memory of rough hands hauling him upright and prying his jaws apart, then a hot, stinging taste redolent of *kireseth*. A thought had wavered at the edge of his fracturing consciousness that it was one of the distillations that suppressed *laran*. They must have forced it into him to prevent him from calling for help with his mind.

Wildly, as if his heart were straining outward, he reached out.

Regis . . .

Almost, he felt an answer. Almost.

Then the nightmares took him.

He'd slept uneasily, drifting in and out of such fevered madness that he thought he was once more in threshold sickness, only magnified a thousandfold. Was this what Regis had endured? He could not tell what was real, the stone walls with their film of greasy moisture or the flames of steel-edged glass that rushed at him, only to shatter into crystals of blood. One moment he seemed to be back at Castle Aldaran, the next, deep in the bowels of the Terran Headquarters Building or at the bottom of Lake Hali, struggling to breathe the fuming cloud-water.

He had screamed until his throat was raw, of that he was certain. Fire had lanced through his chest as if he were breathing, or perhaps spewing forth, the rage of the Sharra matrix. During one of his few lucid moments, he remembered falling down a crevasse along Scaravel Pass, although he could not imagine what he had been doing there. One rib was most likely cracked, and the muscles along his spine burned.

Someone fumbled with the door latch. It clicked open, making a sound like ice cracking. Danilo slitted his eyes against the bar of brilliance as the door inched open. Acid clawed at his throat. He tried to speak, to beg for help, but the only sound he heard was the abnormally loud wheeze of his breath.

The world twisted: a hand in his hair, tipping his face back.

No, don't—

A voice reached him in the spinning darkness, a basso growl. "He can't take much more of this. Our orders are to keep him secure, not turn him into a mewling idiot."

Another voice rumbled an incoherent answer. The hand released him. He fell back on the thin pallet . . . fell endlessly between the stars.

After a time—an hour, a century—his gut settled. He opened his eyes, and the world no longer whirled unpredictably. A low, insistent sound lurked at the edge of his hearing. He should know what it was, that blanketing hum.

Danilo pushed himself to sitting. His mouth tasted like the inside of a banshee's nest, all feathers and rotting flesh. His hands were free, although the skin over his wrists was shredded in strips.

How long had he been here? From the feel of his beard, a tenday at least, most likely two. His joints ached and his muscles felt pasty from disuse, but his vision was clear. He could think.

He was in a stone-walled room lit by a slitted, unglassed window on one side. With dark-adapted eyes, he made out a pallet, a bucket for waste and one of water. The water looked clean. He washed his face and hands.

He had been drugged but now was free of it. The humming sound must be a telepathic damper, like those used during Comyn Council meetings. Untrusting folk, the Comyn were so terrified of one Domain using *laran* to influence another that they insisted on using that infernal device. Still, he reflected as he stood and began to limber his arms and legs, it was better than the *kireseth* they had forced down him.

They. As far as he knew, he had few personal enemies, and those would not hold him in this cowardly manner but would challenge him outright. Regis, on the other hand, had many who wished him ill and who would not scruple to use someone Regis cared about against him.

Danilo paused in his exercises and swore softly. In all the years he had guarded Regis with his life, he had never considered himself at risk.

Who, then? His spine popped as he twisted slowly from one side to the other. *And why?*

Valdir Ridenow, the Pan-Darkovan League, and about a hundred other individuals, for the stance Regis had taken against Federation membership. Any one of the same number of claimants against whom Regis had ruled in the Cortes. The Aldarans, again? Probably not. The Terrans themselves—an agent of the Federation, trying to force Regis to withdraw his opposition?

Danilo threw himself back on the pallet. It all came down to the Federation . . . or did it? He raked his hair, filthy and too long, back from his face. Although clearer than before, his thoughts moved sluggishly. He was missing something vital, something he ought to know . . .

Regis would not give in to threats and intimidation. Danilo broke out in a humorless barking laugh at the thought of Regis being intimidated by a mere human, whether *Terranan* or Darkovan. They were amateurs compared to what Regis had already faced. Dyan Ardais would have spitted them on his sword before breakfast and thought nothing of it.

The thought heartened Danilo, for he had been the target—he refused to think of himself as a *victim*—of Dyan's casual brutality. In the end, honor had won out, no small thanks to Regis. Amends had been offered and accepted. Danilo had mourned Dyan's death.

Hold on, he urged himself. *Regis will not stop until he finds you. He will come. He will. Nothing will stand in his way.*

When the telepathic damper cut out, Haldred Ridenow appeared outside Danilo's cell. Danilo wanted to pummel the man senseless. With restraint, he stepped back from the door, hands well away from his body, poised on both feet. He was not in shape to take on a determined assailant, but the stance, drilled into him over years of training, gave him a semblance of dignity.

Haldred spoke through the slitted window. "I see you're awake. That's good. I've come to fetch you to better surroundings. You're to have a bath, a shave, and decent clothes." His lip curled to emphasize the rank odor.

"Why?" The word came out as a croak. The screaming had been real, not another nightmare. "What do you want?"

"Everything will be explained to you in due time. Are you coming? Or have you grown so accustomed to your prison that you cannot leave it?"

"I will come."

"Then I require your word of honor that you will not try to escape or offer any resistance. Not that you could do much in your present condition, but we don't want you damaging yourself in a futile attempt. And you must submit to a blindfold."

Seeing no other choice, Danilo agreed. Haldred bound his eyes with a cloth and then placed one of Danilo's hands in the crook of his elbow. On uncertain feet, Danilo followed. He had not the slightest trust in his captor's motives, but it was always better to know the enemy's intentions. Haldred was indeed his enemy, although Danilo did not understand why.

They went along a corridor, then up several flights of stairs. Haldred was surprisingly solicitous, warning Danilo of the changes in flooring and supporting him when he stumbled.

Danilo surmised that he had been held somewhere beneath Comyn Castle, possibly in one of the old abandoned dungeons. The Castle itself was a warren with so many disused or forgotten sections that a

prisoner could easily have been hidden without the inhabitants knowing. Regis—was Regis searching for him, even now? Or was Regis waiting for him, having brought about his release?

The dank chill of the air lessened along with the fetor. They paused
while Haldred opened and then locked doors behind them. Underfoot,
bare stone gave way to carpet. At last, Haldred halted.

The next moment, the blindfold fell away. Danilo blinked in the sudden brightness. He had been shut away from the light for so long, he
had almost forgotten what it looked like. In the center of the room
was a freestanding tub filled with steaming herb-scented water. A pile
of towels and a basket containing brushes, a pot of scouring sand, and
several chunks of yellow soap sat within easy reach. Danilo almost wept
at the sight.

A strange expression flickered over Haldred's face, a mixture of
shame and pity. "I remind you of your promise, Lord Syrtis, and leave
you to your ablutions. Ring the bell when you have finished, and I will
return with a barber." Meaning word of honor or not, he would not
trust Danilo with anything as lethal as a razor.

The door latch locked behind Haldred with a click. Danilo turned
away, closing his eyes to focus his thoughts. His mind still felt half-
deadened, as if his skull had been stuffed with banshee feathers, but
he had to try while he had a moment's chance away from that cursed
damper.

Regis . . . he called out silently.

For an instant, he caught a response. Then it was gone, and he could
not be sure if he had imagined it.

Danilo pulled off his grimy clothes and eased himself into the tub.
The water was surprisingly hot. He rested the back of his head against
the rounded edge. He had not realized how many sore muscles one
body could have. Sighing, he closed his eyes for a moment. Despite
the seductive warmth and the soothing herbal aromas arising with the
steam, he was not safe. He must assume these temptations were intended to lull him into a false sense of well-being.

Picking up a brush and chunk of soap, he attacked his hair and as
much of his skin as he could reach. Cuts and scrapes stung under this
treatment, but he welcomed the pain as an aid to alertness.

Once he was as clean as a single scrubbing could make him, Danilo stepped from the bath. He dried himself and wrapped the towel around his waist. Moving carefully, he made a circuit of the room, inspecting windows, searching each piece of furniture and each fold of drapery for anything that might be used as a weapon at such time as he might release himself from his promise.

He found nothing.

Unreasonably irritated, he folded the towel, draped it over the edge where it would cushion his neck, got back into the bath, and reached for the bell. A Comyn lord, even a prisoner, would not dress himself after a bath, and there was no point in providing him a bath without clean clothing.

A moment or two later, Haldred returned, along with two guards and an older man in the robes of a *cristoforo* monk. The monk carried a handful of garments of somber dark gray and a basket containing shaving and grooming equipment. He kept his eyes carefully averted as Danilo dried himself on a fresh towel. The shirt was fine-woven *linex* without ornamentation but expensive, as were the stylishly cut jacket and trousers. The matching boots were a little too large but manageable. Danilo wondered at the finery; this was not ordinary garb, not even for a Comyn, yet it lacked any Domain insignia or even a personality. The man who wore it might as well be a shadow.

A shave and haircut were soon accomplished, the monk being skillful in his duties. No one spoke except for a few necessary instructions.

Haldred inspected the results. "You'll do very well."

"Do for what?"

Haldred's mouth tightened into a straight line. "It is not my place to answer that. Come with me, and all will be explained. Remember your promise."

Despite his determination to take nothing at face value, Danilo's spirits rose as he followed Haldred from the suite of rooms. He recognized where he was. Beneath his feet, Javanne's leaf-patterned carpet welcomed him like a friend.

Two Castle guards stood watch outside the door leading to Danvan Hastur's old chambers. No, Danilo corrected himself, they belonged to Regis now.

One of the guards opened the door. With a brief nod, Haldred departed. So, Danilo thought, Haldred had been nothing more than an errand boy. He forced himself to walk calmly between the two guards, through the outer chamber and into the library.

But the man sitting in Danvan Hastur's enormous carved chair, studying an unfurled scroll held down by paperweights, was not Regis. It was Rinaldo.

For an instant, Danilo stared at his *bredhyu's* brother, not quite understanding but sensing that some fundamental change had taken place. Rinaldo was dressed in Hastur colors and heavy silver jewelry. He seemed at home and not at all as if he were snooping into someone else's private papers.

More than that and worse, far worse, was the absence of any lingering mental trace of Regis in the room. It was as if he had disappeared from the face of Darkover.

Danilo's chest tightened, but he forced himself to stand still. The situation would be made clear soon enough.

"Ah, there you are!" Rinaldo's mouth spread in a smile, but Danilo put no credence in it. Rinaldo did not rise, nor did he motion for Danilo to sit. "You were not too badly treated, I hope? Nothing that will not heal in time?"

"I am well enough," Danilo replied politely, adding with a trace of reluctance, "*vai dom*. But I don't understand why I was held prisoner or what I am doing here now."

He was not so disingenuous as to pretend he did not know it was the Ridenow who had seized him, but he truly did not understand their relationship with Rinaldo.

"I have managed to secure your release under terms that I hope you will not be so foolish as to refuse," Rinaldo said, again with that smile that was not a smile. "My brother has already seen their wisdom." Rinaldo's gaze wavered minutely, flickering around the room as if to indicate the significance of his own presence here. "I am Lord Hastur now, as is my right."

Regis! O sweet Bearer of Burdens, has something happened—

The rush of horror and dismay must have been evident on Danilo's face, for Rinaldo hastened to say, "No, no, my brother has come to no

harm. In fact, he has freely consented to the transfer of power. I suspect he was relieved to lay down a burden he never sought. Now he has
retired to a private life and family, occasionally lending me the benefit
of his advice. You will see him shortly."

Regis, free to live his own life? Danilo's thoughts went spinning. Then
Regis must have come to some arrangement with Valdir, resulting in
Danilo's freedom—but no, that was not what Rinaldo had said. *Rinaldo*
had claimed the credit.

"Will you not show a morsel of gratitude to me for having gotten
you out of that filthy hole?" Rinaldo said.

"I—I thank you, *vai dom*."

Rinaldo's expression softened, gracious now. "It is no more than I
should do for any man who has served my brother so loyally."

Danilo felt the blood drain from his face. *Has* served?

"*Vai dom,* please do not toy with me. I am sworn paxman to Regis
Hastur."

"And now he intends to transfer that service to me." Rinaldo's eyes
glinted like steel. "I have need of assistance, and it is better for everyone that the two of you are no longer so . . . intimate as you were. As I
said, Regis himself agreed to this. I do not require your approval, only
your obedience."

The muscles between Danilo's shoulder blades tightened, as if holding back from striking an opponent. "I made my oath to Regis. I will do
what *he* commands."

"That is sufficient for the moment. I am sorry for your distress, but
I did not wish you to go forward unprepared. In time, we will come
to understand one another." Rinaldo looked as if he would say more,
but just then one of the Castle Guards, a different man from before,
knocked and announced it was time.

"Attend me." Rinaldo swept past Danilo. Four armed Guardsmen
followed them both.

It could not be true, Danilo thought desperately. No matter what
Rinaldo said, Regis would never consent.

They had not gone very far when Danilo realized their destination
was the Crystal Chamber. Their entrance, through the massive double
doors, reminded Danilo of the many times he had accompanied Regis

in just such a procession. A herald cried out, *"Lord Hastur!"* and a string of familiar titles, but the name was Rinaldo's.

Danilo hardly dared to glance around the chamber. He kept his focus on Rinaldo's back, the fur-trimmed blue velvet, the silver links around his neck. Through the hum of the telepathic dampers, he became aware of the waiting audience. His vision wavered in the diffuse polychromatic light. Peripherally, he caught flashes of color, brilliantly hued court dress, jeweled headdresses, chains of copper and silver. The empty spaces were a poignant reminder of the decline of the Comyn.

With surprise Danilo noted a woman, richly dressed but veiled, at the back of the Alton section. He had thought all the Altons gone, all off-world.

One face stood out from the jumble of color and confusion: Valdir Ridenow, his eyes fierce, intent. Gloating.

As Rinaldo's procession approached the Hastur enclosure, Danilo spotted Regis, sitting not in his usual place but on a bench toward the rear, in the shadows. The silver-thread lace on cuff and ruffled jabot gleamed, but his eyes, his face, remained hidden.

Rinaldo settled into the great chair and Danilo took the position indicated, standing half a pace behind and to the right side. Danilo remembered when he had attended Council meetings as Warden of Ardais, Comyn in his own right. Gladly had he laid down that responsibility and resumed the place where he truly belonged.

Beside Regis . . .

But he dared not even turn his head, not until he knew what Rinaldo was really up to. He would not give Rinaldo a moment's weakness to hold over him.

Rinaldo welcomed the assembly, using the familiar traditional phrases. Danilo paid them little heed; this was a formality only, the opening sally.

The introductory remarks concluded, Ruyven Di Asturien proceeded to the roll call of the Domains. What an archaic waste of time, Danilo thought, an empty honor. Then he realized that not so long ago, Di Asturien's daughter had been put forth as a suitable bride for Regis. From where he stood, he could see her without obviously staring. She was sitting between two older female relatives, all of them gorgeously appareled.

A sick feeling crawled up the back of Danilo's throat, fueled by the certainty that more was planned today than Rinaldo had told him. The elegance of dress, the ritual roll call, Rinaldo's ceremonial entrance, all indicated a matter that once would have required the sanction of the Comyn Council.

Crystal Di Asturien—No, Regis would never marry a girl who had made no secret of her desire to supplant Danilo in his affections!

In the moment of inner turmoil, Danilo missed the rest of Di Asturien's remarks, something about how unusual times called for unusual procedures. Then Rinaldo rose, signaling for Regis and Danilo to follow him to the center of the floor.

Rinaldo hung back, leaving Danilo and Regis to face one another. Danilo could not sense anything through the telepathic damping fields. Nor could he read anything in the way Regis held himself or the tautly masked expression on his face.

In a monotone, as if reciting a prepared speech, Regis stated his desire to transfer the allegiance of his paxman to his brother, Lord Hastur, until such time as Rinaldo released Danilo.

Regis! Beloved—bredhyu—*why are you doing this?*

Rinaldo solemnly stated his willingness to assume the obligations of liege lord. Apparently Danilo had no say in the matter. Even if he had wanted to protest, he was too stunned at the moment.

Regis passed a sword to Rinaldo. Rinaldo handled it awkwardly, clearly not a swordsman. Triumph hovered over the corners of Rinaldo's mouth.

Puzzlement stirred in Danilo as he focused on the blade. It was not the dagger he and Regis had used to exchange their first oaths or the sword that had replaced it. Yet Rinaldo acted as if, in accepting this blade, he had severed the bond between them.

Had Regis deliberately chosen an anonymous sword, one that held no emotional significance to either of them? Was Regis trying to tell him that the ceremony was a sham, that he had been forced into it? That in his heart nothing had changed?

Danilo clung to that hope as one of the Guardsmen brought out a second sword, this one tied into its scabbard with stout leather thongs in such a way it could not be drawn.

Rinaldo held out the second sword. "Bear this in my service."

Trembling took hold of Danilo's muscles. He knew he must not falter but stand firm, head up, spine straight, face composed. He had not felt like this since that horrendous time when he had been a cadet. Driven to desperation, he had struck Dyan Ardais, an officer and his Cadet Master. For that offense, he had been dismissed, stripped of rank, and sent home in disgrace. They had taken his sword—not the heirloom his father had given him but a plain Guardsman's sword—and shattered it. In his mind, that terrible breaking-glass sound still echoed, a nightmare that not even Dyan's amends and the subsequent years of privilege could erase.

"In your service do I bear it." The words should have been *in your service alone,* but Danilo could not bring himself to say them. He might accept the necessity of attending Rinaldo, but he would never, as long as he drew breath, take back his promise to Regis.

His hands closed around the scabbard. Half-blind, praying he would not stumble, Danilo followed Rinaldo to the Hastur box.

Regis remained in the middle of the floor.

Danilo glanced back as he passed through the gate. Rinaldo sat down, his anticipation evident.

"You may sit," Rinaldo told Danilo, although he meant it as a command.

The buzz of conversation swelled in the chamber, with more than one curious glance directed first at Regis and then at Danilo. Di Asturien walked with stately pace to stand before Regis. A moment later, Gabriel and Javanne, her gown as resplendent as if she were attending a ball, joined them. Two younger women, Lindirs Danilo knew only slightly, came forward as well. They wore matching gowns of pink silk, and one carried a casket ornamented with copper filigree. The chamber fell still. Even the hum of the telepathic damper seemed muted.

The woman at the back of the Alton enclosure rose. The room was so quiet, Danilo heard the rustle of her skirts as she passed the railing. A veil of silky gossamer edged with gold lace draped her head and shoulders. She wore a formal gown of iridescent silver, cut high and loose in the waist.

Walking with almost painful dignity, Linnea Storn came to a halt facing Regis, between the two young women.

Danilo closed his eyes, wishing he were anywhere else, wishing he were raving mad and that the ceremony about to begin were no more than a fever dream.

Wishing he were dead, rather than witness this moment.

Now Di Asturien was speaking the formal words that had come down, barely altered, from the Ages of Chaos . . . the young woman holding the casket was opening it, and Di Asturien removed the two copper *catenas* bracelets.

Shackles, more like. Unbreakable, eternal.

". . . and with these bracelets, which symbolize the unseen chains that bind you in wedlock, let the bond be sealed," Di Asturien intoned as he fastened the bracelets around the wrists of the couple, first Regis and then Linnea. The clasps clicked shut, echoing loudly in the chamber.

Look at me! Danilo pleaded silently. *Give me a sign you still keep faith with me!*

Regis made no sign he had heard or cared. How could he sense Danilo's desolation through the layers of ancient ritual and the dampers that shut their minds away? How should he care with such a radiant bride beside him—a woman he had always wanted—a woman who had borne him a child and now carried another, a woman he had sought in marriage without even mentioning it to Danilo?

Danvan Hastur was right. The cristoforo *brothers were right. What we had together—what I thought we had—was nothing more than youthful folly. Nothing more.*

This union, this pledging now drawing to its conclusion before him, *this* was the true destiny of men.

"Parted in fact," Di Asturien concluded as he unlocked the clasp between the bracelets, "may you be joined in heart as well as law."

Regis leaned forward to kiss Linnea. She lifted her face to his. Danilo thought his own heart would shatter.

"May you be forever one!" Di Asturien cried.

Beaming, Javanne and Gabriel leaned toward one another in remembrance of their own binding, and throughout the chamber, married couples did the same.

Through Danilo's confusion and pain, betrayal gave way to utter loss.

Forever one . . . joined in heart as well as law . . .

A cheer went up. It was over. Regis and Linnea were husband and wife under the laws of the Comyn.

Holy Bearer of Burdens, help me! How can I endure this?

As if in answer, a sense of stillness, or an exhaustion of the spirit, crept over Danilo. He had been in enough battles to recognize the absence of pain as numbness due to shock. A man might fight on in such a state, unaware of his injuries, until he dropped. Danilo's heart was wounded, gravely wounded, and yet he felt nothing. How could he fight on?

For a single moment, Regis looked directly at him. No trace of emotion showed on his face, but his eyes betrayed him. They glowed with urgency, with agony.

Danilo wrenched his gaze away. So, Regis might have regrets about abandoning everything they had shared. But Regis had set his feelings aside; he had gone through with the ceremony in full knowledge that it could never be undone. He had chosen.

22

Rinaldo showed no interest in keeping Danilo by his side for the festivities. Commenting that he could be as easily attended by servants and protected by Castle Guardsmen, Rinaldo dispatched Danilo back to the Hastur suite to settle into his new chamber and take care of any personal needs, so that he might be ready to direct his full attention to his lord on the following morning. Danilo harbored no illusions regarding the sincerity of Rinaldo's concern, but he was grateful for the excuse to leave before Regis found an opportunity to approach him.

The next days blurred together in a quagmire of misery. Danilo did what he was told. He stood, sat, walked, and schooled his features to the proper degree of attentiveness. He answered questions in monosyllables. He felt nothing.

At night, Danilo lay awake, his eyes open. He found the darkness of his chamber with its single narrow window preferable to the darkness behind his closed lids. It came to him that he might feel relief if he could weep, but no tears answered his prayers. He imagined himself a man pulled from beneath an avalanche in the Hellers, his heart stilled by freezing, with no conception of what had happened to him, so sudden and final was the disaster.

Sometimes, when he peered at the pitted mirror, he did not recognize the man who looked back at him. The lines of his face, the arch of brow and jaw, the flare of nostril, the pattern of lashes, the eyes— quenched, opaque—seemed barely human.

It was not just that Regis no longer wanted him. It was that Regis had found someone *else*, someone better, someone who generated no burden of guilt.

Gradually, Danilo emerged from the initial shock of his grief. He saw, as if through another man's eyes, that Rinaldo meant to be kind. Most of his duties consisted in accompanying his new lord about the city, especially to the Chapel of All Worlds in the Terran Zone and various promising sites for the *cristoforo* cathedral. A priest had been installed in the Castle and charged with the performance of worship services each morning. Rinaldo attended as faithfully as if he were still in orders. Danilo sat at the back of the makeshift chapel, letting the singsong litany wash through him and finding unexpected comfort in the familiar rhythms. He composed a prayer of his own: that when fate and circumstance brought him together with Regis, his heart might be easier and his thoughts less tormented.

Rinaldo seemed to be going to great lengths to avoid situations like the last flurry of summer festivities or the occasional ceremonial function in which Danilo might encounter Regis or Linnea. On those rare gatherings when Danilo caught a glimpse of Regis, Regis was closely guarded, usually by Haldred Ridenow. A private word would have been impossible.

Danilo was initially skeptical of Rinaldo's motives; he doubted that Rinaldo acted purely out of consideration for his feelings. It occurred to Danilo, as he got to know his new lord better, the reason might be simply to give him time to adjust. Rinaldo had acted not from petty spite but from compassion. He had made no attempt to force an artificial intimacy while Danilo was still emotionally vulnerable. Instead, Rinaldo had treated him with courtesy, asking only the obedience of a loyal if unfamiliar servant.

Every morning, Rinaldo and Danilo worked in Danvan Hastur's library. As Rinaldo sorted the various documents and ledger books, Danilo provided detailed explanations and historical context. Whatever his other failings, Rinaldo could be painstaking and meticulous.

A first-year cadet, one of several acting as Rinaldo's messengers, tapped for admittance.

"Come," Rinaldo called. Danilo went to the door, and the cadet handed him a sealed envelope. The paper was smooth and thick, of off-world manufacture, and bore the official insignia of the Terran Federation. Danilo brought the envelope to Rinaldo, who studied it with a frown. The frown deepened as he read the enclosed document.

Rinaldo shoved the papers into Danilo's hands. "You've had dealings with these off-worlders. You know their ways. Is this the usual treatment for a man of my rank? Do they intend an insult, or do they simply not know any better?"

The letter was from Dan Lawton, the looping Darkovan script painfully stiff, the *casta* formal and precise. Lawton acknowledged receiving a communication that Regis Hastur had been replaced as Head of his Domain, without any verification from Regis himself.

Because of the sensitivity of negotiations . . . required assurances . . . appropriate diplomatic credentials . . . mandated observance of autonomous local laws . . . established protocol . . .

As he read on, Danilo wanted to laugh aloud at the audacity of the letter. Someone had coached Lawton on Darkovan law regarding inheritance of Domain-right.

In carefully nuanced language, the Federation declined to acknowledge Rinaldo as successor to Hastur. Lawton indicated he could not in good faith recognize a previously undocumented claimant without ascertaining that his claim was legitimate and not subject to peremptory challenge from his own people. If Hastur spoke for Darkover and if inheritance passed only through biological descent, then Rinaldo must prove he was not an imposter. The *Terranan* stopped just short of accusing Rinaldo of lying about his parentage.

Then came the pivotal point: If Lord Rinaldo would consent to a simple genetic test, a comparison of his DNA with that of Regis Hastur, his authenticity could be verified. The message concluded with formulaic protestations of sincerity.

Danilo stared at the letter. Not in his wildest dreams could he imagine such a strategy for delaying action on Federation membership. Regis must have had something to do with it.

"Well?" Rinaldo demanded. "Is this an affront or just plain foolery?"

Danilo collected his thoughts. "These *Terranan* have strange notions about honor, but I do not believe this was meant to give offense." He generated an approximation of a tolerant sigh. "If you intend to represent the Domain of Hastur in any official capacity, you must comply with their requirements, however petty. Of course, there is no need for you to do so for domestic purposes. No one will dispute your legitimacy, not after Lord Regis has declared it so. But—" this time, with an careless lift of his shoulders, "—the off-worlders know little of civilized politics."

Rinaldo took the letter and read it over. "This implies that my brother will be obliged to submit to the same procedure."

"Yes, that does seem to be the case. I believe it would be possible for Terran Medical to send a technician to collect the samples if it is not convenient for you to go to them." Danilo did not add that, with a little finesse, the process of setting up those appointments might stretch out for some time.

Rinaldo agreed, as much for the purpose of exercising his power over Regis as satisfying the Legate's certification requirements. The cadet was dispatched back to Federation Headquarters with the reply.

Summer passed its height, and the days began to grow noticeably shorter. Many of the Comyn who had journeyed to Thendara for the seasonal festivities prepared to return home while the weather was still good.

Danilo attended Rinaldo in a small sitting room overlooking one of the inner courtyards of the Castle. He stood at his ease a respectful distance from where Rinaldo sat, a book of prayers open on a table. Late afternoon sun cast slanting crimson-tinged shadows across the dwarfed trees that even now intimated the coming brilliance of autumn.

Rinaldo directed the conversation to his own role in extricating Danilo from Valdir's clutches. "Indeed, I was the one who convinced the Ridenow to release you, over many protests."

An expression of thanks seemed to be called for, so Danilo murmured, "I am grateful, *vai dom.*"

"*Dom* Valdir made it clear that your continued freedom is contingent upon your good behavior." Rinaldo stared meaningfully at Danilo, expecting a response.

"What would he," *or you, more like,* "consider 'good behavior'?"

Rinaldo gestured with one long-fingered hand. "You should know. To make no trouble, especially not to conspire with Regis Hastur—"

For all his outward calm, Danilo shivered inside. He had thought himself past hurting, past hoping.

Never to speak with him, to walk with him, to touch him . . .

"—in any manner," Rinaldo went on as if the world had not just shuddered on its axis. "Those are Valdir's demands. As for my own: to serve me loyally and honestly, as you have. To comport yourself in a morally correct and responsible manner . . . particularly in regard to the faith in which you were raised."

Regis! It always comes to Regis!

And then, in a rush of self-loathing: *I wish I had died before I ever met him!*

Rinaldo had gone on, in that gently persuasive voice, "It has troubled me greatly that you and my brother share this . . . sinful practice." He sighed as might a parent over the disobedience of a beloved child. "I have done what I can to save Regis. He has fulfilled my expectations in turning away from—in changing his course to a more righteous path."

Could the truth be any plainer? Regis had abandoned everything they had shared, the love, the passion, the bonds of lord and paxman. What was it these women—Linnea in particular—offered Regis that he, Danilo, could not? Was it merely the ability to bear his children? Or was there something deeper, more fundamental? A flaw or shortcoming in himself?

"I expect some sign of repentance from you as well," Rinaldo said. "If not now, then soon."

Overcome, Danilo bowed his head.

Rinaldo appeared to take the gesture as assent. "As for myself, I can hardly expect my own people to follow where I do not lead."

Danilo lifted his head. "I'm sorry, *vai dom*. I was pondering what you just said, and I failed to grasp your meaning."

"Yes, that's understandable." Rinaldo smiled. "Speaking plainly, I too must marry. I admit, it is a circumstance I never considered in all my years at St. Valentine's. I never anticipated the bliss of the nuptial bed. But my vows no longer bar me from earthly unions, and I must set a virtuous example. Valdir agrees and has suggested a woman from his own Domain. I had considered another candidate, but that did not work out. So a Ridenow bride it will be. That is where you come in."

Danilo felt as if his head were spinning so fast, it might fly off his body at any moment. That a former monk might wish to marry was understandable, but one who was also *emmasca*? Danilo could not wrap his thoughts around the notion. Rinaldo appeared to respond to feminine allure, so perhaps he could function sexually as a male.

"Excuse me again, my lord. You are to wed one of the Ridenow ladies? Then I wish you joy. But what has it to do with me?" *Do you expect me to court her for you?*

Rinaldo's expression turned dour. He settled his hands in his lap, clasping his fingers so tightly his knuckles whitened. "I do not altogether trust the Ridenow, so I wish you to escort my bride hither."

"Are you sure that is wise, my lord? Should any harm come to the lady while she is in my keeping, I could never prove that it was not my doing."

Rinaldo unbent enough to make a scoffing noise. "That is exactly the point. I count on you to make certain nothing happens to her. I have another, even greater reason. Although you have previously shown some lapse of moral judgment, to my knowledge it has involved only other men. You are *cristoforo*, and my bride is not. Therefore I would have you school her in our faith and take her measure for me, since I do not believe I have received a true report of her character from her kinsman."

Danilo could not decide whether he was more appalled or incredulous at Rinaldo's simplicity. Valdir Ridenow meant to use this poor girl and the resulting obligations of kinship to bind Rinaldo even more tightly under his control.

But who, Danilo wondered, was the greater fool—Rinaldo for walking into the trap? Valdir for thinking that marriage to a woman of his Domain could keep Rinaldo from pursuing his own goals? Or he himself, for having anything to do with it?

When Danilo hesitated, Rinaldo pressed his point. His tone was smooth yet implacable. "A *cristoforo* should never deny such a request of another, not when there is an opportunity to bring an innocent into the true faith."

Danilo recognized the futility of argument. He knew Rinaldo well enough to be quite certain that in matters of faith, he was unshakable.

Danilo sensed no duplicity in Rinaldo's request; he did not think he was being set up as a scapegoat. He would simply have to make sure that the lady arrived in Thendara as happy as might be expected.

Danilo bowed a shade more deeply than was necessary. *"Para servirte, vai dom,"* he said, using the formal *casta* phrase. "I am at your service. I will undertake to ensure the lady is treated with respect and that every possible comfort is provided for her along the trail. The best way to accomplish this is to hire Renunciate trail guides."

"Renunciates?" Rinaldo scowled. "Ah, you mean those disreputable women called Free Amazons. I hear they wear men's clothing and reject their proper roles as wife and mother. I hardly think they are suitable attendants."

"Very well, but I will be hard-pressed to find men who are as capable of seeing to a lady's comfort and privacy, not to mention her safety."

"Her—safety. Yes, yes, that's a thought." Rinaldo looked torn between disapproval of women who lived outside social convention and distrust of men apt to act on their baser impulses.

"Many noble families employ Renunciates, especially when their wives and daughters must travel without kinsmen," Danilo explained. "Renunciates are skilled fighters and understand as only women can the needs of a gently reared *damisela*. In their care, no insult would come to your intended bride."

"You have offered your advice, and I am minded to heed it." Rinaldo held out a purse. Judging by its weight, Danilo could buy a small village. "The travel arrangements I will leave up to you."

"If you have no further need of me, I will take my leave," Danilo said. "There is still daylight enough to begin preparations. If possible, we must begin our return journey before snow blocks the passes."

The woman at the gate of the Thendara House of the Guild of Renunciates eyed Danilo without the slightest trace of friendliness as he explained that he wished to hire guides and a protective escort for a young woman traveling from Serrais. It puzzled Danilo that Valdir had not made arrangements for the journey, since there were surely kinsmen to provide her escort.

Although the hour was late, one of the Guild Mothers met with him in the Strangers Room. The old woman, her face seamed with decades of working outdoors, asked Danilo a string of penetrating questions. He made no effort to prevaricate; he carried out his lord's wishes, not his own. He did not know the lady's name or if she had consented to the marriage. Rinaldo Hastur meant his bride no harm and would treat her with kindness if not understanding. This satisfied the old Renunciate. After a little more negotiation and questions about the desired degree of comfort and warnings about the hazards of traveling so close to winter, she named a fee. Danilo thought it high, but considering the weather and the need for security, he decided it was more than reasonable. The Renunciates would be ready in three days, an unusually short time.

Danilo spent the three days gathering what intelligence he could. The markets and taverns buzzed with the recent political changes. Popular sentiment ran strongly in favor of Regis. Although Danilo had expected difficulty in hearing the name spoken aloud, the news lifted his spirits. Regis had been more to him than liege and lover; even stripped of former rank, the name of Regis Hastur continued to inspire hope. A chilling thought came to Danilo, wondering what might befall Darkover if something happened to Regis. Regis would live a long time, wouldn't he?

But what if—what if Regis died with this estrangement still between them? What if the times Danilo had avoided speaking with Regis were the last chance he would ever have?

With this thought heavy on his heart, Danilo departed for the Ride-now seat at Serrais.

23

Under the expert care of the Renunciate guides, the journey to Serrais was unexpectedly easy. The snowfall was light, far less than a winter storm, and they had come well provisioned and warmly garbed.

The head guide was a lanky, flat-chested woman with graying red hair named Darilyn n'ha Miriam. She furnished Danilo with a fur blanket as if he were a delicate Lowlands lordling. Danilo had traveled under much rougher conditions, but he accepted the blanket. He did his best not to stare at Darilyn, which would have been offensive to any woman and especially to a Free Amazon. She had a touch of *laran*, enough to increase her sensitivity to such attentions, and had the physical appearance of one who had been surgically neutered. Danilo had heard of the illegal operation but had never before met anyone who had undergone it. He wondered what had driven her to such a desperate measure and found the answer within himself. Here he was, preparing to bring back a wife for his lord as if the girl were no more than a sack of root vegetables without any voice in the matter. If a woman could sense a man's lustful thoughts and her husband—or father or a stranger on the road—cared nothing for her happiness, what choice did she have?

At least, he thought, Regis had offered the women who had come to him no false promises or seductions. He had been kind because that was his nature, and he was considerate of their pleasure, from all appearances.

Danilo had anticipated a long journey, and he was not disappointed. The Ridenow estates lay on the very edge of their Domain on an upland plateau adjoining the Plains of Valeron and very close to Dry Towns territory. The current Ridenow line descended from both the original Comyn family of that name and Dry Towns bandits who, after taking control of the lands, abandoned their own heritage and intermarried with the surviving heirs. Although many generations had passed and some doubted the story, the Ridenow were still held in suspicion in many quarters. Valdir was undoubtedly the least popular Ridenow in modern times. Time would reveal what sort of man young Francisco would become under Valdir's tutelage.

Danilo and his party arrived during a snow flurry, so he caught only glimpses of the great house. As he passed through the outer gates, he received the impression of a fortress, not a home. As they entered the courtyard, servants and horseboys came running to take charge of animals and baggage. Danilo was accustomed to caring for his own mount on the trail, as were the Renunciates. One of the servants, an under-steward, urged them all to come inside the great house, but Darilyn declined, saying she and her women would sleep in the stables. Danilo wished he might join them, for an evening of quiet fellowship sounded much preferable to ostentatious luxury amid uncertainty and tension.

Danilo was shown to quarters sumptuous with off-world luxuries. This was not surprising, for Lerrys and Geremy Ridenow, brothers to Lew's second wife, Diotima, had been in the forefront of the craze for all things Terran. Moving about the room, touching the costly, exotic ornaments, Danilo wondered at Valdir's rise to power. How very convenient that every other male claimant to the Domain had chosen exile or died, either by assassination, like Lord Edric, or from mysterious causes.

Regis would have had something to say about that.

Danilo paused in his preparations for dinner. He had been so caught up in feeling abandoned, he had not considered all the aspects of his relationship with Regis. They had been lovers, but that had come later. First they had been fellow cadets. Then, very quickly and under terrible stress, they had pledged themselves as lord and paxman. When had his heart truly opened to Regis? Did it matter? Over the following years, they had defended one another, argued, debated, confided, advised, consoled . . . If it was true that he would have given his life to save Regis, it was also true that Regis would have done the same for him.

They had been friends in the deepest and truest sense.

Danilo shivered, as if the season had just turned inside out. Was he willing to throw all that away because current circumstances divided them? Was he so insecure that he still feared being displaced by a woman? Should a man like Regis, bearing as he did so much responsibility, making so many sacrifices, being so set apart, have only *one* friend, *one* councillor, *one* person who loved him for himself?

Sitting in the shadows of the elaborate hangings, Danilo forced himself to acknowledge the truth. He had never been pleased with any of the women Regis had slept with over the years, but he had been able to set his anxieties aside and believe that Regis did not "have *love affairs*" with them.

But Linnea . . . Linnea was different.

I have done them—and myself—no honor in this.

Had the world gone otherwise, had Regis not been born Heir to Hastur and therefore under constant pressure to produce sons, would things have been different? Even then, Danilo told himself savagely, there would have been other people who loved Regis. How could they not?

But not as I have. Not as I do.

Not as he loves me.

Was it too late? Had he lost everything they shared because of one difficulty?

A tap at the door roused him. A servant came to summon him for dinner. Danilo finished making himself presentable.

A small group of men and women, most with the flaxen hair and distinctive features of the Ridenow, stood talking in the near end of the hall. *Dom* Valdir was not in attendance, being back at Thendara, but Francisco came forward to greet Danilo. Francisco, although more confident in his own home, looked younger and less arrogant. Danilo wondered how much of what he had seen in Thendara had been Valdir's influence.

"*Dom* Danilo Syrtis-Ardais," Francisco said, with a friendly smile, "allow me to present my cousin, *Damisela* Bettany Sabrina-Ysabet Ridenow."

A young woman stepped forward and curtsied. In her brocade gown, her flaxen hair arranged in ringlets over her shoulders, she looked very young. A second glance showed her to be well grown but excessively thin. The vacuous expression in her eyes contrasted with a hint of stubbornness in her mouth and chin.

"*S'dia shaya,*" she said, her eyes lowered.

Danilo bowed and returned the appropriate greeting. She hesitated as if unsure what to do next. He said, meaning only kindness, "I am paxman to Lord Hastur, and he has sent me here to escort you to Thendara for your wedding and to prepare you as best I can for your new life."

"But why did he not come for me *himself?*"

Francisco looked aghast. "We have explained that to you, *chiya.* Please excuse my cousin, *Dom* Danilo, she is—this is all very new to her."

"So I see," Danilo replied dryly. *Poor Rinaldo,* he couldn't help thinking as Francisco led her away to the table. Was the girl simple or merely ignorant and ill-mannered?

The dinner itself was small for the occasion, for the Ridenow, like other great houses of the Comyn, were much reduced in numbers. About a third of the guests were neighbors, holders of small estates, and clearly excited to be invited.

As the meal progressed, Danilo noted traces of economy. Despite the costly imported goods in his own chamber, the carpets were worn almost through, the wine was not the best, the room was almost too cold for comfort, and there were not enough servants for the number of diners. Another guest might not have noticed, but Regis had taught Danilo to observe details. Lerrys and Geremy had lived richly among the stars without thought to the welfare of their own Domain.

Danilo had been placed some distance from Bettany, making any conversation between them awkward. Instead, he talked with the other men, the women being meek and, for the most part, silent. If this was the way Bettany had been brought up, no wonder she was graceless and inexperienced. She seemed not to have any immediate family present, certainly no female relatives. Throughout the meal, she picked at her food, played with her napkin, and drank more wine than was proper for a young woman.

The talk ranged from the unusually cold weather to the social season in Thendara to oblique questions about how the new Lord Hastur fared and then back to predictions of a bad winter.

After the meal, any hopes Danilo had of a word with Bettany disappeared as an older woman in the plain clothing of a nurse took the girl in charge and swept her from the hall.

"I am sorry to deprive you all of further entertaining news," Danilo said, bowing to the other men, "but I must see to my horses and my trail guides."

The Renunciates had set up their camp in the stables. Even without a fire, it was quite snug, warmed by the body heat of the animals and out of the wind and snow. He felt their instant alertness as he entered and asked if they needed anything.

Darilyn stood up. "The horses are resting comfortably. The head groom did his best for them with hot mashes and blankets. The hay is not the best, but there is plenty of it. We have not had to dip into our supply of grain."

"I am glad of it," Danilo said. "Is there any reason why we cannot leave for Thendara in the morning?"

The Renunciate offered a small smile. They understood one another. The weather was not bad enough to pin them down here, and the risk of worse would increase every day.

When Danilo returned to main hall, he found Francisco and a few of the men still in conversation. "*Dom* Francisco, I trust the *damisela* will be ready to leave at dawn."

Francisco hesitated, and Danilo saw in that moment of panic that the young Ridenow did not have much influence over his cousin's behavior. Danilo would not have been surprised to learn that Bettany was accustomed to sleeping as late as she liked. It was better to make expectations clear now than to wait until tomorrow morning. Being awakened and dressed at a decent hour, with or without breakfast, would be good for her. He smiled as he headed for his own chamber.

The next morning, the Bloody Sun rose on a cloudless sky. Danilo woke well before dawn, arranged for hot porridge and *jaco* to be sent to the women in the stables, took his own breakfast in the kitchen, and went about supervising replenishment of trail provisions and the loading of the bride's dowry as well as her personal possessions. No one questioned his orders. The house steward, an older man whose mouth seemed permanently set in an expression of disapproval, responded with quiet efficiency. Danilo suspected the man was relieved to be rid of the girl and reassured that she would arrive at her destination with no blemish upon her former dwelling. Apparently Bettany was being sent away without a proper chaperone, since the Renunciates provided the necessary female company.

Just as Danilo was finishing his own work and beginning to wonder what he would do if Bettany did not appear, whether he had license to drag her from her bedchamber and throw her over the back of a horse in her nightgown, she rushed into the stable yard. Her nurse and two other women trailed behind. Danilo bade her a good morning but received only a sullen nod. At least her traveling dress had split skirts for riding astride and stout boots housed her feet. A fur-lined cloak completed her ensemble. Sniffling, her nurse thrust a pair of mittens and matching scarf, obviously knitted with care, into her hands.

"Pah! I don't want those," Bettany pouted. "They're for babies!"

"You will want them before the hour is gone, I assure you." Darilyn looked up from checking the harness on one of the pack animals. With a friendly smile, she took the items and slipped them into the saddlebag of Bettany's pretty white mare. "Here, let me show you how to check the girths and under the saddle cloth to make sure your horse is comfortable for a long ride."

Bettany shook her head. "I am a lady and soon to be the wife of a great lord. Such tasks are for servants."

Danilo expected Darilyn to object, but the Renunciate shrugged. "As you wish. If your saddle slips on the trail or your horse bucks because a wrinkle in her blanket has worn a sore on her back, it is *your* head you will fall upon, not that of a horsegroom."

Darilyn arranged the riders, taking the lead herself and placing Danilo beside Bettany. They set off through the gates at a brisk walk to warm the horses up.

"Why do you suffer this indignity?" Bettany asked him. "Surely, *you* should ride in the position of honor. You are the only man among us, and a Comyn lord. It's demeaning for you to take orders from a hired servant!"

Danilo restrained the retort that rose to his tongue. "Darilyn is our trail guide. Your promised husband has paid for her advice on how to get us to Thendara as safely and comfortably as possible. This is her business, after all. Do you not think we should take her advice?"

Bettany said nothing, only stared ahead. Within a quarter an hour, however, she began complaining. She had a headache, her saddle was too hard, she was cold, she was hot, she was hungry, she was bored. Danilo, who had almost no experience with children, tried at first to encourage her. Nothing he said lessened her distress. Clearly, she had no conception of the distance to Thendara or the importance of taking advantage of every hour of good weather. Very shortly, he was reduced to staring straight ahead, teeth clenched, and doing his best to ignore her.

Finally he burst out, "This incessant whining is making matters difficult for the very people who are trying to help you. Lord Hastur has charged me with your education in the *cristoforo* faith and anything else you might need to know as wife to a great lord. The lessons will begin now. A lady does not complain at every little discomfort! Nor does she sulk and pout like a spoiled brat."

"I'm not spoiled! I can't help being hungry—you would be, too, if you hadn't eaten since yesterday! I'm not *used* to this!" Bettany burst into tears. "I want to go home!"

Darilyn, who had been riding on a circuit of the caravan, reined her sturdy piebald gelding beside the distraught girl. "What is this? Did you not eat breakfast before we set out?"

"What do *you* care?" Bettany glared at the Renunciate and stuck out her lower lip.

"I am responsible for the well-being of every person in my charge, little lady. If you are merely uncomfortable, that is something you must bear in good temper. But if you are not properly nourished, you cannot withstand the rigors of travel. If you become ill and we must stop, we risk becoming snowed in without shelter. You put all our lives in jeopardy. Do you see how your actions affect more than yourself?"

"Oh . . ." Bettany said in a small, contrite voice. "I would not want anyone to *die* because of me."

"Then I will ride beside you and show you how we Free Amazons eat while on a long trail. *Dom* Danilo, would you be so good as to ride point?"

Grateful for the escape, Danilo nudged his horse into a trot until he came to the front of the caravan. Darilyn's kindliness toward Bettany surprised him;. He had thought Darilyn—and all such women, who lived by their own labor and renounced the protection of men—hard and unmotherly. Within a few minutes, Darilyn and Bettany were laughing together. Bettany's chronic petulance disappeared, revealing her to be surprisingly pretty. What her natural temperament might be, Danilo could not tell. She had been taught neither manners nor self-discipline, but there was something more in her that troubled him, an oddness. He could not puzzle it out.

He could not see any man of sense being content with such a wife. He thought of Linnea, with her keen mind and trained *laran,* and more than that, her generosity, her sensitivity . . . all the things he had not wanted to admit but that made her the ideal consort for Regis. In fact, he could think of no other woman who posed *less* of a threat to his relationship with Regis.

Darilyn persuaded Bettany that it was fun to nibble on trail food as they rode along, and the party made good progress. The women set a pace that was not too draining for the animals but took advantage of the fine weather. As afternoon waned, they pressed on, arriving at a good-sized village at a crossroads.

The inn there was run by two Renunciates, friends of Darilyn. One took charge of the horses, patting their necks and speaking to them with such affection that Danilo had no doubt they would be pampered and fed with as much care as their riders.

The common room of the inn was clean and warm, if plainly furnished. By this time, Bettany had passed from her earlier cheer to peevishness and then to sullen silence. She had given up complaining how tired and hungry and cold she was and sat where she had been placed before the fire. The second innkeeper set about providing hot drinks for them all while dinner was prepared and baggage brought up to their rooms.

Danilo carried a cup of *jaco* to Bettany and pulled up a stool beside her. "Here, drink this. It will warm you." He took a packet of honeyed nuts from his jacket pocket and held it out. "Eat these as well. I always carry them on the trail for times such as this. Dinner will be soon, but it is best to have something to tide you over."

Like an obedient child, she sipped the stimulant drink and nibbled on the nuts. Within minutes, her face, which had been very pale, brightened. "These are good. Th-thank you."

"It has been a long, hard day for someone unaccustomed to travel. This must all seem very strange."

"Oh! As to that—" Her eyes turned glassy, then she gathered herself. "I see you mean to help me. Tell me, what sort of man is my new lord? Is it true he is . . . not as other men?"

Danilo sat back, momentarily at a loss as to how to answer. "I am sure he will be a good husband to you."

Temper flashed in her eyes. "Do not treat me like a child to be cozened with pretty promises! I have heard . . ." she lowered her voice to a whisper, "he is deformed. As a man."

Deformed? Danilo felt a rush of outrage. He mistrusted Rinaldo for many reasons, but the poor man's birth was not among them, nor should it be.

"I believe you mean he is *emmasca*," Danilo said firmly. "It is *not* a perversion, but the way he is made."

He paused, surprised at his own vehemence. What he had just asserted was as true for Regis and himself as for Rinaldo. *The way each of us is made.* He did not know the particulars of Rinaldo's anatomy and inclinations, nor did he want to. He knew how difficult it was to reconcile one's nature with incompatible demands. Had Rinaldo undergone a similar struggle, or had he found acceptance in the *cristoforo* community? If the doctrine was harsh in some areas, it could be compassionate in others.

From what Rinaldo had said, he responded sexually to women, at least in theory. He was not ignorant of what passed between husbands and wives. He must have had good reason to think he could perform the role of husband.

Danilo said as much to Bettany, adding, "The marriage bed is not the only test of a man's ability. There are certain normal functions that occur even in young unmarried men—"

"I know—I—" Blushing furiously, the girl looked down.

Danilo took the cup from her and set it down on the hearth. "*Chiya,* I am sorry! I should not have spoken so crudely to you."

Bettany twisted her hands together as tears streamed down her cheeks. Danilo laid one of his hands on hers to comfort her. Her fingers were like ice, but the physical contact brought an unexpected psychic link. He himself was not a strong telepath, but he had always been able to sense the emotions of others. Now he felt her fatigue, her irritability, her fear, her self-absorption. He also sensed a memory so distorted and bizarre that it colored everything else in her mind. In reflex, he pulled his hands away and slammed his *laran* barriers tight.

Brief as the rapport had been, he knew what he had touched. This poor young woman, this difficult child, had been caught up in a Ghost Wind. She must have been away from home at the time, for the plants producing the highly psychedelic pollen grew only at high altitudes. Under the influence of the airborne particles, men were known to have gone berserk. Bettany was lucky to be alive and with any portion of her mind intact.

She had calmed and was staring at him with the glassy expression he now understood. He did not want to touch her again.

"Whatever else he may be," Danilo said, "Lord Hastur is a good man. He has spent most of his life as a *cristoforo* monk, dedicated to a virtuous life. Did they tell you that, as well?"

She shook her head, and he wondered if she had indeed been told but had not understood. He explained, in the broadest terms, the principles of that faith. Rinaldo's constant reminders and regular chapel attendance had sharpened his memory.

The conversation continued through the dinner hour. For the first time, Bettany seemed to be genuinely interested in something besides herself. Perhaps she was relieved or simply attracted to the idea of a husband who was not only rich and powerful but romantically mysterious as well. At least, she was now minimally familiar with the tenets of her husband's faith.

Danilo escorted Bettany up the stairs to the room she shared with one of the Renunciates.

"What I said about my promised husband," she said, "I did not mean it. I was told those things out of spite. *They* wanted me to believe that he could never love me or give me a child. If what you say is true—if the Lord of All Worlds and His saints work miracles for the faithful—then who is to say we will not be blessed as well? Surely, there can be no more devout follower than my husband."

Leaving Danilo speechless, the girl shut the door behind her.

24

As the party neared Thendara, the weather worsened. Clouds blanketed the sun. Both humans and animals breathed out streams of vapor, and ice formed on skin and clothing. Sleet poured down as they crested the pass through the Venza Hills. The horses plodded on, heads lowered and tails clamped to their rumps. There was no shelter along this stretch of the road, and the winds cut through the hills like razor-edged knives. Darilyn, her face pale and set, shouted to keep together and keep moving. Danilo admired her ability to keep everyone organized.

They arrived in Thendara late, as the quick hush of nightfall settled over the city. They were all thoroughly drenched and aching with cold. Bettany's lips had turned blue. She was shivering visibly.

Darilyn sent one of her women ahead to alert the Castle. When they clattered into the courtyard, lanterns were already lit and the cobblestones swept clear of snow. Servants waited in the sheltered alcoves of the doors with blankets in hand.

Within the Castle itself, Javanne Hastur and a handful of maids waited to take Bettany in hand. Javanne stripped off the girl's sodden cloak and wrapped her in a thick shawl.

"Where is her waiting-woman? Has she no kinswoman to attend her?" Javanne demanded of Danilo, as if this lapse of propriety were his fault.

He hesitated to blurt out the truth in front of the girl, that she had been thrust into an unseasonable journey among strangers, without even that small comfort. Javanne pressed her lips together, her posture expressing her opinion, and bustled the girl away.

The Renunciates had finished offloading what did not belong to them and were ready to leave. Danilo offered them a hot meal from the Castle kitchens, but they refused. They looked weary, yet anxious to be back in their own Guild House.

Darilyn and Danilo stood in the lee of the outer wall as he counted out the rest of the fee, adding a generous bonus from his own purse. Instead of taking her leave, Darilyn lingered.

"Is anything amiss?" Danilo asked. He was distracted by the business of their arrival and the safe disposal of Bettany's dowry, so that he was not blocking telepathic contact the way he normally did. She was unsure but not alarmed.

"You are—you were paxman to *Dom* Regis Hastur?"

Pain welled, but only a small pulse, quickly fading in the thought: *Was and still am, in my heart.* Nothing could change that, not all of Rinaldo's fiery words or the gods themselves.

Darilyn said, "I hear he is lately married to Lady Linnea Storn."

"Yes, that is true." Why would the affairs of the Comyn concern a Renunciate? Given Darilyn's touch of *laran* and red-tinted hair, could she and Linnea be distant kinswomen? Throughout the Domains, the illegitimate offspring of Comyn lords often had some degree of psychic talent.

"Would you convey my wishes for her happiness?" Darilyn's usually brusque manner softened. "I met her years ago, you see, when she was Keeper at Arilinn. My freemate and I sought her out when there was no one else we could turn to for help. She was gracious to us when there was no obligation. She accepted us, accepted *me* for what I am. I have never forgotten that kindness."

How like Linnea to have seen past the cropped hair, the mannish clothing, and the surgical mutilation to the heart of the woman. There was nothing mean spirited or prideful in Linnea. She would not judge Darilyn for her choices . . . or Regis for his.

"I cannot say when I will next have the opportunity, but I will speak to the lady and give her your greetings." Danilo bowed in informal salute.

With a whisper of a smile, Darilyn returned to her sisters.

While Danilo was fetching Bettany to Thendara, arrangements for the marriage had been made. The ceremony took place only a tenday later, with barely enough time to sew the wedding clothes.

The intervening time went by in a cascade of autumnal storms, one upon the heels of the next. Ice-edged rain battered the city, sending even the hardiest folk scurrying for shelter. The damp chill penetrated stone and wooden walls alike. Winds swirled through the streets and the courtyards of the Castle. In the brief respites between gusts, common people emerged to rush through the most essential tasks. Street vendors set up their wares with desperate speed and as quickly took them down. On corners and outside taverns, men in ragged cloaks gathered to exchange dire prophecies about the winter to come.

At last, on a particularly blustery day, the waiting came to an end. Danilo's temper was thoroughly frayed, and he wanted the wretched affair to be over; Rinaldo had kept him running between Gabriel, who was in charge of the security arrangements, Javanne and the Castle *coridom,* who were in charge of decorations and food, the musicians, the priest who was to perform the *cristoforo* portion of the ceremony, and almost daily errands to Tiphani Lawton. Danilo had scarcely had a moment to himself, let along to deliver Darilyn's message to Linnea or find a way of letting Regis know, by look or thought, of his desire for a reconciliation. He had scarcely seen Bettany, for she had kept to her rooms, refusing to see anyone but a bevy of dressmakers and jewelers.

Javanne had taken it upon herself to supervise the bride's gown and attendants. Everything would be in impeccable taste, but Danilo could not imagine Javanne as a sympathetic friend.

Danilo wondered if Linnea might be able to help Bettany. If anyone could heal the psychic wounds caused by the Ghost Wind, it was a trained *leronis*. Try as he might, however, Danilo could not think of a way of suggesting it that would not immediately meet with Rinaldo's refusal.

Rinaldo had wanted the wedding to take place in the Crystal Chamber, but Valdir had convinced him of the impropriety of admitting commoners to a place traditionally reserved for Comyn. Therefore, a smaller but no less stately venue was selected, adjacent to the Grand Ballroom. Paneled in rich dark wood with southern-facing windows, ample wall sconces now filled with beeswax candles, and a fireplace capable of warming the entire chamber, the place was suitable for even a royal marriage. Javanne had outdone herself with garlands of hothouse flowers, tied with ribbons in Hastur blue and white. The honey-sweet smell of the candles mingled with the perfume of the flowers.

The wedding was the highlight of the autumn social calendar. Every Comyn and city dignitary in Thendara received an invitation, as did the Terran Legate. When the first guests arrived, Danilo stood in his prescribed place, a pace behind Rinaldo. This way, he need not respond overtly to any greeting, although many guests included him by a glance or a word. It occurred to Danilo that these people valued him in his own right, not merely for his role as paxman to Regis and now to Rinaldo.

Regis and Linnea were among the earliest to arrive, followed by Dan Lawton and his wife. Rinaldo, infused with a celebratory spirit, had ordered Valdir to remove his guards from Regis. To Danilo's surprise, Valdir had complied. Perhaps he no longer considered Regis the primary obstacle to his plans.

Warmly, Regis wished his brother every happiness. Linnea did not curtsy but inclined her head in a Keeper's greeting. She was heavily pregnant, but she carried herself with grace.

Regis paused before making way for the next guest to greet the groom. Unlike the Crystal Chamber, this room had no telepathic dampers. Regis had kept his thoughts shielded, but as his eyes met Danilo's, he lowered his barriers. Linnea stood watch, by her posture and her *laran*-enhanced vigilance ensuring a moment of intimacy.

Bredhyu!

Then Regis was turning away, Rinaldo had already begun his formal greeting to the Terran Legate, and the fleeting rapport disappeared.

While Dan Lawton offered appropriate congratulations, his wife beamed at Rinaldo. Danilo needed no psychic abilities to detect the bond between the two. Was it the sort of flirtation a couple, each married to someone else, might enjoy? No, the connection was far stronger and eerily disturbing. Danilo sensed no trace of sexual attraction, but passion lay at its roots.

The crowd quieted as Bettany entered, accompanied by Crystal Di Asturien and Javanne's adolescent daughter, Ariel. Bettany looked very young and small in a confection of cream-colored lace over satin just a shade darker. Her fair hair had been curled and lacquered so that not a strand moved beneath her diamond-studded veil. Tiny silver bells hung by ribbons from her tiara.

As she halted beside Rinaldo, Bettany's gaze met Danilo's. A glassy light filled her eyes. For a moment, she seemed not to know him, or anyone. Her thin fingers plucked at the lace of her gown. Then she sniffed, lifted her chin, and turned away, as if Danilo were beneath her notice.

The ceremony itself was longer and more complex than Danilo had ever witnessed. As Lord Hastur, the Head of his Domain, Rinaldo must be wed by the ancient Comyn tradition of *di catenas*. He insisted on a religious rite as well.

Rinaldo had asked Regis to officiate for the first portion. The honor should have gone to Ruyven Di Asturien, but no one thought any the worse of Regis for it. For Regis, it was no privilege but a humiliation, a public reminder of his lesser status.

Regis carried out his part with quiet dignity. Linnea stood a short distance away in the front row of onlookers. Danilo sensed her mental presence sustaining Regis. When Danilo opened his mind, it felt as if a door had cracked ajar and sunlight streamed into a darkened room.

The chamber dimmed in Danilo's sight; he felt a surge of—was it welcome? acceptance?—from Linnea.

Then Regis was clasping the *catenas* bracelets on the wrists of his brother and the new bride. Danilo's vision sharpened. One of the fabulously expensive Arcarran rubies set in the bracelets sparkled. It reminded him, uncomfortably, of freshly spilt blood.

The participants rearranged themselves for the religious ceremony.

Tiphani Lawton stood directly behind Bettany. Had he not known Rinaldo's adherence to *cristoforo* morality, Danilo might have suspected him of marrying both women at the same time.

The *cristoforo* priest, a slight man with a straight line for a mouth, intoned the nuptial benediction. Tiphani closed her eyes and swayed dramatically in time with his words. Rinaldo bowed his head as if receiving absolution. Bettany looked blank, her face the color and immobility of a wax doll.

Watching her, Danilo was suddenly overtaken by the certainty that this wedding was a serious mistake, one they would all come to regret. The girl was not bored, as it first appeared. She was trembling. Overwrought, confused. Near tears. Perhaps even aware of the spectacle of Tiphani Lawton behind her.

How could her family have done this to her? Danilo thought angrily. Anyone else would have known the marriage was a sham, her husband incapable of giving her children. Rinaldo was marrying her not for love but out of religious duty and as a way of slacking his long-repressed desires without guilt.

Well, Danilo thought, it was no business of his whom Rinaldo married or why. He did not know whether he pitied more the bridegroom with the glowing, beatific smile or the frightened child who was now his wife.

Or, he added to himself, Tiphani Lawton. The woman had retreated to a corner and was holding forth to a rapt audience. Danilo could not catch her words, only her animated features.

Danilo was more interested in the sight of Linnea and Regis standing close together. Something in his stance, the angle of his shoulder, was tender and protective. She held herself well, despite the awkwardness of her pregnancy, accepting his attention and yet in no way lessened by it. Regis could have done far worse.

The witnesses drifted toward the ballroom, where the reception and dancing would take place. As much with his mind as with his ears, Danilo overheard Regis murmuring to Linnea, "I fear what may come of this, although I do not know why."

A surge of agreement from Linnea: "What are we to do? As the old proverb says, *'The world will go as it will and not as you or I would have it.'*"

"Perhaps." Regis did not sound convinced.

Regis, Danilo thought with a private smile, had never waited passively for the world to do as it willed.

Following the knot of guests, Dan Lawton maneuvered to walk beside Danilo. "Can you get a word to Regis? Every message I've sent has been refused."

Danilo kept his gaze ahead, his expression guarded, and said nothing..

"At least he looks well enough. I feared—" Dan broke off as they came into the ballroom itself. The guests parted to allow Rinaldo and his new bride to enter. "If you can, let Regis know the genetic tests confirmed Rinaldo as a Hastur, so we've had to accept his credentials. I won't be able to ignore him if he starts pressing for Federation membership."

In the ballroom, the musicians had tuned up and were waiting for the newly married couple to begin the night's dancing. Rinaldo had given strict instructions as to which dances and songs were acceptable. There would be no wild mountain *secain* nor any modern, licentious off-world gyrations and especially no Sword Dance. Danilo remembered how Dyan Ardais, in a brilliantly barbaric costume from the Ages of Chaos, had brought a fierce masculine grace and barely sublimated sexuality to the ancient steps. No, this evening would be one of sedate formal dances, preferably ones in which men and women danced only with one another and touched no more than their fingertips.

Rinaldo had clearly been taking lessons, for he squired his new wife through the measures of the opening dance, a *promenada,* without hesitation. Bettany, now the center of attention, smiled up at her husband with the first expression of happiness Danilo had yet seen in her.

The dance concluded to restrained applause. Rinaldo was so pleased with himself that he bade Danilo to dance with any lady he liked. There were not many women with whom Danilo was on cordial terms. Javanne seemed pleased, if startled, when he asked her, and it was not improper because they had been introduced so long ago. Javanne made a restful partner, for she made no attempt at conversation. Danilo enjoyed dancing and wished it were permissible for him to dance with her more than once, but he could not pay special attention to another man's wife.

Bettany had been partnered by Valdir, who escorted her back to her new husband. Rinaldo was talking with the *cristoforo* priest with such absorption that he gave his wife only a cursory nod. Danilo felt a pang of sympathy for the girl. How could Rinaldo fail to see that she craved attention as a drowning man craved air? Moved, Danilo bowed to each of them in turn, including the priest, and then asked if he might request the next dance.

Bettany's fingers felt cold as they rested lightly on Danilo's. The musicians played the opening measures of the next dance, a *passolento* in two lines. Danilo handed Bettany into the position of honor among the other ladies and took his place opposite her. The two lines bowed to one another, moving through the stylized courtly display. Bettany brightened as the two of them swept down the center with all eyes upon her. There was an artless enjoyment in the way she skipped through the close-steps. Her eyes sparkled, and her lips parted. The melody was very old and familiar, and she hummed along like any young woman at her first fancy ball. In that moment of simple pleasure, Danilo saw the girl she had been before the Ghost Wind and might yet be again, given care and understanding, gentle guidance, and, most of all, affection. *Could* Rinaldo love her?

The *passolento* closed with another formal salute. Danilo offered Bettany his arm. "It's good to see you happy, *damisela*—pardon me, *Domna*."

"Happy? Am I happy?" She hesitated, and he slowed his step to give them more time before he must return her to Rinaldo. "I do so love dancing and pretty dresses, but these are things of the moment. At night, in the dark, I am alone with my thoughts. I suppose that will be different now—the being alone. Perhaps *he* will talk to me."

Danilo's heart ached for her poignant hope. "Bettany—*Domna*—if you ever need someone to listen to you, to give you counsel—"

She looked up at him, eyes full of questions. "*You* would be such a friend to me?"

"I doubt your husband would permit it. I meant you might seek out

Domna Linnea. As your sister-in-law and a Comynara in her own right, such a friendship would be perfectly suitable. You will find her kind and sympathetic. She has been trained as a healer of the mind—"

He saw from Bettany's reaction that he had gone too far. Her face, which had softened like a flower in the sun, closed. "I do not need anyone to be *kind* to me. And there is nothing wrong with my mind! I require you to take me to my husband with no more unseemly delay!"

Afterward, Danilo waited out several dances and then, seeing Linnea sitting with a group of ladies, he approached her. Linnea flashed him an expression of relief when he asked her to dance, for what he heard of the conversation concerned this season's fashion in crocheted-lace ruffles.

"I have a message for you," he said as the musicians played the opening bars. "From Darilyn n'ha Miriam."

"Who—oh, the Free Amazon. I remember her. How did you—" Linnea broke off as the pattern of the dance drew them apart, for they were the first couple, casting off.

"I hired her to escort *Damisela*—ah, *Domna* Bettany—from Serrais."

Linnea joined his hands as they circled one another.

"You could not have done better. How does Darilyn fare?"

"She is well and sends her thoughts of you. And her thanks—" they drew back as the second couple moved into the center of the set to circle, "—for your kindness to her."

"Kindness—" Linnea broke off, frustrated. *Danilo, we cannot talk about anything of importance this way!*

With a conspiratorial wink, Linnea passed one hand over her forehead and grasped her rounded belly with the other. She let out a very realistic groan. Danilo, needing no further cue, assisted her to the chairs along one wall, choosing a corner where a pair of old dowagers were snoozing. He waved away offers of help, saying the lady was but a trifle overtired.

Linnea said in a hushed voice, "Regis was so worried—Rinaldo did not tell him that he'd sent you off to Serrais—"

"I didn't think—I've been such a fool!"

"You? No! Regis thought Rinaldo had reneged on his bargain."

"Bargain?"

"You didn't know?" Linnea's expression turned troubled. "Valdir threatened to have you tortured or killed! Rinaldo managed to get you out of his clutches, but only if—if—"

"Regis set me aside. Got married like a proper Comyn lord." Although he knew it was unfair, Danilo could not keep himself from adding, "So what Danvan Hastur and half the Comyn Council could not force Regis to do, Rinaldo has now done."

Listen to me! Linnea shifted to direct mental speech, where no lies or dissembling were possible. *When I sent Regis away last spring, I was hurt and angry. And jealous—of you. I almost threw away something so precious, I would have regretted it for the rest of my life. Don't make my mistake! What the two of you share, I can never be part of . . . and I swear to you, I will never try to come between you.*

Danilo had been bending over Linnea, their heads close together. Now he lowered himself into the chair beside her. Bracing his elbows on his knees, he buried his face in his hands. He did not care who saw him. He had hoped for a word with Regis, a sign, a thought. He had not expected such a revelation, certainly not from Linnea. It was too much, all of it, the whole colossal misunderstanding, the savagery of Valdir's ambition, and Rinaldo—who knew what his aims really were or what he might do to achieve them?

"Danilo . . ."

He had never heard that note of alarm in Linnea's voice before. He lifted his head, stared at her. She hunched over, both arms wrapped around her belly. A high color had risen to her cheeks and even now faded into paleness. He sensed the ripple of energy arise deep within her body, stealing her breath, gripping her muscles.

"I really must lie down, and you had best send for a midwife and let Regis know." It was unthinkable for a telepath to not attend the mother of his children in labor.

She paused, gulping air. "Our little Danilo has chosen a most inopportune time to make his appearance."

Discreetly, Danilo arranged for women to help Linnea to her chamber, for the midwife to be summoned, for excuses to be made to Rinaldo and Bettany. Valdir deserved none.

Regis flashed Danilo a brilliant smile before he hurried after his wife. In the swirl of the festivities, there was no possibility of anything more.

Only when they were gone, when the music faded into a hum, did Danilo realize what Linnea had said about the baby.

Our Danilo.

25

The next morning, Danilo attended Rinaldo in the library, standing in his usual place behind his lord's chair. Rinaldo's marriage had not altered his daily routine. *Poor Bettany,* Danilo thought, *to be paraded about one day and ignored the next.*

One of the Guardsmen brought news that Lady Linnea had given birth to a healthy boy. Rinaldo beamed, as delighted as if it were his own son, and gave Danilo a meaningful look.

He intends that I should be next. Danilo set his teeth together. *It isn't enough that Rinaldo keeps me at his side, making it impossible for me to have a private word with Regis, but he would see me saddled with as loveless a union as his own.*

Now that Danilo understood the true state of affairs with Linnea, how could he repay Regis by placing yet another person between them? Even if Danilo could bring himself to take a wife, it was not likely he could find one who, like Linnea, was willing to share her husband's deepest loyalty with another man.

Something in Danilo's expression must have betrayed his resistance, for Rinaldo responded with a half-smile that, while tolerant and good-humored, indicated he had no intention of relenting.

Rinaldo bade the messenger convey his congratulations to the new parents. Then he returned to the letter he had been contemplating before the interruption. His smile faded, and the creases between his brows deepened.

As the silence wore on, Danilo's curiosity stirred. "My lord . . . ?"

Rinaldo looked up, his frown shifting towards annoyance.

"My lord, is there something I might help you with? A matter in which my experience might be of use?"

"I hardly think that is the case here." Rinaldo pushed the paper away. "I suppose it is difficult to change beliefs people have clung to for so many centuries. I am speaking, you understand, of achieving full acceptance of the *cristoforo* religion throughout the Domains."

"In matters of faith, I believe change comes slowly," Danilo said in an encouraging tone. "People tend to stay with what they were taught as children."

Rinaldo's face tightened again. "I cannot wait a generation! Who knows how many souls may be lost? This prejudice against the true faith is intolerable!"

"There are more chapels in Thendara than ever before," Danilo reminded him. "Surely, given time, the people will come to accept—"

"The common people, but not the Comyn! My own caste, the very men who should be leading this glorious battle, cling to the accursed superstitions of the past! What will it take to make them see that idolatrous worship of Aldones and the rest leads to damnation?"

Danilo flinched at Rinaldo's ferocity. He could not believe that Regis or Lew Alton or any of the other Comyn who faithfully followed the practices of his ancestors, these decent, honorable men, must necessarily face eternal torture. Before he could think of a suitably nonconfrontational comment, he heard an angry voice outside the door, followed by a barrage of sharp raps.

"Out of my way, lout! I will not be put off again!"

The door flew open, and Valdir Ridenow strode in. He was richly attired in the green of his Domain trimmed in gold thread, and his face was flushed.

Drawing his sword, Danilo stepped between Valdir and Rinaldo. The steel sang softly as it came free. A feral smile warmed his lips. Very few things would have pleased him more than an excuse to plunge the blade into Valdir's heart.

Valdir halted, quickly composing himself. Danilo held his position; it was for Rinaldo to command him to attack or to stand down.

Rinaldo waited another moment before speaking. "Danilo, lower your sword. While I appreciate your enthusiasm, I hardly think such a worthy man as *Dom* Valdir has come here with the express intent to assault me."

"As you wish, *vai dom*." Without taking his eyes off Valdir, Danilo replaced his blade in its scabbard. "I beg you to remember that Hasturs have been targets for assassins before this."

He had killed his share of them, defending Regis.

"It seems," Valdir said, attempting levity, "your tame paxman may not be so tame after all."

"I take my oath seriously." Danilo met Valdir's eyes.

Valdir glared back, as if to say, *You were my prisoner once, your life in my hands . . . and can become so again.*

"Enough of this!" Rinaldo's irritation returned in full force. "What do you want, Valdir? I already told your man that I have no time for foolishness."

"The future of Darkover in the Federation is hardly *foolishness*. Now dismiss your paxman so we may discuss the matter freely." Valdir moved toward the larger of the two chairs.

"Sit down if you wish," Rinaldo said tightly, "but I have no intention of wasting my time on affairs that do not immediately concern Darkover . . . with my paxman present or without him."

Valdir did not take a seat. He halted, poised on the balls of his feet. In that moment, he became far more dangerous. Any trained fighter, any experienced politician—in short, any Comyn—would have recognized the threat. Apparently Rinaldo did not, for he reached for the paper and began reading it again.

"I cannot force the Hastur Domain to act," Valdir began, in clear control of himself.

"No," Rinaldo glanced up, "you cannot. Unless you propose to overthrow your precious tradition and place another Domain in ascendancy or find someone to crown as king, you have no power."

"I *do*."

The man was not bluffing. Danilo had seen enough blustering to know the difference. So, apparently, had Rinaldo.

Valdir let the moment stretch out. "I see we understand one another, Lord Hastur. I cannot remove you from the position I have placed you in, and I doubt that taking your lady wife under my . . . *protection* will make any difference to you. Oh, do not look so innocent! You know very well how such things are done—and so does he," meaning Danilo.

"You no longer have the power to advance your pet project," Rinaldo sneered, "and hence must come begging to me like an abandoned cur. I told you before that membership in the Federation is of little consequence compared to the salvation—"

"But these are not my only options. I can convene what is left of the Comyn Council. I can move that each Domain may act as an independent polity unfettered by any previous accord. If, for example, Ridenow wished to join the Federation, we would be free to do so."

Blood drained from Danilo's face.

"Go ahead, then!" Rinaldo snarled. "You cannot coerce me into acting against my conscience!"

"Pardon my intrusion," Danilo kept his face toward Rinaldo, whose ignorance of the implications was appalling. "My lord, how would the Federation respond if only *some* of the Domains applied for membership and others remained opposed?"

"Why, they could do nothing," was the reply, delivered in a careless tone. "How could the Federation accept only *part* of a planet? For that matter, even if all seven Domains wished it, should we exclude the Dry Towns?" Rinaldo snorted in ridicule. "Why not consult the trailmen, as well? Or the *kyrri*?" referring to two of the nonhuman races on Darkover. "Or the *chieri*, assuming any still exist?"

Danilo pressed his lips together to keep from bursting out with the truth. The Federation would jump at the chance to declare the Darkovan government a failed state. They would send military forces to "restore order." Lew Alton had reported on more than one such instance elsewhere, always when intervention was in the best economic interest of the Expansionist Party.

The danger ran deeper than occupation by an interstellar army, dreadful as that might be. Without the Compact, the Council, and the ancient ties of interdependence, there was nothing to stop one Domain from declaring war on another. The armies of Aldaran had marched on Thendara within Danilo's own memory. Every Comyn was taught from childhood about the horrors of the past, incessant warfare when *laran* weapons poisoned water and land, and *clingfire* rained from the skies.

Did Valdir mean to bring about a second Age of Chaos?

Danilo turned to face Valdir, praying his voice would not shake. "You are an educated man, my lord, well versed in history. Do you recall what happened the last time Hastur and Ridenow went to war?"

Valdir paled minutely. If Rinaldo did not appreciate the lessons from that terrible conflict, then Valdir certainly did.

Something shifted in Valdir's demeanor. There was no lessening of determination, only a drawing back from words that could not be un-said . . . and a tinge of consternation. Was he now regretting his alliance with the man he once considered a pliant and useful tool?

"I have taken up enough of your valuable time, Lord Hastur." Valdir bowed, his features carefully masked. "Perhaps we might continue this conversation at a time when you are more disposed to give it your full consideration."

"Perhaps," Rinaldo murmured, "although I cannot tell when that might be."

Valdir bowed again and retreated through the door.

Shaking his head, Rinaldo let out an aggrieved sigh. "Valdir Ridenow is a worthy man in many respects, but he is no better than his fellow idol-worshipers. He thinks only of the worldly advantages of the Fed-eration. I fear his soul will be in grave peril unless he can be brought to see the truth."

He sighed again and picked up the paper. "Meanwhile, I must attend as best I can to those already among the faithful. This—this cannot be allowed to continue!"

"Do you wish to give me any details, my lord?"

"Oh, you will know soon enough. You are well aware that *Domna* Lawton has been among our staunchest allies in bringing God's true word to the people."

"She helped you establish the Chapel of All Worlds," Danilo said neutrally.

"Initially, I was glad of her aid in that enterprise, as well as her counsel in other matters. But she is so much more . . . I believe she is a true prophet, even a saint. Until I met her, I had no idea the Holy One might speak so clearly to one not of our world. Now I am sure it is true."

Rinaldo gestured for Danilo to take the nearest chair. "Did you see the rapture that seized Lady Lawton at my wedding?"

Everyone in the room had noticed Tiphani Lawton's odd behavior. In Danilo's opinion, most of the guests thought it a bizarre off-world tradition for an unrelated woman to pray so dramatically over the head of the bride.

"Until last night, I dared not hope that the Bearer of Burdens might bless me with a sign of divine favor," Rinaldo said, his voice resonant with ardor. "I was taught that miracles come only to those who believe without reservation. No matter how I strove for perfection, I always fell short. I could not rid myself of impure—ah, impious thoughts. Now, surrounded by every worldly temptation, I received an unexpected grace . . ."

He paused, perhaps on the brink of announcing that something amazing and miraculous had happened to him.

"Lady Lawton writes to me now. Oh, that such an affront should come to any of the faithful, but that it should be one blessed with mystical sight! It is insupportable!"

"Why, has some trouble befallen the lady?" Danilo asked.

"Her husband, that *Terranan*! *He* has befallen her! He has accused her—he suspects—it is too outrageous to contemplate!" Throwing down the letter, Rinaldo jumped to his feet and began pacing, kicking chairs as he passed.

"My lord?"

"Read it for yourself!"

Danilo picked up the letter. The paper was Terran manufacture, with the peculiar smoothness that no Darkovan mill could produce. The handwriting was atrocious by Nevarsin standards, as if each letter had been formed by a different child.

The letter was from Tiphani Lawton.

Through the misspellings and incorrectly formed letters, Danilo made out its substance. Dan Lawton had come to the conclusion that his wife's visions were not divinely inspired, as she and Rinaldo knew to be the case, but represented a form of irrational behavior. Although she did not use the word *insanity*, Danilo could read between the lines. Dan wanted her to seek medical care, as if she were ill instead of blessed. She feared what the Terran doctors would do: force her to take drugs that would derange her mind and deprive her of divine guidance. She concluded with an appeal for help that was so overwrought as to be almost incoherent.

Irrational behavior, indeed. Danilo lowered the letter. Even if he had not witnessed her performance at Rinaldo's wedding, her mental instability would have been clear from the letter. Meanwhile, what was he to do? What could he possibly say to make Rinaldo see sense? With Regis, he would have had no hesitation speaking his mind. But Regis would have seen through Tiphani in an instant.

"You see! You see!" Rinaldo snatched the letter from Danilo's hands. "This is why I cannot listen to Valdir! He is in love with the *Terranan,* but I know them for what they are—idolaters who would suppress the truth!"

"Surely a reasoned answer is the best way to lull their suspicions," Danilo suggested, certain that to storm into Terran Federation HQ and carry away the wife of the Legate, even with her willing cooperation, would be seen as a hostile act, one the Federation forces were fully empowered to answer.

"Yes, yes, of course. I must consider how to proceed."

Calmer now after venting his feelings, Rinaldo lowered himself back into the chair. He placed his elbows on the polished surface of the desk and brought his fingertips together, echoing an attitude of prayer. He seemed so deep in thought, Danilo dared not interrupt him.

Then Rinaldo's face brightened. "I cannot, I *will not* abandon her!"

"My lord . . ."

"Do not fear, I will not ask anything of you that is contrary to your *honor.*" Rinaldo inflected the word to sound like an insult. "The moment must be right . . . You will speak to no one about this. *No one.*"

"*Su serva, vai dom.*" Danilo bowed, a shade lower than necessary. Besides, who would he tell that the Head of Hastur and the wife of the Terran Federation Legate were caught up in a shared religious frenzy? Who would believe him?

Winter settled its grip on the city. Each day seemed shorter, bleaker and darker, as if the season hurried to its own death. The storms of autumn gave way to unrelenting cold. Temperatures plummeted, and layers of compacted snow blanketed streets and roof tops. A blizzard, the strongest anyone could recall, blew down from the Hellers. It swept through the Venza Hills to descend upon the city. Streets became impassable, even though crews of men struggled to clear the snow.

The walls of Comyn Castle kept out the worst gales, but the rest of Thendara was not so fortunate. Traffic through the city gates dwindled to a few desperate travelers. Those who reached Thendara brought reports of attacks on human habitations by starving wolves, human and animal, throughout the Kilghard Hills. Giant carnivorous banshees stalked the Hellers passes, venturing down from their usual territories in search of prey. In the city, many muttered that it was the worst winter in memory.

Marriage had not changed Rinaldo's life in any way Danilo could detect. Occasionally, Rinaldo dined with his wife, but more often with Javanne and Gabriel. Javanne looked uneasy, as if she feared Danilo would think her a traitor to Regis by sharing a meal with his usurper. She was in an awkward position as Rinaldo's sister and in her role as Castle chatelaine as well as the wife of the Guards Commander, who served at the pleasure of the Hastur Lord. As far as Danilo knew, Rinaldo had never spoken with Regis after the obligatory visit to admire the baby.

Rinaldo seemed immune to the weather. The monks at St. Valentine's were said to be impervious to the cold, able to sleep on the glacial ice in their sandals and robes. Whether this was myth or a discipline of bodily control, Danilo did not know. Certainly, the monks did not mind the freezing temperatures as the novices and students did.

On all but the bitterest days, Rinaldo went into the city, wearing layers of fur and wool and stout lined boots. He did not insist that Danilo accompany him, but Danilo took pity on the poor Guardsman who would otherwise have had that duty and braved the icy streets himself.

Together they made a circuit of the new *cristoforo* shrines. Now that Rinaldo controlled the Hastur assets, he financed soup kitchens as an act of charity. Exultantly, he pointed out to Danilo how attendance at services had increased. Danilo privately thought these poor wretches were so desperate, they would sit through sermons from Zandru himself for a hot meal.

The days ran on, each darker than the one before, until Midwinter Night drew near. This time was also a great *cristoforo* holiday—the birth-date, they said, of the Bearer of Burdens.

Rinaldo would not permit any of the usual Midwinter celebrations, dismissing them as heretical. Instead, he invited Regis and Linnea as well as Javanne and Gabriel to a late-evening family party. The largest of the parlors had been decorated with strings of dried berries representing the droplets of blood shed by the holy saints, rather than the usual garlands of fir boughs. A generous fire warmed the air, and banks of beeswax candles gave off a gentle, honey-sweet perfume.

Regis arrived early to participate in the customary giving of gifts to the servants. At first glimpse, a fever raced through Danilo. All the things he wanted to say boiled over the cauldron of his mind so that for a moment, he could not even breathe. For a heart-stopping moment, Regis met his gaze.

Rinaldo was watching both of them intently, waiting like a hunter for the slightest lapse. Desperate to do nothing that might betray the depths of his emotions, Danilo threw all his concentration into barricading his mind. Regis answered him with an expression of unconcerned calm.

After the servants went off to their own holiday dinner, the rest of the family came in. Mikhail was not present, having remained at Ardais with Kennard-Dyan. Linnea entered a few minutes later, accompanied by one of the young Castamir ladies. As she and Danilo greeted one another, their eyes met in recognition. A heat rose from her skin, a scent more sensed than felt; she had been nursing little Danilo.

Javanne greeted everyone graciously. Thinner than usual, she wore a holiday gown elegant with lace and silver-thread embroidery but no jewels, as if she had been unable to determine the exact degree of formality of the occasion. Gabriel looked proper and formal in his uniform, with never a word or gesture out of place.

He's angry . . . or afraid. Danilo had known Gabriel since his days as a cadet and could not imagine what would cause fear in the older man. Caution, certainly, for Gabriel's position as brother-in-law to Regis must make his every action suspect.

Servants brought in bowls of mulled berry wine and platters of little seed-cakes that, if not strictly traditional, created an atmosphere of festivity. Rinaldo, playing the generous host, made sure everyone had a full goblet.

"It is time for your gift, my brother." Rinaldo lifted his goblet to Regis. Danilo noticed the hectic, almost feverish light in Rinaldo's eyes.

"I have brought nothing for you," Regis said, "save for my wishes for a peaceful season."

A note in his voice tore at Danilo's heart, a cold whisper slicing through the bright jollity. Danilo had none of the Aldaran Gift of precognition, but he sensed that whatever happened next would change the world forever.

Rinaldo smiled, saying, "Do not distress yourself. I am so happy tonight that nothing can displease me."

The door swung open, and Bettany entered with two ladies in attendance. Her gown, an edifice of brocade and satin, rustled as she moved. A small fortune in Ardcarran rubies set in copper filigree lay upon her exposed bosom and dangled from her ears.

To Danilo's surprise, one of the attendants was Tiphani Lawton. He did not recognize her at first glance, for she wore the long belted tunic over full skirts of an ordinary Darkovan woman. Her hair was caught back in a coil on her neck and covered with a demure coif. But she did not comport herself as a Darkovan woman. Her gaze was bold and direct, and her eyes glowed with brittle fire.

Danilo did not know how to react, whether he should acknowledge her presence. If Rinaldo had managed to spirit her away from Terran Headquarters, Danilo did not want to consider the consequences.

At Rinaldo's gesture, Bettany came to stand beside him. Her color deepened as the other guests bowed to her. Certainly, there was an unwonted freshness to her skin, a new softness to her chin and a fullness to her partly bared breasts.

"Tell them our news, my dearest," Rinaldo said.

She accepted a goblet from a servant and lifted it. "Drink a toast, my lords and ladies, to the son of my lord Rinaldo, which I shall bear come Midsummer's Eve."

For a fraction of a heartbeat, stunned silence reigned. Danilo wondered how it was possible, or how anyone but a *laran*-Gifted healer could determine that Bettany carried a boy child. He could not even begin to consider the political implications of Rinaldo producing an heir. Then Linnea, and a moment later Javanne, recollected themselves enough to utter feminine expressions of joy. Gabriel, moving swiftly to cover the lapse, bowed to Bettany and wished her and her child all happiness.

Regis, his expression unreadable, bowed first to Bettany, as a new mother-to-be taking her place of honor, and then to his brother. "Please accept my most sincere congratulations."

Everyone applauded Bettany and drank several more toasts to her and her unborn child. Then the party split into two groups, the women sitting together, talking about pregnancy and baby clothes, while the men remained standing.

"I know what you are all thinking," Rinaldo said, finishing his goblet and holding it out for a servant to refill. "None of you believed that I—an *emmasca*—could father a child. Admit it, you all believed me incapable."

Gabriel clamped his jaw shut. Regis, meeting his brother's challenging stare, said, "It does happen upon rare occasions, I suppose. Our *chieri* ancestry manifests in the *laran* of some and the six-fingered hands of others. It is said to be especially strong in those who are born as you were, *emmasca*. But the *chieri* are not infertile. They do produce offspring, although very few."

Regis paused, his eyes softening, and Danilo sensed in him one of the few luminous memories from the days of the World Wreckers. A *chieri*, one of the fabled "Children of Light" of the ancient forests, had come forward to help the beleaguered planet.

Danilo closed his eyes, remembering the tall, slender creature, at times like a wild, heartbreakingly beautiful girl, then unquestionably masculine. Keral had given birth to a child, conceived on the same night as Kierestelli and so many others, before returning to the Yellow Forest and the remnants of the *chieri* race. Did Keral still dance under the four moons in yearning, in grief, in ecstasy? And the child, the hope of a fading people, did that child flourish?

Will any of us ever see them again?

"Nothing is impossible to him who puts his faith in the Divine," Rinaldo said. His expression of triumph left Danilo profoundly uneasy.

At least motherhood might bring Bettany a measure of fulfillment. Most well-born girls hoped for nothing more than a comfortable home, a husband and children. Linnea and her sister *leroni* were the exception rather than the rule.

When Bettany moved apart from the other women, Danilo seized the opportunity to extend his felicitation. She responded with a sniff. "My happiness will come from my sons."

After a fractional, astonished moment, Danilo hastened to say, "I hope they will grow to be honorable men."

"They will be powerful and rich! All the world will kneel in fealty to them! Everyone will know that *I* gave them life!"

She paused, chest heaving. Perhaps she was aware that she could easily be overheard. Linnea and Javanne had averted their faces, but Tiphani was staring openly. Bettany turned her back on the off-world woman.

"Everyone said I was worthless. Oh, not when I could hear them, but I *knew*. I heard them whispering in my dreams. Now they will see— I will show them all! Even you with your *kindness*—" and here, Danilo remembered her angry words when he had suggested she seek out Linnea as a companion and guide. Bettany finished with, "*You* won't ever have sons to bow down before mine!"

Danilo did not know which was more appalling, her spiteful delusions or the vision of all Darkover under the rule of her offspring. In such a world, what would become of Mikhail? Of little Dani?

As far as he knew, Danilo had no trace of the Aldaran Gift of precognition, so he could reassure himself that his fears were imaginings born of his own recent captivity and unsettled times, nothing more.

"Oh!" Bettany clapped her hands over her mouth. Her cheeks reddened, and her eyes brimmed with tears. "I didn't mean that! It just popped out! I never know what I'm going to say or feel from one moment to the next!"

"Little one, I did not take it personally. You have not offended me." The only offense came from those who thrust her, ill in mind and unprepared, into such a marriage, but he could not say so to her face.

She lowered her hands. Her lower lip, full and soft as a child's, quivered. She summoned a tentative smile. "There—I am better when I am with you. I think the time on the trail with you and *Mestra* Darilyn and the others was the most fun I have ever had. Now I have no one except those silly maids, and they never tell me anything important. *You* always speak plainly and . . . you're nice to me." With a flutter of her eyelashes, she placed one hand on his arm.

Danilo's chest tightened. By all that was holy, had the girl fallen in love with him? He knew he was reckoned handsome and could have had his pick of women—and more than a few men, too—had his heart not been so focused on Regis. For a hopeful moment, he decided he was mistaken, that she showed him no more favor than was proper to her husband's paxman. Then he saw the sidelong glance and rise of her breasts, felt the caress of her fingers through the fabric of his sleeve, inhaled her perfume, a scent far too provocative for a young bride.

Did she have any idea what she was doing or how many others she placed at risk? She was the wife of the most powerful man on Darkover, and she carried his child, whereas Danilo's freedom and, most likely, his life hung from the slender thread of her husband's good will.

He remembered riding beside Bettany on the trail, her face as he handed her the cup of *jaco* at the inn . . . himself speaking words of encouragement . . . dancing with her at the nuptial ball . . .

Now she was looking up at him with unseemly boldness—no, not boldness. Pleading.

"You will still be my friend, won't you? You'll come and visit me often?"

He removed her hand from his arm and led her back to the other women. "Lady," he said with as much gentleness as he could summon, "that would not be wise for either of us. If you have need of a friend—"

She halted. "You mean Lady Linnea! Why are you always trying to pawn her off on me when it is *you* I want?"

"Because she can help you, truly help you, and I cannot."

"Cannot? Or *will not?*"

Danilo gave Bettany a short bow. He raised his voice so that everyone could hear him as he wished her a healthy child. Bettany looked as if she would stamp her foot. He returned to the other men, and when he glanced back, she had rejoined the women. Linnea, without any sign of having overheard, complimented Bettany on her gown.

Tiphani left the group of women without a backward glance, deserting the lady she purported to attend. Regis, with his usual impeccable grace, bowed to her as to the Legate's wife.

"*Domna* Lawton, I did not anticipate the pleasure of meeting you here. May all the joys of the season be yours."

"Lawton?" She tossed her head, sending the edges of her coif fluttering. "I have left that life behind me. I have a new name, one given to me by the Power we all must answer to. I am no longer Tiphani but *Luminosa*. Through me flows the Divine Light. I have no need for earthly attachments."

Only, Danilo thought wryly, *for the earthly protection of Rinaldo.* But was he her creature, or she his?

". . . only fitting that my unborn son should be attended by the one who foresaw his conception . . ." Rinaldo was saying.

All eyes, for the women had halted in their conversation and now listened openly, turned to Tiphani.

"From the moment of the wedding, the sacred union of masculine and feminine essences," Tiphani said, "I sensed an imminence. You all must have felt the Presence among us! That very night, as I was deep in prayer, I was granted a vision. Light—oh, sweet Divine Light!—filled me. It raptured me beyond any earthly bliss. In the midst of my transport, I saw the Holy Seed flow through me into the womb of the new bride. I was given the knowledge that not only would the handmaiden of my lord Rinaldo be fruitful, but she would carry his firstborn son."

She rushed on, each glowing phrase building upon the one before. Danilo wanted to roll his eyes. He had been taught, as a child of a devout *cristoforo* family, to believe in the saints, but Tiphani Lawton was not among them. Whatever had happened to her sprang from her own unstable mind.

For an instant, Danilo wondered whether the pregnancy was genuine or a concoction of wishful thinking. Such things were possible when weak minds and strong emotions came together. Certainly, the prospect of a legitimate heir would consolidate Rinaldo's power among the Comyn. But how could anyone be sure? Rinaldo was as head-blind as any man Danilo had ever met. Silently, Danilo blessed his choice of Renunciate escorts, for no man could now say he himself had anything to do with her child. The two of them had never been alone for even five minutes.

Unless . . .

Unless she had already been pregnant when he brought her from Serrais. Horrified, he put the thought from his mind.

Bettany jumped to her feet, chattering about her miraculous motherhood. With quiet dignity, Linnea took her aside.

"You must not excite yourself overly, *chiya*. A calm manner and sweet words are beneficial to a woman in your condition. Come and sit beside me."

"You must not address me in such a fashion," Bettany said coldly. "I am Lady Hastur and mother to the future Hastur Lord."

Javanne gasped at this blatant rudeness to a Comynara and former Keeper.

"Your rank is indeed higher than mine, *vai domna,*" Linnea replied with the easy confidence of one who need never bow to anyone. "But I have somewhat more experience in matters of childbearing, have I not?"

"That is all very well, but when my son is born, *your* son will have to do whatever he says."

"I hope our sons will be true and loyal kinsmen," Linnea said. "Let us not argue. If we wish our children to be friends, we must set an example. I have no interest in usurping your precedence, only in your happiness and welfare. I wish to be of help to you."

Tiphani had fallen silent. The men had turned to listen, Rinaldo with a fleeting, black expression, Regis with outright pride, Gabriel with barely disguised relief. Javanne attempted to put a soothing arm around Bettany's shoulders, but Bettany shrugged her off.

"I myself will attend the blessed mother," Tiphani intoned. "We have no need of primitive midwifery or native superstitions. Our guide shall be the Holy Seed itself. Let us retire to pray."

With Bettany at her heels, she swept from the room. An awkward pause followed until Linnea and Javanne joined the men. Little of consequence was said, and the party broke up shortly. Danilo wished beyond words that he were free to leave with Regis and Linnea.

BOOK IV: Regis

26

Late morning sun poured through the windows of the townhouse parlor. After a month of almost continuous snowstorms, the skies had finally cleared. How long the respite would last, no one knew. In the streets, people seized the opportunity to dig out passageways through snow piled higher than a man's head.

Regis, sitting beside the hearth, roused from his musings. The brightness of the day, coupled with the warmth of the parlor, had lulled him halfway into dreaming. On the divan opposite him, Linnea had just rocked Dani to sleep.

Much to her husband's surprise, Linnea had insisted on a separate bedroom down the corridor from his and adjacent to Kierstelli's. Regis thought at first that she wanted to preserve a measure of her former independence. He soon realized the benefits of separating the space in which she devoted herself to her children from the life they shared as a newly married couple. He gave up little of his own customs and preferences, but instead gained from the addition of hers. Each time she came to his bed, she brought a sense of new delight.

Linnea's shawl of soft ivory wool had slipped away, revealing the baby's mouth still pressed to her breast. The sun burnished her hair to a halo of rose-gold. At her feet, Kierstelli sat cross-legged, picking out a melody on the child-sized *ryll* Regis had given her as a Midwinter gift. Sensing his awareness, she looked up and met his gaze without pausing in her music.

A pang brushed his heart. Here he was, warm and comfortable, never hungry, for the cellars and larder were always well supplied. He had at last been freed of the responsibility he had never wanted. He had a wife he loved and respected. More than that, he had a family he had never dreamed possible. To his son, he would be the father he had never known. And yet . . .

And yet, his thoughts kept returning to those who still suffered. The poor, who had little food and no way to buy any, even if they could afford it. The country folk, even colder and hungrier, eating their seed crop from desperation.

And Danilo . . . Always his thoughts came back to Danilo, like an unhealed wound in his heart.

Surely, Rinaldo would value Danilo, would treat him fairly if not kindly. The pain of separation might never pass, but Danilo would be safe and well.

But not with me.

The threat posed by the Federation had receded but was far from resolved. The situation was unstable, dependent on Rinaldo's whim. Since the Midwinter announcement of Bettany's pregnancy, Rinaldo had become increasingly unpredictable, effusive one moment and darkly suspicious the next. Tiphani Lawton now wielded far more persuasive power than Valdir ever had. Valdir and his supporters had not given up their ambitions.

As for poor Bettany, she vacillated from remote and arrogant to childishly needy. In a combination of those moods, she had demanded that Linnea attend her as lady-in-waiting. Regis could not imagine a more perilous situation.

Merilys, who had come to serve Regis and Linnea after their marriage, slipped into the room. She took the sleeping baby into her arms, moving gently so as not to waken him. Regis wondered how she knew when to come, and he decided this knowledge was yet another women's mystery.

When the door closed behind Merilys and the baby, Linnea rearranged the top of her gown, arched her back, and stretched. She looked very young, her movements unselfconscious in their grace, but her expression was somber.

"Regis, with this fine weather, the city will soon be abustle. I will no longer be able to blame being snowed in for not answering Bettany's summons. I fear any further delay will be taken as discourteous at best."

Regis found that his chair had suddenly become too comfortable. He pushed himself to his feet and strode to the window. Over the wall of the garden, he glimpsed people on the street. A rider in the short cloak of a City Guardsman guided his mount between the pedestrians. This district, with its wealthy mansions, was the first to be cleared of snow.

"Then we shall find another reason," he said. "It is an insult to expect you to play nursemaid."

"She has no kinswoman to attend her and is most likely as confused and frightened as any woman pregnant for the first time."

Regis suppressed a smile. "That is compassionate, but it changes nothing."

She came to stand beside him. He felt her ambivalence, her fierce desire to remain with her own baby, to protect both her children.

"What is it, *preciosa*?" he asked. "What troubles you?"

"I cannot set aside the feeling that this poor child needs me. Something is wrong. When I last saw her, at Midwinter, I couldn't monitor her, nor would it have been ethical to do so without her leave. I offered, telling her that Comyn women have done so through the ages. It poses no danger to mother or babe. She grew angry, as if I had insulted her. Should she ask me now, I would not refuse—but I fear the worst."

"And that is?"

She looked up, her gray eyes troubled. "I don't know."

"Do you think she truly wants your help or only to boast that the woman who might have been lady to the Hastur Lord, an Arilinn-trained Keeper, now dances attendance on her?"

From her expression, she thought the same. Carefully, he picked his way through the words so as not to reveal the depth of his fears. "For the sake of our children, I ask you to keep yourself apart from the court and its perils."

It was not so long ago that anyone I loved became a target for kidnapping and threat of worse. The moment Linnea passes through the Castle gates, she becomes vulnerable . . . He could not bear the thought of her in the clutches of his enemies.

But who, he wondered, were his enemies now? Valdir and the other Ridenow? Tiphani Lawton? Or Rinaldo himself?

She shook her head. "What about the risks of defiance? We do not know if this is a passing whim of hers or a test of loyalty. I do not want to move to Comyn Castle, but I would not put you or anyone we care for at risk. Danilo is still in Rinaldo's custody, no matter what it's called."

"That's all the more reason for you to stay here. Bettany cannot command you. She may be Lady Hastur, but she is not queen. I will speak with my brother. If this is his wish rather than hers, if he wants to be sure of me, then I will find another way of demonstrating my compliance."

Linnea arched one eyebrow. *You have never been compliant.*

Regis wanted to laugh and scowl at the same time. True, if old Danvan Hastur, with all his manipulative wiles and force of personality, had not been able to bend Regis to his wishes, then a monk dressed in Hastur robes had little chance. And yet . . . *Grandfather could not force me to marry, and here I am.*

"I do not wish to raise a rebellion against Rinaldo," Regis said, trying to keep his voice light. "If anything, I owe him a brother's love and all the help he will accept. He may have odd ideas, having been raised by Nevarsin monks, but he is not unintelligent. He is perceptive and idealistic. With time and good advice, he will come around."

"You trust him more than I do." She fell silent for a moment. "Still, you are right in one thing. Your brother means to do right. If you can persuade him that I am unsuitable as a waiting-woman, that would be the best solution to this problem."

"Then I will try."

— ✦ —

It still seemed odd to be out in the city without Danilo beside him. Regis felt half-dressed, as if he had left home without his boots. He did what he could to appear inconspicuous. Muffled in a cloak of muted green, his distinctive white hair covered by the hood, he hardly resembled the legendary Regis Hastur. He rode, rather than walked as he once might have, not his Armida-bred mare but a stout gelding, big enough to shoulder its way through a crowd. The dun was shaggy with winter coat, each sturdy foot covered with feathering. It stepped out eagerly, pleased to be free of the stable on such a fine day.

Regis followed the maze of cleared streets, angling toward the Castle. Compacted snow rose like walls to either side, broken at intervals by doors. A handful of children dressed in layers of rags scampered laughing across the top layers, hurling snowballs at one another.

A clearing marked a major intersection where a scattering of vendors had set up their stalls. There was no produce, only hot *jaco* and fried bread twists. An old woman sold knitted mittens from a basket. She offered a pair to Regis. Gravely, he inspected the tiny, even stitches, the soft *chervine* wool. The old woman's expression, dignity mixed with hunger, touched him. Blessing the foresight that had provided him with a purse, he fished out a silver coin. It was more than the mittens were worth, but not so much as to offend her pride.

A little way farther, Regis heard men's voices, rising and falling in rhythmic chant. He drew the gelding to a halt. A strange procession approached. At first, Regis thought it a collection of monks from St. Valentine's. Those in the vanguard wore long brown robes belted with rope, but none were tonsured. The rest, a dozen or so, carried standards with crudely painted *cristoforo* symbols, jingled bells, or pounded on hand drums. They sang,

> *"Lord of Worlds,*
> *Remove our sin.*
> *Lord of Worlds,*
> *The Light Within."*

Regis had heard the chant every morning and every evening of his years at St. Valentine's. At the time, he had thought it tedious and simple-minded. Now, the fervor and insistent rhythm troubled him. The singers seemed to be not so much penitent as demanding. Reluctant to encounter them more closely, Regis loosened the reins and touched the horse with his heels.

A Castle Guardsman took the horse at the gate. A second escorted Regis to the Hastur apartments and his grandfather's—now Rinaldo's—study. The room seemed little changed since Regis himself had occupied it.

Rinaldo sat behind the massive desk. Tiphani Lawton stood beside him, in the place where Danilo should be. She wore a robe somewhat like a monk's, not of coarse brown homespun but stripes of silky white, red, and black.

Where's Danilo? By all the Seven Frozen Hells—

The next instant, Rinaldo caught Regis up in a brother's embrace. Quelling his sudden alarm, Regis tried to return the greeting as heartily as it was given.

Rinaldo released Regis, clapping him on both shoulders. "It's good to see you! This weather has kept us apart, you in your snug little den halfway across the city and me immured in this drafty old Castle."

"I hope I find you in good health. And you, *Mestra* Lawton." Regis bowed to Tiphani.

She lifted her chin. Her features had altered, pared to starkness but still beautiful, her hair cut short and slicked to her skull.

"I no longer bear that tainted name," she announced. "I now answer to the name granted to me by the Most Holy—*Luminosa!* All glory be to God."

"All glory be to God," Rinaldo repeated.

Regis wondered what the Terran Legate had to say about his wife's psychiatric condition now. *Better not to open that subject,* he thought as he took a seat at Rinaldo's invitation. Before the conversation could resume, however, there came a tap at the door.

"Come," Rinaldo called, and Danilo entered.

With an effort, Regis kept his expression calm, as if Danilo meant no more to him than a passing acquaintance. His heart turned into a falcon caged within his chest, beating frantic wings as it tore at its prison. He longed to open his mind to his *bredhyu*. Rinaldo was head-blind and would never notice . . . but Tiphani might. From their earliest meeting, Regis had sensed her psychic sensitivity, perhaps *laran*.

Be still. Say nothing. Do nothing to risk him.

Danilo moved across the room, graceful as always, whole of body and unharmed. He went to the desk and placed a packet of papers before Rinaldo.

Danilo bowed first to Rinaldo, then to Tiphani Lawton—Regis could not think of her as anything else, certainly not that pompous name—and then, without the slightest hesitation, to Regis himself.

Regis relaxed minutely. Danilo's silence had been more eloquent than any greeting. If they had indeed grown apart, if all feeling between them had died, a few meaningless words would have come easily.

Paper crinkled as Rinaldo folded the sheets and set them aside. He turned back to Regis with another smile. "What is the news from the other side of town? How does your wife and your new son? I expect he is trotting about the house by now."

Regis smiled. "Not for some months yet, I think. Babies grow more slowly than that. He still needs his mother's tender care. For his sake, she should remain close by him, at home."

"Of course! I am glad to hear she is such a devoted mother, and you such a solicitous husband and father. You see, my brother, the blessings that come with obedience to Divine Law?"

"I am indeed content in my marriage," Regis said, keeping his eyes upon his brother and not on Danilo.

Confusion flickered across Rinaldo's features. "I do not see why the issue of a mother leaving her own young children should arise—"

"The note," Tiphani said, placing one hand on Rinaldo's shoulder.

"I thought Lady Bettany had sent an apology." Rinaldo scowled. "I *told* her!"

"Do not think harshly of your poor wife." Tiphani's voice turned honey-sweet. "Pregnancy can addle the wits of any woman."

Pregnancy had not made Linnea any less rational. Regis listened politely as Rinaldo explained that, of course, Bettany had not thought of the implications of her invitation.

"In any event, it is not necessary. Lady Hastur is well tended here in the Castle. She wants for nothing, certainly not feminine companionship." Rinaldo glanced at Tiphani.

Regis felt impelled to repeat Linnea's offer, that should Bettany desire *laran* monitoring of her pregnancy, Linnea would be at her service. He did not add that it was an extraordinary privilege to have such care from a Keeper.

Tiphani set her lips in a tight line. Rinaldo's expression, which had been open and earnest, darkened. "With all respect to your lady wife, who seems a model of womanly virtue," he said, "it would not be proper for one who once practiced sorcerous arts to attend my own wife. I cannot allow the innocent souls of both mother and unborn child to be exposed to such an influence, even if unintended."

"*Laran* is not magic," Regis said, caught unawares by the accusation. "We Comyn are not witches. Our Gifts may seem supernatural, but they can be understood rationally and used honorably."

"So you have been misled to believe," Rinaldo said. "I cannot fault you, although you must have learned otherwise from the good brothers at Nevarsin."

Regis recalled that so deep was the *cristoforos'* animosity to mental powers that every stone of the monastery had been laid by human hands, without the assistance of *laran*. "I intended no offense. No harm would come to Lady Hastur in my wife's care."

"I do not doubt *Domna* Linnea's good intentions, but even the strongest mind can be seduced by temptation."

The atmosphere had chilled during the discussion. Tiphani broke the tension, turning to Regis. "We need not discompose your household, Lord Regis. Lady Hastur is in the best hands imaginable, for when the spirit is under Divine guidance, no ill can come to the body. Daily I receive instruction as to her care. No malign influence is permitted to approach her, only those individuals sanctified by the One True God. All will be well, I assure you."

Ice brushed the back of his neck as Regis remembered her tear-streaked face and passionate words: *"I took the filthy thing away from Felix as soon as I realized. Oh, God, it's all my fault! If only I had not been weak in letting Felix have his way! If only I had watched him more closely—"*

Her ignorance had almost killed her own child. Was she now making some bizarre atonement . . . or convincing herself that she was fulfilling a holy mission?

Rinaldo nodded beatifically. Regis could not think what to say. He had faced more challenging situations than he could count, but this declaration left him speechless.

"Surely," Danilo said to Tiphani, moving smoothly into the pause, "your husband can have no objection to your being of such service."

Tiphani shot him a look of unadulterated spite.

So that's where the lines of alliance were drawn. *Be careful, Danilo. Few people are more dangerous than those who believe God speaks through them.*

"Have no fear," Rinaldo said as he patted Tiphani's arm. "I have given you my protection. No one will force you to return against your will."

She shook off his touch. "It's not so simple."

"No, indeed," Regis broke in, "for you are still a Federation citizen, *Mestra* . . . Luminosa, and your husband is the Legate. My brother may be Lord Hastur, but he does not speak for the other Domains. This Castle is the joint property of all the Comyn, controlled by no single house."

It was a clumsy move, speaking to Tiphani but really directing his remarks at Rinaldo: *"What do you think you're doing, harboring a runaway Terran against the wishes of her family? Are you trying to provoke a conflict with the Federation?"*

Rinaldo glared at Regis as if confronting a delinquent student. "You go too far, my brother! How dare you speak so disrespectfully to me, your elder and Head of your Domain?"

"You asked for my counsel once," Regis replied. "Is it disrespectful to speak a truth that might—" He paused, meaning to say, *"prevent a catastrophic decision?"* but, deciding better, finished, "—be put to good use?"

"*Dom* Valdir is always lecturing me on the importance of diplomatic cooperation. I am only one Domain among many . . ." Rinaldo went on, his voice becoming more thoughtful. "There is nothing to stop others from taking independent action, siding against me with Lawton and the Federation. As for the Telepath Council, they are nothing more than a

band of commoners infected by *laran* witchery! No, no, what I need—
what all of Darkover needs—is a strong leader to speak for everyone."

"That is not as easy as it sounds," Regis commented, "even with loyal
supporters and sound advice." He meant Danilo's service and his own
counsel, but Tiphani took it as an oblique compliment and preened.
"As for your situation, *Mestra* Luminosa, you yourself have the power to
resolve the current issue between the Federation forces and Hastur."

"By making peace with my husband, you mean."

Regis nodded. "Is it prudent to involve the most powerful house on
Darkover in a domestic problem?"

"You know nothing of the matter!" She glowered at him. "How full
of advice you are, for everyone but yourself! Regis Peacemaker, Regis
Kingmaker—is that how you intend to make your mark on history?"

"I have no such aspirations," Regis said. "In fact, I would be quite
content if history forgot me entirely."

"We must honor those who have gone before us," Rinaldo stepped
in.

Tiphani, still seething, took her leave so that she might attend to Bettany. The mood remained somber for a time, punctuated by comments
of no consequence.

Then Regis said, "This tension between you—" he did not say *Hastur,* for he meant Rinaldo personally, "—and the Terran Legate is not a
good situation. It can too easily spread to include our entire Domain, as
well as others and the Federation itself. Would you hear my advice?"

"I am always happy to hear what you have to say. However, I question whether you truly understand the matter."

"As far as I can tell, it is a family dispute that ought not to involve
powers of state. Let the Lawtons work out their differences free from
outside interference. Establish a neutral ground where they may speak
with one another without intimidation."

"That is impossible. The matter has spiritual as well as political
implications."

"You mean because the woman is a coreligionist and says she receives visions? Voices, whatever? Rinaldo, those are symptoms of a
sickness of the mind. If she is ill, she needs proper treatment." *And not
blind trust from someone who only reinforces her delusions.*

"I repeat, you do not fully comprehend what is at stake. At first, I could not understand why I had been driven from St. Valentine's into this hotbed of licentiousness. But now, since the Lord of All Worlds has sent Lady Luminosa to guide me, I see my true calling. I am meant not merely to instruct a few boys who, like you yourself, will soon forget their good precepts. My destiny is to cleanse a city, a Domain . . . an entire planet."

Lord of Light! He means it!

Danilo flinched and as quickly recovered himself. Rinaldo gave not the slightest indication he'd sensed the surge of dismay. He continued speaking about the poor, helping them through the winter, or opening the roads to pilgrimage.

Regis peered into his brother's earnest, open face. *He is a good man, for all his early years of isolation from the world. He means to do right in the world, he just has no understanding of what that is . . .*

Rinaldo had fallen under the influence of those who were not so altruistic: first Valdir Ridenow, with his desire to see Darkover a Federation member, then Tiphani Lawton, a disturbed woman only too willing to incorporate Rinaldo's faith into her own grandiose delusions.

My brother needs my help more than ever before. How could he turn his back on Rinaldo, a *chervine* kid among wolves?

27

Winter ended as abruptly as it had begun, as if the sky had exhausted itself. Snow gave way to sleet. From one tenday to the next, the layers of filthy snow shrank. True to his promise, Regis met every day with Rinaldo, except on *cristoforo* fast days. Regis had no idea there were so many saints or occasions for suspending normal business, but he welcomed those occasions to remain with his family.

Despite his lingering grief at being separated from Danilo, Regis found an unexpected peace in the small domestic joys of sitting quietly with Linnea, listening to Kierestelli sing or teaching her the game of Castles, or playing with baby Dani. All those years when he had resisted the pressure to marry, he had no idea what he was refusing. How could he have? He had grown up in a cold and joyless house with only his distant, demanding grandfather and a loving but overworked older sister for comfort. No wonder he had regarded the *catenas* as shackles.

For all his contentment, Regis sensed a growing tension in the city. He saw it in Linnea as well, in the faint signs of restlessness, the flicker of vigilance in her eyes when she thought he was not watching. This idyllic time could not endure. All things changed. Nothing was certain but death and next winter's snow. The milder weather would open the mountain passes . . . and summer would come, with whatever Comyn might observe the traditional gathering in Thendara.

Something else was coming, carried on the seasonal change. The world was no longer frozen solid.

Rinaldo proved an apt pupil; he had been a scholar at Nevarsin and had a good mind, even if he had been trained to memorize without critical understanding. At times, Regis thought his brother's negative attitude toward the *laran* Gifts of their caste had softened. Regis advanced the argument that such abilities, when trained and used properly, could do much good: in healing, in communication across long distances, in mining precious minerals or manufacturing and delivering firefighting chemicals. Once or twice they discussed the possibility of opening the old, disused Comyn Tower if they could find a Keeper and enough *leroni* for a working circle. In the end, however, Rinaldo refused to commit to the plan.

On the subject of relations with the Federation, Regis made greater progress. Rinaldo had all but broken off contact with Valdir Ridenow. Except for his closeness to Tiphani Lawton, Rinaldo had little interest in off-worlders and their material benefits. The Federation seemed to have enough internal difficulties without pressing the issue of Darkovan membership, but no one could predict how long that might last. Sooner or later, Darkover's strategic importance, its location in the galactic arm, would bring it to the attention of the Expansionist Party.

"We cannot accept the meddling of Godless outsiders," Rinaldo stated. "Valdir is right about one thing: the Federation, with its promise of an easier life, has destroyed the moral fiber of our society. Luminosa has seen this in a vision."

Dan Lawton sent increasingly formal demands for the release of his wife, invoking the power of his office as Federation Legate. With all the diplomatic skill he possessed, Regis went about convincing his brother of the unwiseness of interfering between the Lawtons. He brought up the issue yet again at breakfast in the central parlor of the Hastur apartments. It was not the most cheerful of mornings, for the first edge of a storm front obscured the red sun. A damp chill pervaded the chamber.

Even the warmth of the *jaco*, served unsweetened in monastery style, seemed fleeting. Danilo was out on some errand or another.

"Is it not written that a husband is responsible for the keeping of his wife?" Regis asked. "How can he do that when, for all he knows, she is held here against her will?"

"Ridiculous!" Rinaldo snorted.

"Yes, but her husband does not know it. Nor does he know of the work she does here or the companionship she provides to Lady Hastur. He is not an unreasonable man, and he is genuinely concerned about her health. If he were able to reassure himself that she is well, he might even approve the arrangement."

Grudgingly, Rinaldo admitted that Dan Lawton had a legitimate reason to speak with his wife. Regis proposed to arrange a meeting at the Renunciate Guild House. The Guild House had a private room used to negotiate trade contracts, to which men might be admitted. The neutrality of the venue, along with Rinaldo's promise that she would not be coerced into returning to the Terran Zone, should satisfy Tiphani.

"Lady Luminosa," Rinaldo corrected.

"So she is called . . . *here,*" Regis conceded, "but her husband knows her only by her former name."

Servants came in to clear away the remains of the meal. In the tension of the conversation, Regis had hardly touched the buttered pastries or cold meat pie. Rinaldo made no comment; perhaps he thought Regis was practicing abstemiousness.

Rinaldo waited until the bustle faded behind closed doors. "What you propose sounds reasonable, but I do not see the point of it. I have no intention of relinquishing Lady Luminosa, should her husband prove obdurate. It would be wrong to create any expectation that he might be allowed to take her back and subject her to—whatever it is they do there."

"The Terranan are not monsters," Regis said evenly. "They have freely shared their medical and technical expertise, to our advantage. Moreover, they have laws governing their citizens, rights that cannot be taken away."

"I have granted her sanctuary with the inviolable Word of a Hastur."

Rinaldo's voice shifted to a tone Regis was coming to know all too well. In this mood, Rinaldo would not be budged.

Regis was reluctant to let the matter slide. The woman's influence over his brother had grown since Midwinter. He saw no possibility of awakening Rinaldo to the extremeness of her pronouncements; that Rinaldo listened to anyone else was a victory in itself.

"You must honor your word," Regis said. "At the same time, it is unkind to leave Dan Lawton in ignorance about his wife's well-being."

If Linnea were separated from him for this long without so much as a word, Regis would tear apart the Castle walls with his bare hands to find her. Or want to, at any rate.

Perhaps recalling the teachings of St. Christopher, Rinaldo considered the point. Regis offered to take word to the Legate himself, saying, "He trusts my integrity. If I explain the situation, I believe that will put his worries to rest."

"That is a compassionate thing to do." Rinaldo wrote out a safe-passage request to allow Regis to enter the Terran Zone.

Since the day was young, Regis rode the dun gelding directly to Terran Headquarters. A wind had sprung up, damp and ice-edged, slicing through his cloak. He wondered if the fairer weather of the past tenday had been a deceit, winter's mockery, and that true spring would be a long time arriving. At least Linnea and the children were warm and secure. He thought of Mikhail, still at Ardais and well out of Thendaran politics. And Danilo . . .

Here I am, he chided himself, *a mother barnfowl making sure all my chicks are safe!*

Outside the Terran Zone, Regis paid a street sweeper to look after the horse. He passed the checkpoint without incident. One of the Spaceforce guards escorted him to the Headquarters building. In the man's friendly manner Regis read a hope that tensions between Federation and Castle might be thawing. Regis did not disabuse him of the notion.

Headquarters had not changed, not the glass and gleaming steel or the men and women in form-fitting uniforms, or the faint reek of ozone and machine oil; it might have been yesterday that Regis had last walked here with Danilo beside him.

As soon as Regis presented himself to the Legate's office, he was ushered into the inner chamber.

Valdir Ridenow was sitting in one of the two chairs informally placed around a low table.

Dan Lawton stood to greet Regis. Valdir rose as well, an unreadable expression on his face. "Lord Regis, how very good of you to call."

"*Mestre* Lawton," Regis said formally, then inclined his head to the Ridenow lord. "Lord Valdir."

"Lord Regis. Legate Lawton, I believe this concludes our business." With a slight bow, Valdir took his leave.

Once the door was safely shut, and Regis and Dan had seated themselves, Dan leaned forward, bracing his elbows on his knees.

"My god, Regis, what's been going on? One day, Darkover is ready to petition for full Federation membership, and the next, it looks as though we'll be formally evicted!"

"I believe that my brother, as Lord Hastur, has not yet settled on a course of action," Regis replied. "Before we say anything more on that subject, may I ask what *Dom* Valdir wanted? Please tell me it was not to petition for separate Federation membership on behalf of his Domain."

"I doubt the Federation would accept the application even if he did. I can tell you this, for it is public knowledge. *Dom* Valdir and his cousin Haldred have applied for Federation citizenship. He came here today to ask me to expedite the processing, and there is no reason I should not do so. Is there?"

Regis shook his head to cover his surprise. Had the Ridenow given up the cause of Darkovan membership, seeking instead the rights and protections of the Federation? What would come next—exile to the stars, as Lerrys Ridenow had chosen?

"I didn't come here to investigate Valdir Ridenow," Regis admitted. "I'm acting as my brother's agent. I think he's tired of getting complaints from you."

"I've run out of polite ways to say, *Return my wife or else*. What does he think he's doing, holding a Federation citizen? If he wanted to convince the Senate that Darkover is a barbaric planet that must be pacified for the safety of the entire galaxy, he's made a good start."

"I don't think that's what he has in mind. He's not holding Tiphani against her will."

"He's standing in the way of her getting proper medical care, that's what he's doing!" Dan shoved himself to his feet and began pacing. "You should have heard the way she was going on before she made a break for it! I knew she'd been exposed to some bizarre cults on Temperance, but I never dreamed—"

Dan reined in his outburst. "I'm sorry. It's not fair to inflict my feelings on you, but I've had no one else to talk to. Oh, the medics here have diagnoses aplenty for what's wrong with her, but no help for how it makes me *feel*!"

"Helpless. Desperate. Responsible."

Comprehension flickered in Dan's eyes. He lowered himself back into his seat. The color in his cheeks seeped away.

"Regis . . . I didn't think."

Regis made a dismissive gesture. "I've been granted leave to tell you that your wife is well—in body, at least—and content to remain where she is. My brother regards her as a valuable advisor, not to mention a companion for his wife."

"Then heaven help them both! Encouraging her delusions is bad enough, but to be guided by them is insanity!"

"My brother doesn't see it that way, but he has offered to arrange a meeting on neutral ground." Regis detailed the proposal, adding, "I hope you can persuade your wife to accept treatment."

"Tiphani is an adult. I can't force her to come back. Or to get help, unless she's a danger to herself or someone else."

"Giving advice hardly constitutes a criminal assault," Regis observed. "If she feels secure, she will be more amenable to seeing you and Felix, and that may open the door to reconciliation. How is your son, by the way?"

"Confused. Angry. How else should he be?"

"As are you, for good reason. But Felix, having lost his mother, now needs his father more than ever."

Dan lowered his head, his features hidden. Regis thought how easy it was to become mired in a problem that had no solution.

At last, Dan said, "Thanks, I needed that reminder. I hope things work out for Tiphani and she receives the care she needs and returns to her old self. Meanwhile, I can't set everything else aside. I have a son who needs me, as you pointed out, and work commitments." His gaze was steady, his eyes shadowed. "And friends—"

With a quick gesture, Regis forestalled whatever Dan was about to say. "You're a good man and a good Legate with a deep sensitivity to Darkovan culture, but you will be of no use to either us or your Federation if you don't remain neutral." Regis paused to let his words sink in. "Certainly, grant individual citizenship, negotiate trade agreements and leases for the spaceport, and conduct your usual business. But *leave the internal affairs of the Domains to us.*"

"Have I ever done otherwise?"

Regis shook his head. "No, but these are unusual times. We will come through them, and Darkover will reach a new accord with the Federation. I have opinions as to what that relationship should be, as do others. Until then, let us work out our own concerns without any appearance of taking sides."

"As much as I can, I will." Dan paused, his brow furrowed. "Except that . . . you know I tried to delay formal recognition of your brother as Head of Hastur."

"Your technicians took a tissue sample from me for comparison. I appreciate your efforts, Dan. It was a difficult, confusing time. But what you did was hardly interfering with our domestic affairs. You were within your mandate to establish his identity."

Dan shook his head. "It's not that. When we did a genetic analysis of your brother, we mapped all his chromosomes . . ."

Regis still couldn't figure out what his friend was getting at. Then he realized, *all his chromosomes* included those that determined gender. "I know Rinaldo is *emmasca*. He has never kept it secret. The condition may cause other anomalies as well . . . Are you saying he isn't human?"

"I am saying there is no way he could have fathered the child his wife is carrying. It's biologically impossible. He is genetically sterile."

"Then who—"

Did that innocent-seeming child have a lover? Counting backward from Midsummer, she could not have been pregnant when she married

Rinaldo. The implications of a son with no Hastur blood succeeding to the Domain were staggering.

It would break Rinaldo's heart to discover the betrayal.

Dan lifted his hands in a gesture of surrender. "I have no idea, nor will I offer any advice as to what action, if any, you should take."

"I hardly know what is necessary . . . or prudent."

"Was I wrong to tell you?"

Regis shook his head. "The information is safe with me. I must ask you not to tell anyone else."

"Only the doctor who performed the analysis knows. I will speak to her and have the records sealed."

After a few parting comments, the two men wished each other well, and Regis took his leave.

"Tell Tiphani we miss her and hope to see her . . . when it becomes possible."

After the artificial illumination of Headquarters, daylight seemed blessedly muted. Regis strode briskly past the Terran Zone perimeter, his mind still spinning. The air tasted of stone and metal. As he passed the checkpoint, the guard waved, a brief lift of one hand, and then returned to his work.

Regis reclaimed his horse with an additional tip to the street sweeper. Before he could mount up, however, Regis sensed he was not alone. He stilled himself, reins gathered in his left hand. His right hand slipped beneath his cloak to the dagger at his belt.

Air stirred behind his left shoulder. Regis heard a faint scuff of boot leather on stone . . .

The dagger slipped free. Regis turned, shifting his shoulder to swing the cloak out of the way—

And faced Valdir Ridenow, an arm's-length away.

Valdir froze, hands well away from his body. "Lord Regis, we have lived through perilous times, you and I, but do you really think I would assassinate you in the middle of a street?"

"I do not know what you are capable of." Regis slipped the weapon back into its sheath, but kept his fingers curled around the hilt. "Have you something to say to me? A farewell before you take ship for the stars?"

Valdir flushed. "I have no intention of abandoning my caste or my world. Federation citizenship is available to all as our right. It was a precaution only."

"I truly do not care whether you are a citizen of the Federation or the Fourteenth Planet of Bibbledygook." It might be better for Darkover if Valdir *did* go far away. "What do you want?"

"A word."

"Only one? Why would I grant you that much?" An evil mood had infected Regis. Seeing the other man's face, taut and proud, he relented.

"Very well. I am listening."

"It's too early for ale, and this street is far too public," Valdir said. "I know a place in the Trade City where we can get a back room."

"Please don't insult my intelligence." Although Regis could hold his own in a fair fight, old habits still held. He was not fool enough to go anywhere private with a man who had shown himself to be unscrupulous or to allow Valdir any closer than arm's-length. Danilo would have a fit if Regis gave such a scoundrel the chance to slip a blade between his ribs.

"Here? Out in the open?" Aghast, Valdir glanced to either side. The horse's body granted little visual privacy, and every few moments, a pedestrian passed close enough to overhear them.

"I advise you not to say anything you do not wish made public," Regis said dryly.

"You have no reason to trust me . . ." When Regis made no reply, Valdir went on in a rush, "Lord Regis, we've had our differences in the past. I never thought to say this to your face, but I—we—no, I cannot shift any part of the blame to my cousins. They only followed where I led."

Was Valdir trying to *apologize,* to admit he'd made a mistake?

"I know you think my methods improper—" Valdir said.

Criminal, more like.

"—but I am not a man who shrinks from what must be done. I was right in principle, if not in my choice of an ally."

"My brother, you mean."

Valdir's expression hardened in response.

"You thought you could manage him," Regis persisted, "like a puppet. But he has priorities of his own and no interest in your precious Federation. You put him in power, and now you must deal with him."

"He won't *listen*! It's impossible to have a serious discussion with him! He's unstable, out of control! I don't know what he'll do next—no one is beyond his reach."

Regis straightened, the joints of his spine crackling with tension. "Why should I help you with the mess you've dug yourself into? Why should I do anything at all for you?"

"I acted only as I thought best," Valdir repeated.

For a long moment, the two men stared at one another. Regis remembered Dyan Ardais saying very much the same thing. The man called Kadarin had doubtless thought so, too.

"Better men than you have done terrible things *for the good of Darkover*. How does that lessen the harm they caused or restore the lives they destroyed?" Black rage boiled up in Regis. "You put Rinaldo where he is and made sure I had no power to oppose you. You married off your own kinswoman to him, though she was a child with no understanding of what that meant.

"You set Haldred as my jailor," Regis stormed on, "you cut me off from friends. You kidnapped two innocent men, one hardly more than a boy, a deed so lacking in honor that it should haunt you to your grave.

"And you threatened to murder my paxman . . ."

Valdir blanched.

"So now you come whining to me that my brother has a mind of his own? I say, you can choke on it. There are more important things at stake than your petty ambition! Go home to Serrais and tend to your people, or get yourself to Vainwal like your kinsman Lerrys. Or freeze in Hell, for all I care! Just don't expect any sympathy from me!"

Regis swung into the saddle, leaving Valdir standing alone.

The ride back to the townhouse settled his temper somewhat. The sky still threatened, but the storm was not yet upon him. The last portion of the trip, he found himself longing for the sunlit parlor, Linnea's steadfast warmth, and the laughter of the children, as if these could stand as bulwarks against the cruelty of the world.

The moment Regis entered the foyer of the townhouse, he knew something was wrong.

"Oh, Blessed Cassilda, you're back!" Merilys rushed through the interior door, face red, hands fluttering.

"What's happened?"

"*Domna* Javanne—"

The sound of incoherent sobbing came from within, carrying the unmistakable imprint of Javanne's *laran*. Regis thrust his cloak into the hands of the trembling servant and hurried inside.

The uproar led him straight to the family parlor, no longer a haven of tranquility. Javanne hunched on the divan, wailing. Linnea sat beside her, one arm around Javanne's shoulders, speaking soothing words. Neither child was present, but surely Kierestelli must have sensed the jangled waves of grief and fury.

Gabriel—

Javanne looked up, saw Regis, and burst out in renewed weeping. He hesitated, feeling helpless in the face of such feminine outburst. If Linnea could not calm Javanne, then what could he do?

But Javanne was his sister, and she had been as kind an older sibling as she could. He lowered himself to the divan on Javanne's other side and took her hand in his. Her skin was moist from wiping away her tears.

"*Breda,* you are safe with us. Let us help you."

Javanne's shuddering lessened, but she could not speak, only shake her head.

Linnea said, "She held herself together long enough to tell me that Rinaldo has dismissed Gabriel as Commander of the Guards."

"Why, for what cause?" Regis asked. Gabriel was one of the most capable and respected Guards officers in a generation.

"None that Javanne knew." Linnea's brows drew together and her lips tightened. "Regis, how can your brother do such a thing? He does not have the authority!"

"I'm afraid he does," Regis said with a twinge of regret at how easily and dispassionately his grandfather's lectures returned to him. "He is Lord Hastur and, nominally at any rate, Regent of the Comyn. The Comyn Council no longer exists, and with Lew Alton off-world, no one else has the rank to challenge him."

Javanne straightened up, struggling visibly to control her sobs. "He—he—"

"The Lanarts have some claim to Alton," Regis said thoughtfully. "Gabriel has a basis to challenge the decision, and many would stand with him."

"See, it's not so bad—" Linnea began.

"You don't understand!" Javanne burst out. "He's *taken* Ariel!"

28

*T*aken *Ariel?*

Javanne took one deep breath after another, but managed to keep from bursting into renewed tears. Over her head, Regis met his wife's eyes. Linnea's bone-deep fear shivered through him. His first coherent thought was that Valdir Ridenow was up to his old schemes, and what could he want with Gabriel and Javanne—

No, Valdir tried to warn me.

"What do you mean, *taken?*" Linnea prompted Javanne.

"I left her alone—with her governess—in our quarters. Only for an hour, while I tended to—there's so much to do, and Bettany's useless! When I got back, Ariel was gone—the governess half out of her mind—a note—"

Javanne fumbled in a pocket and drew out a paper. Hand trembling, she held it out to Regis.

"*Dear sister,*" he read the scholarly script aloud for Linnea's sake.

"*Be at ease concerning the welfare of my niece. She is well, and her spiritual development is now properly*—" with each phrase, his heart sank lower "—*in the care of Lady Luminosa. Every means will be taken to ensure her continued safety, but it would be imprudent to interrupt her religious education.*

"*Rinaldo Felix-Valentine, Lord of Hastur*"

"May all the demons in Zandru's Seven Hells curse him!" Javanne cried. "Oh, my poor little girl!"

"It seems," Linnea said, filling the brief pause, "that Rinaldo has learned his lessons from Valdir Ridenow all too well. I cannot think why he would want to set aside such a capable and loyal Guards Commander as Gabriel—"

"Because my husband *is* loyal, that's why! Loyal to the Comyn," Javanne muttered.

"—except to prevent Gabriel from stopping him," Linnea finished.

Memories flooded Regis of the sickening fear when Danilo and Mikhail had been held prisoner. He would have done anything, given anything—even his own life—to save them. Danilo was an adult and Mikhail almost so, but Ariel was just a child . . .

Blessed Cassilda, what kind of monster would do this to a little girl?

"He won't harm her. He still needs your cooperation," Linnea was saying to Javanne in that cool, rational tone of hers. "Until we can find a way to release her, you must pretend to go along."

Javanne gave Linnea a glassy-eyed stare of incomprehension. Her desolation shocked Regis into action. When he had developed near-fatal threshold sickness, she had reached him with her mind. She had talked him through the worst of it until his life was no longer in danger.

Regis grasped Javanne's shoulders and forced her to look at him. She flinched at the first contact, but she did not resist. Her eyes reflected things that were not there.

Breda. Gently he opened his mind to hers, inviting her permission to make contact. She lowered her barriers.

He moved through the brittle flare of her terror, the confusion and grief—not only the loss of her daughter but the festering resentment over Mikhail, the son taken from her years ago to be the Hastur heir Regis needed. He sensed love twisting into bitterness and blame, at herself, at Mikhail for deserting the family—*running away to Ardais to save his own cowardly skin—no longer a son of mine!—*

I must do something to ease her hurt, he thought, but had no time for it now.

At least Mikhail is beyond Rinaldo's reach. For the moment.

Regis turned his attention back to the churning morass of his sister's emotions. *You are Hastur, and Comynara, grand-daughter of the greatest statesman of our time.*

The crazed light in her eyes shifted, now a clear blue mirror. He conjured images of a woman whose sense of honor and duty had made her a credit to her Domain, one who had taken on responsibilities far beyond her age. A competent, resourceful wife and mother . . .

Regis startled at Linnea's light touch on his arm. He had lost all sense of passing time. Javanne slumped beside him, pale and drained but calmer. Merilys entered with a tray bearing a pitcher of *jaco,* a tureen of soup, a plate of cheeses, and a basket of nut-studded rolls. At first hesitantly and then with ravenous speed, Javanne devoured the meal.

"I will speak with Rinaldo," Regis assured her. "He still respects my counsel. I will make him see reason."

"We must think carefully on how to proceed," Linnea said.

Javanne got to her feet. "I had best return to the Castle, so messages can reach me without delay." She looked a little unsteady as she took her cloak from the servant.

Regis asked one of servants to order a litter for Javanne's comfort. When it came, she paused at the door, gave Regis a hard look, and then departed.

"If you were anyone else, I doubt she would trust you." Linnea dropped into a chair and closed her eyes. The skin around her mouth had gone white.

Regis took one of her hands in his, feeling the chill in her slender fingers. "I must go to my brother. I cannot allow my sister to suffer like this."

"You must not go." Linnea shook her head. "Not yet."

He knelt beside her, peering into her drawn face. Her eyes burned against the paleness of her skin. "There is no one else he will listen to."

"Ah, my love, for a man who has grown up in a hotbed of Comyn politics, you are an incurable idealist. Don't you see? He'll come after *our* children next if you dare breathe a word against him. Your plan to guide him has failed."

Our children. Baby Dani—and Kierestelli.

His muscles went soft with horror. He wanted to contradict her, but in the pit of his belly, he knew she was right.

Regis could not accept that Rinaldo was beyond persuasion. He must give his brother a chance. What else could he do, he who had placed Rinaldo in a position of such power?

Something red and hot, implacable, surged up behind his throat.

Never again will I bend to the will of one who would make hostages of those I love!

"We must get the children beyond his reach," Regis said. "You'll have to go, too."

She lifted her chin, and he saw the negation in her eyes. "That would set the hunt on us for certain. I must remain here, visible. But you must take Stelli to safety."

"Leave you—at the mercy of kidnappers?"

"I am not helpless." She drew herself up, and an invisible mantle of power shimmered around her shoulders. "I was a Keeper, and no man touches me without leave. I will be able to keep Dani close to me and protect him, but I cannot see to both children. Stelli is more vulnerable, for she is at the right age for Rinaldo's school. Regis, promise to take her to those who will understand her—not the Terrans!"

Regis clambered to his feet. He could not afford the luxury of deliberation. The situation called for speed.

Where would his daughter be safely beyond the reach of even a Hastur Lord? And who would nurture her spirit?

Regis summoned a servant and ordered a horse to be made ready immediately. The Armida black was too old, so it must be the dun gelding. He would travel as he had before, in plain clothes, with his face and hair hidden.

"I'll be but a moment." He paused at the door to look back at Linnea. "See that she's warmly dressed."

Linnea did not ask where he was going. They both understood that no one, not even she herself, must have that knowledge.

Regis never knew what Linnea told the little girl. When, a quarter of an hour later, he swung her up on the saddle in front of him, Kierestelli looked at him gravely and said nothing. Linnea had bundled her in a servant's cloak. She was so light, like a bird. With a pang, he thought how easily those winged creatures could be broken.

Linnea had packed a set of saddlebags such as any man out for a casual ride might carry. She handed Regis a leather belt, heavy with hidden coins. Kierestelli reached out a hand to her mother; Linnea touched the girl's fingertips, and Regis felt the connection between them.

Be brave, my treasure. I do not know when I will see you again, but you will always be in my heart.

The dun pulled at the bit, snorting in excitement. Regis stroked the heavy neck; the beast would need all its strength for the road ahead. Linnea swung the gate open.

A hundred phrases rose to his tongue and died there.

If I don't come back—

Aloud, he said, "Do what you can to hide my absence. I may be a tenday or more."

She nodded, a quick decisive dip of her chin, a pulse of warmth caressing his mind, and then the dun surged through the opening and the gate closed behind them.

The most difficult part would be getting out of the city. Too many of the Guards knew him, but most recognized only the trappings of a Hastur Lord, not his features or posture. They would expect him to have an escort, for he rarely left his own walls without Danilo or a Guardsman.

No alarm had yet been raised. Unless Rinaldo meant to seize hostages from all his family members—a thing Regis could not contemplate even now—there would be no reason to forbid Regis from leaving the city. If questioned, Regis would simply have to bluff his way through as he'd done in his younger days.

As luck would have it, as Regis neared the Traders Gate, a procession approached from outside, some in costumes resembling monk's robes, others in rags.

> *"Lord of Worlds,*
> *Remove our sin.*
> *Let the cleansing*
> *Now begin."*

Mingled with the ringing of bells, the chanting grew louder. Farmers drew their carts aside, worsening the congestion at the gate. Until that moment, Regis had never thought any good might come from Rinaldo's pilgrimages.

The Guardsmen rushed to tackle the disorder, leaving a space wide enough for a single horse. Regis touched his heels to the dun, and it surged through the opening. Once beyond, Regis maneuvered through the milling pilgrims, farmers, wagons, and laden pack animals. A white-bearded fellow in a shepherd's coat pulled his *chervine* team to a halt to let him pass. "The lass looks ill."

Regis nodded his thanks. These simple people saw him not as a Comyn lord but as a father with a child in his arms.

In a surprisingly short time, the open road lay before them. There was still no sign of alarm or pursuit. Regis lifted the reins, and the dun shifted into an easy, ground-covering jog.

Kierestelli huddled against his chest, enduring the jarring gait without complaint. As they climbed the long slope into the Venza Hills, Regis drew the horse to a walk, letting it breathe. Near the top of the pass, he halted.

"Let's rest here. Would you like to walk a bit?"

She jumped lightly to the ground. Regis was glad to stretch his legs. He'd been too long in the city and too little in the saddle. Joints and muscles unaccustomed to long riding would be sore tomorrow.

The child looked back on the city. "I'm not coming back, am I, Papa?"

What did Linnea tell her? Or what had Stelli herself guessed?

"Of course you are," he hastened to reply. "I will come for you when the trouble is past."

She seemed all at once bewildered and wise, terrified and unshaken. He did not want to frighten her with tales of men who would threaten children. He would have given anything to reassure her that the world was a safe place and everyone wished her well.

It would be a lie, as he himself had learned at an early age. When this crisis had passed, there would be other threats. No child of his could ever be carefree, not until the four moons fell from the sky. There would always be a compelling cause and a man willing to use violence to advance it.

This was why the Comyn had adopted the Compact, to limit violence to weapons that placed the user at equal risk. No *clingfire* would rain destruction from the skies, no bonewater dust would poison generations to come. No *laran*-fueled inferno would turn cities to ashes and spaceships to crumpled wreckage.

Was Rinaldo guilty of another violation of the Compact by seizing little Ariel, who had no means to defend herself? Regis thrust the thought aside. He would deal with his brother once this precious daughter was safe.

While these thoughts jumbled in his mind, Kierestelli had been studying him. In her silvery gaze, he read trust but also a growing wariness. She understood, in a deep, wordless fashion, that she was being taken away from those who wished her harm . . . because the adults she depended upon could protect her in no other way. He wanted to deny it, to weep with helpless anguish.

"If . . . anything happens, no one must know who you are," he said as they mounted up again. Thendara's towers disappeared behind the curve of the sharply rising hills.

"Am I to have a new name? Am I to forget you and Mama?"

Such questions from so young a child. His heart ached.

"I hope you will never forget us as we will never forget you. But a new name is a good idea, don't you think? A temporary name for the time you are away. Would you like to choose it?"

"I will think of one."

Days passed, falling into a rhythm of travel. Skills Regis had not used in years came back to him: how to set a pace that both rider and horse could maintain, when to rest, where to find water and food. At first, they came upon an inn or small village at the end of each day's travel. Here they found stabling for the horse, hot meals for themselves, and sometimes a bath. As the lands grew wilder, human dwellings became scarce. Regis was leery of using the public travel-shelters for fear of being remarked and remembered. They might also encounter bandits who, caring nothing for shelter-truce, would see him as one man to be easily overpowered, his goods and horse seized. In the end, he took the risk. If he had been alone, he might have chanced finding what shelter he could. The nights were still cold and wet with freezing rain turning into snow, and he decided the greater danger was to Kierestelli's health. Fortunately, they never met other travelers. Some god—Aldones himself—watched over them.

They reached the River Kadarin on a sullen gray afternoon. The water was turbulent with its own storms. Froth laced the slate-dark water. The far shore was rocky, the trees leafless and stark as a thicket of thorns. A bitter wind whipped down from the Hellers. The dun tossed its head, tail clamped against rump. It didn't like this place.

Me, either. Regis remembered stories of wolves ravening through the wild lands beyond the Kadarin. Human wolves roamed there as well.

The bank curved into a natural cove where a ferry boat was tied up at a wharf. A hut and outbuildings stood nearby, and a thread of smoke curled upward from a crude stone chimney.

Regis called out a greeting. An old man emerged from the hut in response. His beard was a wisp of river foam, his back bent, and his movements spare and nimble. He halted a few paces from the horse and swung his head from side to side in an odd searching gesture. Cataracts whitened his eyes.

"We seek river passage, friend. Is the ferryman about?"

"He stands here before you."

Before Regis could stop her, Kierestelli jumped to the ground. She showed no fear, only curiosity. Awe lighted the ferryman's weathered features.

"Forgive me, Child of Grace! I never thought to behold one of the beautiful folk!"

Kierestelli turned back to Regis with puzzlement in her eyes. "Papa, what does he mean?"

Blessed Cassilda, he thinks she's a chieri!

"We must cross the Kadarin as soon as possible," Regis said.

"Aye, and on to the Yellow Forest." The ferryman nodded, as much to himself as to anyone else. "Long have I searched for them, back in the days when I still burned with dreaming. But they would not be found. Not by me, oh, no, not by the likes of me. But you, you with this child I mistook for a moment . . ." He tilted his head, and Regis had the uncanny feeling that the old man saw far more in him than a tall man in a hooded cloak, that the ferryman saw through the Hastur beauty to the very heart of his cells and the *chieri* lineage of the Comyn.

". . . I think *they* will find *you*."

Uneasy, Regis glanced at the river. The ferryman was not only half blind, but half crazy as well. Still, who could tell about anyone who lived here, on the border of the wild lands? And who was the greater fool, the old man with his dreams of searching for a lost, ancient race in the trackless forest, or Regis for believing him?

Regis hesitated as the boatman shuffled off toward the ferry, gesturing for them to follow. Then Kierestelli pulled at his hand. She appeared to have no doubts. He decided to trust her instinct. In the end, what choice did he have? They could not cross the Kadarin on their own.

The boatman made the ferry ready and gestured for them to board. He turned his face toward the river, although how even a sighted man could make out anything in the shifting currents, Regis did not know. Kierestelli jumped, light and nimble, onto the ferry's flat surface.

The dun snorted and balked at the edge of the wharf. Regis took hold of the reins and brought the horse's head down. Speaking soothingly, he stroked the tense neck. As far as he knew, he had no trace of the Ridenow Gift of empathy with animals, but he had handled horses all his life. The terror in the dun's eyes faded. Its muscles relaxed, and it dipped its nose. It moved forward, lifting each foot high. Its hooves made a hollow sound on the wooden deck

The boatman cast off the mooring lines and poled the ferry away from the shore. Seized by the currents, the craft rocked and tilted. The gelding tensed but held steady. Kierestelli positioned herself at the rail and peered over the purling waves.

At first, it seemed the currents were shoving and pulling the little craft and that all the boatman's efforts had no effect. They would surely be carried downstream or overturned to drown. The old man showed no fear. His expression, eyes half closed, nostrils flaring as if to catch the river's scent, resembled that of a hunter closing on his prey . . . or a lover wooing his lady.

The motion of the ferry changed. The sounds of water and wind blended like music. They glided across the river, slipping through the waves like dancers moving through the figures of a set. Kierestelli clapped her hands and the boatman grinned.

When the ferry reached the wharf on the far side, Regis almost felt sorry the crossing was over. He paid the boatman more than the usual fee. The dun leaped free of the boat and clattered across the wood-plank wharf, eager for solid land.

Before them lay tangled thickets and broken rocks rising to hills covered by twisted, leafless trees. The air was less chill than over the water but also less welcoming. It seemed to Regis that winter had never lifted from this forest.

Regis lifted Kierestelli to the horse's back and then mounted behind her. She stared at the ferryman for a long moment, but he was already turning the boat.

"He thought I was one of the Beautiful Folk of the Forest," she said in her piping child's voice. When Regis made no immediate answer, she went on, "That's where you're taking me, isn't it?"

Even before it came into view, Regis scented the Yellow Forest. They had been traveling for days, camping cold and rough at night, forcing their way through narrow openings and up jagged trails. Regis had begun to wonder if he had made a terrible mistake, if he had risked both their lives on a panic-born impulse. More than once, he thought they were lost. Under the overcast sky, the hills looked the same in every direction. Each time his courage wavered, however, the ghost of a trail would beckon and the horse would step forward, as if on the way to its own stable.

On the fourth afternoon, the air, which had previously carried only the smell of cold wet earth, grew warmer. They had been following a path along the side of a hill, dipping and then laboriously climbing again. Gnarled black-barked trees and underbrush had blocked their view. As they came around the next curve, the vegetation thinned. The path widened, dry and gravelly, as it led upward.

They crested the rise. Regis drew the horse to a halt and breathed in astonishment. The entrance to a wooded valley stretched before them. The trees shimmered, their trunks gray, their leaves pale yellow. A breeze turned the foliage into a rippling carpet of gold.

The Yellow Forest.

The next moment, the light shifted and the forest was no longer a jewel-bright garden but only a patch of trees clinging to last autumn's leaves. They looked old, withered. Soon they would fall, from the battering of winter storms or the simple erosion of time. New growth would take their place, according to the natural cycle. There might be a dozen, a hundred such valleys through these mountains.

Regis felt his heart sink within his chest. The air, which had seemed so sweet, turned ashen. Hope had illuminated the scene below, but only for a moment.

They were almost out of food and probably lost. Kierestelli had not complained, but he could see in the gray tinge around her mouth that she was near the end of her strength.

Regis nudged the dun with his legs, and the horse started downhill, tucking its hindquarters. Knowing better than to hurry the beast, he let it set its own pace.

The bottom of the slope led to an apron of gravel and wind-twisted weeds. The gelding's hooves rang on the loose stones. The place felt empty, without even the cry of a far-off raptor or the skitter of insect or rodent. The forest seemed to be holding its breath. As Regis halted the gelding a few paces before the edge of the trees, he sensed a flicker of—vitality? awareness? or simple wariness of any encounter in such a remote and lawless place?

"Halloo, the forest!" He raised himself in the stirrups. "I am Regis Hastur, and I seek the Folk of the Yellow Forest!"

He paused, not sure if he truly wanted an answer. Then a notion came to him that whether or not the last of the *chieri* lived here, he ought to request permission before entering.

"I ask your leave to search for them here."

He waited for a long moment, and then another. There was no response. Of course not. What had he expected, that the trees would part and open a path for him? That one of the Beautiful Folk would step forward, hands raised in welcome? Keral himself?

Keral . . .

The *chieri* had come down from these mountains to seek Regis, to offer help during the crisis of the World Wreckers. At first meeting, Keral had seemed a tall boyish figure with the exquisite beauty that marked Regis and all his kin. The *chieri* was deceptively strong and yet possessed an endearing uncertainty. How much courage it must have taken to leave everything safe and familiar, to journey into a land of strangers and their machines.

Keral, no longer in neuter phase but fully female, dancing in ecstasy, silken hair rippling around the slender body . . .

Keral's radiant smile as he gazed down upon his own baby, the first chieri *to be born in so many years . . .*

After the departure of the World Wreckers, Keral and his child had gone back to the Yellow Forest, or so it was supposed. His mate, a Terran doctor, had disappeared about the same time. Keral's child would be the same age as Kierestelli . . .

The dun had started moving forward of its own accord, neck arched, each foot placed with ceremonial precision. Regis sat, hands quiet on the reins, trusting the animal's instinct.

They passed the edge of the forest, moving through dappled shade. Dry leaves crackled under the horse's tread. A breeze ruffled branches overhead. Again came that hint of sweetness in the air, that stirring of life . . .

With it came a faint mental touch, so delicate that Regis could not be sure he had sensed it. Kierestelli shifted her weight, pressing against him. She took the reins from his hands. In trust, he closed his eyes, lowered his mental barriers—reached out with his *laran.*

Regis? Is it you, my friend?

Keral!

As quickly as it had come, the contact vanished. Regis shuddered with the recoil. No easy fading this, but a severing, brutal in its finality. Only a moment ago, his mind had been filled with the *aliveness* of the forest and the presence of Keral. Now he felt only an aching absence.

He would have given up in utter desolation, would have surrendered to a loss too great to bear, had the horse not kept going. The beast never paused in its careful stride.

How long they continued like this, Regis could not have said. He lost all awareness of the swollen Bloody Sun creeping across the sky beyond the canopy of wind-kissed leaves. Unshed tears left him half-blind. After a time, he became conscious of someone singing. He could not make out words, only a melody compounded of hope and regret, of joy remembered and echoed.

The singer sat in the saddle before him, his own daughter.

The horse came to a halt in a clearing. Slanting light touched the grasses and the low brush that, against the order of the season, bore a profusion of star-bright flowers. Regis breathed deeply, inhaling their perfume.

Kierestelli gestured that she wished to get down. Regis dismounted and helped her to the ground. She walked to the center of the clearing and halted. He hesitated, unsure if he should follow. Beside him, the gelding stood as if rooted in the layers of fallen leaves, head up, ears pricked, nostrils flaring.

Suddenly Kierestelli laughed and glanced back at Regis, her face alight. The next moment, something flickered in the forest directly ahead, a shift of light-filled shadow.

A *chieri* stepped into the clearing. Regis caught his breath, but it was not Keral. This creature was far older, more ancient even than the trees behind him. Like Keral, he was tall, willowy thin, and seemed to dance rather than walk across the grass. He wore a flowing garment of the same opalescent silver as his hair. Bones arched, delicate and strong, beneath milky skin. The eyes that watched Regis with wary regard were likewise pale, almost colorless. And cool, neither welcoming nor hostile. Measuring.

"Child of Grace . . ." Without conscious intent, Regis formed the traditional greeting. He wanted to rush forward, to fall on his knees before this being of a race that had traveled the far reaches of space before his own kind had learned to walk upright.

Keral had been a child, lost and overwhelmed in the land of men. This *chieri* was old, experienced, and in his own territory.

But Regis was Comyn, and Hastur. Whether his own lineage descended from the first Hastur, son of Aldones who was Lord of Light, or whether from the interbreeding of lost Terran colonists with this ancient race, his heritage was still a proud and honorable one. Respect he would offer, for respect was certainly due, but not groveling.

He came forward and bowed. "*S'dei shaya,* Noble One." *You lend us grace.*

"What seek ye here?" The voice was light and clear, the words an ancient form of *casta.*

"I am Regis Hastur, friend to the one of you known as Keral, and I seek protection for my child."

For a long moment, the *chieri* stared at Regis. Meeting that gaze was like looking into the heart of a living starstone.

"Keral has told us of your people, who kill their own young."

Regis held himself erect, although he wanted to cover his face in shame that humans could threaten children, even babes in their cradles. His throat closed around the cry—*"No, not all of us!"*—but it was true. Whether by direct assault, by abuse or neglect, his kind did not always cherish their children or protect them from those who meant harm. He had lost enough of his own *nedestro* offspring, had seen the horrendous damage done to those who survived, even Lew's daughter Marja, even Lew himself . . . even he, Regis . . .

The truth, then.

Regis opened his mind to the slender, gray-eyed creature before him. *Chieri* were telepathic. Let this one look into his heart and see the good and the ill, the honor kept and betrayed, the hopes cherished, all his failures revealed. Under that uncompromising regard, he had little confidence in his own worthiness, but he had every faith in Kierestelli's.

Not for my sake, but for hers, I ask this.

He offered the image of his own brother, learning the ways of power from the likes of Valdir Ridenow . . . *allowed* that power by Regis himself.

The time for making excuses for Rinaldo, for rationalizing and temporizing, had passed. No matter how much Regis wanted to think well of his brother—and there *was* goodness in Rinaldo, albeit colored by fanaticism—Regis could no longer stand by, tacitly cooperating with the abuse of power.

If you will keep my child safe so that I may act without fear of retaliation upon an innocent, then I will stop him.

Silence, waiting. Then: *How?*

In that question, Regis sensed the *chieri's* abhorrence of violence. *Chieri* did not kill, Keral had insisted; they did not even eat meat.

Truth, came from the *chieri's* mind. *Truth, not fine words.*

"I do not know," Regis said aloud, "I will find a way."

The *chieri* shifted his gaze from Regis to Kierestelli. A gust of air, warm with the scent of flowers, ruffled the silver-gilt hair. Kierestelli took a step and then another, and then she burst into a run. The *chieri* scooped her up in his arms. With a smile of heartbreaking radiance, he glanced once at Regis, then faded into the forest.

"Wait!" Regis had anticipated time to say his farewells, to reassure Kierestelli that he would come for her once the danger was passed.

To tell her that he loved her.

The *chieri* had disappeared, leaving a rustle of dead leaves and a sudden chill in the air. With a shiver, Regis wondered if he would be able to find this place and its inhabitants again. He envisioned himself riding through these hills, straining to catch a hint of gold in the trees, each time returning with a heart filled with ashes. He saw Kierestelli grow more and more apart from the human world, cherished but always an outsider. He felt the bitterness festering within her spirit as if it were his own.

He said he would come for me, but he never did. Is that how she would become a woman, how she would think of her father?

Memory nudged him, offering comfort: What had the ferryman said?

"They *will find* you."

29

Through the return journey, slower because of the weariness of the horse, Regis tried not to anticipate what he would find. On those occasions when he allowed his thoughts to leap ahead to Thendara and what might have unfolded in his absence, ill-omened images assailed him.

His absence had gone unnoticed . . . he had been declared a traitor . . . Linnea and the baby were safe, and Ariel back with her family, all forgiven . . . Linnea was imprisoned, Danilo executed—no, the thought was too devastating to contemplate—*Javanne and Gabriel were outlawed . . . the Federation had intervened and Rinaldo was now a prisoner . . . there was open fighting in the streets, the Terran Zone blockaded . . . Rinaldo was beside himself with worry, eager for a reconciliation . . .*

It was enough to drive a man mad.

Regis stopped at an inn along the Venza Road. The dun had been flagging since noon, and he himself was in need of a bath and shave. Regardless of the disguise in which he had left Thendara, Lord Regis Hastur could not come riding into the city looking like the roughest of mountain men. With luck, he would be able to slip past the gates with as little notice as he had left. If not, he must maintain at least the semblance of a proper Comyn lord.

The inn looked snug and well-kept. Regis kept his hood raised as he negotiated with the innkeeper for a room, a bath, and stabling for the horse. The man, whose stocky frame, rounded cheeks, and watchful eyes attested to the success of his enterprise, asked no questions beyond the desires of his guest, but he demanded payment in advance. Regis added a generous tip from his dwindling supply of coins. The innkeeper grinned and called for the stable boy.

"See to see to the horse, lad, and give it an extra ration of grain. I'll warrant it's seen hard travel this past tenday. Clean its feet well, mind you, and check the leg tendons for heat. As for you, m'lord," he handed Regis a key, "upstairs and second on the left. Our very best room. Will you be wantin' dinner in your room or down here, beside the fire? And hot water for the bath now, or after you've eaten?"

Regis glanced around the common room. It was almost empty except for a serving maid, most likely the innkeeper's wife, and a pair of men in farmer's thick-spun smocks, bent over their drinks. The fire's warmth spread through the room. Chips of cedar had been added to the logs to freshen the air, mixing with the smells of fresh bread, roasted meat, and ale.

The two farmers had taken no overt notice of Regis, and he did not relish hiding in his room until morning. He took a seat in the darkest corner, his back to the wall. The innkeeper brought him a trencher of steaming slices of meat and boiled redroots, two thick, butter-smeared slabs of bread, and a crockery tankard brimming with ale. Regis blew away the froth and sipped, savoring the darkly rich brew. Warmth and contentment spread through his belly. The meat was a bit tough, but the roots were succulent and well-seasoned. A few more customers came in, locals by their greetings.

Regis waved the serving maid away when she would have refilled his tankard. The voices of the other men drifted over him. He should retreat upstairs before too many more came in. Just as he gathered himself to make an exit, bits of the conversation startled him into immobility.

"Ye're daft to believe it, I tell yer," one of the farmers pronounced. "Why, there's not been a Comyn king since before me grampa's time."

King?

"Aye," his mate chimed in. "What would the folk in Thendara want with a king?"

"Especially the likes of—what was his name? The young one that were killed about the time Sharra rose up in Caer Donn? Darrak? Derik?"

"That were he. Last of the royal line, he were." One of the newcomers went on to express the opinion that the only sane thing the Elhalyns had ever done was to agree to the Hastur Regency.

Regis hardly dared to believe what he had just heard. Poor Derik had died without issue, and whatever was left of his kin were distant and scattered. The Elhalyn were not extinct, however, so perhaps one of them had come forward. What kind of Regent would Rinaldo make? He had not been able to dissuade an inexperienced upstart from claiming the crown.

Remembering his own feelings when faced with pressure to claim the throne, Regis was not sure whether to be amused or appalled at such folly. What, after all, was there to be king over? A handful of remaining Comyn, who had been rendered irrelevant by the upheavals of the last decade? A planet on the edge of colonized space, a marginal world struggling to preserve its identity?

As for himself, he was just as happy to let whatever idiot Elhalyn who wanted all that meaningless spectacle have it, so that steadier men could get on with the business of guiding Darkover into the future. That meant taking Rinaldo firmly in hand, one way or another. With these black thoughts, Regis slipped up the stairs to his room.

Regis slept surprisingly well, woke before dawn, and arrived at the city gates just before they opened. The sun crested the eastern hills and swept the valley of Thendara in clear rosy light. The night had been cold but not freezing, and newly sprouted vegetation lined the road. He had been gone over two tendays, and in the interval the last dregs of winter had faded.

A crowd had assembled outside the gates, farmers and carts laden with spring vegetables, a caravan of fur merchants with their Renunciate escort, and a handful of other travelers.

The gates swung open, and the line moved forward. The Guardsmen were letting people through with only a greeting. As Regis passed, a Guardsman brought the procession to a halt.

"Lord Regis? Is that you?"

For a moment, Regis considered and discarded the notion of denying it. One glimpse of his youthful features and white hair would put a lie to any claim of mistaken identity. He stated he'd been on the road, on Hastur business, which was true enough.

The Guardsman accepted his explanation without comment. If he thought it odd that a Hastur should travel without an escort, mounted on such a common-looking horse and wearing such clothing, he kept his opinion to himself. Regis decided against asking about the news for fear of appearing suspiciously like a returning fugitive.

Regis had not gone very far into Thendara, heading toward the townhouse, when he heard a man addressing the passing traffic. He nudged the dun through the pedestrians to the corner where the speaker stood on a platform. The reaction of the listeners ranged from acceptance to outrage, with much muttering.

At first, Regis could not make out the words that dismayed so many. When those nearest the platform moved off, he was able to get close enough to hear clearly. He recognized the speaker as a Guardsman who had once performed similar duties for the Comyn Council; now the man wore Hastur livery with a baldric bearing several glittering badges.

"Hear ye! Hear ye! Know all those present, by the order of His Majesty, King Rinaldo Felix-Valentine, that as of this day, no man shall hinder the free practice of the *cristoforo* faith . . . Hear ye! Hear ye! Know all those present . . ."

Rinaldo . . . King?

Had the entire world taken leave of its senses?

Regis urged the dun through the swirling crowd. The horse, startled by the determination of its rider, lunged forward. Pedestrians scattered. A woman hissed a curse as she snatched her toddler out of the horse's path.

Once free of the crowd, Regis kicked the dun into a hard gallop. Its hooves clattered on the paving stones. The saddlebags flapped like leather wings against its flanks.

The gelding slid to a halt in front of the town house. Regis jumped to the ground and shoved the reins into the hands of the startled groom.

"Lord Regis, what—"

Regis was already racing to the house. He scrambled up the steps and through the front door.

"Linnea!" he shouted with all the breath left in him.

Everything in the foyer looked as should, with no sign of forced entry.

Linnea!

He darted into the sun-lit parlor where she liked to nurse the baby.

Empty—

Heart pounding, he started toward the stairs. A slight, feminine shape appeared along the shadowed corridor. His heart lifted, but it was Merilys who stood there.

"My wife—" Regis grabbed the girl by the shoulders as if he could shake the answers from her. "Is she—my son—"

Cario, I am here.

Linnea emerged from her own bedroom, a shawl in disarray around her shoulders, little Dani in her arms. His face was flushed with sleep, one cheek reddened where he had pressed himself against her breast. A bubble of milk gleamed at one corner of his tiny mouth.

Regis could not speak. It was enough to breathe.

With a glance that said, *We will discuss things privately,* Linnea summoned the *coridom.* The steward arrived a moment later. Linnea excused herself while Regis was giving instructions for the servants to be properly cautioned not to comment on their master's unorthodox appearance and sudden return.

Linnea came back without the baby a moment later, her dress and hair impeccable. Merilys carried a breakfast tray into the parlor, tidied the hearth, and then departed with a curtsy.

The moment the door closed behind the servant, Regis caught Linnea in his arms. Her body felt brittle with unvoiced questions.

"Stelli is safe," he murmured, "and will remain so as long as the Red Sun rises."

Her muscles softened, and she let out a deep breath.

"But you—I should never have left you here!" he cried.

Linnea's gray eyes darkened. "Where would you have me go? Not to High Windward, not traveling with a baby this early in spring. The roads would be barely passable for the hardiest traveler, let alone a woman with an infant."

She had a point. High Windward was no longer a fortified stronghold, and even when it had been, it had fallen to a determined assault. Linnea would not risk so many other lives by seeking sanctuary there. Once Rinaldo realized she had fled, it would be the first place he would send for her.

Only one place on Darkover was truly immune from either royal command or military assault.

Now Linnea shook her head with a firmness Regis had come to recognize. "I will not endanger my friends by bringing them into this quarrel. Since the Ages of Chaos, the Towers have remained neutral. They must continue to do so. Let us speak no more of this. I will remain here, at your side."

She set about pouring the *jaco*. "From the uproar of your return, I gather you heard the news."

Regis took a cup and lowered himself to the divan. She sat down beside him.

"When I first heard, and that was rumor only," he said, "I thought it must be some halfwit who's been hiding out in the back corridors of Castle Elhalyn all these years, now seized with delusions of royal glory. It didn't occur to me it might be Rinaldo. What was my brother thinking, to get himself crowned? The monks at Nevarsin never preached royal ambition."

"They were quick enough to promote the notion of a *cristoforo* king," Linnea said darkly. "Some of Rinaldo's new 'councillors' produced historical records that the Hasturs had once held the throne."

Regis felt a sudden, heavy tension in his jaw muscles. "Of course, no Elhalyn candidate came forth to protest."

"This isn't an usurpation in the strict legal sense. Rinaldo took the matter to a senior judge of the Cortes, who ruled that he has a legitimate claim."

"The same judge, no doubt, who presided at the crowning."

Linnea raised one slender eyebrow. "Along with every Comyn in the city . . . except you."

Regis had hoped his absence might have gone unnoticed. He had not planned on missing such a public event.

"Of course," Linnea said, "we were both expected to attend the ceremony. I cannot tell you how tempted I was! In the end, though, we both declined with regrets."

"Hmmm. How did you manage that?"

A smile twinkled behind her eyes. "With dexterous diplomacy, worthy of the most convoluted Tower politics. A touch of milk-fever required my seclusion and your attendance on me. The refusal was remarked, of course. For several days, I expected a summons for you to present yourself and explain."

"But none came?"

She shrugged. "It seemed my subterfuge had been successful, or Rinaldo was so occupied with his own concerns that other things took precedence."

"My brother would not overlook my refusal to witness his coronation and thereby endorse it. Another Comyn would use such a lapse as grounds for a blood feud."

"Rinaldo was . . . annoyed. Disappointed. Furious. Incredulous. Concerned. All in turn, and no reaction lasting very long. Still, you should tread lightly."

"That is, until this mockery of a kingship has been nullified and things put to rights."

Linnea got up and moved restlessly about the brightly lit chamber. She seemed a fey, wild creature, and Regis realized that he did not know her well. They had had a few brief, intense encounters and a short span of married life, little more.

"Just because Rinaldo's coronation was hasty and unexpected does not mean it can be easily undone," she remarked. "Unless he himself chooses to abdicate, he is King of the Domains. Or would you set aside law and tradition because the particular personalities do not meet with your approval?"

She was right. He must not waste time and resources on the colossal anachronism of a king in this age. He must try to understand Rinaldo's intentions, reason with him, and guide him. And if he could not . . .

Regis surged to his feet and strode to the window. He looked over the walls to the city beyond. "What about my brother's court? Who has replaced Gabriel as Guards Commander?"

"At first, it was to be Haldred Ridenow, but at the last minute, Rinaldo changed his mind and appointed Bertram Monterey."

"I don't know him."

"He's only a junior officer, but he is a devoted *cristoforo* and absolutely loyal to Rinaldo."

"How is Gabriel taking all this? And my sister?"

"Javanne expected you to storm the Castle and rescue her daughter, and when you didn't . . ." Linnea winced.

My poor sister, to have lost two children. First Mikhail to me as my heir, then Ariel . . . "Do you now fault me for seeing to Stelli's safety first?"

"I have not changed my mind. You did the only thing you could, no matter how disappointed Javanne might be."

"I suppose you will now remind me of the impossibility of eating nuts without breaking their shells." Regis could not mask the anguish in his voice.

Linnea's brows drew together, troubled but resolute. "If it had been Stelli instead of Ariel in Rinaldo's clutches, I might *feel* differently, but I would *think* the same."

"I wish my sister had your strength of mind. I fear she will never forgive me for betraying the bonds of our kinship."

I have lost Danilo and my brother, and now Javanne as well . . .

"There is an even greater reason for me to remain here, despite the risk," Linnea said with quiet intensity. "Regis, you act as if the weight of the world rested on you alone."

"The failure is mine," he said stubbornly. "So must the remedy be."

Linnea regarded him with that deep, searching gaze, but she made no attempt to breach the fragile shell of his isolation.

A heartbeat later, he had gathered himself. "Given what you just told me, I must waste no more time in dealing with my brother."

"What will you do?"

"Try to reason with him, certainly. He must be brought to see this concentration of power cannot be good for Darkover."

"And if he will not listen to you? What then?"

"I will fly that hawk when his pinions are grown," Regis retorted. "Do you mean to cripple me with prophecies of failure?"

She sighed but did not argue further.

Regis went to make himself presentable for a visit to the Castle. He did not know what awaited him or what arguments or actions he might be forced to take. If Rinaldo would not listen to reason, what then?

What then?

30

By the time Regis arrived at Comyn Castle, he had acquired an escort of three off-duty City Guardsmen, all seasoned officers. The sincerity with which they offered him their service as an honor guard bespoke their hope that now all things would be put right. Eventually, Regis would need a paxman, and Gabriel might be willing, but in the urgency of the moment, these volunteers provided the necessary security.

The three Guardsmen sliced through knots of pedestrians. Even the occasional rider steered clear, so they made much better time than Regis could have on his own.

They passed the outer gates of Comyn Castle and entered an open-air courtyard. In summer, the garden would be a haven of flowers and arching green branches. Now the benches were rain-wet, and the buds of the branches had only begun to open. The place seemed to be holding its breath.

The three Guardsmen who had attached themselves to Regis, although none had been on active duty since the coronation, were well informed. At this hour Rinaldo was within the Castle, not visiting one of the many new *cristoforo* shrines about the city. The new king held court daily in the same elegant hall used for his wedding, adjacent to the Grand Ballroom.

Regis would have preferred a private place where each might speak in confidence, most likely the study that Regis still though of as his grandfather's. He had not anticipated the effect of Rinaldo's newly royal status.

A pair of Castle Guards stood at attention outside the Grand Ballroom. They looked barely more than cadets, and they offered no objection as their senior officers escorted Regis through.

The hall had been newly furbished with hangings and carpets. Paintings and sculptures of various *cristoforo* holy images, many of them gilded or bejeweled, dotted the walls. Between these religious objects and tapestries that looked as if they had recently been dragged from the Castle storage rooms, there was hardly an inch of bare wall. Regis, who had never cared for ornate embellishments, felt as if the true beauty of the place, the stones so beautifully cut and placed, and the panels of translucent blue, had been crusted over and obscured.

Regis drew himself up. The decoration was trivial, although it revealed much about the man who had ordered it. He must not allow it to distract him from his own purpose.

With his escort on each side and behind him, Regis marched down the central aisle. Onlookers stared as he passed. The faint, rankling buzz of a telepathic damper blurred his *laran* senses.

A dais had been erected at the far end. Rinaldo occupied the massive carved chair used by Danvan Hastur when he presided over meetings of the Comyn Council. In fact, Regis realized, the configuration of the room approximated that of the Crystal Chamber. The arrangement of the seating formed a roughly octagonal shape, angled toward the throne. Rinaldo seemed to be saying, *As the Comyn once ruled the Domains, I do now.*

The assembly drew back as Regis approached. He knew some of them, city dignitaries, members of the Telepath Council, and a few minor Comyn. All were formally dressed, and many looked pleased with themselves.

Rinaldo's courtiers are showing off, vying for power and royal favor, Regis thought with disgust. Here and there, he heard whispers and expressions of surprise.

Ignoring several attempts at greeting, Regis drew near the dais. Rinaldo was wearing a long robe in Hastur colors, the fir tree embroidered in silver thread. His belt and ornamental chain were of gleaming copper. A crown perched on his head, bright with Ardcarran rubies and sapphires. Danilo stood in the proper position of a paxman, features waxen, mouth set. His eyes came to life when he saw Regis, but he gave no other sign of recognition.

A man in a suit of opulent bronze brocade knelt at Rinaldo's feet, hands placed in the attitude of a vassal pledging his loyalty. Rinaldo bent forward, his face intent. A *cristoforo* priest, who had been standing beside the dais, came forward.

Regis slowed his pace. The ceremony was akin to that used among the Comyn from ancient times. Regis himself had, at various occasions, both given and accepted oaths in just this fashion, but never with the participation of a priest . . .

The meaning of the ritual became evident a moment later: The new vassal had just publicly converted to the *cristoforo* faith. Regis set his jaw to suppress a shudder. In Darkover's long past, kings and regents and Comyn lords had demanded—and received— fidelity of word and deed, even unto death. A man's religious beliefs were matters for his own conscience. They had never been the price of royal patronage.

The ceremony concluded as Regis reached the dais. Rinaldo's head jerked up, his expression momentarily unreadable. The newly sworn liegeman withdrew with alacrity.

Regis schooled his features into a pleasant smile and bowed. He lowered himself to the exact degree due to a kinsman of slightly higher rank. It was the salutation of a Comyn lord to the Head of his Domain, nothing more. How easily such niceties came to him, but, then, he had been drilled in the intricacies of Comyn politics since the time he could walk. If the nuances were lost on Rinaldo, they would be obvious to those few Comyn present.

"Regis! Brother!" Rinaldo exclaimed. "Where have you—I mean—we bid you welcome!"

Regis permitted himself an answering smile. "It gladdens my heart to see you well, my brother. Or should I say, Your Majesty?"

"It seems we have much to say to one another."

"Then we had best do so privately."

Rinaldo surged to his feet and raised his voice, addressing the assembly. "No more for today! Out, all of you!" As he strode out the door behind the dais, he barely managed to avoid knocking over the startled priest. Danilo followed closely, as a paxman should. Regis thought he saw a fleeting smile lighten Danilo's mouth.

Rinaldo rushed along the Castle corridors at such a pace that Regis did not catch up with him and Danilo until they halted outside the study door.

"You're not needed," Rinaldo snarled at Danilo.

"As you wish, *vai dom*," Danilo bowed with impeccable grace and backed away.

Rinaldo slammed the door and rounded on Regis. "What do you mean, disappearing without a word and then returning in such an ostentatious manner, interrupting my court?"

Regis made sure his own voice was under steady control. "I should as soon ask you, my brother, what *you* mean by defying custom in claiming the throne no Hastur has wanted for generations. I might inquire whether you feel yourself more worthy than Grandfather," *or myself, for that matter,* "or what sudden and overpowering need our people have for a king. But none of these questions will accomplish anything except to widen the rift between us."

"If there is a rift," Rinaldo said tightly, "it is *your* doing. You promised to advise me, and then you vanished! My agents could not find you anywhere! Where did you go? With whom did you meet?"

His eyes narrowed. *"What exactly were you up to?"*

Regis had never before heard such naked hostility in his brother's voice. "Let us sit down and discuss matters like civilized men."

Trying to appear more calm than he felt, Regis walked over to the two chairs before the hearth, thus drawing Rinaldo away from the desk. There was no point in placing such an imposing piece of furniture between them; it would only serve to heighten the antagonism.

Rinaldo hesitated for a moment, then threw himself into one of the chairs. He was clearly angry at having lost the initiative.

Regis moved into the breach. "I was attending to necessary family business, if you must know. Am I not free to do so? Or do you intend to take care of our entire Domain single-handedly?"

When Rinaldo glared at him, Regis shifted to a more conciliatory tone. "You trust me enough to ask for my advice. Can you not trust me to handle my own affairs and fulfill my other responsibilities?"

Rinaldo had the grace to look abashed. "I was wrong to be angry when I did not understand. I had thought—erroneously, I see—you would be by my side. Everyone said it was an insult that you did not attend my coronation."

"I am here now, and we have much to discuss. How did it come about that you are now king? What crisis required such a drastic step?"

Not to mention usurping the old faith with a relatively minor sect and then demanding conversion as proof of loyalty?

"If you are going to lecture me on how change takes time, save your breath!" Rinaldo snapped. "I have already heard more of such nonsense than I can stomach. I have been charged with the spiritual welfare of our people. The rightness of my calling has been verified by miracles—or do you think an *emmasca* siring a son is an event that happens every day?"

"That is indeed an extraordinary thing," Regis admitted, choosing his words with care, "but not one that requires a supernatural explanation."

Rinaldo leaned forward, his face alight with the fervor Regis had come to know. "I had been granted worldly power, but I needed more of it to fulfill my mission. We Hasturs are the most powerful Domain on Darkover. Men listen when we speak, and our word is accepted as an oath. At first, I thought that prestige was enough, but I was wrong. The very people I have been sent to succor refused to alter their vile practices. All my pleas and exhortations could not reach them."

"You have been Head of Hastur for only a short time," Regis pointed out. "Even Grandfather could not sway tradition in a single season. A better strategy might be to lead by example, by attraction rather than by force."

Rinaldo responded with a dismissive gesture. "That is all very well when debating women's fashions or the mode in musical entertainments. It is criminally negligent when men's souls are at stake! Who knows how many have already died in sin, condemned to eternal torment, when quicker action on my part might have saved them?"

Regis was startled into momentary silence, although upon reflection, what had Rinaldo said that did not follow from everything that had gone before?

"How can you hold yourself responsible for the fate of all men?" Regis asked incredulously. "Is not each free to choose as his conscience dictates?"

Rinaldo replied, as if this were the most reasonable thing in the world, "Why else have I been placed in a position of authority over so many?"

Regis thought bitterly that the real reason Rinaldo had been given such power was that he, Regis, had so readily relinquished it. He wrenched his own thoughts back to the present problem. With those sentiments and ambitions, Rinaldo would naturally seek the means to compel what he could not persuade.

"It is a very serious matter to assume a crown," Regis said. "Long ago, wiser men than you and I decided that the best way to influence the course of history was by wise counsel and restraint, by inspiration instead of command."

"They must have been fools! No, no, of course not. They were men without divine purpose. They could afford to work subtly. I have not the luxury of such patience. I see you do not approve, my brother, just because you yourself would never take such a bold step."

"If—" Regis began.

"If you had been here, and if you had counseled me otherwise, my decision would have been the same. Come, do not look so grim. A coronation is not a funeral! Think of the good we can accomplish!"

Regis thought of Javanne, half out of her mind, of Gabriel thrust from the office he had held so honorably for so long. Of Ariel, torn from her mother. Of Linnea, begging him to take Kierestelli to safety. Of Danilo . . .

"Power cannot coerce good will," Regis declared, "nor can bad means serve good objectives. That is the lesson we have learned in our long and bloody history from the Ages of Chaos."

"Ah! This is why I need you here to advise me, to be sure that I use the power of the crown in a worthy manner. I know what I am called to accomplish. I have been given the means. All I lack is guidance as to prudent yet effective methods."

Regis bit back a caustic reply. He should take his own advice: *Persuade, reason, shift gradually . . . do not provoke a man so set in his opinion by outright confrontation.*

"Your goals are noble indeed," he said slowly, "and there is no question that you now have the power to do much good. You have spent the better part of your life among men of faith and discipline, so of course you are disappointed in the failings of those who have not had such benefits."

Rinaldo nodded, the tension in his features lightening.

"I suspect that men are more stubborn about their faith than almost anything else, even their choice of wives." Regis kept his tone easy. "They will fight for their religion when they will fight for nothing else. I believe the Federation worlds have strict laws against the imposition of one faith over another."

"Yes, that much is true." Rinaldo looked thoughtful. "Lady Luminosa said as much. Even when the One True Faith is reviled, it is never proscribed."

"It would be a terrible thing," Regis suggested, "if its followers were forced to turn against their own consciences and worship false gods."

Rinaldo nodded agreement.

"That being the case," Regis went on in the same tone, "might not men of other faiths feel the same way? Most of our people know little or nothing of *cristoforo* ways. Who knows what lies they may have been taught? Surely, once the truth is known, and the virtues of the faith have been demonstrated to them, they will eagerly embrace it."

And if they did not, Regis would have bought time to soften his brother's stance.

Rinaldo expelled a sigh, half frustration, half resignation. "I suppose you are right. But I cannot allow anyone of prominence in my court to follow any other religion. How could I trust their counsel? How could I be sure they were not under the influence of demons masquerading as this absurd pantheon?"

"How can any man be sure of any other?" Regis returned, thinking of all the betrayals and shifting alliances in his life. If a man behaved honorably, did it matter which god he answered to? He already knew what Rinaldo would say to that.

For a moment, the two brothers fell silent. Regis debated whether to press the issue or let it go, resting with what he had already achieved. The next opportunity for moderation might come slowly, in its own time, but it would surely come. Briefly, he considered bringing the conversation to a close with whatever cordiality might be expressed.

I have failed Javanne once. I cannot leave without trying to restore Ariel to her.

"I mentioned that I was absent on family business," he began, and he saw Rinaldo's interest rouse. "There is still more of that to be discussed. And, hopefully, an accord reached."

"The Bearer of Burdens reminds us of the holy nature of blood connections," Rinaldo replied.

Regis knew he was taking a risk, that he might well cross an invisible line and send his brother into another fit of self-righteous indignation. Carefully, he said, "You and I, for all the estrangement of our early lives, have reached an understanding. But we are not the only members of our family. We have a sister who is also a devoted wife and mother."

"A woman of virtue. Yes, I do believe our sister is that. I have never heard a word spoken against her."

Regis wished his heart were not pounding quite so loudly. This was an argument he must win, but not by *laran* Gift or skill with steel, not even with cleverness of words.

"As a loving parent, she is of course concerned with the welfare of her children," he ventured.

Rinaldo nodded, apparently not yet seeing the thrust of the argument.

"She is worried about her daughter. No, she is beside herself." Thoughts flowed more clearly now, words rising to his lips. Compassion, Regis realized with no little surprise, was a stronger foundation from which to argue than confrontation. He reminded himself that he had not yet heard Rinaldo's side of the story or his rationale for separating children from their parents. Perhaps Rinaldo truly believed he was doing good.

"Brother, I do not know the details of how our niece Ariel came to be taken from her mother or the child's feelings about the matter, but I do know how much it distresses Javanne. As her nearest kinsmen, it is our obligation to ease her suffering. Can we not work together for her sake?"

Rinaldo protested, "Surely she understands as do the other parents—"

Blessed Cassilda, there are others?

"—it is for the children's salvation to be properly instructed—"

Rinaldo broke off at the clamor of voices and footsteps outside the door. Tiphani Lawton burst into the room without knocking. Her lips were unnaturally pale, her hair had been slicked so tightly to her skull that it appeared painted, and she wore a bizarre combination of the brown robe of a *cristoforo* monk and a costume from a musical entertainment. An enormous yellow stone, off-world amber, swung between her unbound breasts on a chain of copper.

"I was told—Holy saints, he *is* alive!" She did not look at all pleased to see Regis sitting companionably with Rinaldo.

Regis did not rise, as he would have had he encountered her as the wife of the Terran Legate. Instead, he inclined his head in her direction. "I am well, as you see."

Rinaldo's expression shifted to anxiety as he got to his feet. "Lady Luminosa, you lend us grace. Is anything amiss? How fares my wife and unborn son?"

"All proceeds in accordance with Divine Will," she hastened to reply. Rinaldo's question had broken the momentum of her entrance. "I heard—" she stumbled, recovered herself, "I felt myself summoned to Your Majesty's presence."

With the practice of years under his Grandfather's tutelage, Regis suppressed his incredulity.

"Of course," Rinaldo said warmly. "Your inspiration never fails our holy mission, even before I myself have recognized the need. Now all is made clear. My good brother here has heard slanderous tales about the new school we have established for the uplifting of moral values in our children. I was about to assure him that this strategy is not only beneficial but necessary."

Tiphani settled herself with a lift of her chin and a smile that was more triumph than pleasure. She moved so that Regis would be forced to look up at her. Before she could draw breath to speak, however, he broke in.

"*Mestra,* nothing would give me greater pleasure and edification than to listen to you, but I am here on pressing family business and have not the luxury of time. Please accept my thanks for your dedication." Then he stood, towering over her. Instinctively, she moved back.

"I—I—" Tiphani stammered, glancing from Regis to Rinaldo. She was enough a diplomat's wife to know when she was being dismissed. As she took her leave, she gave Regis a venomous glare. Regis responded with a neutral bow.

Alone again with his brother, Regis picked up the thread of his argument. "No matter how worthy or virtuous the goals, if an action harms innocents, it cannot be good. Can we not find another way of accomplishing what you desire, one that does not cause our sister so much anguish?"

"I have been graced with this power and the vision of what it was intended for. I must not flinch from using whatever means come within my grasp."

"I have heard very much the same more times than I ever wished," Regis said, unable to keep a shading of bitterness from his voice. Some of the men who had uttered those sentiments had been his friends, others his enemies. Most of them were dead now, leaving piles of bodies and smoking ruins in their wake.

"Javanne is not an obstacle but your sister, a woman of your own flesh and blood who grieves the loss of her daughter," Regis went on. "*You* have the means to ease her pain and restore her family."

With a restless gesture, Rinaldo shifted in his chair. He looked at the fire, about the room, anywhere but his brother's eyes. "I cannot rely on men of uncertain faith to reform an entire world. You yourself said change comes slowly, and men must learn to accept new things. What better way to accomplish this than by the education of the young, who have not yet been polluted by false doctrines and sinful practices?"

"Rinaldo, that is besides the point. You—or if not you yourself, on your orders—forcibly removed these children from their families. You can disguise what you did in all the fancy language you like, but it is still kidnapping!"

With an effort, Regis reined his temper under control. He was only a breath away from words that could not be unsaid. From Rinaldo's expression, both stricken and adamant, it would not take much to push him too far.

"There are better ways of promoting tolerance of the *cristoforo* faith," Regis said in a more moderate tone. "I myself can testify that indoctrination imposed unwillingly upon the young rarely works. If it had, I would have converted during my student years at St. Valentine's. The monks certainly tried to convince me of the error of my ways."

"You always were a recalcitrant student," Rinaldo said, softening.

"I believe the correct term is *blockhead*." Regis returned his brother's grin. "Remember, too, that I went there at Grandfather's wish, if not my own. Can you imagine the situation if he had been forced to send me?"

Rinaldo considered this. "From what I know of our grandsire, he was a formidable opponent and not a man to bend to circumstance. He would have raised half the Domains against us."

Regis let the comment stand. "He certainly would have made his disapproval known. Who then would have listened to the truth of the holy saint's teachings?"

For a long moment, Rinaldo did not respond. There was no real answer to the question, and to press the point would surely lose any sympathy Regis had thus far achieved. Moving slowly, as if his joints pained him, Rinaldo crossed to the fireplace. He laid one arm along the mantle. The gentle orange glow from the hearth warmed his features.

"I can't give up now, and yet I can't go on. I hoped we could begin a new generation, one dedicated to truth and virtue. Free from the idolatrous traditions of their elders. But it is not so easy, is it? When I think of how I might feel if my own son had been taken from me and taught—" he broke off, his breath catching in his throat. "Can these others, Javanne and the rest, feel any less?"

He turned back to Regis. A fire burned behind his eyes, but perhaps that was only the reflection of the hearth. "What am I to do? How can I keep faith with my calling? How can I reconcile the cloister and the crown?"

Regis stood up and moved into the heat of the fire. They were of a height, Rinaldo and himself, so that their gazes met levelly. On impulse, he placed his hands on Rinaldo's shoulders, almost a brother's embrace. The physical contact brought no hint of *laran* communication, yet Regis felt a deep emotion resonate through Rinaldo's spare frame.

"Be generous of spirit, as I know you are. Send the children back to their families. By all means, keep the schools open, but offer the teaching freely to any who desire it. Then . . . when your son is born, become an example and inspiration to others."

Regis saw the hardness lift from Rinaldo's eyes. The brother he had longed for emerged from the mask of despotic fervor.

The moment could not endure. Rinaldo sighed. "I will have to explain this change in policy to Luminosa. It was at her urging that I took this step. She was convinced it was Divine Will. I see now that cannot be, for the Holy Bearer of Burdens would never add so greatly to the pain of the world."

Regis restrained himself from pointing out that Rinaldo, not the wife of the Terran Legate, was the king. "It might be better to create an advisory council so that in the future, no one person can unduly influence your decisions."

"Yes, yes, I had thought of that. But she has always seemed so sure, her vision so clear."

"I'm certain it is . . . to *her*."

Rinaldo nodded. "I see your point. You have saved me from a grievous misstep this day. I have missed your counsel recently. You will not fail me again?"

Regis shied away from the reassurance his brother so clearly wanted. "If you will heed my own recommendation, seek out people of wisdom and experience, even if—or especially if—their beliefs and opinions differ from your own. That way, you will be able to choose among the different arguments the one that seems most wise and just."

Rinaldo agreed this was a good plan, and the brothers parted amicably.

31

Regis could not leave the Castle without reassuring Javanne of the results of his discussion with Rinaldo. He wound his way through the maze of stairs and corridors, passing from one era to another as the architectural styles changed. Once or twice, he was stopped by Castle Guards and asked his business. No one challenged his right to visit his own family. Other than the Guardsmen and a few servants, the halls were empty.

There are too few of us Comyn to lose even a single one.

When Regis arrived at the apartments where Javanne and Gabriel had set up their housekeeping, he found Gabriel sprawled in a chair, staring at nothing in particular. Regis felt a spasm of sadness to see him thus, a man of action forced into idleness.

"Regis!" Astonishment lit Gabriel's face, immediately coalescing into a frown.

"I heard about Bertram Monterey," Regis said. "I'm sorry."

"Regis! Lord of Light, you just *disappeared*! With no word, nothing! Where in the Nine Hells have you been?"

Regis cast about for an acceptable explanation and failed miserably. "I'm here now."

"We would have suspected Rinaldo had you killed if Linnea hadn't been so calm about it. Javanne's ready to wring your neck the next time she sees you. She went to you for help, and you just *left*—Do you have any idea what's been going on? Ariel—"

"Yes, Javanne told me. I'm sorry I couldn't do anything sooner. Is she about? I have good news."

"She's hiding in the linen closet, counting kitchen towels," Gabriel growled. "That *Terranan* woman is everywhere, bossing everyone about. Not that Javanne has the heart to run the Castle now." Regis had never heard his brother-in-law so downcast.

"As for Bertram Monterey, that rabbithorn!" Gabriel went on. "Rumor has it that he's placed *cristoforo* agents in key positions. You don't know whom to trust."

He paused, his expression hardening. "I never thought to say this, Regis, but I'd be happy to leave Thendara. I was proud of my work here and even prouder of the cadets I'd trained and the Guardsmen I led. Now that's all gone. There's no more honor, not in the Comyn, not anywhere in the city. I'd take Javanne away to Armida tomorrow if we could get Ariel back."

"It's not like you to run away from a fight," Regis said. "If things are as bad as you say, we need all the sane men we have. *I* need you—your experience, your strength. Since Rinaldo has taken Danilo, would you consider acting as my paxman?"

A series of emotions passed over Gabriel's features. He turned away. "I have no desire to abandon everything the Comyn have stood for, the old ways of respect and decency, but I have my family to protect."

"As do I." Regis grasped Gabriel's shoulder. "My brother is my family, too. Rinaldo is easily led astray by others, but he still listens to me. I can reason with him. We'll sort this out. Meanwhile, I need a strong man to guard my back, someone I can trust—"

Suddenly the door flew open. Javanne rushed into the room. She wore a gown that had once been green but had faded to gray, covered by a dust-streaked apron. Her hair was tucked beneath a pleated cap. The muscles around her eyes seemed too tight.

"There you are! I heard—" She swung from Regis to confront her husband. "Regis is here and you didn't send word to me!"

"I came directly from speaking with Rinaldo, and he has agreed to release the children," Regis broke in.

"Just like that?" Javanne demanded. "When will this miraculous event take place?"

"You doubt my word?"

"Not at all. But I have more than enough reason to doubt *Rinaldo's.*"

"Regis, do you know where they are?" Gabriel said. "Somewhere in the Castle? One of those temples? A hovel in the city, one of those areas no sane man walks unarmed? Spirited away to Nevarsin?"

"They could be *anywhere!*" Javanne threw herself at Regis, hands raised as if she would tear his eyes out. "If it had been Mikhail, your precious Heir, instead of my daughter, you would have saved him! Why are you doing this to me? I hate you! I hate both of you!"

Gabriel caught Javanne in his arms, holding her with surprising gentleness. "Hush, love, you don't mean that."

"It's not fair!" She allowed herself to be led to the divan, where she collapsed, burying her face in her hands. "She is lost, lost! And all you men do is *talk*! What good is that to my sweet girl?"

Javanne spoke truly. What was Rinaldo's agreement but empty words?

Regis knelt, but she would not look at him. "*Breda,* I swear to you, I will restore your daughter. She is my kin as well."

"I wish you'd left Rinaldo at Nevarsin!" Javanne wavered on the edge of hysterical tears. "I wish he'd never been born!"

Gabriel rested his hands comfortingly on his wife's shoulders and said to Regis, "Or that you never had the notion to hand so much power over to someone not trained to handle it."

"Trained?" Regis shot back. "As Grandfather trained me? I would not wish that on my dearest enemy, let alone my only brother."

"Who has run amok—"

"Yes, but under the influence of men like Valdir Ridenow!" Regis said. "I admit I failed to prepare him. What else should I have done? Become king myself? That's absurd!"

"As absurd as Rinaldo doing the same, with far less ability or rightful claim?" Gabriel rumbled. "Gods, Regis! When good men fail to do their duty, tyrants step into the breach. You failed all of us, and now it's our children who suffer."

"I told you. I handled that," Regis protested.

Gabriel stared at him. "I'll believe it when Ariel is home again."

Regis repeated, "Rinaldo gave me his word."

Javanne lifted her tear-streaked face. Her voice, although hoarse, was steady. "And what is that worth without honor?"

"Regis," Gabriel said, his voice now shading into weariness, "I have always thought well of you. I know you've faced down things I can't imagine. If you can restrain that tyrant of a brother who dares to warm the throne with his backside, so much the better. But you place too much faith in Rinaldo's willingness to be guided. You think he is without ambition? That is your own modesty speaking. Open your eyes and see what he really is."

"Grandfather was right: You have never taken this business of governing seriously." Javanne's voice regained its former edge. "As a member of the Comyn, you have a responsibility to our people. But it's not my business to lecture you on your duties."

"Please do not do so," Regis said tightly. "Grandfather did nothing else for most of my life."

"But never in a way that you heeded!" she cried.

"I have done what I can! I am not a god, no matter what the legends say."

"No," Gabriel said quietly, "but you are a Hastur lord, which is close enough for most people. Take care to watch your back."

"That," Regis said with a meaningful look, "is why I need you."

Gabriel sighed, and for a moment, Regis felt sympathy for the older man's position. With a wife as sharp-tongued as Javanne, and Javanne at her distraught worst, the decision could not be an easy one.

"You have my voice and my sword," Gabriel said. "I will not make any formal vows—" meaning those of a paxman, "—but I will help you as best I can."

Regis reached out to clasp Gabriel's forearms, a soldierly embrace. Javanne leaned forward to kiss Regis on the cheek. Although she held herself with composure, her body felt as brittle as eggshells.

Regis halted beneath an arched doorway. Before him, a narrow stairway led into shadows, and a corridor angled away to the left. He did not recognize the passageway. What a fine situation for a grown man, Comyn and Hastur, to become lost in his own Castle!

He sat down on the lowest stair and considered what he must do next. His thoughts vacillated between optimism and self-doubt. He tried to cheer himself up, reassuring himself that the fears of his sister and brother-in-law were misplaced. He was making progress with Rinaldo. Soon he would be able to bring Kierestelli home, and all would be well.

All would be well. How many times had he thought that and been wrong?

Gabriel was right, Rinaldo's excesses were the responsibility of the man who put him into power. It was up to Regis to deal with the results.

Desperately, Regis missed the friendship of men of his own caste. Lew Alton was off-world, along with his only child, Gabriel had turned distant, almost hostile, and Dyan Ardais was dead. Some things he could not say to Linnea, and Danilo . . .

Regis had become accustomed to the aching emptiness in his life. Danilo did not always agree with him, but his advice and the inexpressible comfort of his support had always been there.

He glanced up and knew where he was. All his temporizing and self-justification fell away. He and none other had put Rinaldo into a position of unbridled power. He had closed his eyes to Rinaldo's obsessions. He had lulled his own conscience with false reassurances. Why should Rinaldo heed anything he, Regis, said?

More than that, he had left his sister's child and the children of others in the clutches of unscrupulous men while he spirited his own daughter to safety. For too long, he had delayed and made excuses for Rinaldo. He must rescue the children himself.

Only a few moments ago, he had been alone in the endlessly twisting Castle corridors. Now he emerged into the more populated public areas. At every corner, he encountered more courtiers. Some—an Eldrin cousin here, a Castamir or MacNoire there—he knew slightly, but none well enough to trust. All of them wanted some favor, some influence with the king.

Regis strode through the knots of sycophants, ignoring their greetings, and out the Castle gates. As Gabriel had pointed out, the children

could be anywhere in the city. Barring interrogating every Guardsman
loyal to Rinaldo, there was only one way to find them.

He needed Linnea's help.

With a sigh, Linnea broke the psychic rapport. Regis blinked, his vision
clearing. They had been sitting together, a circle of two, their starstones
glittering on the table between them, for what seemed like days. He
arched his back, feeling the stiffness in the joints. How did Tower workers concentrate their *laran* for hours at a time?

"For one thing, a circle has a monitor to safeguard their well-being,"
Linnea said, yawning. Shadows bruised the delicate skin around her eyes.

Regis rubbed the bridge of his nose to ease the ache behind his eye
sockets. "Did you sense anything?" *Or was this a waste of time?*

"Mmmm." She went to the sideboard and carried back the platter of
food she had placed there before they began. Regis had chafed silently
at her preparations. Now the smell of nuts dusted with powdered crys-
tallized honey made his mouth water. Linnea was already tearing apart a
spiral bun and devouring the morsels. She paused long enough to take
a draft of the honeyed wine.

"That's better," she said. "Now I can talk without falling over."

Within moments, the worst of the headache eased as the food and
sweetened drink replaced the energy Regis had expended.

"To answer your question, I did get a flicker. A taste, as it were. It
would have been easier if Ariel's *laran* had awakened, assuming she has
any. Her twin sister is already studying at Neskaya?"

"Yes, that would be Liriel."

Linnea's brow furrowed. "Odd that one would have so much talent
and the other none. I suppose some twins are no more similar than
any other siblings. Ariel is still here in the city, I'm sure of that much.
She's not in the Castle or the Old Town. Somewhere in the Trade City,
I think." She wiped her fingertips on a napkin and peered anxiously at
Regis. "I wish I knew more, dearest. I'm guessing as it is."

He touched the back of her wrist lightly and felt the pulse of warmth
in her wordless response. "It is more than I had before." He tried to
stand up, found his knees had turned to jelly, and sat down again.

Linnea kept her face grave as she instructed him to rest. "*Laran* work burns tremendous amounts of energy." Pointedly she looked at the crumbs remaining on the platter. "You'll be better shortly, but not if you don't give your body time to recover. An hour now—lying down, if you can—may well spare you the inconvenience of fainting later."

Although he wanted to begin the search right away, Regis saw the wisdom in Linnea's argument. He lay down on his own bed. Minutes crept by, and then he sat up with a jerk and realized he'd been sleeping.

Regis pulled on the clothing he had worn for the ride to the Yellow Forest. The shirt and pants were travel-stained despite the best efforts of Merilys to clean them. He slipped on his oldest boots. Their quality was out of keeping with the clothing, but he was not willing to sacrifice comfort, not to mention sure footing, when he had no idea what he might encounter.

Weapons? Regis frowned. All his training urged him to go armed, if only with a dagger. A sword would be better. Would carrying one create more of a risk—of discovery, of unnecessary violence—than a benefit?

Perhaps the Terrans are right and we are *savages who resolve our differences by sticking each other with bits of pointed metal.*

The world went as it would, and not as men would have it. He could not risk coming up against an armed assailant without a weapon, but he needed freedom of movement. He settled for a dagger, easily concealed beneath his cloak, and a boot knife.

With the hood of his cloak covering his distinctive hair, Regis slipped out the servants' entrance and down the street. Within a short time, he left the wealthier district. The foot traffic was heavier here, people going about their business in the fair spring weather. No one took any particular notice of him, not even the Guardsmen watching the intersections.

As Regis entered the Trade City, searching for a building that might serve as a "school," Javanne's accusation returned with all its sting. He had never taken the time to get to know any of her children except Mikhail. The older sons, Gabriel after his father, and Rafael, he knew only slightly. Both had trained as cadets. He wasn't sure he would recognize Liriel, the girl who had gone to Neskaya Tower.

As for Ariel herself, he knew what she looked like, a shy, pretty child. But did he really know anything about her?

Ariel . . .

Small shops offered an array of Terran imports, Valeron pottery, and clothing. The area was an uneasy amalgam of the two cultures.

He couldn't very well knock on doors, asking if anyone had seen a parade of kidnapped children. There was no help for it but to continue up one street and down the next, through the maze of byways and alleys, hoping for a clue. The search would be tedious and methodical, but it was all he could do.

His route took him deeper into the Trade City, past the Street of Four Shadows, where the few licensed matrix mechanics did their business. Here and there, Regis spotted an ale shop, and once he noticed a pair of men, *Terranan* by their coloring and dress, enter a discreetly marked brothel. He did not like to think of his niece, or any child, in this place.

The street Regis had been following, little more than an alley, twisted and doubled back, paralleling the way he had come. He spotted a broader avenue ahead, and the lacy pattern of trees. Perhaps it led to a residential area.

As Regis neared the opening of the alley, a familiar figure passed by on the intersecting avenue. He drew back, flattening himself against the stone wall, but there was no alarm. He had not been seen. Anxious to not lose his quarry, he crept forward. There she was, walking with a firm stride, her head high.

Tiphani Lawton. Even without her imperious bearing, there could be no mistaking that outlandish costume.

Regis dared not follow too closely. Only a few people were abroad, not enough to hide his presence should she glance back. He tried to move in a casual way, as if he were in no hurry.

A short distance along, Tiphani veered toward a two-storey building. Regis halted a half-block away. From his vantage, the structure looked old but well kept, with a few windows set high in the dark stone walls. The wooden double doors were bound in brass, a luxury for metal-poor Darkover.

Tiphani stopped on the threshold and raised one hand to knock. The door swung open.

Haldred Ridenow stood there.

Tiphani stepped inside. Haldred glanced up and down the street, then shut the door.

Regis proceeded along the street, examining the house as closely as he could without being obvious. He discovered a narrow lane running along the back and far side of the house. While broader than the usual alleys, the lane was hidden from easy view of the street. Even more fortunately, the back wall had not been smooth-finished. Irregularities studded the stone blocks, forming holds for feet and fingers.

A balcony ran along the center third of the building. It looked disused, in poor repair, as did the door to one side and the clouded window. Regis peered up, calculating a route. He had done some mountain-climbing as a youth, but always with ropes and a guide. It occurred to him that he had considerably more experience getting out of tightly locked places than in breaking into them.

About half an hour later, Tiphani Lawton left the building in the direction of Comyn Castle. Regis slipped back into the side passage. He had identified only three ways into the house: the front door, guarded by Haldred, the servants' entrance, hazards unknown, or the balcony. He might not get a better chance, and any choice was better than standing here like a scarecrow. He folded his cloak over his shoulders to free his arms, grasped the upper edge of a head-high stone, set one foot on the nearest rough patch, and hauled himself upward.

Inch by painful inch, Regis climbed. He moved one hand, digging his fingers into the crevices of the rock. His feet found tiny, almost invisible ledges. He forced himself to test each hold before committing his weight to it. A fall would—no, he must not even think of it. Within a few heartbeats, he was sweating. Silently he cursed himself for not keeping more fit. His shoulders throbbed, and his hands were already scraped raw in half a dozen places.

Halfway up the wall, Regis froze at the muted sound of men's voices below him. The words were indistinct, yet they seemed to be coming closer. He felt naked, vulnerable, his hold on the wall fragile. One glance would brand him as would-be thief, suspended halfway up the back of a residence, where no honest man had any business. He was now too high to jump down without injury.

A moment later, the voices receded. The walls of the lane had carried and amplified the sound. Regis took a trembling breath and continued upward.

The final part of the climb lasted only a few minutes, but it felt like an eon before Regis reached the balcony. Wooden slats, many of them weathered into splinters, made up the floor. With difficulty, he shuffled to the side where the framing looked more sound. As he grasped the likeliest of the beams, the foot bearing most of his weight lost traction. Boot leather skidded over stone, the noise alarmingly loud.

Suddenly his entire weight hung from one hand. Fire shot through his shoulder as ligaments and muscles stretched under the shock. Somehow he held on.

Panting, Regis grabbed the beam with his free hand. His feet, which had been flailing wildly, slammed into solid wall and held. He inhaled sharply, then pushed with his legs as he pulled with his arms. He might not be as fit as he'd been as a cadet, but he didn't weigh much more.

The burst of effort raised his body enough so that he could hook one elbow over the edge of the beam. From there, he dragged himself up.

The balcony was in even worse shape than he'd feared. It was by Zandru's own luck that it hadn't collapsed, plummeting him to the ground. As it was, he found several splinters among the abrasions on his palms.

"Who? Who's there?" The words in halting *casta* came from inside the door. The voice was a child's.

"It's all right," Regis said, keeping his voice low and soothing. "I won't hurt you."

"Have you come to take me home?"

Regis smiled, although the child, a boy he thought, could not see. "Yes. Now stand back from the door."

Bracing himself, Regis inspected the door. It was weathered, although still sound enough to keep out the elements. The lock was cheap, but it held when he leaned his weight into the door. The frame, however, was warped, spongy in places. The wood was not only weakened by the elements but most likely rotted as well. Regis studied the door frame and the beam on which he perched. He might choose wrongly and go crashing down or attract attention from within the house, but he must take that chance.

He selected his target, just below the level of the latch, braced himself on the soundest part of the railing, and landed a hard, percussive kick. From inside came a smothered shriek. The door flexed under the blow, but the frame fractured in places into powdery fragments. Regis closed his eyes and delivered a silent prayer to whatever god looked out for chivalric fools. Then he reached inside. His fingers found the lock.

"You can't open it that way," said the boy. "I've tried."

Of course, the door would be locked to prevent escape, not entry. A second kick, although not as well-placed as the first, weakened the door frame further. The third landed dead-on with all the power he could muster. The door tilted open, hanging on its hinges.

Regis pushed his way through the opening. The room beyond was comfortless and chill, the meager fireplace bare, the only furnishings two narrow beds and a chair.

On one of those beds, with its stained straw pallet, Felix Lawton sat bolt upright.

"How long have you been here? The others—there *are* other children here, aren't there? Have you seen them?"

Felix lowered himself to the bed. "It's been a couple of days, but I can't be sure. She made me drink this awful stuff. Drugged, of course." He let out a bitter cough of a laugh. "I—I heard voices, and someone crying. A girl. I don't think I imagined it." He paused and they both listened. "What happens now?"

"Now," Regis answered with a ghost of a smile, "we get you out of here."

Felix glanced toward the splintered wooden debris where Regis had wrenched the door aside.

Regis shook his head. "I don't think we can manage that way. Not without a rope." Felix's captors had left him neither blanket nor anything else that might be used to escape, except his own clothing. "Besides," Regis added, "I'll need your help with the others. Are you with me?"

Felix straightened his shoulders and nodded.

"Come on, then."

As Regis had expected, the latch had no lock. Darkovans did not lock their doors within their own homes. Instead, a bar had been installed on the outside. Regis took out his dagger and maneuvered the slender blade through the gap between the door and its framing. It took several attempts to lever the bar free. When he succeeded, the bar clattered to the floor outside.

Regis and Felix held still, barely breathing, listening for sounds of alarm. The last echoes of the bar falling died into silence. Gesturing for Felix to stay back, Regis lifted the latch. The door opened with a creak.

A corridor ran the length of the house, lined on either side with closed doors. Each door, like Felix's, had been fitted on the outside with a bar. A window of cloudy, poor-quality glass admitted a diffuse light at the far end. The floor was bare wood. Once, it must have been very fine, but age and lack of care had dulled its luster. An arched opening midway along one wall led to a staircase going down.

Regis moved silently to the nearest door. There was no response when he tapped. The bar slipped easily from its brackets. The room, very much like Felix's with bare pallets on simple frame beds, a single

32

With an inarticulate cry, Felix Lawton rushed forward. Regis caught him and held him close. Silent, barely suppressed sobs racked the boy's body. Felix was thinner than Regis remembered, his muscles taut. He was trembling too badly to form coherent words. For a moment, Regis feared the boy's starstone had been taken from him, but the boy's *laran*, although turbulent with terror and relief, was steady.

Regis stroked the boy's hair, lank with grime. Felix's cheek was clammy, as if he were on the verge of shock.

This could be any child. This could be my child.

I'm here, Regis sent a pulse of mental reassurance. *It's all right. You're not alone.*

Felix looked up, his eyes red-rimmed but dry. "I didn't think anyone knew where I was."

Or, Regis caught the boy's thought, *that anyone would look for me.*

Felix added, "I was an idiot to believe my mother when she said she had a surprise for me. I thought maybe she missed me—she's been over at the Castle every moment she isn't fighting with Father. I never thought she'd—she'd—"

rickety chair and little else, was empty. There was no sign of food or water. When Regis asked Felix how long it had been since he'd eaten, Felix shrugged.

The next two rooms were empty but in use, from the rumpled ticking on the pallets. A sense of urgency grew in Regis. The longer they delayed, the greater the chance of discovery. Tiphani might have gone, but Haldred was still in the house.

"Downstairs, maybe?" Felix whispered.

"Let's go, then. Stay behind me. We don't know what's down there, but in case it's trouble . . ." Regis touched the hilt of his dagger.

Felix flashed Regis a crooked grin. Clearly, having a course of action steadied the youngster.

Keeping to one wall, Regis led the way down the stairs. As they stepped on to the landing and changed directions, muffled sounds wafted upwards. Children's voices rose and fell in unison, although Regis could not make out their words.

They descended another few stairs. The ground floor came into view. There were no bedrooms here, only a wide hall tiled in faded mosaics, a smaller door that must lead to a parlor or formal dining room, and there, at the far end, a set of double exterior doors. Carvings swirled across the dark wood like frozen shadows.

Regis slipped his dagger free. There was no sign of Haldred or anyone else, but he could not tell how long their luck would hold. He glanced back at Felix and lifted one finger of his free hand to his lips. Felix nodded, eyes huge and somber.

With only a whisper of footsteps, they crept down the remaining stairs. Felix might not have had cadet training, but he carried himself well.

The sounds of the children grew louder, then stopped. Regis froze. A man's voice took over, in that same rhythmic cadence. Regis recognized a devotional chant from Nevarsin.

The hallway was still clear, but they were exposed, with nowhere to hide or run. Regis motioned Felix to stay close as he hurried across the mosaic floor. Before he could reach the double doors, however, the side door opened. Regis spun around just as a man, dour-faced and broad of shoulder, entered the hall.

Haldred Ridenow.

Haldred hesitated, caught momentarily off-guard. Dagger in hand, Regis moved into the lapse. Haldred was already reaching for his sword when Regis closed with him, dagger aimed for his throat. Haldred yelped, his voice echoing in the near-empty hall, and jumped back.

Regis followed closely, circling. With his free hand, he grabbed Haldred's wrist and twisted hard. In a fluid, circular movement, Regis spun Haldred around. Haldred staggered, but Regis held his arm twisted behind his back so tightly that their joined hands were almost at the level of Haldred's shoulder blades. Regis knew from experience that even a little more leverage would produce excruciating pain. He laid the edge of the dagger, less sharp than its point but effective nonetheless, against Haldred's neck.

Gasping, Haldred managed to hold still. "What—what are you doing here?" he muttered through clenched teeth.

"Rescuing the Legate's son. My niece. A few others. You'll know them, I expect." Regis nudged Haldred toward the double doors. "In there, are they?"

"You'll never get away with this!"

"Who taught you to talk like that? Valdir?"

"That weakling!" Haldred struggled, then gasped in pain.

"Do that again, and I'll slice your throat," Regis hissed. "Felix, can you open the doors? Good. Then you and I, Haldred, are going through them slowly. Do you understand me?"

Haldred gulped noisily. Regis took the movement for assent.

Felix shoved the doors open. Regis half prodded, half dragged Haldred through the opening. The room was spacious and bright, its windows of unblemished glass. A fireplace of chalky stone held a small fire. The chamber had been designed for elegance as well as comfort and might have once been used for dances. Now rows of benches filled the center, all facing a freestanding altar.

A man in sandals and a brown *cristoforo* robe stood with his back to the blaze, absorbing its warmth. He was short and balding, well-padded around the middle.

A handful of children in sacks of brown cloth huddled on the benches. Their feet were bare and their eyes dull. Regis spotted Ariel among them. Several had the bright red hair of the Comyn.

"Savage!" the priest screamed. "How dare you disturb us—or carry weapons into this place of holy learning! Sacrilege, I say!"

Regis had neither the time nor the temper to answer. "All of you," he called to the children, "we're taking you home! Felix, get them together—"

His next words were cut off by the clamor of men's voices and booted feet over tile. Two men armed with swords pelted down the hallway. From his vantage, Regis could not see if they had come from outside or elsewhere in the house. One or two of the children shrieked. The others whimpered and clung to one another.

Regis whirled Haldred around so that the newcomers could see the dagger. "Stop there or he dies!"

One of the men scowled, ready for a fight. Regis wasn't sure he could carry through his threat, or what he might do against three swordsmen with just his dagger. He couldn't risk Felix, and the children on the benches looked too intimidated to move on their own.

The second man raised his hands well away from his weapon. "It's Lord Regis . . ."

"Get back, both of you!" Regis barked.

"You men, why are you standing there?" the priest demanded. "Do your duty! Seize the intruder!"

Regis ignored him, keeping his eyes on the two swordsmen. "We're going to move very carefully toward the street. All of us. Do you understand?"

Both men nodded, the first more reluctantly. The priest made incoherent mutters of protest. From his peripheral vision, Regis caught the expression on Felix's face and it heartened him.

"Good," he said. "Then you'll oblige me by taking off your sword belts and laying them on the floor." They did so and backed away at his command.

"Stop!" yelled the priest. "Where are you going with those students?"

"I'm taking them back to their families."

Felix helped the smaller children to their feet and ushered them toward the hallway. A few went willingly, but others cowered on their benches. Ariel was one of those too frightened to move or apparently to comprehend what was happening. The priest took a step to block their passage, but Regis warned him back.

Half the children had crossed the hallway when the outer doors flew open.

"Spaceforce! Freeze!" The words blared out in accented, mechanically amplified *casta*.

The next instant, half a dozen men in the black leather uniforms of the *Terranan* police rushed through the doors. They moved like hunters closing on the kill, swift and powerful, focused.

They all carried blasters.

Stung beyond reason by this blatant violation of the Compact, Regis cursed aloud.

Haldred took advantage of the momentary lapse and wrenched free. He stumbled, fell, and caught himself on hands and one knee.

Pandemonium erupted in the hallway. Black-clad Terrans seemed to be everywhere. Their shouts reverberated, distorted by echoes. The children who were already in the hall panicked and darted this way and that. One of the girls started screaming like a banshee.

Haldred lurched to his feet. He shouted out orders to the two swordsmen. For the first time, Regis saw the blood smearing Haldred's throat. The wound did not look deep, but there was enough blood to terrify the children. It must have happened when Haldred struggled free.

One of the guards, the one who had recognized Regis, reached for his dropped sword. Blaster fire, silent and swift, caught him. He screamed and toppled over. Steel rattled over tile as the sword fell from his hand.

Yelling, the priest tried to herd the children back into the school room.

The second Darkovan guard snatched up his weapon. Wild-eyed, he lunged at the nearest Spaceforce man. Too late, the Terran's head whipped around. The sword edge cut through leather, then snagged on bone. The Terran's knees folded under him.

The Darkovan rushed in, jerking his sword free for a killing stroke. A blast beam sliced across his belly. He stiffened, head thrown back, mouth gaping, and toppled to the floor. The stench of charred flesh filled the air.

"Enough!" Regis bellowed. "Stop!"

The next moment, Haldred grabbed the dagger with one hand. The two men wrestled for control of the weapon. Regis reeled as Haldred's other fist slammed into his jaw. His vision fractured, but he managed to hold on to the hilt.

Without releasing the dagger, Regis swiveled and lashed out with a circular kick. The blow was badly aimed, with little power behind it. The toe of his boot struck the side of Haldred's thigh, hard enough to hurt but not disable.

Grunting with pain, Haldred tried to pull free. Regis clamped his hand over Haldred's, anchoring it to the hilt. All he could think was that with Haldred out of action, the Terrans would break off their assault. There would be a chance for parley and an end to the killing.

"Filthy nine-fathered *ombredin!*" Haldred counterattacked, pummeling Regis with his free fist. At the same time, he jerked and twisted their joined hands.

Slippery with sweat, the hold broke. Haldred grabbed the dagger in both hands and lunged at Regis. Regis jumped back, barely in time. The tip caught a fold of his cloak but missed his skin.

Felix rushed toward the fallen Terran, calling out the man's name. Regis shouted out a warning, but he could not reach the boy. Haldred blocked the way.

As Felix crossed in front of Haldred, the Darkovan grabbed him. A quick, savage move spun the boy around and pinned him against Haldred's torso, facing away. Haldred's forearm squeezed tight against Felix's throat. With his other hand, Haldred jammed the tip of the dagger just below the boy's ear.

Not my own dagger!

"Drop your weapons or he dies!" Haldred's hoarse shout rang out.

As if in a dream, Regis saw the Terran commander turn toward them. Saw the blaster swing up in a move too quick for thought.

Acting by instinct, Regis hurled himself at Haldred. He grappled the other man around the hips. The impetus of the blow broke Haldred's balance. They went down, slamming into the tile floor, rolling, flailing, Haldred yelling.

The next few moments blurred in a tangle of arms and legs, shouted orders in a *Terranan* dialect, then a silence and a sudden, dense weight. Regis tried to free himself, but Haldred was too heavy. He shoved and twisted, fighting for leverage.

With a wordless shout, Regis pushed again. The weight lifted as Haldred's body rolled aside.

Dazed, Regis pushed himself up on one elbow. Two of the Space-force men dragged Haldred away, one by either arm. The blaster had sliced Haldred's torso from one shoulder to the opposite hip. Layers of fabric had crisped away to reveal a blackened, gaping cavity. Exposed vertebrae gleamed wetly at the back of the wound. Regis gulped, his guts clenching. No living creature could have survived such an injury.

The Terran commander knelt beside Felix. The boy's head lolled to one side, one arm flung out limp and graceless. He wasn't moving, wasn't breathing.

Blood pooled beneath his body.

"Oh, god," one of the Terrans babbled, "ohgodohgodohgod."

Regis crawled over and touched one shoulder, rolling Felix toward him. Blood smeared one side of the boy's neck and chest.

The hilt of the dagger stuck out below his ribs.

Regis jerked the front of Felix's shirt open. His fingers closed around the cord and then the silken bag. He hesitated only for an instant before opening the drawstring.

Thrusting his fingers between the layers of soft insulating fabric, Regis felt the hard crystalline shape. He watched Felix's face for any hint of change.

No reaction.

No movement, no fleeting expression of shock or pain. Nothing.

A moment, a blink, and we are dust . . .

Lord of Light, what could he say to Dan? *Sorry* was so pale and futile a word.

And none of this would have happened had he, Regis, not been so weak as to allow Rinaldo the throne . . . Tiphani taking her own son to be indoctrinated . . . the predictable incursion of the Federation forces . . .

Sick at heart, Regis drew out the psychoactive gem. The starstone was warm from contact with the boy's body. A pale flicker like the dying echo of fire still danced in its depths.

"No pulse!" the commander blurted. Someone else said, "He's not breathing," and another, "—can't resuss—dagger too close to the heart—pull it out, might kill him—"

The commander barked: "Medics here, stat!"

"—never arrive in time—"

Regis blotted out the voices, the hovering figures. The only thing that mattered was that twist of brightness.

If Linnea were here—or even the most novice monitor—she would know what to do, how to start the boy's heart and lungs. Regis had no training in such techniques, no way to reach anyone who did.

I cannot do this.

I cannot let him die.

Words reverberated through his mind: *Light calls to Light.*

Memory thundered through him, how he had opened himself— offered himself—to the power that men called the Lord of Light.

And something had answered, had filled him, flowed through him, *used* him to defeat Sharra.

Regis pressed the starstone against Felix's red-streaked chest. Head bent, eyes closed in concentration, Regis shaped his thoughts into a prayer.

Save him . . . take my strength, use my Gift. Aldones, father of my fathers . . . let my life pass into this child . . .

Regis felt a quickening, a flicker of electric energy, in the stone under his hand. His fingers were sticky with Felix's blood—blood as carrier of life—blood as conductor and amplifier of power . . .

And then he had no more words, only, *Please, please . . .*

Power answered. It rang like a crystalline bell in his mind, faintly at first, then louder. Time slowed. Between one breath and the next, the resonant clangor grew until it drove away all other awareness. The sound was beautiful past bearing and more terrible than night. It flooded him, jarred him from his moorings, shredded all resistance.

He had become a single vibrating crystal: the Hastur Gift, the living matrix.

He could shape, direct, use this power as he wished. Or he could let himself be shaped and used by it. With it, he could stride like a god across the face of the world, blasting away all who stood against him. He could remake whole planets to his own desire.

Between his hands, the boy's life force guttered.

He did not know what to do. He let go—

Light surged through him. He no longer grasped it; he shrank to a speck in an ocean of blue-white brilliance. Knowing it would burn him up like tinder, he gave himself to the light.

Without sight or hearing, he sensed patterns within the effulgence. A form coalesced, at first only a tracery, a suggestion of lines of force. Then details emerged . . . the metallic signature of a long, slender object, the resonances of liquids, gelatinous cells bright with renewed life-energy . . .

As if the boy's body had turned to glass, Regis made out the dagger as it sat, nested in torn and punctured tissues, the tip almost touching the heart, the severed blood vessels, the nerves still paralyzed by shock.

Live . . .

Power reached through him, not his own will but something deep and sure. An invisible spark propagated through the muscles of the heart. At the same time, the edges of the arteries clamped down. The blood-filled space between the dagger and the pericardial sac took on a new, elastic density, holding the blade in place.

The heart chambers contracted, the first beat rough, but the next smooth and strong, rippling from top to bottom. Blood pounded through the major vessels. The diaphragm shuddered, then clenched under a cascade of nerve signals.

The light faded. Regis dropped into his own body, at once too hot and too cold, too solid and too fragile.

Beneath his palms, Felix's chest rose in a heaving breath.

Rough hands hauled Regis to his feet. He began to protest, then realized these men had no idea what had just happened. The Terrans saw him as one of the hostage takers, in league with Haldred. Still caught in a maelstrom of grief and guilt and the exhilaration of the healing, he tried and failed to summon words.

"I've got a pulse!" The man kneeling on the other side of Felix looked up with an expression of astonishment.

Felix groaned and feebly lifted one arm.

"Lie still, son," the commander said. "Help's on the way."

"Sir? What about this one?" asked one of the men holding Regis.

"Let him go," the commander answered, his voice thick. "He's not with—Sweet heavens, it's Lord Hastur." He got to his feet, brisk and efficient, and confronted Regis. "What in blazes are *you* doing here?"

Regis glared back. Outrage flared, fueling his words. "Trying to rescue these children. Which I would have done without bloodshed if you had not come barging in. You are in direct violation of the Compact and, need I add, of Federation policy."

"You savages! Do you think you can kidnap the Legate's son, a Federation citizen, with impunity? That we would sit back and do nothing? It's a miracle the kid's still alive!" *And he still might not make it.*

Shaking off the grip of the two Spaceforce men, Regis drew himself up. He had not contradicted the commander's use of the title, *Lord Hastur*. It was time he took back those responsibilities as well.

"There will be consequences," Regis promised, "to the ones responsible for this outrage. But your presence here, your disregard for local sovereignty is not only illegal but inflammatory. It will be seen as an act of aggression, an abrogation of all we have worked to achieve between our two worlds."

"When the safety of a Federation citizen is at risk, we have the right—"

"You have the right to ask Darkovan authorities for assistance, but you do *not* have the right to single-handedly start a war! Is that what you want? Have you forgotten recent history? Do you think we are such backward savages," Regis deliberately echoed the words of the Spaceforce man, "that we have no means to defend ourselves? Have you so quickly blotted out how the spaceport at Caer Donn was destroyed?"

The commander blanched.

"I will see to it those Darkovans responsible for this tragedy are held accountable," Regis continued, more quietly now. "What you must do is remove your men and their weapons as quickly as possible."

Just then, a trio in the uniforms of the Terran Medical Corps pelted into the foyer. Regis had no idea how they had arrived so fast. The commander directed them first to Felix, then to the other wounded. They set about examining the boy with their instruments. Regis did not understand a fraction of what they did, only that they meant to stabilize him for transport.

"He's a lucky kid," the head medic told the commander. His gaze flickered to Regis in his gore-stained shirt. He added in Terran Standard, *"What about that one? He looks like one of the local aristocrats."*

"It's not my blood," Regis answered in the same language.

A few minutes later, the medics had brought in a rigid carrier for Felix and secured him to it. Regis approached the head medic. "Tell Dan—" his voice caught, then held firm, "tell the Legate how very sorry I am."

"Nothing—to be sorry—" Felix stumbled, before the medics maneuvered his carrier through the doors.

"And these?" The commander indicated Haldred and his two comrades. One of them was still alive, huddled on the floor while a medic applied an anesthetic spray.

"If you're willing to treat him, it would be seen as a gesture of goodwill," Regis conceded. "As for *him,*" with a nod toward Haldred's corpse, "I'll inform his family."

"With your permission, I'll transport the bodies back to HQ. This will require an internal investigation. We will treat the remains with respect, and the families can claim them as soon as the forensic reports are done."

Regis was in no mood to dispute such a sound plan.

With practiced efficiency, the Spaceforce team took charge of the wounded and the dead. Regis turned to the priest and issued a string of orders regarding the children. The *cristoforo,* visibly shaken by the turn of events, obeyed meekly. Soon nothing remained of the fight except bloodstains and the reek of charred flesh.

The Terran commander paused at the outer door. "I'm taking a big risk in trusting you to keep your word. How do I know you'll punish those responsible? That you won't exonerate them because they're your own people?"

Regis glared at the man. "I have said it. I am Hastur."

There it was, his word an unbreakable promise. It was a burden he would bear for all his days.

Something in his tone, his bearing, or perhaps his eyes, reached the Terran. The commander lowered his own gaze, nodded, and retreated back into the street.

Regis held out his hand to Ariel. She stared at him, eyes white-rimmed, mouth set in a tight line. Slowly she slipped her chill fingers into his. Now that the last traces of power had drained from him, Regis felt lightheaded, as if his bones belonged to someone else. He could not rest, not yet.

He lifted his gaze to the waiting children. "Come, little ones. It's time to go home."

33

They looked like a bunch of refugees, some of the children barefoot, others wrapped in oversized cloaks from the storerooms. Regis had worried about how the younger ones were going to walk all the way back to the Castle, but before long, he was able to hail a wagon half-filled with bales of unspun wool. The driver, an elderly, leather-skinned man, said it was no burden to his team to carry such little ones. He lifted the children one by one to perch on the soft bales. The younger ones giggled, as if this were a fine adventure. Ariel huddled beside Regis, clutching his hand.

When they arrived at the Castle gates, Regis dispatched a Guardsman to fetch Javanne. He dared not trust anyone else with the children, for fear of turning them over to Rinaldo's agents.

A few minutes later, when the children were still clambering down from the wagon and thanking the driver, Javanne burst through the gate. Gabriel followed close behind. Ariel gave a piercing cry. Regis lifted the girl from the wagon and into her mother's arms. Javanne pressed her daughter close, rocking her with exclamations of relief.

Gabriel caught Regis in a kinsman's embrace. "You did it! I truly did not believe you could—but you freed them!"

"All is not well," Regis said somberly. "The Legate's son is badly injured and Haldred Ridenow—I'm afraid he's dead. And a couple of other men, I don't know their names."

"Zandru's demons! What happened?" Gabriel fixed on the blood-stained shirt. "Are you hurt?"

Shaking his head, Regis glanced toward the children, now clustered around Javanne. She'd put Ariel down and was herding the others together, clucking over their thinness and pallor like a mother barnfowl.

"Spaceforce sent a rescue party," Regis lowered his voice. "They were armed with blasters. As you can imagine, the result was some nasty fighting. I'll tell you more later. For now, we need to notify the families, and I must deal with my brother."

"He's in council with Lord Valdir and half a dozen others."

Leave it to Gabriel, even when relieved of his command, to know the inner workings of the Castle.

"I can't waste any time," Regis said. "For all I know, Rinaldo's already gotten word of what happened. Gabriel, I need your help."

"You've got it. Regis . . . there will be Nine Hells to pay. You and I both know it."

"That's why this madness has to stop now, whatever it takes, before any more men die. Before we reach the point of no return with the Federation. Before there is too much anger, too much bloodshed, too much reason for retaliation."

"Aye, that's true," Gabriel muttered. "Once the *Terranan* impose martial law, they'll never let go. We'll become little more than a heavily armed spaceport."

Once given a task, and with Ariel firmly in hand, Javanne regained her composure. She rattled off orders to a stream of servants. Within the hour, the children would be restored to their families. Knowing her, they would first be fed and properly clothed.

With Gabriel a half-pace behind, Regis stormed across the inner courtyard and into the main Castle. Servants and an occasional courtier scurried out of their way. Once a Guardsman began to intercept them but withdrew, bowing respectfully. Regis was not sure whether the man had recognized him or Gabriel as the former Commander, and he did not care.

As they approached Rinaldo's council chamber, the Guardsman on duty outside the door held his ground. Gabriel stepped to the fore.

"Commander—" the Guardsman protested.

"Move aside, Esteban. That's a direct order. One way or another, we're going through that door. I don't want to lose another good man to this idiocy."

The Guardsman's mouth dropped open. He let them pass. Gabriel knocked loudly and then, without waiting for a response, flung the door open.

The chamber was modest, once used for informal Comyn gatherings. A table had been set up in the center, with Rinaldo at the head. Maps and documents were laid out, along with a tray containing a carafe of wine, unwatered by its deep hue.

Rinaldo looked up sharply as Regis and Gabriel entered. To either side sat Valdir Ridenow, two courtiers from minor noble families, and the *cristoforo* priest who had conducted the conversions at Rinaldo's court. Danilo stood a pace behind and to the side of Rinaldo, but the chair to Rinaldo's right was conspicuously empty.

"Regis!" Rinaldo exclaimed. "Blessed saints, what has happened? Has there been an attempt on your life?"

"It's not *my* blood." Regis heard his own voice ringing through the chamber, then a terrible stillness, a waiting, an expectancy. Every head turned in his direction, some with expressions of amazement, others with dismay. Danilo shifted, his hand going to the hilt of his sword. Valdir's eyes reflected the despair of a man confronted with his own worst fears.

Regis waited another heartbeat. "Some of this blood belonged to Haldred Ridenow. The man *you* sent to guard those children—children *you* abducted from their families against every principle of honor and decency!"

Several of the council cried out in protest. One started to rise. In a lightning move, Gabriel clamped one hand on the man's shoulder and forced him back to his seat.

"I?" Rinaldo faltered. "I had nothing to do—"

as if he had been physically struck. Danilo looked nauseated, almost ill. Gabriel's face turned ashen.

Rinaldo fell back into his chair. "My son . . . born too soon?"

Tiphani lifted her face, and Regis thought he had never seen such bleak confusion, not even when Felix had been so sick.

Felix! Had she heard—did she yet know?

A few mute movements of her lips, and then she forced the words out: "The babe is gone, vanished from my lady's womb!"

Appalled silence hung in the air.

"Is—is it certain?" stammered one of the courtiers. Tiphani looked as if she would break down again.

"My son . . . my son . . ." Rinaldo swayed like a man who has suffered a fatal wound.

"How can this be?" the other councillor recovered himself sufficiently to ask. "A babe spirited away, unborn?"

"It cannot be natural," the *cristoforo* priest intoned.

The words passed over Regis like so many puffs of air, devoid of meaning. As angry as he had been with his brother only a few moments before, now his heart responded to the bewilderment on Rinaldo's face.

And Tiphani, for whom he had never cared, whom he held responsible for the whole bloody disaster and Zandru only knew how much friction yet to come with the Federation, surely she deserved a morsel of compassion as well. She did not even know of her son's desperate condition.

As gently as he could, Regis said, "My brother, these are matters that call for a lady's tender care. Let me send for my wife. She has training in healing—"

Tiphani's head shot up, her eyes filled with too much white. "Trained, yes, in that nest of sorcery you call a Tower! Do you not see, my lord," to Rinaldo, "how she could have cast her evil spells out of jealousy—"

"No, no, my dear," Rinaldo replied with surprising calm as he patted her hand. "My brother's wife is a woman of virtue, and she has not been anywhere near Bettany." In a quicksilver shift of mood, like the sudden fall of night over Thendara, his features darkened. "*She* has not . . ."

His gaze lit upon Danilo.

"Lady Luminosa is correct. This tragic affair smacks of wizardry!" the priest repeated. "As I said before, it cannot be natural!"

"You don't know what you're talking about!" Regis snapped. Cloistered away from women, new to the ways of the world, what monk could be acquainted with the ills of women? But this was no time to educate the man about false pregnancy. "If you will not have Linnea's help, then let us send for a healer-woman. *Mestra* Tiphani is overwrought—"

"Call me not by that vile Terran name!" Tiphani spat.

"—and will need support to bear her own tragedy."

"What could be worse than the supernatural death of the king's unborn son?" she demanded, her voice rising shrilly.

"Please, calm yourself—" Rinaldo said.

"Tell me!" she shrieked at Regis. She looked as if she would claw out the eyes of any man who crossed her. Danilo moved to intercept her.

In that brief hesitation, Valdir growled, "Your son was almost killed, you heartless vixen—and my own kinsman is dead! The *Terranan* raided the house in the Trade City—because *you* took your son there!"

"Lies! Foul lies, spread by this scheming usurper!" Tiphani pointed at Regis.

Regis gazed back, and for a moment, his heart ached for her, so lost in self-righteous fury that she could not understand what had happened.

Then awareness flickered across her face. She lowered her hand. Her tone shifted from strident to hoarse. "What . . . *what have you done?*"

"I, lady?" Regis said. "I tried to save your son and would have done so, if the Federation men had not opened fire. I am sorry, more than I have words to tell you."

Tiphani began to weep soundlessly. She turned away, blocked by the solid bulk of Gabriel. He put his arms around her with the same tenderness he would have used with a younger sister.

Rinaldo rose like the slow gathering of a storm cloud. "These things do not happen by chance."

"No, they happen by human folly," Regis responded. "By arrogance, greed, and ambition. By power without the wisdom to use it wisely."

"This terrible winter and now this even more terrible loss," Rinaldo went on, his voice breathy with passion, "these trials are surely sent to punish us for our wickedness."

He fixed Regis with his icy gaze, then glared at Danilo. "We have tolerated evil among us for too long, even in the highest places. Can you gainsay this, Danilo?"

Lord of Light! I was a fool to think that if Danilo and I were parted, he would be safe!

"Confess now or risk your immortal soul!" Rinaldo cried. "Confess that you have influenced *Domna* Bettany and tried to sway her from the path of righteousness!"

"I have done nothing to harm the lady or her babe," Danilo protested. "I have tried as best I could to be her friend."

"You!" Tiphani shrilled. "You *dared*—"

Rinaldo cut her off. "You took advantage of my wife's inexperience. You used her vulnerable condition—you seduced her thoughts—not that you would know what to do with a woman's body!"

"If that is so," Danilo answered with a flare of heat, "then she can be in no danger from me."

"She can be in very grave danger," came the silky rumble of the priest. "Spiritual danger, far more potent than mere physical lust. Your perverse inclinations, hidden but never abandoned, have struck down the unborn prince!"

"There is no evil in any form of love if it is given honestly," Danilo said, his voice steady. "I cannot believe that a just god would so punish an innocent child."

"Aha! There we have the heart of it!" cried Rinaldo. "I have known all along, but I have refrained from taking action for my brother's sake. I had hoped you would repent, but now I see that is impossible. The evil has taken too deep a hold. It is *you*, Danilo Syrtis-Ardais, who are the cancer at the heart of this city!"

Rinaldo pointed at Danilo. "There is the sinner whose transgressions have brought retribution on us all. Seize him!"

Before the Guardsmen could respond, Valdir jumped up. "This is going too far! I have no love for your paxman, Your Majesty, but he is no way responsible for the actions of the Federation. I will have no part in this!"

"Rinaldo, I consider it no edifying sight for Comyn to trade insults like a pair of gutter rats," Regis interposed. "But this matter, as Lord Valdir said, goes too far. Mourn the dead, see to your lady wife, but more than that, I will not permit. Touch Danilo Syrtis at your peril."

"How dare you speak to me in this manner?" Rinaldo cried. "I have endured this pestilence among us because he was a favorite of yours and the Holy St. Christopher urges us to be compassionate—but Danilo Syrtis overstepped the limits of decency in speaking as he did. And in our very presence! That he should—oh, most insufferable effrontery—link the word *love* to such base carnal deviance in one breath and *God* in the next!"

"He did no such thing," Regis countered, keeping his voice even, his words measured, "but only spoke as a man of sense."

Rinaldo gestured to the guards. "Seize him, I said! If my brother gives you any trouble, lay hands upon him, too!"

"Danilo has committed no crime," Regis insisted. "He has acted in good faith to you."

"His own words reveal the blasphemy in his heart." Rinaldo's expression turned adamant. "Any man who sins in his thoughts sins *in fact*."

"You cannot truly believe that," Regis said, growing even more deeply troubled. "How can a man be damned for thinking about an act he then chooses not to commit? If that's the case, we are all lost!"

"But we *are* lost!" Rinaldo's eyes went wild and opaque. "Don't you see?"

"I see that your mind is made up," Regis said.

"He should be hanged as a warning to other sinners, but *you* would make trouble. Your loyalties have never done credit to your rank or education. I must be content to expose him for a day or two in the stocks. That will do him a measure of good and will demonstrate that the eternal Divine Law is no respecter of high estate."

"In this weather? He would be dead before nightfall!" Now Regis had no doubt of the force of his brother's delusions.

Blessed Cassilda, my brother truly has gone mad. Danilo, bredhyu, *you were right in your suspicions. How I wish I had heeded you then!*

"If you intend to send Danilo to the stocks, you had better be prepared to put me there, too."

"Don't tempt me, my brother," Rinaldo said. "If I thought for a moment the people would stand for it, I would do just that!"

I allowed him this power, I welcomed it . . .

"I know what you have been plotting." Rinaldo's expression twisted into slyness. "You want my crown for your own. Yes, yes, I see your ambition in your eyes. You deserve to be punished, for you have sinned as well. Oh, don't tell me that those disgusting lusts are sinful only for *cristoforos*. God's commands apply to everyone. Your only hope is to repent and chastise the flesh, which is weak. You should welcome a night in the stocks for the good of your immortal soul."

Between his teeth, Regis muttered, "If I believed for a moment that you really meant it—"

"Believe it!" Rinaldo snapped. "Believe I mean every word of it, *my brother*. God has sent a pestilence upon this land and I am the instrument of its cure—"

Entirely out of patience, Regis interrupted, "Oh, go and preach to the crows! I've had enough! Danilo, I hereby revoke the transfer of your oath to this—this—to my brother, and require of you all allegiance and service as my paxman."

His face somber and unrevealing, Danilo inclined his head, the salute of a Comyn lord to one of higher rank, to Regis.

"*Vai dom*. I am yours to command." *As I have always been.*

"You—you can't do this! I am Lord Hastur, your sworn liege! *I am King!*" For a breathless moment, Rinaldo glanced about the chamber. The other members of his council refused to meet his eyes. Tiphani had stopped sobbing, her face as pale as marble.

"Lady," Regis said to her, "my counsel, if you will have it, is for you to return to your husband. He cares deeply for you. In the days to come, your son will need both his parents."

She stood there, stunned, until Gabriel led her to the door and delivered her into the care of one of the Guardsmen. Although she left the chamber docilely enough, Regis caught the look of pure malice that she directed, not at himself, but at Rinaldo.

Regis broke the awkward silence. "Rinaldo, you and I are not finished. What I have to say to you next concerns not only Hastur but all the Domains. According to law as well as custom, any such action must be witnessed by the Comyn. In the absence of a formal Council, we will accommodate tradition as best we can."

"What are you talking about? I am King! You cannot make me do anything! As for the Comyn, they are without consequence. I do not grant them any rights whatsoever over me."

"But *I do.* I summon you to answer me in the Crystal Chamber. There, as has been custom since the Ages of Chaos, we will discuss the future of Hastur. I will not insist we meet immediately. You and your lady wife deserve time to mourn your loss," for although there had never been an actual pregnancy in fact, it had existed in their minds and hearts. "Therefore, the hearing will take place tomorrow at this very hour before all members of our caste who can be assembled."

Rinaldo gaped at him. Regis thought ruefully that if he had been decisive to begin with, matters would never have deteriorated to this point. But that opportunity, like last winter's snows, was gone past recall.

"I warn you," Regis went on, "to take no precipitous action during this time. I have issued a summons to you, and a truce now exists between us until the matter is resolved."

Around the room, heads nodded. The Guardsmen looked frankly relieved.

"If you do not behave with honor or if you fail to appear at the Crystal Chamber," Regis added, aware of the tightness in his jaw, "then all the world will know you have agreed to whatever I decide in your absence. Think hard on it, *my brother,* for you may not care for the result."

Regis did not wait for an answer. Giving the council members a scowl worthy of his grandfather, he strode through the door, with Danilo and Gabriel a half pace behind.

34

"**H**ave you gone mad?" Gabriel asked Regis as the three men hurried from the main part of the Castle and crossed a series of courtyards to the nearest gate.

Regis felt the subtle, sustaining touch of Danilo's *laran*. *I could not do this without him, any more than I could have come this far without Linnea.*

"No," Regis answered with a ghost of a smile. "For the first time in far too long, I have gone sane."

The gate was locked from the inside, but it was unguarded. Regis lifted the latch. "Gabriel, you must return to Javanne and tell her what happened. I will need both of you present tomorrow. You have a rightful claim to represent Alton in Lew's absence."

Gabriel's eyes darkened with understanding. "By all the gods, you mean to do it."

"In full view of the Comyn, whatever is left of us. In order for the outcome to be binding, the challenge must be seen as legitimate beyond question."

"We'll be there," Gabriel said. "And Mikhail as well. He sent word he expects to arrive late today, bringing Kennard-Dyan with him."

The news gave Regis an unexpected lift to his spirits. Danilo breathed, "What a stroke of luck."

"Mikhail left Ardais as soon as he received word about his sister's abduction," Gabriel explained. "He meant to comfort his mother, although he could not have known what would come next. He has an extraordinary sense of timing, if I say so myself."

"He will be most welcome," Regis said. With a bow, Gabriel withdrew back into the Castle.

Regis and Danilo headed for the town house in silence. Regis drank in the comfort of having Danilo once again by his side. There was still work to be done, work that only Danilo could do.

"Danilo, once you accomplished wonders gathering together a temporary Council when we debated the question of Federation membership," Regis began, hearing the heaviness in his own voice. "I would not have it said I dealt with my brother secretly or through subterfuge. As it is, there will be too many vacant places in the Crystal Chamber—"

"Don't," Danilo said.

Regis paused, raising one eyebrow in question.

"Don't ask me to leave you so soon. I've hardly—" Danilo's voice caught in his throat. His eyes were wide and dark, filled with emotion. When he spoke again, his voice was so soft that no one but Regis could have heard: "I've clung to hope for so long, without even a word."

They had come to a halt, standing very close, leaning toward one another without conscious intent. Regis felt the warmth of Danilo's breath on his face. He thought of Linnea at home, of this moment, of Kierestelli hidden in the Yellow Forest. Of Felix's blood, sticky beneath his fingers. Of the flare of light and power beyond his own.

Too much, it was too much for one human heart to bear alone.

Not alone, came Danilo's thought.

Regis drew in a breath. Danilo raised his hand, quick as a dagger in the hands of a master, and brushed Regis on the lips with one fingertip. It was only a fleeting touch, but enough to shatter doubt.

Bredhyu.

Always.

"Now let me take you home," Danilo said, with the hint of smile. "I cannot in good conscience allow you to wander the streets unguarded."

Still, Regis did not move. "Home. To Linnea." And to all the questions implicit in those few words.

"Home," Danilo agreed, "to whatever has changed and not changed. For many years, we have both known that you must marry. I wished it were not so, but it is the way of the world. You are Hastur. Your destiny was laid down before you were born."

Regis did not know whether to laugh or weep. "Then I should have chosen my parents more carefully."

Danilo did not rise to the old joke. "I would not have you other than you are. In any way." He paused. Then: "You once said you would not marry any woman you could not respect and cherish, who did not return those feelings. I think you have found her."

Understanding rose slowly, trailing inexpressible relief. Danilo and Linnea might never be close, but neither would question the other's devotion. Or place in his heart.

Although the day was mild for spring, a chill wind curled through the street. Danilo, dressed only in indoor clothing, shivered. Regis glanced back at the Castle.

Danilo followed the movement of his eyes. "I would not willingly set foot in the Castle again, except at your side. Tomorrow, either I will be able to retrieve my possessions or it will not matter."

Regis unclasped his own cloak and draped it over Danilo's shoulders. Danilo looked as if he would protest, that he could not accept the cloak while Regis had none, that Regis looked like a wild man with his stained, torn clothing and disheveled hair. The blood on his shirt had dried to a crust.

Danilo said nothing to repudiate the gift of lord to liegeman, of lover to beloved, and the two went on together.

When Regis and Danilo arrived at the townhouse, Linnea asked no questions, although she must have had many. She took a brief, hard look at the two of them, then summoned servants and issued orders for hot baths, hot food, and hot spiced wine, enough for a company traveling in the Hellers in winter.

Danilo bowed to her. "Lady Linnea, I thank you—"

"Danilo, we are friends. We have no need of such formalities." Linnea did not touch Danilo, for as a Tower worker and Keeper, she had been trained to avoid any but the most deliberate physical contact, yet the warmth of her voice was as welcoming as an embrace.

"Lady, I was not sure—"

"There will be time enough for discussion once you are settled. Food and hot water will take a short time. I shall return presently with someone you want to see." With a smile, she glided from the room and shut the door firmly.

As Danilo turned to Regis, his expression melted like ice in spring, giving way to wild joy. The next moment, they were in each other's arms, holding one another as if they could never let go. Danilo was thinner than Regis remembered him, his muscles rigid from long-held tension.

"Regis, when you did not appear at the coronation, I was so afraid—" Danilo said in a choked voice.

"I never thought—I'm sorry I put you through that—and the whole dreadful business of becoming Rinaldo's paxman."

"You owe me no apologies."

"I—"

Danilo put an end to further protest. Time fluttered on gossamer wings for Regis as Danilo captured his mouth with his own.

The kiss began hard and urgent, driven by pent-up longing. Desire catapulted into tenderness and demanding physical need and relief and feelings beyond words.

Without breaking away, Regis ran his hands over Danilo's body. He pulled the front of Danilo's shirt loose. Danilo's skin was taut and fine-grained over hard muscle and the soaring arch of bone.

Regis buried his face in the curve between Danilo's neck and shoulder. Heart racing, heat throbbing in his blood, he inhaled the musk of arousal and clean masculine sweat.

With an effort, Regis wrenched away, not wanting to have Linnea return and find them so. She was a telepath, surely she could feel the sexual hunger between the two of them. Reaching, he sensed a wall like polished quartz where her mind should be. She had closed off her psychic awareness, even as she had physically closed the door.

They fell on the divan, tugging at each other's clothing. Regis could no longer tell where his own sensations ended and Danilo's began: the fire that fueled every touch, demanding again and *more* and *deeper,* the convulsive opening of one heart to the other. Only the flimsiest barrier separated them, like the border between a flame and its reflection.

As their bodies joined, Regis felt an electric pulse blaze up in him like living lightning. It soared through them both, swift and bright and vital. One moment, it seemed to rush from Danilo into himself, past throat and heart and groin. The next, it was Regis who poured himself out and felt Danilo's ecstatic response as keenly as if it were his own.

Afterward, they lay panting and replete, half on the divan, half on the floor. Danilo chuckled, soft and deep in his chest. Regis, who had been sprawled with his head on Danilo's chest, stirred.

"Best to get dressed," he murmured, reaching for his underclothes. "There will be time again, later."

Danilo regarded him with a slow, provocative smile. "We have all winter to make up for."

"Count on it." Regis snatched up Danilo's pants and tossed them at him. "But first, there's work to do. Make yourself decent. Or would you rather be in your current state when my wife walks in?"

When Linnea did return, both men were fully dressed. Even the divan cushions had been replaced in their proper order. A discrete touch of *laran* and a tap on the door signaled Linnea's request to enter.

She carried the baby on one hip and a towel draped over her shoulder. "Come and meet your namesake, Danilo."

Danilo took a step closer. Amazement tinged with awe spread across his face, and Regis was struck yet again by how handsome, how expressive he was. How quick to delight as well as to despair.

When Linnea held out Dani, Danilo raised both hands with an expression of consternation. A moment later, she had arranged him on the divan with the baby on his lap. Dani looked up, eyes wide. The two Danilos stared at one another. Regis watched, unsure whether his son was on the brink of glee or wailing. Then the baby's mouth curved in a blissful smile, and Danilo too was laughing.

Baby Dani gave a little burp. Linnea swept him back into her arms, facing the towel on her shoulder, just in time for him to bring up a small amount of milk.

"Now, enough of that," Linnea laughed. "The bath water is hot. Off with you!"

A short time later, Regis had bathed and eaten, and was sitting before a comforting fire with a steaming goblet. For the sake of a clear head, he had insisted on *jaco* instead of wine. Danilo was still upstairs, soaking, and the bustle of the household had quieted.

"Tell me what happened." Linnea pulled up a bench to sit beside his knee, almost close enough to touch.

Regis told her as directly as possible, leaving out nothing important, yet not dwelling on personal emotions. She would sense what lay beneath his words. She listened, gray eyes somber, holding him like an anchor through the storm of reliving the rescue and its aftermath.

"It is too bad I was not permitted to monitor Bettany, or that sad part of the affair would have been settled earlier," she commented.

Regis shook his head. "I doubt Rinaldo would have accepted your findings. He was firmly convinced of the miraculous nature of his wife's conception. I wronged poor Bettany in my thoughts when I learned the *Terran* medical tests had confirmed that Rinaldo was sterile."

"At least he did not blame her pregnancy on some other man. Regis, you don't suppose he suspected Danilo?"

"How could he do that and then condemn Danilo for being a lover of men?"

"Your brother is hardly rational, with his faith in supernatural intervention," she replied. "The real miracle is that Felix Lawton wasn't killed. If he lives and if he is still in need of a teacher, I must help him."

As Linnea spoke, she allowed her own feelings to surface. Like all Comyn, she found a violent assault on a child unspeakable. She and Regis had first opened their hearts to each other following the murder of two of his own *nedestro* children.

Regis remembered thinking, *A child of Linnea's would be too precious to risk to fate . . .*

Hard on that thought came another, darker still: Would there ever come a time when it was safe to bring Kierestelli back? Dared he risk it? Ever?

He had kept his mind guarded, but Linnea must have sensed his fear. She said, "Since Bettany is not pregnant, and never was, the Domain of Hastur once more passes through you. You already have an Heir in Mikhail. He is well-grown and trained to protect himself. But little Dani—must we expose a helpless babe to those dangers?"

"You suggest that I leave Mikhail as Heir to Hastur in order to protect our son?" Memory, bittersweet, brushed his thoughts. "When I took Mikhail from my sister, I swore that I would not set him aside, not even if I produced an Heir of my own flesh. I will not go back on my word or dishonor my sister's sacrifice."

Linnea held herself still, her only concession to relief the slow closing of her eyes.

"We should not tell anyone," Regis said. "At least, not until Dani is grown enough to understand. Mikhail will do well enough for the present as Kennard-Dyan's paxman."

"He'll learn the wise uses of power much better from that perspective," Linnea agreed.

"Yes, and although Dani must of necessity be exposed to the politics of the Comyn—or whatever takes our place—I would hope—" Regis stumbled, caught between his own tormented childhood and his dreams for his son, "that he not grow up as I did in the shadow of such crushing responsibility."

"He will always be your son, Regis. As much as we and Danilo can manage it, he will grow up in a loving family."

Within his heart, Regis felt the easing of a tension he had not known existed. He could not, as the old saying went, put banshee chicks back into their eggs or change the world into which he had been born. But he could do his best to make sure none of his children ever endured the same.

He, and Linnea . . . and Danilo.

In a short time, Danilo would come down. He and Regis could never return to the life they had lived here together. Would Danilo resent the trust and intimacy that had grown between Regis and Linnea or Linnea's a role as his wife, in which Danilo had no part?

It came to Regis that each relationship—wife and *leronis,* paxman and *bredhyu*—had its own intrinsic honor and value. Loving one person could in no way diminish his devotion to the other.

Linnea rose, smoothing her skirts. "You and Danilo will have much to discuss. What's left of today will be hectic, to say the least. I will leave you to it. I have my own work, making sure Danilo's chamber is comfortable and that he has everything he needs."

As mistress of the household, Linnea had the right to arrange quarters as she chose. Nevertheless, Regis felt a tinge of dread. Would she use this power to place herself between him and Danilo? Then she gave a little teasing laugh and he realized he was seeing the world through the lens of the day's horror.

"Of course," she said, "Danilo must have his old chamber next to yours, as is proper for a paxman. I'm quite comfortable where I am."

"Linnea—"

"Regis, this will not be the first time I have shared a lover with someone else, although never before with another man . . . or one who was as dear to me as you are. In the Towers, we learned how to manage such things. The best practical arrangement to begin with is for each of us to have our own chamber. Later, we'll work out a schedule and psychic shielding."

Regis had forgotten how forthright she was. "I'll leave the arrangements to you . . . with my thanks."

She walked briskly to the door, then paused and turned back. "Regis. Promise me one thing."

He heard the unsureness in her voice and waited.

"You will not walk into the Crystal Chamber without me."

She asked not only because she was Comynara in her own right. Not only because as one who had once been Keeper at Arilinn, her voice still commanded respect. Not only because she might be of support to him. Not only because, if things went badly and turned violent, she had the right to face that danger with her husband.

Danilo would be there, as paxman and Comyn. Linnea's presence would state, in clear and irrevocable terms, her own rightful place.

Am I truly an equal partner?

Smiling, he nodded.

———— ✦ ————

A short while later, Danilo came into the parlor, flushed from the heat of the bath. His hair, still wet, tumbled over his shoulders. Regis recognized the shirt, a bit large but clean and pressed, as belonging to the *coridom*. Linnea must have borrowed it for him.

"There's hot wine as well as *jaco*," Regis said, gesturing.

Danilo poured half a goblet of wine and sat down. "I suppose *jaco* is more sensible, but, Holy Bearer of Burdens, I need this more. I still can't believe I'm here."

"You are," Regis grinned. "Or else we're both hallucinating. Are you easy, Danilo? Is there anything we need to discuss before we turn our minds to plots and schemes?"

Danilo hesitated, studying the garnet surface of the wine. "There's nothing more to be said. Life itself will unfold. But—even if you set me aside," lifting his gaze, his eyes filled with light, "what you have given me is more than I ever dreamed. You came for me, even as you did so many years ago at Caer Donn. You restored my honor as well as my life."

You were willing to die for me.

"Having risked that, do you think me such a blockhead as to cast away the finest paxman of our generation?" Regis tried to keep his tone light. "We are what we are to one another. Even as Linnea and I are."

Danilo looked away, blinked once or twice, nodded. Inhaled. Cleared his throat. "So we are to resurrect the extinct Comyn Council once again?"

"I'm afraid so. I would prefer not to rely on the ghosts of the old order, but not even Varzil the Good could convene the Telepath Council in the Crystal Chamber. To be seen as legitimate beyond question, these proceedings must have the full and indisputable authority of the Domains. I must also speak with Dan Lawton without delay, to forestall a military coup by the *Terranan* before I can get things straightened out."

"Well," Danilo replied with a ghost of humor, "what is one more miracle on a day such as this?"

The crimson sun sank behind the rooftops of Thendara. Shadows deepened, staining colors into gloom. Regis and Danilo, muffled in woolen cloaks, made their way to the Trade City.

The day had been clear, and not a cloud blurred the twilit sky. Darkness, dense and swift, swept across the heavens like great soft wings. Leaping out in sudden brilliance, the crown of vast white stars and the two smaller moons glittered like gemstones set asymmetrically against the galactic plane.

The two men stopped outside a walled compound that revealed nothing to the outer world except that its owner was rich enough to ensure his privacy.

"You've outdone yourself, Danilo," Regis muttered. "I don't think even Valdir Ridenow would look for me here."

Danilo pulled the bell rope. The gate cracked open. A servant carrying a torch ushered them through a small garden and into the house beyond.

Regis and Danilo followed the servant into a richly furnished room. Lights came on, not the tallow candles of poor people or even the *laran*-charged glows of the Comyn, but a bank of yellow globes of Federation origin. Regis recognized a hanging of Thetan sea-silk, a carpet with an intricate Dry Towns pattern, and a chair that could only have come from the pleasure world of Keef. Historically, Darkovans had little interest in off-world goods, except practical things like lenses and small metal implements. For the most part, the Comyn discouraged interstellar trade. As he surveyed the chamber, Regis could not deny the beauty with which off-world and Darkovan cultures could combine.

A moment later, their host entered, followed closely by Dan Lawton. The host, a member of the Pan-Darkovan League, wore a floor-length robe of emerald wool belted with a chain of enameled medallions of curious off-world design.

"*Vai domyn*," he said, bowing first to Regis and then to Danilo, "you lend grace to my humble establishment."

"*Mestre* Bartolomeo, thank you for your hospitality." Regis inclined his head toward Dan Lawton. The Terran looked a decade older than the last time Regis had seen him. "I regret we meet under such circumstances."

After a few more words, their host withdrew. Regis and Dan sat in two of the elaborate chairs, with Danilo standing near Regis in the attitude of a paxman.

Regis took the lead, quickly dismissing the last traces of formality. "Dan, I am so sorry about Felix. How does he fare?"

"You were with him when—" Dan's voice roughened. He swallowed. "He came through the surgery and is stable. Jay Allison thinks he'll make a full recovery, although it will be slow. There's been nerve damage. Jay says he would have died of blood loss, but the dagger seemed to have sealed off the severed vessels. That's not supposed to happen. You—whatever you did, I'm grateful."

Regis nodded, feeling inadequate to the moment. How could he take credit for something that was not his doing? The healing power had flowed through him, but it had not been his.

"I wish there had not been a need," Regis said aloud. "It would have been far better if you had kept your word to stay out of our affairs. I'm sorry your son was involved, but the matter should have been handled through Darkovan authorities . . . regardless of your parental interest."

"Does that matter now? You clearly hadn't been able to maintain order. Your own people were out of control, kidnapping children, with disorder in the streets, and religious fanaticism running riot. The Federation respects local autonomy, but we can and will intervene under certain circumstances. I know you asked to speak with me, and I agreed to this meeting because of our old friendship. I cannot and will not allow personal factors to interfere with my duties as Legate."

What was Dan trying to say? That he meant to declare martial law in Thendara or place the entire planet under emergency Federation authority?

The repercussions would be indelible, provoking consequences—accusations, confrontations, escalating violence—that could not be easily undone.

"Any action should be carefully considered." Regis tried to keep his tone conciliatory. "We have worked together before, each of us on his own side. In this case, there is enough blame to go around. After all, the fighting was initiated by Spaceforce police, not those holding the children. If you break the agreements governing relations between the Domains and the Federation, you will be seen as the aggressors."

Dan's mouth tightened. *"My* son was taken captive by *your* people."

"That's not true. The other children were taken by my brother's agents, but they were all Darkovan, so the matter remains within our jurisdiction. Felix, on the other hand, was abducted by his own mother. I thought you knew."

"Where did you hear that?" Dan's chin jerked up. "Why would Tiphani do such a thing? The accusation is ridiculous! Where's your proof?"

"Felix himself told me." Regis paused, letting the words sink in. "I brought her the news, but she was . . . distraught. I'm not sure she understood. She might respond better if you spoke to her."

"She—she's not at the Castle?"

"The last time I saw her, she was being escorted back to the Terran Zone. I cannot say of my own knowledge if she arrived there, but she's not foolish enough to return to my brother. They did not part on amicable terms."

"Then I don't know where she is," Dan said, clearly miserable. "I've listed her as a missing person and initiated a search. The gate logs show she entered Headquarters Building, visited our quarters briefly, and then left again. I assumed she went back to Rinaldo."

"Do you agree that this new information changes the situation? It must affect your actions with respect to our autonomy if no Darkovan was involved in Felix's abduction."

Dan drummed his fingertips on the wooden armrest of his chair. The light in his eyes had shifted from raw emotion to rationality. "You're right, damn you. I can't charge Tiphani with kidnapping her own son, not without a legal order transferring custody to me, and that wouldn't be retroactive." He glared at Regis. "All right, you've made your point. What do you want?"

Regis got up and began to pace, letting the movement loosen his muscles and his thoughts. "It's not so much what *I* want as what is best for us all. I'm grateful that you have trusted me enough to keep the Federation off our backs this past year. I must ask you to do so for just a little longer."

"While whoever is responsible for these outrages perpetrates more of them?"

Danilo reacted to the Terran's impassioned tone. With a restraining gesture, Regis slid back into his seat. "I don't think that will happen. In any event, the situation may be radically altered soon."

Dan stared at Regis. A long moment passed, and then another, during which neither man spoke. Then the Terran said, "You aren't going to tell me what you're planning, are you?"

"I dare not. You will know everything in a little while."

"And you want me to keep Spaceforce out of Darkovan Thendara until then?" Dan nodded slightly, his expression thoughtful. "What are a few more days—or weeks, for that matter—in the grand scheme of things? This is a volatile time for us, as well. It would be foolish to endanger everything we've worked for without giving you a chance to make it right."

Make it right, Regis repeated silently. If only it were that simple.

Regis went to the door, Danilo following like the shadow of a cloud-leopard. "I hope," Regis said, one hand upon the latch, "that when this is over, we will have the chance to talk. To really talk."

I do not have so many friends that I can afford to lose one needlessly.

Silence answered him. It was too much to ask, and the gulf might never be bridged. That was a risk he must take, for there was no course of action left but to go on.

The door closed behind him with a faint, decisive sound.

35

Regis arrived early at the Crystal Chamber. He and Danilo had planned to ride to the Castle, with Linnea traveling in a litter. She had refused, quite emphatically, and a horse had been furnished for her as well. Danilo had arranged for an armed escort, Gabriel and the three Guardsmen. With their stern faces and practical, unadorned blades, they presented a daunting sight. Pedestrians and riders alike drew back as they approached.

Their passage did not go unmarked. The party had not gone far when a parade gathered in their wake. Followers cheered, "Lord Regis! Lord Regis!" Regis would have preferred a less conspicuous procession, but once he was recognized, there was no possibility of anonymity.

They were the first to arrive, except for the Guardsmen stationed at the entrance. Nothing more had been seen of Tiphani Lawton, nor had Regis heard anything of Valdir Ridenow's latest plans. In this atmosphere of shifting loyalties, anything was possible.

Light streamed through the ceiling prisms to cast rainbows on the pale stone floor. The enclosures for the various Domains appeared untouched by the passing years. Aldaran would remain vacant, as it had for the last centuries. Rinaldo's advisors would surely have informed him that as king, he was entitled to take the seat of Elhalyn. Yes, there hung the banner of that Domain, the same Hastur blue, the silver fir-tree crowned with the emblem of royalty. Danvan Hastur's ornate presence-chair now occupied the front row of the Elhalyn box.

While Danilo circled the Chamber, performing his usual security check, Linnea searched for any hidden *laran* devices such as a trap matrix and then set the telepathic dampers.

The Comyn began to arrive, using their respective private entrances rather than the double doors through which Rinaldo would make his formal appearance. Draperies fluttered here and there at the back of the enclosures. Regis could not sense anything through the hum of the telepathic dampers, but for a moment, he received the distinct impression of someone lingering behind the curtains of the empty Aldaran box. The next moment, the fabric stilled, and he decided he was mistaken. It had been a stray current of air, nothing more.

Regis looked around the room, noting among them Ruyven Di Asturien, an elderly Castamir lord, Francisco Ridenow resplendent in the gold and green of his Domain, and Kennard-Dyan Ardais with Mikhail at his back. Bettany was absent, but Regis would have been surprised to see her. She must be closeted away with her ladies, grieving for a child that had never existed. What would such a loss do to her?

Gabriel sat in the Alton section, looking grim. Javanne, although as a Hastur she had the right to sit with Regis, had chosen to remain beside her husband. Likewise, Danilo could have claimed Domain-right for Ardais, but his oath and the bond he shared with Regis took precedence over status.

Regis reflected, *That is all any of us really wants—to serve the ones we love.*

As the scattered audience settled, Mikhail flashed Regis a grin.

Aldones Lord of Light, Blessed Cassilda, any god who is listening! Keep him safe—and Linnea, and Danilo. Keep them all safe on this day.

Regis took his seat in the Hastur box, with Danilo behind him. As if they had been waiting for his signal, the others came to order. Conversation diminished into whispers and then silence. The Chamber seemed to be holding its breath.

The doors swung open, and a Guardsman cried out in ringing tones,

"His Majesty, Rinaldo Felix-Valentine Lanart-Hastur, First of that Name, Warden of Hastur and Sovereign of the Seven Domains!"

As one, the greatly reduced assembly stood. All heads turned toward the doors. A procession entered the Chamber, led by a pair of Castle Guardsmen. Their formal uniforms, encrusted with badges and decorations, glittered in the multihued light. After them came Rinaldo's council, including Valdir Ridenow, and finally Rinaldo himself.

Rinaldo proceeded across the central area at a slow, stately pace. Regis thought his brother could hardly have moved briskly under the layers of fur and jewel-studded velvet and the thick, ruby-set copper chains. Rinaldo's crown outshone the gold of the crown on the Elhalyn banner, which overlaid but could not obliterate the Hastur fir-tree.

Permanedál, ran the ancient motto of the Hasturs. *I shall remain.*

Yes, my brother, I am still here.

Rinaldo lowered himself into the carved and gilded presence-chair. He took a moment to arrange his lace-trimmed sleeves. An expression of satisfaction lighted his angular features.

"Kinsmen, nobles, Comynarii, I bid you welcome." Rinaldo pitched his voice to fill the Chamber. "Lord Valdir, will it please you to call the roll of the Domains?"

So, Regis thought, Rinaldo been studying the ritual forms. Valdir was to be rewarded for his loyalty with a meaningless ceremonial privilege. As the Ridenow lord began the recitation, Regis reconsidered. Valdir was no fool, to be bought with an empty gesture. He was biding his time, watching for the right opportunity, and young Francisco was following his every move.

On more than one occasion, the opening of a session had resulted in a challenge to the rightful holding of one or another of the Domains. This time, however, the roll call proceeded smoothly, marked only by the silences when there was no one present to respond.

We are so few, Regis thought. *How can I risk even one of us?* Even if this day went as he hoped, what place would Rinaldo have in Thendara, with all the enemies he had made? Perhaps he might be content with a minor role at Castle Hastur, or he might prefer to retire to Nevarsin . . .

Regis dared not think that far into the future. Anything might happen before tomorrow's sunrise.

When the roll call was done, one of Rinaldo's aides handed him a prepared speech. In flowery legalistic phrases, he declared the Council valid only for this session and only to hear one complaint. He had, he stated, no intention of permanently reconvening it or investing it with any other authority.

"My younger brother, whom you all know, has requested this audience. Since there is no other business at hand, I am now prepared to hear what he has to say. I hope—" and here Rinaldo cleared his throat, brows drawing together, "—the results will not constitute an abuse of anyone's time."

Regis approached the railing of the Hastur partition and paused, one hand on the gate. The Chamber seemed immense. When he stepped onto the floor, the clatter of his boot heels was far too loud. Acutely aware of the intense interest of the audience, he lifted his chin, squared his shoulders, and faced his brother.

"Know ye by all present," he used the formal words, "that I, Regis-Rafael Felix Alar Hastur y Elhalyn, do declare you, Rinaldo Felix-Valentine Lanart-Hastur, unfit to rule the Domain of Hastur. How answer you?"

Rinaldo half-rose in his chair, then regained his composure. He might be impulsive, and devout to the point of zealotry, but he was not a simpleton. He realized that an outburst would only strengthen the case against him.

Muted exclamations rippled through the Chamber, as quickly hushed. Everyone wanted to hear what came next. Some of those present, old enough to have witnessed the intricate web that was the old Comyn politics, showed no surprise. Others startled, and one of the younger lords—Francisco Ridenow—gaped openly. No one present had been alive when Danvan Hastur had assumed the position of Regent for the incompetent King Stephen, but they had all grown up with the tale. No matter what the outcome of the challenge, history was unfolding before them.

What Regis had *not* said, and what every Comyn understood, except possibly Rinaldo himself, was that Rinaldo could claim the throne only as Head of Hastur, based on the preeminence of his Domain. Regis, on the other hand, traced his lineage through his mother, the only sister of the last Elhalyn king. Rinaldo might be recognized as his father's legitimate son, thanks to the actions Regis had taken, but his Domain-right was to Hastur, not Elhalyn.

"I have issued a lawful challenge," Regis repeated. "If you do not answer, you admit the validity of my charges and forfeit your place."

"I admit no such thing! I hereby dismiss this gathering!" Rinaldo gestured to the Guardsmen. "Sergeant-at-arms, clear the Chamber!" He pointed at Regis. "Arrest that traitor!"

"Stand as you are!" Gabriel thundered. "That is an illegal order, one you are oath-bound to disregard!"

The Guardsman, who had hesitated to lay hands on a Hastur Lord, even on the direct order from the King, hurried back to their places.

"Your Majesty," Ruyven Di Asturien said with grave courtesy, "even a king must answer such a challenge. None of us may hold himself above the law. The very name, *Comyn,* means 'equal.' Regis has the right to demand an accounting of you." When Rinaldo made no further objection, Di Asturien continued, "Lord Regis, on what basis do you accuse His Majesty?"

"I declare that my brother has abused his authority by either authorizing or by failing to prevent the abduction of a member of his own Domain, my niece Ariel Lanart-Hastur, as well as other Comyn children."

"I deny these charges unequivocally," Rinaldo announced. "They are spurious and without merit. This has nothing to do with my fitness to rule Hastur! Regis makes these wild statements out of envy, because he seeks to wrest from me the crown *he* lacked the courage to take for himself. Envy, I say! *I* have achieved what *he* never dared! The crown is mine, and nothing he says can change the fact!"

Uproar swept the Chamber. Raised voices echoed off the walls, jumbling together.

Kennard-Dyan, his face flushing in outrage, surged to his feet. "We Comyn do not tolerate tyranny in our midst—not even from a Hastur! It would be better to disband our caste entirely than to submit to such dishonor!"

A few, Mikhail among them, cheered.

Regis knew he must act before the situation got further out of hand.

Rinaldo would not hesitate to use force, and some Guardsmen were still loyal to him.

"Kinsmen, listen to me!" Regis raised his arms for attention. "Calm yourselves! We are not living in the Ages of Chaos! We must not be ruled by the passions of the moment but by honor and reason!"

The clamor died away, leaving the Chamber once more with that ghostly emptiness.

"*Dom* Regis has brought grave complaints against Your Majesty," *Dom* Ruyven said. "They cannot be summarily dismissed. What say you to the charge of kidnapping your sister's child?"

"She was not *kidnapped*. She was given the honor of being one of the first students in the school that I myself established for the spiritual betterment of our children. As Head of Hastur and as King, I had every right to do so."

"You had no right to seize my child!" Gabriel's features congested with outrage. "King or not, you have no authority over my daughter!"

"Or my nephew!" came a voice from the other side of the Chamber.

"Or my granddaughter!" That was one of the Eldrins, hurling the words like the opening of a blood-feud.

"Do you admit your guilt?" asked *Dom* Ruyven. "Think carefully, *vai dom*. Your intentions may have been noble, but that does not change the serious nature of these accusations. Not even the greatest of our ancient kings dared commit such an offense."

By the set of Rinaldo's jaw and the stormy angle of his brow, he had little patience for the question. He was not going to concede. Wars had been fought for less cause.

Valdir, who had been watching the interchange, gestured for permission to speak. Regis needed no *laran* to recognize the man's simmering frustration. Everything in Valdir's posture, from the coiled tension in his shoulders to the angle of his jaw, conveyed menace.

"A school for Darkovan children is commendable," Valdir said, "and Your Majesty can argue that you have the right to compel attendance. But you did *not* have the right to take a Terran child and provoke Federation military intervention. Did you think the Federation would sit idly by while the Legate's own son was abducted? They sent a rescue party, a tactical strike team armed with blasters. And, as you well know, they *used* them."

"Blasters?" the Eldrin lord exclaimed.

"In the Trade City?"

"But the Compact forbids—"

How did Valdir know about the blasters? Regis had carefully avoided mentioning them when he stormed into Rinaldo's council meeting.

"The Terrans have shown their willingness to ignore the Compact on more than one occasion!" Skillfully, Valdir maintained control. "That's why I've argued for full Federation membership, so that we can stand among them with full rights. Now, thanks to this debacle, they'll be screaming for justice—justice they won't hesitate to take into their own hands. Whose responsibility will that be? Who will answer their charges?"

Valdir had not given up his dream of Federation membership. He had used Rinaldo only as long as the puppet king did his bidding. Now, when threatened with retaliatory martial law, he would not scruple to place the blame on Rinaldo. He would throw the Council into chaos, discredit the Comyn as rulers of the Domains, and then step in as the one man who could speak for Darkover.

In another moment, the Comyn would be all too happy to hand over Rinaldo, as the guilty party, to the Terrans.

Poor, deluded Rinaldo! He probably had no idea what was happening. Regis pitied his brother. It was like watching a drowning man as the tide carried him ever farther from the shore.

Regis faced Rinaldo once more. Throughout the Chamber, men paused in midsentence to listen. "My brother, I appeal to you and to the honor of the Hasturs. Our father and grandfather and all our ancestors, from the beginning of recorded time, devoted their lives to our world and its people. For their sake, you must step down. Only then can we convince the Federation that we are capable of handling this matter ourselves."

For every Valdir Ridenow, there was a Varzil the Good, the visionary who brought about the Compact and ended centuries of horrific *laran* warfare. Dyan Ardais, Kennard-Dyan's father, had sacrificed himself for the greater good as he saw it. His actions might have been disastrous, but his integrity had been beyond question; in the end, he had seen his error and paid for it with his life.

As he spoke, Regis searched for the phrases that might reach Rinaldo, bringing forth that same altruistic spirit. Surely, the *cristoforos* strove to emulate their own holy saints, men who placed the welfare of others above their own.

Regis shaped his argument in accord with that hope. He reminded Rinaldo of Nevarsin's long tradition of service and humility. He tried to speak only to Rinaldo, to focus only on convincing his brother, not anyone else, and in so doing, he captured the entire audience.

The words slipped off the shield of Rinaldo's single-minded determination like paper swords against a wall of stone. Within moments, Regis heard the rhythmic beat of men running in formation, converging on the Chamber. Rinaldo's picked Guards would arrest or eliminate any man who stood against their King.

Despite the telepathic dampers, Regis read the thoughts behind Rinaldo's simmering fury: *Rebels and traitors, and Regis the most vile of them . . .*

"I am no traitor!" Regis insisted. "When I have I ever dealt with you dishonorably? Have I lied to you or cheated you? Have I taken what was rightfully yours? I could have left you at Nevarsin, hidden away by your own family as if you were a shameful thing. Or brought you to Thendara as a *nedestro,* without rank or place."

Something shifted behind Rinaldo's eyes, like a stray beam of sun through storm-gathered clouds.

Regis stepped closer and held out his hands. His throat thickened, but he forced the words through. "You were the brother I longed for, the brother I chose to stand at my side, the brother I was proud to acknowledge. Compared to you, the privileges of Hastur meant nothing. Can you understand how important you were to me? How much I wanted to love you? You are the only brother I will ever have, just as I am yours."

Rinaldo's pale face took on a faint tinge of color and wetness gleamed in his eyes.

"Let us not be adversaries, each striving for power over the other," Regis pleaded. "Can we not work together, each of us with our own gifts to offer our people?"

As if in a daze, Rinaldo passed one hand over his face. He mumbled a few words, a prayer, perhaps. As he swung open the gate and stepped onto the Chamber floor, he cried, "My brother! Everything you said is true! You have never been anything but generous and truthful. Yet . . . I do not know how to answer you. Have I not been given this power," looking down at his heavily ornamented ceremonial garb, "by the Lord of All Worlds? Must I then break faith with either my brother or my God?"

"With neither of us," Regis replied. "You will find a way to honor your spiritual calling. You will open the hearts of men by example, by goodness and compassion, not by fear and coercion. Is that not the way of St. Valentine, whose penitential life we once studied together?"

"The holy saint preached forgiveness as a path to salvation." Tears spilled over Rinaldo's cheeks. "I had all but forgotten that lesson. God will indeed find a way. Truly, I am a flawed instrument. For whatever harm has come from my best intentions, I must make restitution."

Regis was moved beyond speech by the grace of his brother's surrender. He had hoped but not expected that his words would make a difference. When he had used hard tactics, challenging Rinaldo's position, he had met with equal resistance. Only when he had spoken from his heart and laid open his longing for a brother's love had he succeeded.

The Chamber hushed in respect. Weeping openly now, Rinaldo stepped forward to embrace Regis.

"You snake!" A woman's voice split the silence. "Seducer! Pervert! You've ruined it all—everything God has called us to accomplish!" Tiphani Lawton burst through the curtains at the back of the Aldaran enclosure.

"You can't have him!" she shrieked at Regis. "He's *mine*—God gave him to *me!*"

She reached the railing. Regis and Rinaldo, now only an arm's-length apart, turned in unison. Danilo shouted out a warning. Already, Gabriel had risen from his place, and the Sergeant-at-Arms laid one hand on the hilt of his sword.

Tiphani stumbled onto the Chamber floor. She pawed at the folds of her robe.

With a savage cry, she brought out a Terran blaster and aimed it at Regis.

Regis stared at the gleaming cylinder. Behind him, Linnea yelled, "Go!" and Danilo hurtled over the railing.

Rinaldo grabbed Regis by the shoulders and spun him around, shielding Regis with his own body.

White fire erupted from the muzzle of the blaster.

Regis could not move. His breath had turned to ice in his throat. The stench of charred flesh enveloped him. Dazedly, he wondered if they had both been hit, or only he himself.

Rinaldo's body stiffened. He landed in a graceless tangle, almost bringing Regis down with him. Regis caught his balance. Danilo flew past him, racing across the floor to tackle Tiphani. She waved the blaster, firing wildly. Danilo reached her an instant before the nearest Guardsman did.

Pandemonium erupted in the Chamber, people shouting, benches toppling, robes swirling as people rushed about. Gabriel reached the floor, and Valdir as well.

Between them, Danilo and the Guardsman wrestled Tiphani to the floor. The blaster went skidding across the smooth-worn stone. Tiphani spewed forth off-world curses. She lashed out with her fists, kicking hard.

"Uncle Regis!" Mikhail appeared beside Regis, taking his weight as Regis stumbled. "Are you hurt?"

Regis dropped to his knees beside his brother. Rinaldo lay on his back. His colorless eyes were open, filled with rainbow light. Regis stretched one hand over Rinaldo's face, hovering his fingers over the pale, serene features, searching for a hint of breath and finding none.

The next instant, the telepathic dampers cut out. *Laran* sensations flooded through Regis, a maelstrom of emotions and wild, desperate thoughts.

"Regis."

He lifted his head and met Linnea's gaze.

I'm so sorry! Anguish rang through her telepathic thought. *If only I'd disabled the dampers sooner, I would have known what that woman was up to!*

"No, love," he said. "None of us could have anticipated . . ." He lowered his gaze to his brother's features, so still that Rinaldo looked ageless. "Least of all he, who trusted her."

He turned his eyes away, folded his grief like a fragile thing in his heart, and stood once more. Someone must take charge, see that Tiphani Lawton was properly restrained, decide what to do with her, give orders about the . . . the body.

Around him, psychic currents surged like storm-whipped turbulence. His own feelings—grief and fury and things he could not name—clashed inside him.

I can't do this.

As if in a mad dream, Regis watched Francisco Ridenow pick up the blaster. Francisco looked down at the gleaming metal for what seemed an eternity, weighing it. A strange, hard light glimmered in his eyes. Then Valdir grasped him by the shoulder and took the weapon away.

A short distance away, Tiphani had gone limp, sobbing in the arms of Gabriel and another Guardsman.

Regis. Linnea laced her fingers, cool and strong, through his. Danilo strode toward them. Their minds linked . . . held.

The roiling insanity receded. Regis knew who he was. What he was. What he must do.

Regis felt as if he had been hurled down from a great height, certain he would smash into the rocky ground, only to find himself caught in an invisible net. Each strand was gossamer light, the thousand tiny threads that bound his life to those he loved. Together, they sustained him.

36

Regis would not allow Rinaldo to be buried in an unmarked grave at Hali with the generations of Comyn. Rinaldo had never been one of them; the softly green hills of Hali would have meant exile for a spirit longing for home.

"I myself will take him to St. Valentine's," Regis told Javanne, "and let him rest in the everlasting snows along with the holy men of his order."

They had been sitting together in the Hastur apartments in Comyn Castle. With regret he had bowed to the necessity of moving back, although he refused to give up the townhouse. In the next room, Linnea was supervising the rearrangement of the furniture to be safer for an active toddler. Ariel, who had not stopped clinging to her mother since her return, sat on the floor beside Javanne, shoulder touching knee.

Javanne opened her mouth, then closed it with a sigh. The events of the past winter had left her gaunt, her tongue sharper than ever. Although pleased with Gabriel's reinstatement as Guards Commander, she continued to hold Mikhail at a distance.

"It would not be fitting for a Hastur to be buried at Nevarsin," she said, "but then, Rinaldo was never properly one of us. He had not the slightest sense of Comyn honor."

"Let us not speak uncharitably," Regis said, gentle with the pain beneath her words. "He was our brother."

Javanne shrugged. "At least some good has come out of this. You are now settled and married, and no one can accuse you of shirking your duty. What is one *nedestro* more or less, when the Hastur succession has been properly secured?"

"Mama, can we go now?" Ariel moved restlessly against her mother's skirts. Since her rescue, she had not been able to sit still for more than a few moments. Linnea said that with time and care, the girl might become less nervous, but Regis saw no sign of improvement. He feared she might never fully recover.

"In a moment, dearest," Javanne murmured. "Regis, will you excuse us? There is so much to do, preparing for the move back to Armida. We must travel while the weather is still clement."

Regis did not ask if she would miss Mikhail. He rose, kissed his sister on the cheek, and bade her good day. After Javanne and Ariel left, Linnea came into the parlor.

As chatelaine of the Castle and mistress of the Hastur suite, Linnea had set about arranging the sleeping and living quarters to accommodate both privacy and shared family activities. Danilo's chamber was by mutual accord adjacent to that of Regis, while Linnea preferred to be closer to the baby. Her frank approach to intimacy and psychic shielding had eased the transition, and the three adults had come to a working understanding.

"I cannot say I will miss my sister-in-law's meddling," Linnea said, a trace less kindly than her usual manner.

"Javanne is unhappy," he reminded her, "although I do not entirely understand why. The hardest thing to sympathize with is how relieved she acts that Rinaldo is dead."

Linnea stood beside Regis and gazed up at him with her calm, assessing gray eyes. "She did not love him."

"Did she even know him? Did I? Did any of us? Or did I see only a brother to shoulder the burdens I never wanted?"

"My dear, how long will you carry that guilt? It is not your fault that things turned out as they did. Perhaps your choices were not always the wisest, but you made them out of love and generosity." She did not add that the same could not be said for others, namely Tiphani Lawton and Valdir Ridenow.

For the moment, he reminded himself, neither Tiphani nor Valdir posed any threat. Tiphani had been turned over to the Terran authorities and was soon to be shipped to another planet, Sirius IX most likely, for the treatment of the criminally insane. Dan had let her go without protest; Regis could not imagine his friend's distress. At least the issue of Federation membership looked to be permanently stalled. The Terrans would be hesitant to meddle in Darkovan affairs for a long time to come.

Felix was making a good recovery and had already begun private lessons with Linnea. Eventually, the boy might need the disciplined community of a Tower, Arilinn most likely, with Jeff Kerwin as his Keeper, but that decision lay in the future.

As for Valdir Ridenow, he had stated his intention to retire to Serrais, taking Bettany and Francisco with him. Regis would rather have seen the girl entrusted to the Bridge Society healers or sent somewhere she might receive help and understanding. Clearly, the current Ridenow lord felt it was more important to forget the entire affair.

Poor child, I wonder what will happen to her. And Francisco, growing up under Valdir's tutelage . . .

Recalling his thoughts to the present, Regis kissed his wife on the forehead. "You are right, of course. Danilo spouts similar wisdom at me on a daily basis."

"As well he should," she replied with an impish smile. "Perhaps the two of us will accomplish what neither one of us alone can. Getting you to see sense."

"I?" Bemused by her playful turn, he raised one eyebrow.

The light in her eyes dimmed and Regis knew she was thinking of Kierestelli. In response, he said aloud what was in his mind, that he would go directly from Nevarsin to the Yellow Forest and bring their daughter home.

Linnea summoned a smile. "I'm sure you will try."

"What do you mean?" Regis shivered inside, as if a gust from the everlasting snows touched his heart. The Storns were an old mountain family and undoubtedly had Aldaran blood. Linnea had never said she possessed the Gift of foreseeing, but . . .

Regis thought of his daughter, slim and graceful as a *chieri,* among the towers of Thendara, the raucous life of the city, the strangeness of the Terran Zone. He thought of men with blasters, with swords. "Are you saying it is not safe for her?"

She turned away. "Let it rest, love. We have endured more sadness in this last year than many people do in an entire lifetime. Go, bestow this last gift upon your brother, and know I will be waiting for you."

Brother Valentine, once called Rinaldo Felix-Valentine Lanart-Hastur, was laid to rest in the burial area dedicated to those who had given their lives in holy service. The entire monastic community attended, except for one or two elderly monks too frail to make the journey. They climbed the rocky slope, following a path between the arms of glacial ice. Chanting, they shared the weight of the rough wooden coffin. Those who were young and strong took longer turns, but even the lame carried their brother in imitation of the Holy Bearer of Burdens.

The ceremony, conducted by the new Father Master, a tall, soft-spoken man named Conn, was brief. Regis found himself unexpectedly moved. After all that had gone before, he feared the traditional words might ring hollow. The priest recited the prayers with such tenderness that even Danilo had tears in his eyes when the final *"May it be so"* drew the mourners together. Afterward, Regis waited with Danilo as each monk and novice paused to say a word of consolation. Some had barely known Rinaldo, but others remembered him as a youth, a child, a teacher, a friend.

How they loved him, Regis thought with a heavy gladness. *I should never have taken him away.*

He and Danilo were in light rapport, as they had been almost continually during this pilgrimage. Danilo said aloud, "Do not take that sorrow on yourself, *bredhyu.* A hundred things might have happened differently. Old Lord Hastur could have educated him as befitted a Comyn or else buried all record of his existence, leaving him to a life of contemplative prayer. Rinaldo himself made many choices along the way."

Rinaldo could have resisted Valdir's seductive offer of power and Tiphani Lawton's delusions as well.

"Sometimes I think the saddest thing in this whole affair is how few people in Thendara will remember him in the years to come," Regis sighed. The procession of monks was already winding their way down to the monastery. Although it was still full afternoon, a frigid wind swept down over the ice.

They stayed that night in the monastery's guest house, warmed by a fire, hot food, and thick blankets. Neither felt the need for speech. When the fire had died into glowing embers, Regis lay in his single bed, waiting for sleep, listening to Danilo's breathing.

I shall never return to Nevarsin.

Once he could not wait to be free of this place, its harsh discipline and creed of chastity, not to mention its climate. Now he thought of all he had been given, not just the education of books and writing, but the struggle within himself, the clarity to discern the truth and the strength to act upon it. The condemnation of homosexuality had all but destroyed him, and yet, was he not a stronger, more honest person for having wrestled with it? If he had not come to terms with his feelings for Danilo, would he have had the resolve to insist upon a wife for whom he felt genuine love and respect?

For a tenday, Regis scoured the hills in search of the Yellow Forest, and he did so alone. Danilo had been reluctant to allow Regis to ride off by himself, but Regis refused to explain what he was doing or why he must go alone. Kierestelli's safety no longer depended on no one else knowing where she was hiding, but in all likelihood, the continued existence of the *chieri* did. Regis in no way distrusted Danilo, but the secret was not his to divulge. The Yellow Forest, sanctuary for a dwindling and near-magical race, had been revealed to him alone.

Revealed once, but not now. Every time he thought he recognized a hillside, a mountain or grove of green-leafed trees, the path led only to more of the same. The Yellow Forest had turned invisible, its entrance just beyond human senses. He called out until his throat was raw as he trotted his horse up and down the place where he thought it must be.

Nothing.

Nothing, like an echo that betrayed *something*.

Each passing day fueled his anxiety. He imagined Danilo, waiting for him at the village on the far side of the Kadarin, fretting and fearful. Imagined Linnea back in Thendara, her heart aching for the loss of her daughter, and then that strange resignation.

Had she known what would happen?

She would never ask, never cast even a whisper of blame on him. She understood, as he was only now beginning to, that Kierestelli, like her namesake, had never belonged to the world of greed and betrayal, hatred and manipulation, the world that kidnapped children for dogmatic ends. The world that so callously obliterated the brightest of hopes.

The world he must return to and serve as best he could.

When Regis arrived home, he learned that Valdir and Francisco had departed for Serrais, but not Bettany. Her kinswoman, Istvana Ridenow, had come to Thendara, packed up the girl and her belongings, and taken her back to Neskaya Tower.

"Really, it was Danilo's doing," Linnea told Regis.

Danilo, coming into the parlor where breakfast was laid out, mumbled that he deserved no credit.

"It was kindly done," Regis said. "From what you've told me, no one at Serrais cares about her."

"Or is equipped enough to deal with such severe mental trauma," Linnea put in. "Did you know she'd survived a Ghost Wind? Danilo suspected, and Istvana confirmed it. There's strength in that young woman and more than a trace of empathy."

"I couldn't stand by and see her life thrown away," Danilo said.

"You have feelings for her?" Regis asked, surprised.

"No more than for any human creature in pain," Danilo explained, "although Bettany fancied herself in love with me. Poor thing, with no one to love. She'd been rejected and betrayed so many times, I couldn't turn my back on her."

"Danilo was marvelous," Linnea said. "She wouldn't have anything to do with me, but he kept her talking—"

"—and crying," Danilo added.

"—until Istvana came. Kinswoman or not, when Istvana sees a poor lost chick, she swoops in like a mother hen. We trained together for a time, and I know. Bettany ate up all that attention as if she were starving."

"She was," Danilo said quietly.

You could not give her the affection she needed, so you—and Linnea—found someone who could. Regis felt a rush of pride and love. He did not need to ask what Linnea's part had been. How she'd gotten word so quickly to Neskaya, he didn't know and suspected he never would.

Above the city of Thendara, the great crimson sun of Darkover crept toward midday. Winter was drawing to a close. Shadows stretched like pools of darkness from the walls of Comyn Castle.

Regis Hastur, the Lord of his Domain and Regent of the Comyn, stood on a balcony of the Castle and gazed over the spires of the Old Town to the Terran Trade city, the rising steel edifice of the Terran Empire Headquarters complex and, still further, the spaceport.

Even without the sounds of hushed footsteps, Regis knew by the lightening of his heart that Danilo and Linnea had come into the room behind him. He closed his eyes, opening the space in his mind where their thoughts met. Linnea's skirts whispered as she moved. She interlaced her fingers with his. With a click of the latch, Danilo closed the door and came to stand beside them both.

They would, none of them, be the same people they were before Rinaldo had touched and twisted their lives, but they no longer lived in the same world. The Terran Federation remained a vastly powerful, unstable force. Regis now took up the role of Regent, with everything that implied. The questions of his marriage and the heritage of Hastur were settled, although how the relationship between Mikhail and little Dani might evolve, no one could say.

As for Kierestelli, enfolded into the hidden world of the *chieri* and warned never to reveal her identity, Regis could only pray that her life would be as rich as his and as blessed with love.